In the Rogue Blood

Books by James Carlos Blake

IN THE ROGUE BLOOD

———◆———

James Carlos Blake

AVON BOOKS ◆ NEW YORK

For
Dale L. Walker

This is a work of fiction. Names, characters, places,
and incidents either are the product of the author's
imagination or are used fictitiously. Any resemblance
to actual events, locales, organizations, or persons,
living or dead, is entirely coincidental and beyond
the intent of either the author or the publisher.

AVON BOOKS
A division of
The Hearst Corporation
1350 Avenue of the Americas
New York, New York 10019

Copyright © 1997 by James Carlos Blake
Interior design by Kellan Peck
Visit our website at http://AvonBooks.com
ISBN: 0-380-97492-4

Library of Congress Cataloging in Publication Data:

First Avon Books Printing: September 1997

AVON TRADEMARK REG. U.S. PAT. OFF. AND IN OTHER COUNTRIES, MARCA REGISTRADA,
HECHO EN U.S.A.

Printed in the U.S.A.

FIRST EDITION

10 9 8 7 6 5 4 3 2 1

Why does your sword so drip with blood,
    Edward, Edward?
Why does your sword so drip with blood,
    And why so sad go ye, O?

—FROM AN ANONYMOUS SCOTTISH BALLAD OF THE MIDDLE AGES

I stood upon a high place,
And saw, below, many devils
Running, leaping,
And carousing in sin.
One looked up, grinning,
And said, "Comrade! Brother"

—STEPHEN CRANE

The essential American character is hard, isolate, stoic, and a killer.

—D. H. LAWRENCE

Lo que no tiene remedio se tiene que aguantar.

—AN OLD MEXICAN DICHO

CONTENTS

vii

CONTENTS

I

THE FAMILY

1

In the summer of 1845 Edward Little was sixteen years old and restless in his blood. He knelt beside a tree stump next to the stable and carved intently upon it in the first gray light of day. He had often sat on this stump and watched the sun lower into the trees and wondered how great the distance from where he sat to where the day was still high noon. His family fled to this blackwater wildland just east of the Perdido and nearly two days' ride north of Pensacola in the fall of '42 when Daddyjack hied them out of the Georgia uplands following a barndance fracas that left a man dead and occasioned the local constable to initiate inquiry. The killed man was named Tom Rainey. He was a childhood acquaintance of Edward's mother and made bold to ask her for a turn on the dance-floor. She shook her head as much in warning as in refusal, but before he could turn away, there was Daddyjack before him redeyed with drink and much offended by Rainey's familiarity toward his wife. Hard words abruptly gave way to grappling and folk jumped clear as a table overturned and then Rainey was staring down in wide-eyed wonder at the knife haft jutting from his breastbone and tight in Daddyjack's grip. Edward was thirteen and had seen men die under felled trees and from a mulekick to the head and in wildeyed fever in their bunks, but this was his first witness to mankilling and his blood jumped at the swift and utter finality of its decree and at the resolute set of Daddyjack's face as he gave the blade a hard twist before yanking it free. Rainey staggered and his face sagged as he gaped at the scarlet bloom on his shirtfront and then his eyes rolled up white and he dropped dead. Daddyjack got the family out of there fast as people fell away from the door. The boy was drymouthed and nearly breathless with the sense of having just seen something of himself, something at once dreadful and exhilarating and ascendant and not to be denied, some fierce region of his own being that awaited him like a badland horizon red as Hell.

2

Their covered wagon had lurched along toward Florida on narrow muddy traces that wound through deep pine forests and traversed marsh prairies and skirted shadowy swamplands where the moss hung heavy and the evening haze flared with will-o'-the-wisp. Daddyjack's horse trailed on a lead rope and their two dogs trotted alongside. At the infrequent crossroads there was sometimes an inn where Daddyjack would rein up the team and step inside to sample a cup of the local distillate while Edward and his brother John watered the animals and listened to the conversations of passing travelers. More than one group of pilgrims they met was headed for the Republic of Texas. The emigrants had all been told the place beggared description and they spoke as if they'd already seen it with their own eyes—the towering pinewoods and fertile bottomlands, the long curving seacoast and rolling green hills, the vast plains that ranged for countless miles out to the western mountains. They'd been assured a man could make a good life for himself in Texas if he but had the grit to stand up to the Mexican army and the roving bands of red savages. It was anyhow sure to become a state before long, Mexican objections be damned. Daddyjack overheard a bunch of them one time and as he hupped the mules back onto the southern track he shook his head and muttered about fools who thought they could get away from themselves in Texas or any other damned place.

One drizzly afternoon on the drive to Florida, when Edward and his brother and sister were sitting with their mother in the back of the wagon as Daddyjack drove the mule team through the blowing mist with water running from his hatbrim, she whispered to them that Jack Little was a murderous man never to be admired and much less trusted. They were the first words she had uttered in over a year and for a moment Edward was not certain if she had actually spoken or he had somehow heard the thoughts inside her head. "That man will eat you up," she hissed. "All you. If you don't kill him first."

The girl nodded with tightlipped accord and stared fiercely at her brothers. The brothers exchanged uncertain looks. Daddyjack's voice rasped into the wagon: "I'd rather go on not hearin your mouth a-tall than have to hear such crazywoman talk."

She said nothing more that night or for the next three years, but the fervor in her eyes did look to Edward like the gleam of lunacy.

3

Their mother was a fairskinned supple beauty with sharp features, but neither Daddyjack nor the children knew—not the woman herself knew—that her roiled green eyes and darkly auburn hair were inherited from a murderous brute who begat her atop a thirteen-year-old girl as the rest of his bandit party whooped over the flaming wagons on a cold South Georgia afternoon and the girl's family lay about in twisted slaughter. The childmother never recovered from the ordeal's visitation of madness and she spoke not another word for the brief rest of her life. She wandered in the scrub for days before an tinker came upon her and carried her in his wagon to the next town on his route where she was housed by a grocer and his wife until they realized she was with child and passed her on to the grocer's spinster sisters. A few weeks after the birth of her daughter she hanged herself from a rafter in her room. Her suicide was the favored conversational topic among the locals for some time but the gossipry soon made even the details of her death as uncertain as all else about her. In time all tales told of her were but fancies.

The infant was taken to raise by a childless Methodist minister named

Gaines and his sallow dispirited wife who were on their way to settle in
the high country. The reverend christened her Lilith and told everyone
she was his niece who had been orphaned by the cholera. She grew up
a quiet observant girl who read the Bible and practiced her hand by cop-
ying passages from the Song of Solomon, which the reverend's good wife
was disturbed—and the reverend himself secretly piqued—to learn was
her favorite portion of the Good Book. She had just turned twelve and
offered no resistance when the preacher deflowered her one late evening
as his consumptive spouse coughed away her life in an adjoining room.
Six weeks later, on the night following his wife's funeral, he lay with the
girl again and wept even as he grunted with the labor of his lust. He told
her it was the Lord's own will that they commit their flesh one to the
other and she smiled at his tears and said it was wonderful that the Lord
willed such a pleasurable thing—and then laughed at his gaping astonishment at her brazenness. He took her to his bed nearly every night
thereafter.

By the time she was fourteen she was pleasuring boys from every corner
of the county in exchange for a bit of specie or at the least some general
store gimcrack she fancied. She delighted in watching them fight over
her. Her reputation began to draw passing drummers and tradesmen off
the main road. The Reverend Gaines was the last to know. When he
discovered he was no longer the sole recipient of the girl's favors he was
enraged by her perfidy and took to praying aloud every evening for the
Lord to redeem her corrupt and bastard soul. He determined to see her
married and gone as soon as some dupe might be found who would ask
her hand.

And here came tall and burly and thickly mustached Jack Little, making known he was from Tennessee and a hewer by trade and in search
of a wife. He said his father hailed from County Cork. The preacher
invited him to supper and introduced him to his orphaned "niece." Lilith
was now fifteen and as eager to get free of the reverend and the whole
damned state of Georgia as he was to be shed of her, and although nobody knew a single certain fact about Jack Little except that his accent
had little in it of Tennessee and that he was hale and hankering to be
wed, she perceived him as an opportune means for effecting her escape
into the world.

They married three weeks after their introduction. Immediately following the ceremony the Reverend Gaines announced that he had sold his
house and holdings to Jack Little and was returning to the itinerant life

of spreading the Blessed Word. Within the hour he was departed for places unknown. Jack Little gestured awkwardly toward the house and told his bride, "I wanted to surprise you." Her wet-eyed speechlessness he took for joy. In fact she stood stunned by the world's unending ironies and the cursed character of her luck. Her husband smiled at her evident happiness.

The moment Jack Little shut the bedroom door behind them on their wedding night she assumed her frailest face and her eyes brimmed as she told him she was heartsick and more ashamed than he could ever know because two summers ago she'd had an accident, had slipped and fallen astraddle the gunwale of a rowboat and sundered her maidenhead and thus robbed herself and him too of the dearest present a bride could give her husband. She wept into her hands. He gave her a narrow look but decided to make no matter of it. He'd been intimate with no women in his life but whores and needed to believe she was cut from finer cloth and so refused to entertain suspicions. In bed she responded with such fervor to his urgings that he counted himself lucky indeed to be wed to one so freshly young and uninhibitedly eager to pleasure her husband. He felt he might be in love.

He went to work at a timbercamp a few miles into the deepwoods. John was born in early winter and a year later came Edward. In the summer of the following year Lilith was in her sixth month with Margaret when a scowling pair of yellowbearded brothers named Klasson showed up in town carrying long rifles and inquiring after a man called Haywood Boggs. They claimed he was a bad actor who'd murdered their uncle four years earlier in western Kentucky and was now said to be living round-abouts. Their description of Boggs was discomfitingly familiar and some-body finally pointed them toward the logging trace that led to the timbercamp.

Three days later Jack Little drove a team into town with the stiffening bodies of the Klassons laid out on the wagonboards behind him. A crowd of townsmen including the constable gathered to behold the rawly dark rifleball hole over the glazed left eye of one corpse and the other's battered and misshapen head set in a jelled pool of blood and brainstuff and swarming with fat blue flies. The camp foreman had come along on horseback to verify Jack Little's story of what happened. The Klassons had appeared at the camp on the previous morning and dismounted with rifles in hand and hailed for a man named Boggs. When the foreman stepped forth and said there was no such fellow amongst them one of the

Klassons spotted Jack Little and threw up his rifle and fired and put a hole through the high crown of his hat. Woodcutters scattered for cover as the other man fired and missed too. Jack Little ran into the side shed where he kept his rifle charged and dry and grabbed it up and rushed back out and set himself and shot the first man dead as he was raising his gun to fire again. He ran to the second man who was almost finished reloading and cracked him across the face with the flat of his riflestock and knocked him down and then drove the buttplate into his skull a half-dozen crunching times to assure no further threat from him. The fray was done by the time the rest of the woodjacks came running in from the timber to see what the shooting was about.

He had never seen either man before in his life, Jack Little said, and he could offer no explanation for their attack. The constable scratched his chin and shrugged and for lack of warrant to do otherwise he ruled it a matter of self-defense. By right of the local law Jack Little had first claim to everything in the dead men's outfits from horses to guns to saddlebag possibles. He kept the guns but sold the horses and the possibles for a tidy sum. And that was the end of it. In a tavern that evening everybody agreed that the Klassons had mistaken Jack Little for somebody else. "They surely did make a mistake," one fellow said, speaking softly and looking about to make sure Jack Little wasn't around before he added: "Even if they didn't." There was a chorus of ayes and laughter and much sage nodding of heads.

4

Eleven years passed. The only book in the house was a Bible left behind by the Reverend Gaines. The mother used it as a primer to teach the children to read and letter while they were still quite young and she saw to it that they kept those skills in practice. Daddyjack instructed the brothers in the ways of using tools from the time they were big enough to heft a hatchet. As soon as they were of a size to lift and aim a long gun he taught them to shoot his Kentucky flintlock named Roselips and the two caplock Hawkens he'd taken off the Klasson brothers. Both of the Hawkens had octagon barrels and double-set triggers and stained maple stocks with oval cheekpieces. One was a halfstock .54 caliber and the other a massive fullstock .66 caliber piece that weighed over fourteen pounds and which the brothers were thrilled to learn could blast a ball through a double plank of oak at two hundred yards. He taught them to measure out a charge quickly by pouring enough black powder to cover a rifle ball in the palm of their hand. They laughed at each other when the big gun's recoil knocked them down. From their earliest years they were strong and rangy. Working an axe gave them long muscles like ropes. John was the taller, Edward the quicker, and both had wrists like pickhandle heads. Like their father they naturally inclined to violence and made easy practice of it. They regularly bloodied each other in fistfights sparked by sheer exuberance while Daddyjack looked on and lauded every punch landed. He taught them the proper way to drive a knee to the balls, how to apply an elbow to the teeth and a backfist to the throat. How to gouge out an eyeball. How to break a nose with a head butt and stomp on an instep and uncouple a knee with a kick.

When they began accompanying him into town to get supplies they discovered the yet greater joy of fighting somebody besides each other and before long even bigger and older boys trod lightly in their presence. One Saturday in town a sixteen-year old tough fresh from North Carolina got into it with John in an alley. The other boy had the advantages of thirty pounds and three years in age and thumped John steadily in the first few minutes while the surrounding crowd of spectating boys cried out for blood. Then John's persistent counterattacks began to tell. When he butted the other boy in the face and broke his nose the fellow's eyes flooded with tearful panic and he pulled a claspknife and cut John across the chin. Edward jumped on him from behind and pulled him down and wrested the blade from him and slashed the boy's fending arms and hands while John stove his ribs with one kick after another and the other boys yelled "Kill him! Kill him!" They might have done so if a big-shouldered storekeeper hadn't come out wielding a shovel and sent the lot of them scattering. That night Daddyjack stitched up John's chin and the next day showed them how to defend against a knife and how to fight with one.

"There's always plenty a reason to fight in this world," Daddyjack told them. "For damn sure to defend yourself and your own. Truth is, you can fight for any reason ye fancy. But heed me now: Whatever you fight about, be willin to die over it. That's the trick of it, boys. If you're ready to die and the other fellow's not, you'll whip his ass sure every time."

"What if the other fella's ready to die as you, Daddyjack?" John asked.

"Well now," he said, showing his teeth, "that's when the fur does fly and the fight gets interestin."

The brothers grinned right back at him.

Through those eleven years Jack Little remained ignorant of his wife's wanton past, but then one afternoon he was in the farrier's shop repairing a grindstone mount when a passing drummer who was having his horse newly shod asked of the small assembly if any of them knew whatever had become of the little redheaded whore.

"You boys know the one, from back about ten year ago when I was last around here. She was hardly moren a babychick but she used to do it in the woods and charged but half-a-dollar. Sweet thing would settle for two bits if twas all you had. Had the nicest titties and roundest little rump this side of New Orleans. What in thunder *was* her name?"

The men cast nervous glances to the rear of the shop where Jack Little had been overseeing the smith's apprentice in straightening the grindstone's axle and was now staring at the back of the drummer's head. The smitty tried to warn the drummer with his eyes but the man was stroking his thin imperial and looking at his feet in an effort to recall the girl's name. "Ah, yes," he said, "Lily. Foolcrazy darlin Lil. Why, that girl had a way of—"

Jack Little was on him in a bound, clubbing him in the neck with the heel of his fist, punching him to the floor, kicking him in the face and ribs and crotch and he would have killed him sure if a handful of men had not wrestled him out of there and held him fast while the drummer was carried off to an inn where he would recover sufficiently over the next few days to manage the reins of his team and leave town forever. When the men let go of Jack Little he glared at them all but none would meet his eyes nor speak a word. He heaved the grindstone onto the wagon and giddapped the mule for home.

Edward and John were slopping the pigs when he drove the wagon into the stable and came out with a coil of rope and a rawhide quirt and dropped them at the base of an oak and stalked into the house, his face dark with rage. A moment later they heard their sister scream and he came out dragging their mother by the hair with one hand and fending off ten-year-old Maggie with the other. The woman was struggling like a roped cat and the girl kept trying to bite the hand that gripped her mother's hair and Daddyjack swatted her off her feet. He dragged the woman to the tree and held her down with a knee on her chest and tied her wrists together with one end of the rope. The girl went at him again swinging both fists and he backhanded her once more and John rushed

in and pinioned her in his arms and pulled her away and she was screaming, "Let her be! Let her be! Let her be!"

He lobbed the free end of the rope over a branch and caught it and
jerked up the slack and then hoisted the woman a good two feet off the
ground by her bound hands and made fast the end of the rope around
the tree trunk. She kept trying to kick him as he grabbed her dress by the
neckline and ripped it open and yanked it off her arms and tugged it
down over her hips and off her legs, stripping her naked. She was turning
slowly at the end of the rope as he snatched up the quirt and began
whipping her with hard fast strokes.

She yelped with each strike of the quirt as it cut into her back and
breasts and belly. She was quickly striped and streaked with blood from
teats to thighs. John looked stricken but kept his tight hold on the girl
and she was crying and screeching, "Stop it! Stop it!" And though Edward too was horrified, he felt something else at the same time, something
attached to the horror and yet apart from it, something his twelve-year-
old heart could not have named but which thrilled him to the bone even
as his throat tightened with shame.

Daddyjack beat her for less a minute and then flung away the quirt
and embraced her about the hips and pressed his face between her breasts,
sobbing and mixing his tears with her blood. Then he eased her down
and untied her hands and massaged the circulation back into them and
brushed the sweated hair out of her eyes as she lay still and watched him
without word. He told Edward to fetch a cloth and a bucket of water and
when he brought them Daddyjack helped the woman to her feet and
gently swabbed the blood and dirt off her back and buttocks. Each time
he touched a laceration she bit her lip and tears spilled down her face.

"Give me it," the daughter said, holding her hand out for the cloth,
and Daddyjack let her finish the cleaning as he supported the woman
upright. The daughter made a thorough job of it, mopping even the blood
that had trickled into her mother's patch of private hair. The worst wound
was at the left nipple which the quirt tip had torn loose and the only
whimper the woman let was when the daughter dabbed the blood from
it with the cloth.

Dadddyjack then cradled her up in his arms and carried her into the
house and set her gently on the bed and covered her lower privates with
a blanket. He had the girl bring him a threaded needle and ordered the
boys to stop looking upon their mother's nakedness and they reluctantly
left the room. He gave the woman a folded cloth to bite on and then

sewed the nipple back in place as best he could while the daughter held the lantern close for him. The boys listened intently at the door but never once heard her cry out. It was a successful but clumsy surgery and the woman would bear the ugly scar to her death. When Daddyjack was done she looked bloodless pale but her eyes were red as fires and she watched him looking on as the daughter gingerly applied grease to her wounds.

Once the woman had been tended, Daddyjack took the girl outside and led her and the boys to the creekbank and sat them down and explained that he'd whipped their mother because she had been a whore. "She dishonored me as much as herself," Daddyjack told them, "and lied to me about it. Dishonored you too, all of you, since you got to live with the fact of being born of a woman who whored. What I did to her she's had comin for a long time."

"You ain't God!" Maggie abruptly shouted, startling Edward and John who looked at her like she might have lost her mind.

Daddyjack pinned her with a glare. "Missy," he said, "you ain't never goin to be near big enough nor old enough to talk that way to me. I won't shy from stretchin *you* on that tree if you don't show proper respect." The girl defiantly met his hard look as John sidled over and put a hand on her shoulder and she held her tongue. In recent months John had assumed an attitude of guardianship toward their sister that Edward found somewhat puzzling because Maggie had never given the least sign of wanting or appreciating anybody's protection.

"I blame naught but my own foolishness for marryin her," Daddyjack said. "I thought because she was so young and her uncle who raised her was a preacher she couldn't be but pure. That was damnfool thinkin and I admit it, but just the same, that son of a bitch ought have told me she'd been a whore, and he ought not have lied about her being orphaned by the cholera, which I finally come to get the truth of from people who knew it, people from down in the lowland where she was born. Come to find out she was born tainted. Her momma was a crazywoman who murdered her husband and then drowned herself when your momma was just a babygirl. That's right—that's just exactly what they told me. I never did let on to your momma that I knew. Figured it didn't much matter. Figured just because *her* momma was crazy didn't mean *she* had to be."

He paused to spit and to study the sky a moment.

"Now I know it *does* matter," he said. "I believe your momma like as not has some of the same craziness her own momma had. I'm tellin you so you'll know for a fact she ain't a right woman. I reckon it's something in the blood. It's what made her be a whore and then lie to me about it and taint my honor and yours too." He fixed Maggie with another look. "You ought to pray Jesus she ain't passed that bad blood to you as well, missy, though it's startin to look to me like she surely did."

Maggie flushed and looked away.

"She's still your momma, though," he told them, "and she's still my wife and that's a fact and nothin'll change it. Ye can pity her if you've a mind to, since she caint help what she is anymoren a rabid dog can do other than it does, but I say ye be wise never to believe a word from her mouth."

5

He did not raise his hand to her again for the rest of the time they lived in Georgia, though every now and then he'd plunge into a drinking binge of two or three days during which he glowered at her a good deal while muttering to himself. For her part she refused to speak. During the following year she said not a word to anyone, although she carried on with her obligations as always, including her conjugal duties to Daddyjack. She communicated with the brothers through gestures and facial expressions, commanding their attention with a clap of her hands and directing them to their chores with a jut of her chin or a pointed finger, putting an end to their horseplay in the house with a hard-flung sopping washrag and a stern gaze. At first Edward was amused by her dedicated muteness but he soon tired of it and he sometimes wanted to shake her and demand she quit the silliness. He thought she might be every bit as crazy as Daddyjack had said.

Maggie required neither gestures nor broad looks to understand their mother. She seemed able to read her eyes, to know her thoughts without the need of speech. John was fascinated by the uncanny bond between the women. He remarked upon it to Daddyjack one day when they were hewing oak. Daddyjack said he had noticed it himself but was not impressed. "It's lots of crazywomen old and young can shine with each other like that," he said, "especially if they of the same blood. Like mother like daughter is what they say, and I believe it's a true fact."

If Daddyjack was bothered by his wife's refusal to speak he did not let it show except sometimes late at night when Edward was awakened by the heaving and panting of their couplings and the ripe sweetsour scent of sex filled the small house. Daddyjack's voice would be low and rough in the darkness, exhorting her: "Tell me, woman! Tell me how much you like it! *Tell* me, damn you!" His mother would moan softly and the bed would toss even more convulsively and moments later Daddyjack would issue an explosive breath and collapse upon her and they would lie there gasping loudly in the dark for a few moments before pulling apart into their separate silences.

Throughout their marriage Daddyjack and Lilith had regularly attended the Saturday night barn dances held all about the county, but after the whipping she would dance no more. Daddyjack said he was damned if they'd quit going to the shindigs just because she refused to kick up her heels. He continued to hitch up the team every Saturday evening and drive the family to the dances. He told his wife that as far as he was concerned she could sit on a bench against the back wall till her ass grew roots but he was going to have himself a time, by Jesus. And he always did, dancing with girls who'd heard the story of the Klassons from the time they were children and were both terrified and thrilled to be whirling in his arms as their fathers and brothers watched after them anxiously and hoped Jack Little would turn to someone else's womenfolk for the next dance. His own daughter was now approaching an age and fairness of face and figure to draw attention, and she did love to dance, but it was clear to every man and boy in the place that her daddy kept a sharp eye on her even as he danced on the other side of the room and few were the young fellows brave enough to risk his ire by asking Maggie for a turn on the floor more than once of a Saturday night. Then came the night Rainey asked Lilith to dance and Daddyjack put a knife in his chest. Then came Florida.

6

They made their homestead in the deep timber, well off the main trace, on Cowdevil Creek near its junction with the Perdido River. The shadowing forest towered around them. They cleared a tract and built a two-room cabin and a stable. Lilith and Maggie planted a vegetable garden in a clearing that caught sun for part of every day. The mosquitoes were unremitting and the summer humidity made warm gel of the air and alligators ate the dogs in the first few weeks. Yet game was plentiful and they never lacked for fresh venison or wild pig and the creek was thick with catfish and bream and snapping turtle. They often spotted black bear lurking at the edge of the surrounding woods and they sometimes heard a panther shriek close by in the night. Huge owls on the hunt swooped past the house in the late evenings with a rush of wings like maladict spirits. They kept the stable and the henhouse bolted tight after dark. They hewed timber and trimmed it and sledded it to the creek and rafted it to the river where a logging contractor showed up on a steamboat every six weeks or so to buy it and float it downriver to sell to the lumber companies.

"It's a good place we got here, boys," Daddyjack said one evening when they all sat on the porch steps at sunset and he was mellow in his cups. Maggie sat in a chair with her feet up on the porch railing. "Ever man needs a place to call his own," Daddyjack said. "You boys remember that. Without a place to call his own a man aint but a feather on the wind."

But his drinking had now become dipsomaniac and his demons more frequently slipped their chains. In his sporadic besotted rages over the next three years he would accuse their mother of having coupled with that Rainey fool like a common yardcat, with him among others, from the time she was hardly more than a child. "The whole county probly knew about it, by damn! All these years they were *laughin* at me, laughin at Jack Little, the fool who married the whore! Probly *still* laughin!"

She endured his bitter tirades with a stonefaced silence that only stoked his fury, and, if he was drunk enough, he'd strike her. At such times John felt pulled between allegiance to Daddyjack and an impulse to protect their mother. But he could never bring himself to intervene. His sister would look at him with such accusation he felt cowardly. Edward warned him not to mix in their parents' scraps and not to pay heed to Maggie, who was likely to be crazy as their mother.

"Crazy's got nothin to do with it," John argued. "She's our mother, dammit! He ought not to hit her!"

"And she's his *wife*," Edward said. "It ain't for us to push into it."

At times now Daddyjack denounced their mother for her girlhood whoring even when he was fully sober. The hate that passed between his parents had become so rank Edward believed he could smell it like rotted fruit.

And yet they still mated. Not as often as before but more ferociously than ever, snarling like dogs over a bone, like they were set on drawing blood from each other. Edward knew John and Maggie heard them too, though they never spoke of it. His sister had lately become moody and increasingly reticent with her brothers and was even more closedmouthed than usual following a night of their parents' loud coupling. Her brooding troubled John but Edward simply shrugged at it, remembering Daddy-jack's admonition: "Like mother, like daughter."

One early morning they woke to find Maggie gone. She'd slipped out in the night and saddled Daddyjack's horse and made off as quiet as a secret thought. Daddyjack admired her nerve even though she'd taken his horse. "Wasn't the least bit of moon out last night," he said. "And I heard a painter yowlin in the south wood just before I blew out the lamp. Girl might be loony as a coot but she got more grit than many a man I could name."

Then he saw the look on his wife's face, saw she was pleased that the girl had absconded, and his good humor vanished and he cursed her for having raised a worthless thief of a daughter.

John wanted to go in search of her right away. It was his guess she had gone to Pensacola, the nearest town of size. Daddyjack agreed. "It's the surest place she'll find a whorehouse to work in," he said, and gave his wife a spiteful look. He stroked his mustaches in thought for a moment before deciding to let the brothers go after her. "I don't care if she comes back or not, but I want that horse. You catch sight of it you fetch it home, hear?"

A few minutes later they were mounted bareback on the bridled mules and ready to go. They each carried a small croker sack of food and a knife on his belt and each had three dollars in his pocket. "Don't be long about it," Daddyjack said. "If she's there you ought find her right quick."

"What if she's hid out, Daddyjack?" John said. "I guess it's lots of places she could hide in a town."

"Don't matter if she's hid out or not," Daddyjack said. "If she's there you'll find her. Blood always finds blood. If she went clear tother side of the damn world and you followed after you'd find her. Blood *always* finds blood. Now yall get goin."

All show of pleasure had fled their mother's face. She hugged herself tightly and regarded the brothers with a darkly fretful look that John was oblivious to in his distraction over Maggie and that Edward pointedly ignored it, reasoning that if she wanted to say something she could damn well open her mouth and do it. "Let's go," he said, hupping the mule forward with his heels.

7

Pensacola was loud with celebration on the sultry afternoon the brothers rode into town. It was America's Independence Day and the first Fourth of July for Florida since gaining statehood four months earlier. A brass band blatted in the main square and boys dropped firecrackers from the red-tiled Spanish rooftops onto the sand streets below and laughed to see how they frighted the animals. The brick sidewalks were thronged with uniformed soldiers and swarthy sailors, toothy Negro dockhands, straw-whatted farmers, burly timberjacks and sawyers, finely outfitted gentlemen escorting ladies in frill dresses shading themselves with lacy parasols. Jugs flowed freely and yapping dogs raced through the crowd.

"Whooee! They kickin they heels, aint they!" John said.

Edward grinned back at him. "I'd say we picked the right day to be here, son."

On a high wooden platform a dark-suited man in white muttonchops orated about Florida's glorious future while overhead fluttered the American flag and alongside it a flag striped in five bright colors emblazoned with the words "Let us alone." A salt breeze blew off the bright harbor just a block beyond the square and rattled the palm fronds and the brothers hupped the mules to the foot of a long wooden pier. They dismounted and walked out onto the dock and stood looking at the cargo ships laying ready to receive lighters bearing lumber and cotton and naval stores. A flock of pelicans sailed past just a few feet over the water and a flurry of screeching seagulls hovered above the docks. When they first settled in Florida the brothers had sometimes smelled the sea when the wind came strong from the south but this was their first view of it. In contrast to the close and deepshadowed world of tall timber the vast blue expanse of ocean and sky made them lightheaded.

They hitched the mules in front of a tavern on the corner of the square, agreed to meet back there at dusk, and split up to conduct their search, Edward in the side streets and John in the square. As Edward wended his way through the crowds he fixed closely on every blonde woman he spotted. Then he rounded a backstreet corner and heard "Hey, handsome!" and looked up to see a pair of pretty girls, a freckled redhead and a dusky mulatto, grinning down at him from a wrought-iron balcony. They were in bright white underclothes and the sight of their legs in tight pantalettes and their breasts bulging over the tops of their corsets nearly staggered him. "Get on *up* here, you rascally-looking thing, you!" the redhead called, and both girls laughed and beckoned him and the redhead squeezed her breasts and blew him a kiss.

He went inside and a goateed man wearing a checkered vest and a pistol in his waistband told him he could have the girl of his choice for five dollars and he had a plentiful selection. He had a gold front tooth that glinted in the light. Edward said he didn't have but three dollars and the man said all right then, since they weren't too awful busy at the moment he could have a special rate of ten minutes for three dollars. Edward handed over his money and picked the redhead.

His first time had been the year before when he and John were hunting up along the Escambia and came upon a pair of women scooping mussels from the glassy river shallows and towing a dugout behind them on a bowline. The older was the mother of the younger and offered her daughter's sex in exchange for the deer carcass they were carrying home on a shoulder pole. The brothers were quick to strike the bargain even though the girl was a softbrain with an drifting stare and a wet vacant smile. She was younger than their sister and her breasts were still only buds and she lay inert on the weedy bank while the brothers took their turns on her. They then gave their attention over to the woman who shied away and said no, not unless they added to the bargain. She had a thin white scar along one side of her face but was striking nonetheless and had full breasts under her worn wet shirt. Edward was about to offer his knife but John said they wouldn't break her neck, how was that for adding to the bargain? The woman looked from one brother to the other and then told the girl to go sit in the dugout. She lay down on the grass and pulled up her skirts and John fell to her. After Edward had his turn they loaded the deer in the dugout and watched the women pole the boat around the riverbend and then slapped each other on the shoulder and laughed.

He went back out on the street with the sweetpowder taste of the red-head's skin on his lips and her perfume on his hands and he was feeling very much a man of the world. He would have bought himself a cigar if he'd had any money left. He continued to search for Maggie until the evening vermilion sun glanced redly off the roof tiles and eased behind the palms and then the streets were in deep shadow and the first sidewalk lamps were being fired. He returned to the mules and found John already there and looking glum because he'd found no sign of their sister either. Edward told him about the whorehouse and the passel of pretties who worked there but John scowled and said they had come to find Maggie and not to look for a good time. Edward had anyway been cheated at a price of three dollars, John told him. Edward asked how he knew that and John said, "Hell, I guess everbody knows that but you." John did not in fact know any such thing but he was angry because they had not found their sister and was in no mood to hear about Edward's good time in a cathouse. Edward did not press the matter but the idea that he had been cheated was enraging.

They decided to eat supper before renewing the search and went into the tavern and ordered two platters of fried oysters, a loaf of bread, and a bucket of beer. After they'd cleaned their plates John ordered another bucket and when they finished it he suggested they try a taste of something with more bite and Edward said why not and they called for a round of whiskey. They raised glasses to each other and tossed the drinks down in a gulp. It was their first taste of spirits other than the vile stuff they sometimes bought from a downriver swamp rat named Douglas Scratchley and they expelled their breath slowly and grinned at each other. Edward said, "Well now, I guess I know why Daddyjack likes *this* so much."

At the mention of Daddyjack, John's mood darkened again. "He run her off, I'll wager. I wouldn't be surprised if she got to talkin smart at him and he hit her. She wouldn't of stood for it if he did."

Edward shrugged and said he wouldn't mind if John treated them to another drink. John said he'd didn't have enough money left to buy them even a smell of good whiskey. "If you hadn't gone and got yourself cheated in that damn cathouse we'd right now have the means for another."

The reminder rekindled Edward's anger. "Did that picaroon truly cheat me?"

John allowed that he truly had. Edward said he'd be damned if he would stand for it and got to his feet so abruptly his chair teetered and nearly overturned. "I guess I'll just go see that son of a bitch." John said he guessed he'd go with him.

In the central square a different brass band was playing by torchlight for a large appreciative crowd and the sidewalks still teemed with roisterers of every stripe. The air felt heavy and cool. When they got to the brothel the place was doing livelier business than it had been doing that afternoon. A queue of patrons extended out onto the front walk, and through the open door Edward saw a different man now taking the patrons' money and directing every man in turn up the stairway each time someone else came back down.

He stopped a man coming out the door and asked him what the rate was. The man smiled and said, "Two dollars, son, same as always." He asked how much time with the girl that bought and the man laughed and winked at the grinning onlookers. "Why, just as much time as you need to empty your breech, boy, so long as you don't make a damn courtship of it."

"What're ye thinkin to do, lad," a man in the line called out, "sit and take tea with the lass, maybe, before ye get on with it?" Loud guffaws down the line.

Edward asked the first man if he knew a fellow with a checkered vest and chin whiskers and a gold front tooth and the man said, "Walton? He went to get some eats while I was still in line. He'll be back by and by."

The brothers went down the street and crossed over and came back without attracting attention and took up positions near the mouth of an alleyway and kept a lookout in both directions. They hadn't been waiting ten minutes before they spotted the checkered vest heading toward them on their side of the street. John ambled to the edge of the sidewalk and spat into the street and busied himself brushing off his shirtfront. Just as Walton was about to cross over, Edward said, "Mister Walton, can I have a word with you, sir?"

When Walton paused to fix suspiciously on Edward in the dim light John grabbed him from behind in a tight bear hug and yanked him into the shadowed alleyway and Edward leaped forward and snatched the pistol from the whoreman's waistband. Walton bucked and spun and lost his hat and crashed through broken crates and empty barrels, cursing and trying to shake John loose but John held to him like a hog dog. Edward grabbed Walton by the shirtfront and hit him in the face with the pistol barrel four fast times and Walton's knees gave way and John let him fall and Edward joined him in kicking the whoreman in the head. The men across the street were all looking now and one of them yelled "Hey! What the devil there!" Edward quickly went through Walton's pockets and dug out a handful of money. As some of the men started toward them the brothers raced away down the alley and around the corner and into the crowd milling in the square.

At the bar of the tavern they learned they had twenty-one dollars and they agreed it was sufficient compensation for the whoreman having cheated Edward. The barkeeper said, "What you boys do, strike it rich?" and laughed. Edward bought a bottle of bourbon and the brothers went

out and mounted their mules and casually rode through the crowded
square, not hupping the animals to a trot even when they spotted a handful of roughs from the cathouse shoving their way through the packed
sidewalk. The men were studying faces and looking in the door of every
public house they passed. Edward eased Walton's pistol out of his belt
and cocked it and held it close against his belly as the mule made its
unhurried way through the clamorous street but none of the roughs
caught sight of them and a minute later they were back on the north road
for home.

8

"We should of stayed and looked some more," John said. Darkness had
given way to a hard blue dawnlight. They had ridden through the night
and were deep in the pines, off the Escambia trace and well north of
Pensacola and no longer concerned that they might have trackers behind
them. "She might of been there. That many people, she could of been in
there amongst them and we never saw."

"She wasn't there," Edward said. "She'd been there we would of seen
her. Listenin to the music, dancin, you know her. I'd say we looked that
crowd up and down pretty good. Anyhow, we'd of stayed and we'd of
sure had dealins with them boys from the cathouse."

"I ain't afraid of them."

"Didn't say you were and I ain't either."

"Then what do they matter?"

Neither said anything for a minute, then John said: "Could be she
wasn't outside. Could be she was inside somewhere. Workin maybe."

"Doin what? I was in that cathouse, Johnny, I saw the kind of girls
they have. She couldn't of worked in one of them houses if she wanted,
not till she gets bigger grown."

"A lot you know about it," John said, his face tight. "Been to one
damn whorehouse in your life for ten minutes. I'll have you know some
of them places have girls younger than her. Anyhow, I didn't mean she
was bein no whore. It's other sort of work she can do."

"Hell, it wasn't nobody but whores and barkeeps workin yesterday in
all that celebratin. The plain and simple of it is she wasn't there."

"Then where in the hell *is* she?"

"Somewhere west, probly. Mobile maybe."

John spat hard and said nothing more for a while. Then he said: "Dad-dyjack sees that bottle he'll sure thank you for it and drink it all himself."

Edward pulled the whiskey out of the croker sack and admired its color against the light. "Believe you're right," he said and uncorked the bottle and took a swallow and passed it over to his brother. They paced their drinks so that the bottle lasted them most of the remaining ride. They didn't take the last drop of it until they were within ten miles of the homestead and they asked each other if they seemed drunk and told each other not so anybody'd notice and both of them laughed.

9

They smelled the smoke before they covered the last mile of the trace through the heavy trees and came out into the clearing and into the acrid haze lingering over the blackened remains of the house. Only the rock chimney and part of the back wall were still upright in the ashes. The stable stood untouched but the pigpen was open and the pigs were gone. The brothers slid down from the mules and stepped carefully through the ruins and kicked at the larger chunks of black-crisped wood. They studied the ashes closely and came on the stockless and warped remains of the Kentucky rifle and the smaller Hawken but found no trace of bodies. They looked at each other and John's face was pale and strained but Edward felt only a strange excitement he couldn't define. The slight whis-key buzz in his head had given way to an excited curiosity and a feeling that his life had already been altered more profoundly than he knew.

"Sons."

Her voice was behind them and they turned to see their mother stand-ing at the edge of the woods. John breathed "Damn" at the sight of her. Her face was bruised and one eye swollen purple and her hair was in disarray and the upper part of her dress was ripped. She spread her arms wide as if to receive them to her bosom and the torn dress parted to reveal one pale breast and its darkly scarred and twisted nipple.

"He *killed* her," she said, her eyes were whitely wide and seemed fixed on some horror in her mind. "He lay with her, yes, yes he did! He fouled his own *daughter*. He *lay* with her I say! And she told him she would tell, she said she would tell her brothers—tell *you*—and so he *killed* her and sank her in the creek for the gators and the gars to eat all up. He did! He *did!*"

Edward said, "What the *hell*, woman!" He was certain she was gone utterly mad. But John's eyes were as wide and anguished as the woman's and his fists quivered at his sides and Edward thought the look of him more frightful than the woman's crazy words.

She slowly came forward with her arms out to them, speaking fast and breathlessly. "He *told* me so. After you went off. Told me and laughed and beat me and said he would kill me too and say I tried to murder him in his sleep. Tied me to the bed and beat me. Cut his ownself so he could show you how I tried to kill him. But I got loose. I run out and hid in the woods and waited and waited for you and he set the house afire and he tromped around in the woods huntin me and he . . . oh Jesus."

Her gaze had gone to something behind them and her arms closed tightly over her breasts. They turned and saw Daddyjack limping out of the woods from the other side of the clearing and coming on with the big Hawken in his hand. The crotch of his trousers was stained red and he wasn't looking at the brothers but only at the woman as he came now at a gimping trot and cursing her loudly for a hellish whore. The woman whimpered and began backstepping stiffly toward the trees. Daddyjack stopped short and threw up the Hawken and fired. The ball passed between the woman's legs and belled back the skirt of her dress and pulled her down.

And now John was running at Daddyjack with his knife in his hand and howling and Edward ran after him calling for him to stop. Daddyjack watched them come and swung the Hawken by the stock neck and caught John on the shoulder with the barrel and knocked him to his hands and knees. His eyes were wild as he gripped the Hawken by the barrel with both hands and stepped up to John with the rifle raised high over his head like a club. Edward cried "NOOOOO!" and the pistol was in his outstretched hand and cocked and pointed and it cracked flatly in a small huff of smoke and the ball pierced Daddyjack's left eye and exited behind his right ear in a bloody spray of brain and bone and he went sprawling onto his back with his arms flung wide and his teeth bared and his remaining eye wide and unbelieving.

The woman sat on the ground and stared at her sons as they gaped upon the body of Jack Little, her hands over her mouth, covering the smile so bright in her eyes.

10

They carried the body a half-mile into the timber and took turns digging a deep grave under a wide wateroak overlooking the creek. The Hawken leaned against the tree trunk and its powderflask and ball pouch lay alongside. Edward searched Daddyjack's pockets and found tobacco and a pipe and matches and a money pouch containing six dollars in paper currency and silver. And he found the razor-keen snaphandle knife with a tapered seven-inch blade that had killed Rainey up in Georgia those years ago. Scratched into the wide top part of the blade were the initials "H.B." Edward folded the blade back into the haft and put the knife in his pocket.

The crotch of Daddyjack's pants was stiff and dark with dried blood but there was no rip in the cloth nor sign of a bullet hole and Edward's curiosity would not be denied. He undid Daddyjack's belt and began to tug down his pants.

"What are you *doin?* John said. "Don't do that!"

Edward tugged and grunted and got the pants past Daddyjack's hips. His privates were wrapped in a bloodsoaked bandanna. Edward removed the covering and exposed a nearly severed phallus and a slashed scrotum from which one testicle was missing.

"Sweet Baby *Jesus,*" John said softly. Then said: "Damn it, pull up them britches! Oh, goddamn, pull em up!"

They gently eased the body into the grave and Edward dropped down in the hole and closed Daddyjack's remaining eye and carefully placed his hat over his face and then climbed out and they shoveled the dirt over him. They worked without talking while a flock of crows squalled loudly in the high branches. When they got back to the ruins the sun was almost down to the treetops and their mother was gone with both mules.

11

They built a fire in front of the stable and got a hatful of eggs from the hen roost inside and boiled them for supper in a small blackened kettle they found in the ashes. Edward cleaned and loaded the Hawken. He recharged the pistol too but lacked a bullet of proper .44 caliber size and so packed it with a load of smooth gravel he'd scooped from the creekbank.

They were agreed to abandon the homestead. They neither one desired to remain on this burnt piece of ground that held their father's accusing bones and the likely possibility of visits from agents of the local order. Daddyjack had often gone to the nearest villages for supplies and a bit of conviviality in the taverns and was the sort people did not forget, the sort they would surely begin to ask after in his prolonged absence.

They sat before the fire and stared into the wavering flames and listened to the hoots and croakings and splashes and the sudden beatings of wings in the surrounding night. The sky was thinly overcast, the moonlight ghostly pale. A heavy mist off the creek drifted in through the trees and made a yellow haze around the fire.

"The son of a bitch," John said.

Edward glanced at him but said nothing.

"Listen," John said, "I know the woman's truly bout half-crazy, but it aint real hard for me to believe some of what she said. It aint real hard to believe he got good and drunk and all hotted up and got him a notion about Maggie. He was always lookin at her legs when she'd put them up on the porch rail the way she used to. You know good and well he did."

Edward said nothing but he recalled that all of them had watched Maggie's legs when she put them up like that and they'd all grinned whenever they caught each other looking.

"But *kill* her? I cant hardly believe that! Sweet Jesus, his own *daughter*. Bad enough he'd . . . you know, *do* it to her. But he couldn't of *killed* her." He spat into the fire and turned his face away. "Could he done that, Ward, you reckon?"

Edward did not look at him. "I don't know."

"God damn it," John said softly. And then after a while said: "That was a hellacious good shot."

Edward looked at him. "I never even aimed. Goddamn luck is what it was." He grimaced and spat viciously. "Shit! *Luck* don't hardly seem a fit word for it."

"Does to me," John said. "Luckiest thing ever to me." He paused and dug in the dirt before him with a stick. "You didn't have no choice about it. You know that."

Edward shrugged.

"It was him or me."

Edward stared at the flames.

"He was fixin to bash out my brains."

Edward spat into the fire and said, "I guess."

"Guess all you want but he was. You hadn't shot him it would of been me you buried yonder."

His voice was strained and Edward glanced at him and saw that his face was unnaturally pale in the firelight. They watched the fire slowly burn down. The darkness gathered closer.

"If you feelin sorry for it," John said, "well, I know you only did it cause of me."

Edward blew a hard breath. "You aint got to say anymore about it."

"I know I don't. I just wanted to say *that*."

"All right, you said it."

"All right then."

Edward well knew that what was done was done and would never be undone, not by any power on this earth. No matter how much his brother might set himself at fault and no matter how much they might talk of it and no matter what he might do in the rest of his life, none of it would ever change the fact that he'd fired the ball that blew the brains out of their daddy's head. It was a truth as unchangeable as his blood and bones and there wasn't a thing to be done about it, not now or ever.

He was feeling something else as well, something he couldn't put name to. Something to do with the way their mother had looked at them as they carried off Daddyjack's body.

After a while they went into the stable and bunched some of the straw into beds and took off their boots and lay down. Neither spoke for a time and then Edward said, "What I cant believe is he cut hisself like that. Not like that."

"I believe he went crazy," John said. "He was always sayin how momma and Maggie was crazy, but it could be he got craziern either a them ever was."

"You'd have to awful goddamn crazy to cut your ownself like that."

"Could be he was."

"I don't know. Maybe."

They lay without speaking but neither fell asleep. John said: "I wonder where all she's headed?"

Edward thought about that a minute. "Hell, I'd say."

John leaned away from the straw and spat. "Well then," he said, "I guess it's a damn good chance we be seein her again, aint it?"

12

And now in the first gray light of dawn Edward carved intently with the snaphandle knife on the stump beside the stable. He finished just as the sky began to redden and John rose from a fitful night's sleep. They rolled their blankets and tied them tightly and hung them across their backs like arrow quivers and they put the rest of the eggs in a croker sack. Armed with the Hawken and the pistol and their knives they set out for the western trace. John paused at the treeline and took a rearward look at the burnt house. But Edward did not look back. He was sixteen years old and restless in his blood and he had carved his farewell into the stump alongside the stable: "G.T.T." Gone to Texas.

II

THE BROTHERS

1

They hiked upriver and reached the shallows on the follwing afternoon and there forded the Perdido into Alabama. They walked till sundown and made camp by a willowcreek. They built a fire and talked very little as they ate the last of the boiled eggs and then they rolled up in their blankets and slept. The next day they crossed the Tensaw on a lumber barge and another few miles farther west they paid ten cents each to cross the Mobile on a pulley ferry. Purple thunderheads towered to the south over the Gulf. The scent of the sea mingled with the smell of ripe black bottomland and coming rain. Seahawks circled in the high sky.

The ferryman was a garrulous graybeard with a pegleg and a jawful of chaw. The ropy muscles of his arms stood sharply as he worked the pulley rope and told of having lost the leg to a crocodile in the wilds of southern

Florida when he was down there in search of Spanish gold.

"Not a alligator, mind, I mean a goddamn *crocodile!* I was fordin a mangrove saltpool and never saw the sumbitch till it bit my shin right in two. Sounded just like a dog snappin a chickenbone, only lots louder and for damn sure no chicken ever let out a holler like I did. Ever bit of fifteen foot long and I never saw it till it had me. It's lots of people don't think it's much difference twixt a gator and a crock. Hellfire, it's only the same difference as twixt a bobcat and a painter is all the difference it is. Get yourself bit by a gator then go get bit by a crock and you'll know the difference mighty goddamn quick."

Edward said he had seen a gator kill and eat a redbone in less time than it takes to tell. "Dog was trottin along the bank and the next thing you knew it wasnt nothin there but a bull gator with a mouthful of bloody hide and a big grin of teeth."

"Gator's fast all right," the old man said, showing his skewed and blackened teeth in what could have been either grin or grimace, "but crock's faster and you'd care a whole lot less to get chewed on by one, I can by damn assure you of that." He spat a brown streak of juice at a turtle sunning itself on a chunk of driftwood and missed it by a whisker-breadth and the turtle plopped into the blackwater and disappeared.

He asked where they were headed and when Edward said Texas the old man's mouth turned down and he shook his head. "Aint nothin get me to go to no damn Texas. Ever Texan I ever met been craziern a beestung cat. All them Mexicaners they got there don't make the place no likelier neither. And they's Comanche everwhere you turn. They got ways to kill you the devil hisself aint thought of. No, thankee! You boys can have all my share a Texas and ye welcome to it."

The ferry bumped against the western bank and the old man hopped off and made the painter fast to a cottonwood trunk. The brothers slung their bedrolls over their shoulders and bid him farewell and hiked up onto the trace and headed south. The old man stood spitting chaw juice and watching them until they were out of sight round the bend.

2

The sky grew darkly purple with thick rolling storm clouds and early that afternoon a hard rain came sweeping down. It fell for two hours and then abruptly ceased and the clouds broke and the sun shone through. Steam rose off the tamped earth of the river trace and their clothes were dry by sunset.

They put down for the night in a clearing hard by the river. They built a good high fire and some of the wood was yet damp and popped like pistol shots and threw high trailing sparks. They cut thin willow branches and sharpened them to long fine points and sharpened too a dozen smaller greensticks . Each then took up a flaming hickory brand and a willow spear and went to the riverbank and stepped down to the edge of the reeds where colonies of frogs were ringing in a steady clamor. They held their torches forth and saw a horde of red eyes shining in the cattails. They worked quickly and with practiced smoothness, gigging frogs on the spearheads and wrist-whipping the willow lance backward to send the frogs arcing up to the higher ground to writhe and spasm in the glow of the fire. In minutes they took four dozen and then put aside their gigs and torches and cut the legs off the frogs and pitched the remains in the river. They stripped the skin off the legs and pinned several legs on each greenstick and roasted them over the fire until the juices dripped and hissed in the flames. Then they sat back against the broad trunk of a huge oak and ate loudly, smacking lips and licking fingers and tossing the thin bones into the river reeds and pausing but to burp. When they were done with eating, Edward took out the pipe and pouch of tobacco he'd removed from Daddyjack's body and filled the bowl and fired it with a match and took several billowing puffs before passing the pipe to John.

They passed the pipe back and forth and smoked in silence for a time. The wavering light of the fire played on their faces. Then John said: "What if we was to run up on her?"

Edward looked at him. "On who?"

"Momma. What if we come up on her twixt here and Texas?"

"You been thinkin on *that?*"

John shrugged "Kindly. I'd like to know how come she just up and went like she did."

"Cause she's craziern a drunk Indian is how come."

"Well, I don't reckon it'd hurt nothin to ask after her."

Edward looked at him. "I tell you what—I hope to hell we *do* find her, cause I want them mules."

John stared at him for a moment. "I guess she figured she had right to em."

"Well *I* figure we got as much right to em as she do. Leastways to one of them. Wouldnt have to walk all the way to Texas if we had us a damn mule."

They stared into the fire for a time and then John said: "What-all you figure we gone *do* in Texas?"

Edward looked at his brother and shrugged. "What *you* figure?"

"I aint give it a lot a thought."

"Well I aint neither. I figure we just get there and then we see what-all we do."

"That's all right by me," John said. He studied the cloud-streaked sky for a moment and then hawked and spit in the fire. "Still, I been thinkin on it *some* the last coupla days. I been thinkin how maybe, well, it'd be nice we had us our own place."

Edward stared at him.

"Why not?" John said, his tone defensive against the argument he perceived in his brother's eyes. "You've heard all them pilgrims talkin about the timberland in Texas. They say it's ever bit as good as in Florida, better maybe. We could get us a piece of it and work that sumbitch into somethin good. Who knows more about axin trees than we do? Tell me somethin we don't know about sawyerin. We could have our own mill is what we could have. If Daddyjack wasnt no good for nothin else he sure enough taught us all there's to know about cuttin wood."

Edward fell to repacking the pipe. They had never spoken of it but he had always sensed that John desired nothing so much as to work his own land and raise a family and live in the way of most men. The Florida homestead would have been his elder brother's natural birthright, but now they both of them stood unrooted and Edward knew the circumstance weighed more sorely on John than on himself. As he tamped down the pipe and struck a lucifer to light it, he knew too that he could not favor his own vague and restless yearnings above fidelity to his brother, who was all that remained to him of loyal kinship in the world. If nothing else would do for John but to settle in Texas and work a tract of timber, then that's what they would do.

Still, there were arguments to be made.

"What if it's noplace left to homestead?" he asked. "What if we got to pay cash money for this here piece a property ye be so set on?"

"No place *left?* In *Texas?* About the biggest damn place ye ever laid eyes on? Where they say the timber just goes on and on as far as you can see and then goes yonder more?"

"I'm just sayin what *if?*"

"Well, it's like sayin what *if* the sun falls down tomorrow is what it's like sayin. It just don't make sense."

"What *if*, Johnny?"

"Then we'll work for wages, goddamnit, till we've saved up the stake we need," John said. "It's others who done it and you know it well as me. You think it's somethin others can do that we can't? You and me together, Ward, we can do any damn thing and just show me the man says we can't."

So ardent was his brother's faith that Edward had to smile.

"Listen Ward, Daddyjack was right about one thing. A man with no place to call his own aint but a feather on the wind."

Edward's grin widened. "Is that why I been feelin so light in the ass lately?"

John laughed. "Go ahead on and make all the jokes you want, but you know it's true. You and me, we aint gone stay no feathers on the wind, not us. Hell, Ward, we can have us a nice place, a damn *business* is what we could have us, if we do this right."

"Whatever you say, big brother," Edward said. "Whatever you say."

3

They followed the river trace downstream for the next two days in a steady rain that eased to a drizzle as they slogged into Mobile like apparitions of the drowned. The streets lay deep in red mud and the air was heavy with the smell of clay. They checked the hotels first thing and found that no one named Lilith Little had lately been registered in any of them and none of the desk clerks recognized John's descriptions of her.

They decided to check the liveries and in the first one they entered they saw one of their mules standing in a stall.

"Hey Foots," Edward said. The mule swung its head to look at him and twitched its ears. The Remus mule wasn't there.

The stableman had got up out his rocker with a grin when the brothers entered but their apparent recognition of the mule wiped the false cheer off his face. A white bulldog stood at his side growling low with its nape bristled and teeth showing. The stableman hushed it with a snap of his fingers. He was tall and beefy and was missing the larger portion of his nose which looked to have recently been bitten off or somehow torn away and the wound was raw and gaping.

"You boys need yourselfs a mount?"

"Done got one," John said. "That mule there's ours."

The man looked over at the mule and then back at the brothers. "That a fact?" He regarded them closely and then spat to the side. "I guess yall got a paper on it?"

John looked at Edward and Edward stared back at him and then they both looked at the stableman.

"We don't know about a paper," John said.

The stableman crossed his arms. "Then yall got no proof the animal's yours."

"Don't need no damn paper to know what's ours," John said.

"Reckon not," the stableman said. "But knowin and provin's two different things. The law don't care a good goddamn what all you know, only what you got the proof of. You want that animal, you got to prove it's yours or you got to pay for it."

"*You* got a paper on that mule?" Edward asked.

The stableman sighed and went to a battered desk in the corner and dug a key out of his pocket and worked it noisily in the drawer lock and opened it. He thumbed through a thin stack of papers and extracted a sheet and called the bulldog over beside him and told it to stand fast and then beckoned the brothers to the table and the light of the overhanging lantern. "I reckon you boys can read?"

John reached for the paper but the man put his big hand over it and held it flat on the table. "You aint got to touch it to read it."

The signature at the bottom of the bill of sale said Joan Armstrong but John recognized his mother's hand. He looked up from the paper and nodded at Edward. The stableman described her as having hair reddish dark like a roast apple. "Face of a angel but for them eyes. Them eyes seen things no angel ever did I'll wager you that. And somebody done recent put a shiner on one of them. Tell me true, boys: You know the woman?"

Edward looked away and spat. John said, "We might know her."

"Thought you might," the stableman said, looking closely at them both. He told the brothers she'd been there two days ago. "Walked in here with the mule on a lead and said she wanted to sell it. I said how much and she said whatever's fair. I said did she have a paper on it and she said no. I said who's it belong to and she said it belonged to her husband who up and died real sudden and didn't leave her much and that was why she had to sell the animal. You boys tell me now—was that a lie, do you know?''

"No," John said. "It wasn't exactly no lie."

"Not exactly," the stableman echoed. He pursed his lips and nodded as though mulling a fact of significance. "She was some galled at bein asked for a paper," he said. "Asked me did she look like a dishonest person. Well, my momma didn't raise no peckerwoods but she raised me never to offend a lady neither, so I said no mam, I'd be proud to buy the animal if she'd be so kind as to sign this here bill to make it all nice and legal and above the board, as they say."

"Says here you paid but twenty dollars," Edward said.

The stableman chuckled. "I started at twelve but she wouldn't have it. But I could see she was in kind of a hurry to be on her way so I hemmed and hawed and raised the offer one slow dollar at a time and she practically called me a damn thief. I said she was free to go to some other stable and see could she do any better and she said we were probly all in cahoots. I do believe she been around some. But like I say, she looked in a hurry, and when I said twenty was as high as I was ever goin to go she took it."

"Was there a girl with her?" John asked. "Bout yay high."

Edward looked at his brother. They had neither one spoken of their sister since they'd abandoned the charred homestead. He himself did not want to believe that what their mother had told them was true, he did not *feel* that it was, and he was surprised to know that John still had his doubts as well.

"Didn't see no girl. Come in by her sweet lonesome."

"Twenty dollars is some less than that animal's worth," Edward said.

"That's a true fact," the stableman said. The raw nose holes flared over a broad grin. "It's some of us with a natural-born talent for business."

Edward took the pistol from his waistband and said, "I'll give you twenty dollars and this here gun for it," Edward said.

The stableman laughed and shook his head. "Got a sense of fun, don't ye boy?" he said.

Edward's eyes narrowed. The pistol muzzle was pointed at the ceiling but now he slid his finger over the trigger and put his thumb on the hammer. The stableman glanced at the pistol but did not yield his smile.

John put his hand on Edward's arm and said, "Leave it be. He got the paper and that's the damn law. Let's go." Edward stood fast a moment longer and stared hard at the stableman but the man refused to be stared down and simply grinned at him. Edward spat to the side and tucked the pistol in his pants and the brothers went out into a sprinkling rain.

The stableman went to the door and looked after them and called: "You boys come back and see me you decide you need yourselfs some mounts. I give the best deals in town and that's a fact."

4

The dark sky rumbled steadily as they went about the town and looked in the few other liveries but the Remus mule was in none of them nor Daddyjack's horse. None of the stablemen had seen any woman or girl fitting the descriptions the brothers gave.

By the time they'd checked the last livery the rain was falling hard once again, pocking the muddy streets and clattering on the rooftops. They went in a tavern and the lantern flames guttered in their sooty glass in the sudden flux of air they admitted through the door. The roof drummed with rain and the room was close and dimly lighted and rank with the smell of dampened men too long unwashed. Shadowed faces turned their way and conversation fell off as the brothers stood and slung water off their hats onto the floor. They went to the bar and ordered whiskey and gulped it down and ordered another and sipped at it mutely as the talk in the room gradually renewed. When they finished the second drink they went outside and stood on the small porch and watched the rain.

"Well, it aint like to let up anytime soon," John said, scanning the heavy sky and then looking down the street to westward. "Last I heard, Texas was still yonderway. Sooner we get goin again the sooner we be there."

'I aint leavin without that mule," Edward said.

John looked at him.

"Well I aint. I aint lettin no thievin smitty have that mule for twenty dollars. I don't care she signed a paper on it."

"Well hell, bubba, when you decide *this?*"

"In there just now." Edward was looking toward a side street and John followed his gaze and recognized the street as leading to the stable where they'd see the Foots mule. He looked at Edward and said, "That stable-buck looks a rough ole boy."

"He cheated her of that mule and I aim to get it back. And he don't scare me none."

"Didn't say he did and he don't me neither," John said. He looked down the street again. "You want that mule, I say let's get it."

Edward regarded the overcast sky. "Be full dark soon. Best wait till then." He caught John's look at the tavern door. "I aint scared a him but probly better we don't front him half-drunk, either."

John shrugged and nodded. They'd wrapped their firearms in their blankets to protect them from the rain and now uncovered them and checked the locks to make sure they were still dry and then wrapped the guns again. They sat on the porch with their backs against the wall and waited for nightfall and when it came they got up and trudged down the thickmudded street.

The rain had again slackened to a drizzle amid continuing growls of thunder but the clouds were yet thick and roily and riding low. Sporadic lightning shimmered the street with blue light and black shadows. The wind was stronger now and shook water off the trees in heavy splattering sheets. They could hear the river's swollen rush. The smell of raw clay was strong on the air. The buildings along the main street were closed and dark but for the taverns and pleasure parlors whose windows showed wavering lamplight and resounded with music and laughter. A pair of horsemen draped with slickers went sploshing past, joking loudly about Mobile's sporting ladies.

They rounded the corner and saw a cast of pale yellow light in the livery and eased up to the door and looked inside. The stableman sat in his rocker sipping from a jug and addressing the bulldog lying at his feet with its chin on its paws. They stepped inside and the dog flexed to its feet with its back roached and fangs bared, growling low.

The stableman set the jug on the floor and rose from his chair and John leveled the Hawken at him from the hip and the man stood fast and looked mournful. Edward took a coiled rope off a stall gate and tossed it to him and told him to tie the dog short to a post. The man did it and then Edward ordered him to hand over the key to the desk drawer and sit back down in the rocker. He bound the man snug to the chair with a length of rope while the bulldog snarled and slobbered and strained against its short leash but did not bark. John fashioned a rope hackamore for the mule and slipped it on the animal while Edward went to the desk and opened the drawer and found the bill of sale and folded it and put it in his pocket.

"We could take any of these mounts we want," Edward told the stableman, "but we aint here to steal from you, only to take what's rightly ours. You paid twenty dollars for old Foots, but it was cheatin money cause you know good and well this mule's worth more, so it's only fittin you lose what you paid."

As John began cutting a wide strip off a burlap bag the stableman said, "You thievin me, boys, no matter how you shine the light on it. You gone have the law on you. You sure you want that?"

"How you gonna prove to the law you even had a mule stole?" Edward said. He patted his pocket. "Where's your damn paper on it?

"You ever decide you want to make us a fair offer on it," John said, "you come see us in Pensacola." He winked at Edward over the stableman's head. "That's our home and that's where we headed."

John rolled the burlap strip and gagged the man with it. Edward stepped outside to make sure the going was clear and then John blew out the lantern and the brothers doubled up on the Foots mule and rode down the street and out of Mobile in the falling rain.

5

They rode steadily through the night and most of the next day, taking turns sleeping one behind the other, pushing westward, putting distance between themselves and Mobile. The rain fell and fell. They were sodden to their bones. At first light they began scanning the murky landscape behind them for signs of pursuers. The sagging sky looked made of clay. On the trail along the bottoms the water was to the mule's belly. They kept a sharp eye for moccasins. The only sounds were of the mule's huffing breath and splooshing forward progress, the rain pattering the trees and dimpling the water. A dead pig drifted past, its upturned eye dull as stone, and then a dozen white chickens, bloated and giving off feathers to the breeze. When a catfish as big as a boy broke the surface alongside them the mule frighted and Edward was unseated and nearly kicked in the head and he swallowed mouthfuls of muddy water as he struggled to his feet while John got the animal steadied again.

Late that afternoon the rain abated but the sky remained leaden. As the mule slogged through water to its knees they spotted something large bobbing beside a canefield some thirty yards ahead and close to the road. It looked to be a heavy cut of timber but as they drew near they saw it was an empty coffin. Within the next half-mile they came upon four more and all of them empty. The air assumed the odor of rot. Now the road curved around a wide cypress stand and they saw more than a dozen coffins afloat where a graveyard had flooded and the rising groundwater had forced the coffins up out of the softened saturated earth. Most of the coffins were lidless and empty and some were hardly more than a few rotted boards still clung together on a rusted nail. Cadavers in various states of decomposition carried on the slow current of the flood. Most were the color of the earth itself and some were snagged on shrubbery and in the cane and those with upturned faces showed empty black eyeholes and rotted yellow grins against the gloomy sky.

Now they saw two men in black slickers on a nearby rise applying a prising bar to a coffin and the lid screeched and came asunder and one of the men bent over the box and cried out, "Luck!" He dropped to his knees and lifted a moldered hand into view and pulled a ring from its finger and rinsed it in the water and held it up for the other man to see. But the other had caught sight of the brothers and now unslung his rifle and pulled off the rag he'd wrapped around the breech to keep it dry and he held the weapon pointed at them from his hip.

The brothers passed slowly within thirty feet of them and Edward jerked on the hackamore to pull the curious mule's eyes away from the graverobbers. John held the cocked Hawken propped across his thighs with his finger on the trigger. The men were bonefaced and grizzled and there was nothing in their darkeyed aspect save hard wariness. No one spoke and John kept his eyes on them until he was turned around almost completely on the back of the mule. The graverobbers watched them in turn until the brothers went around the next bend and out of sight.

6

They camped that evening in a small clearing on a stretch of high ground thick with shrubbery and hardwoods and flanked by a swift creek running high on its steep banks. Edward hacked branches off a water oak and sliced off the wet bark and used the inner wood to kindle a fire while John went to the creek and shot a large snapping turtle for their supper. They cut steaks out of it and roasted them on sharpened greensticks propped against the firestones. They built up the flames and took off their boots and set them close beside the fire and then stripped naked and hung their clothes and blankets on frames fashioned of willow branches around the fire to dry while they ate. When their pants and shirts were dry they put them on and rolled up in their damp blankets and went to sleep.

Edward dreamed that he was back in the cabin in Florida and sitting across the table from Daddyjack who was hatless and wildhaired and stared at him with one sad eye and a socket gaping empty and hung with streaks of dried bloody gore. He did not seem angry so much as curious and somewhat puzzled. Edward's heart was pounding. He told Daddy-jack he was sorry, he truly was, but he'd had to protect his brother. That's good, Daddyjack said, I aint chiding you for it, brothers ought always to look out for each other. Then he made a face and shook his head and Edward did not understand and asked what he meant and Daddyjack shook his head again. He turned in his chair and looked out the window into the darkness beyond and Edward saw the ragged red-black hole in the back of his head where the pistol ball had come through. Daddyjack pointed out into the dark and said, "The bitch knows." And then his mother was at the window and looking in at them and smiling exactly as she had the last time he'd seen her.

He woke in darkness. His face was wet and a sprinkling rain ticked on the foliage. The vague quartermoon shone dimly through scudding violet clouds. The fire had burned down to a bed of bright embers and raised a ghostly smoke in the drizzle. There was a rustling of shrubbery and he distinctly heard someone say in a whispered rasp, "Here. Fire looks like."

John whispered "Ward" in his ear and lightly touched his face. Edward nodded and rolled out of his blanket and put on his boots. They started toward the trees along the creekbank but they'd gone only a few feet when a rifle blasted from the trees behind them and Edward felt himself clubbed high and hard on the back and he staggered forward and fell crashing through saplings down the bank and into the high water of the rushing creek.

Water seared in through his mouth and nose and he gagged and felt himself being pulled along the bottom by the current and he could not get upright and was sure he was going to drown. He grabbed wildly and caught hold of a root and arrested his downstream tumble and found footing and at last managed to thrust his head out of the water and gulp down air. He grabbed a willow branch and pulled himself grunting up the bank and sprawled on his belly and choked and spewed a gush of creekwater and lay there gasping. The long muscle along the top of his shoulder ached deeply and he felt the warm flow of blood over his collarbone but he could flex and rotate the arm and knew no bone was broken.

He lay still in the grass and listened, trying to mute his heavy breathing and tasting the acrid and muddy vomit in his mouth. It seemed to him he had heard another rifleshot while he was in the water but he wasn't sure. Now he heard voices in the darkness farther up along the creekbank but could not make out the words. Now somebody was coming his way, pushing though the foliage with no concern for stealth. Edward slipped Daddyjack's snaphandle knife out of his pocket and opened the blade with a flick of his wrist and crawled deeper into the shadow of a large bush and there crouched and breathed shallowly through his open mouth and watched the slightly lighter patch of sky above the bushtop and listened as the man drew closer.

When the man's silhouette crossed the patch of sky Edward silently rose up behind him and clamped a swift arm hard around his head with a sureness that came to him as naturally as breathing. His arm stifled the man's cry as he thrust the knife into his neck and twisted the blade and felt it scrape the neckbone and then he yanked it out and blood jetted hugely and spattered on the shrubbery and abruptly ebbed to a hot pulsing flow smelling of cut copper. It ran off the man's neck and down his rainslicker and onto the front of Edward's shirt. The man abruptly went slack and the dead weight of him was unlike any heft Edward had ever felt. He let the body fall. His heart banged against his ribs like a thing becrazed. The blood was warm on his chest and thick on his hands, the smell of it ripe on his face. He had to restrain the impulse to howl.

He was dizzy, weak in the legs. Sharp pain jolted through his neck all the way to his left shoulder. He put his fingers to the muscle joining neck and back and felt the wound. The rifleball had entered above the shoulder blade and exited just over the collarbone, which flared with white pain to the touch. Blood pulsed from the wound. His shirt was sopping.

A rifleshot sounded from the direction of the campsite and a man yelped in pain and Edward dropped to his haunches. A voice yelled, "Harlan, help me! I'm bad hurt!"

He sheathed his knife and sidled over in the darkness to the dead man who he dearly hoped was Harlan. He stripped the man of powder flask and shot pouch and took up the fallen rifle and made sure it was loaded and started making his way back toward the campsite. He moved through the brush in a careful lightfoot crouch, hearing his own breath and the dripping leaves, smelling blood and raw earth.

He was within a few yards of the clearing when the wounded man called for Harlan again. Then his voice went higher as he said, "Oh Jesus, son, don't *kill* me. I wasn't lookin to—" There came a soft thud and the man groaned deeply.

Edward stood up and peered over the bushes and into the clearing where their campfire still cast a dull orange glow. John was standing over a retching man in a black slicker who lay on his side with his hands at his crotch. On the far edge of the clearing lay a man in a yellow slicker in such awkward attitude as only the dead can assume.

Edward stepped out of the brush and John spun around white-eyed with the Hawken held like a club and he saw it was his brother and lowered the rifle and expelled a hard breath. "God *damn*, bubba!" he said. "I thought sure you'd been shot." He quickly looked around and lowered his voice. "There's anothern out there yet."

"That's so," Edward said. "But he aint no trouble."

"How come's that? I didn't hear no shot."

"Snapknife don't shoot."

"*Snapknife?* Damn, son!" John's face was alight with admiration and more—with a wild elation of a sort as old as Cain. "Hell, little brother," he said, gesturing toward the yellow-slickered man, "we put down the lot, you and me! The lot! And them with the jump on us."

Edward felt himself returning his brother's grin. The man at John's feet drew their attention with a low moan. "Hey now," John said, "lookit here what we got." He put his boot against the man's shoulder and pushed him over onto his back and even in the weak light of the coalfire there was no mistaking the mutilated nose of the stableman from Mobile.

"Him and a coupla friends come all this way in the rain to shoot us for a damn mule that wasn't rightly his to start with." John grinned down at the stableman and said, "Your daddy oughta taught you to hunt some better."

The stableman looked at Edward and raised a supplicant hand. "Please," he whispered. Edward saw the dark stain over his belly where John had shot him and he knew the wound was mortal.

"What you want, hardcase?" John asked the stableman. "Another kick in the walnuts? You want me put you out you misery?" He raised the rifle to drive the buttplate through the man's terrified face and Edward said, "Johnny don't."

John looked at him, rifle poised.

"It aint a need," Edward said. "Not no more." His wound spasmed sharply and he clutched at it and yawed.

John hurried to him. "Damn boy—you bleedin!"

He dropped his rifle and eased Edward to the ground next to the coal-fire and helped him off with his blood-sopped shirt and examined the wound as best he could in the weak amber light.

"I'm all right," Edward said. "It just give me a smart is all."

John confirmed that the round had passed cleanly through the muscle over the collarbone. He told Edward to stay put while he fetched water from the creek. Edward was holding tightly to the wound and staring into the orange coals when he was startled by the stableman's loud groan.

Then the man's last breath gurgled from his throat and faded into the night.

John washed out his wound with creek water and fashioned a tight bandage for it from the stableman's shirt. They heard the whickering of the men's horses and found the animals tethered back in the trees just off the trail and brought them to the creek to drink. In the Mobile men's pockets they found two boxes of matches and a honed claspknife and less than five dollars. Among the dead men's possibles they found bundles of smoked mullet and ears of roasted corn and they built up the fire again and sat beside it and ate.

After a time John said, "I never thought it'd feel, I don't know . . . like *this*."

Edward saw the high excitement still showing bright in his brother's eyes.

John said, "Killin a man, I mean. I always thought, well, I don't know anymore what I always thought. . . . But I never thought it'd feel so . . . so damn *right*." He started to grin and then remembered who the first man was that his brother had killed and his grin fell away and he shifted his gaze.

Edward had himself been about to grin but just then thought of Dad-dyjack too. "I guess," he said, "it depends on who the fella is."

"Yeah. I guess."

They ate in silence for a time and then John asked if he thought others would come looking for these three.

"Don't believe any law will," Edward said. "I don't know who these other two are, but no-nose didn't say nothin about either of them bein law. I figure he might of tried to get the law on us but it wasnt interested in nothin so small-account as a mule the feller didn't have no papers on anyway. Still, it might could be some kin'll come lookin for em. We best be gettin on.''

The sky was dawning hard and gray as they stripped the Mobile men of their slickers and weapons, powder and shot. John took the stableman's black slicker for his own. The man who was sprawled at the edge of the clearing showed a nearly perfectly round hole over his left eyebrow and when Edward turned him over to take off his yellow slicker he saw the larger exit wound in back of the skull. He thought it was a hell of a shot under the circumstances. Johnny always was the shooter.

He replaced his shirt with the man's unbloodied one and then the brothers rinsed the slickers in the creek and put them on against the continuing drizzle. The yellowslickered man had been carrying a Spanish musket forged more than a century before. John examined it and snorted in disdain and flung it in the creek. The other two longarms were well-kept Kentuckys of .45 caliber with patch-and-ball boxes built into the stocks and complemented with nearly full powder flasks. One of the men had in addition carried a .54 pistol that John quickly claimed on the grounds that Edward already had a handgun and never mind that he lacked the .44 ammunition for it. They recharged the weapons and made ready to ride.

The best of the horses was a sorrel mare. The brothers flipped a coin for her and Edward won. He named the animal Janey in memory of a pretty girl he'd once met at a barn dance but never saw again. All the saddles of the party were worn and cracked. John mounted a sound but nervous bay and led the third horse, an aging dun, on a lead rope. Edward trailed the mule.

At midmorning the sun broke through the clouds for the first time in days. The high waters receded steadily and by early afternoon they were riding mostly through mud. John pistolshot a large rabbit and dressed it and they cooked it on a spit and ate half of it and saved the rest for later. John checked Edward's wound and saw that it was still swelling and oozing blood. At sunset they camped under an enormous oak on high dry ground and ate the rest of the rabbit and watched the western treeline blazing as if afire.

Next morning Edward was in high fever. The engorged wound showed the color of spoiled meat and the skin was drawn tight. He could raise his left arm only with grimacing effort. "It's nothin to do but burn it,'' John said. "Should of done her yesterday.''

He built up the fire and set a rifle ramrod in it until the metal turned bright red. Edward sat close by and positioned a stick between his teeth and gripped the belt over his belly tightly with both hands. Using the old bandage as a glove John picked up the glowing ramrod and said, "Bite down, bubba." He pressed the tip of the rod into the rear opening of the wound. The flesh hissed and smoked and Edward shrilled through the stick crunching between his teeth and the tendons in his neck stood like wires. John then inserted the rod in the front of the wound and the hiss was not as loud and to compensate for cooling he this time left the iron in a little longer before withdrawing it. Edward exhaled a shuddering breath and slumped forward and the cracked stick fell from his mouth coated with bloody saliva. The sickly smell of roasted flesh was like grease on the air.

John wiped the cleaning rod on his trouser leg and said, "Reckon we ought do it once more just to be sure she's done right?"

Edward looked up at his brother's wicked grin and smiled weakly. "You sorry son of a bitch."

"Takes one to know one, little brother," John said. "Takes one to know one."

7

Early that evening they came upon a family camped beside a cottonwood grove within sight of the trace. The western sky was a bright red streak smudged with thin purple clouds. Blackbirds squawked in their high roosts and tree frogs clamored without pause. The brothers asked if the pilgrims might spare a bit of coffee and were invited to take supper with them.

They hailed from South Carolina and were on their way to East Texas. The man was a farmer named Campbell, large and slow of speech. His face was badly misshapen, one cheekbone jutting sharply and the other sunken, one eye set higher and deeper than the other, the nose askew, the lower jaw out of line and the upper lacking both front teeth. The scars belied any notion that he'd been born with that face. The man had sometime been beaten near to death.

Farmer Campbell's voice welled from deep in his nose. He said he'd had his fill of Carolina and had long thought about going west but had been shy about putting his daughters in danger of the damned Indians. But he'd been keeping up with the news from Texas real close and figured that the Texians were sure to accept annexation to the Union, which Congress had approved back in winter. "Soon's it becomes a state the U.S. Army's bound to clear the savages off the land so's a man can make decent use of it," he said. "Hell, could be the Texians done annexed already. Course now, the damn Mexicans still got to be reckoned with. But they aint no big worry. Sonsabitches couldn't hold Texas against Sam Houston and two hundred Texians ten year ago and now they threatenin to go to war with the whole U. S. of A over where the border rightly sets. Well, they keep runnin they goddamned mouth like they doing and they just might find they aint got to worry about no border no more cause they won't have no damned country to have a border *for*, by Jesus!"

"You, Douglas Campbell!" his wife snapped at him. "You quit that awful language and all that blaspheming in front of your daughters!" The little girls were about nine and ten years old and seemed amused by their father's profanity. The farmer shrugged and winked at the girls and they hid their smiles behind their hands. The mother sighed in exasperation and busied herself filling the supper plates.

When Campbell asked where they might be headed Edward kept his attention on his plate of cornbread and beans and possum stew although he lacked his proper appetite and was still feverish. John told the man they were on their way to New Orleans. He said they had an uncle there who made furniture and was going to teach them the trade. Edward looked sidelong at his brother and marveled at his easy way with falsehood. They had agreed not to tell anyone their true destination in case someone should come along behind them making inquiries after two boys who'd but recently killed three citizens of Mobile.

At the end of the meal Edward tried to brace himself on his left arm to push up to his feet and a spasm of pain bolted from his shoulder up through his neck. The woman caught his grimace. "Why, son, you're hurt!"

Edward tried to make naught of it but Campbell too was solicitous and said if Edward was suffering an injury he ought to let his old woman have a look. "She's a natural-born healer if ever there was one," he said. Edward demurred but John said, "Let her see it, bubba. I aint real sure how good I done on it."

The woman helped Edward off with his shirt and made close examination of the wound and then turned to her husband and he stepped up and took a look at it and then looked at the brothers as if seeing them for the first time. Then he sat down and busied himself packing and lighting his pipe.

The woman commended John's handiwork with a cauterizing iron but neither she nor Campbell asked how Edward had come to receive such a wound. She ordered the elder daughter to form strips of bandage from a sheet of clean linen stored in a trunk and told the younger to boil a kettle of water and to use a bit of it to make a cup of red root tea. She fetched a handful of wild potato leaves from the wagon and ground them in a small amount of water to form a salve. When the hot water was ready she soaked a clean strip of linen in it and gently washed the wound and patted it dry and applied the leaf salve to it and rewrapped it in a fresh bandage. The younger girl presented Edward with a steaming cup of red root tea and the woman instructed him to drink it every drop. "It's willow bark," she said. "It'll rid what fever you still got."

Campbell and the brothers kept by the dying fire and drank coffee after the woman and the girls bedded down in the wagon. None of the three spoke for a time and then Campbell asked in a low voice if the boys might appreciate a taste of something a little stronger than just coffee. Edward and John exchanged grins and John said he believed a drink of something stronger would set real well. Campbell looked toward the wagon as if to ascertain that the woman was indeed asleep. He put a finger to his lips and stood up and went to a corner of the wagon and quietly detached a rucksack hanging there and brought it back to the fire and from it he withdrew a corked jug.

"My old woman thinks a sip of spirits is a swallow of the devil's own spit," he said. "She probly right. But hell, ever now and then a feller's got to have him a taste of good shine, else he's like to lose his sap altogether. Aint that right, you boys?" The brothers assured him that he was absolutely right. They were all speaking in whispers.

"Specially if it's a wounded man among them," Campbell said, pouring a generous dollop of moonshine into each cup. "Wounded man got to have all the medicinal help he can get." The brothers said he was as right as can be about that too.

"So happens I been carryin a real bad wound myself for moren a year now," John said with solemn mien. "Happened last year at a dance. Sarah Jean Charles refused to take a turn with me. Wounded my poor heart worse than a Indian arrow and I aint recovered yet." Edward grinned and the farmer lightly slapped his thigh and covered his mouth with his hand to stifle his chortle. The three gently touched cups and took a drink and there followed a succession of soft appreciative sighs.

They drank like that for a while, sipping steadily and smacking their lips. The farmer poured another round and passed tobacco to Edward who packed his pipe and lit it and passed it to John. They smoked and drank in contented silence and then had another round and again toasted each other without words. The moon was high when the farmer poured out a last drink for everybody and they touched cups and drank and then put down for the night.

In the morning the pain of Edward's wound was much abated and he had no fever at all. The Campbell woman examined it and pronounced that it was crusting nicely and then she bound it anew with a fresh bandage. The brothers took breakfast with the family and the woman packed a chunk of cornbread and a few hocks for them to take with them. They presented Campbell with the old dun in gratitude for his hospitality and his wife's treatment of Edward's wound and they thanked the daughters for their kindness too and then they rode off with the rising sun at their backs.

8

West into Mississippi. Days of fierce sunshine and thick wet heat. Ripe lowcountry smells. They meandered over low hills and through dense pinewoods, through forests full of moss-hung oaks and magnolia trees bursting with white blossoms. Some afternoons the clouds banked huge and dark over the Gulf and thunder rolled and lightning branched brightly and wind shook the trees and rain swept in and churned fresh orange mud. Sometimes it rained in the night and the brothers cursed and slept fitfully in sopping blankets. But in the mornings the clouds came asunder and the sun broke red through the trees and the rivers did not top their banks again in the rest of that sultry summer.

They knew no haste and rarely hupped their mounts to a trot. They sometimes stayed put at a campsite for days. They shot deer and gorged themselves on the roasted haunches and smoked the backmeat in thick strips. They climbed trees to achieve a vista and have a closer look at the clouds and holler their names across the treetops. They swam in lakes and netted catfish from the creeks with their shirts. They napped in the high summer grass. They slept in pastures lit pale as bone by moonlight, under skies black as mystery and blasting with stars. They claimed various blazing comets as omens of their own bright futures. They told each other of the beautiful women they were destined to be loved by, the great wealth they were bound to amass.

They were ferried across the Pascagoula by a labor gang working to repair a bridge and with them shared their bounty of smoked venison and from them learned the game of three-card poker which some called monte. The ante was two bits. Edward was incapable of losing. When somebody held an ace he held a pair of treys. When somebody had a pair of queens he held the four-five-six. John thought he'd won a hand when he laid down three sixes but Edward gleefully showed three eights and took the pot. He won one hand after another and laughed as he pulled in the money. The workmen's eyes went narrow and their mouths drew tight.

When Edward beat three aces with the seven-eight-nine of hearts to win for the eighth time in a row and increase his winnings to nearly twenty dollars, the aces holder threw down his cards and said, "You cheatin sumbitch!"

Edward sprang to his feet and kicked him in the throat before the man's knife cleared its sheath. John quickly mounted up and held the others at pistolpoint, his heart kicking wildly, while Edward scooped up the money and then stepped up onto the sorrell mare and can'tered off with the mule in tow. John sat his horse and kept the cocked pistol on the workmen until he was sure Edward was well away and then he reined about and lit out at a gallop to catch up to his brother. They laughed and whooped and rode hard till the sun was below the treeline and then they swung off the trace and into the deeper woods and there made a fireless camp and took turns keeping watch through the night but no one came after them.

9

They came upon a house-raising early one morning as the sun was just beginning to show through the trees. Several families had come together to help a neighbor put up his new cabin in a wildflowered clearing within sight of the trace and flanked by a wide shallow creek. John halloed the folk and asked if they might spare some coffee and the brothers were invited to step down to breakfast. They sat at one of two long puncheon tables and ate their fill of fried catfish and grits with red gravy, cornbread with molasses, boiled greens. They drank steaming cups of chicory. The tables were loud with talk and laughter and the children were enthralled by the two strangers, peering at them shyly and then covering their giggles with their hands when John or Edward winked or waggled their brows at them. They were generous workhardened folk, several of the families having settled in the region shortly after Jackson put down the Creeks, others of more recent arrival. The newest family, they whose house was today being erected, had come from the Alabama highlands to farm Mississippi's rich bottom country.

When the talk came round to the brothers John offered his lie about the uncle they were going to apprentice with in New Orleans and delivered his low opinion of Mobile and told of the floods he and Edward had come through in Alabama and told too of the graverobbers they'd seen at their grisly trade. Some of the men cleared their throats and cast sidewise glances at the women among them and the women concentrated intently on the plates before them and Edward gave his brother a look to warn him off any such further talk. They mopped their plates clean with chunks of cornbread and then looked at each other and John told the men at the table he and his brother would be proud to lend a hand and their offer was gratefully accepted.

Over the preceding days the building party had felled the timber they would need and trimmed it clean and cut the logs to length and hauled them by oxen to the cabin site. Today they would raise the cabin itself.

The house would be a two-room round-log with top-saddle corner notches and no dogrun. Edward and John grinned at the simplicity of it and the work went fast. At Daddyjack's side they had erected houses of square-hewn logs, using broadaxes with offset handles to keep their hands clear of the logs as they squared them. All that was required here was to notch the logs and raise the walls by rolling the logs one atop the other by means of skids, one pair of men hauling on the logs from above with ropes as another two men pushed them up the skids with sturdy poles from below. As the brothers worked with the party putting up the walls, other men rived shingles with mallets and froes and shaved them down with drawknives. Against one of the end walls, a group of older children under the direction of an elderly man erected a makeshift catted chimney to be later replaced with one of stone. The warm morning air shook with the steady clatter of axes and thumping of mallets. By the time the women rang the dinner iron the walls and most of the chimney were up and the roof frame was in place.

The men converged on the well to rinse themselves amid much familiar joking and shoving with each other and remarking upon the brothers' impressive skill with an ax. Then everyone sat to a dinner of venison stew and roast potatoes and blackeyed peas and yams and cobbed corn and biscuits and gravy and strawberry cobbler. The tabletalk was full of news of who in the region had married and who had been born and who had died. Most of the deaths reported had come by way of violent accident. One man's skull stove by a kick from a mule. Another man misstepping as he crossed a plank bridge and he and the young son riding his shoulders plunging into the quickmoving river where both did drown. Another's saw slipping wildly from its groove to gash his thigh to the bone and bleed him to death as he limped for home. Among the other news passed at the table was an announcement of a barndance to be held at Nathaniel Hurley's farm on Saturday evening next. John whispered to Edward that he surely wished they could be here for that, considering all the pretty girls about. When the men had done with eating they took another few minutes' ease with their pipes and cigars and then went back to work.

While one party of men completed the roof, another, including John and Edward, cut openings in the walls for windows and door, and still another set to chinking the walls with clay. The brothers demonstrated their mastery of a variety of saws and by the end of the day had secured reputations among these men as true craftsmen in timber. The sun was still above the trees when the cabin stood finished. The men clapped each other on the shoulder and each man gathered his tools and set them in his wagon and then everyone sat to a supper of bacon and beans, greens and cornbread.

Then the fiddles and banjos were brought out and everyone gathered on a wide cleared patch of ground and a redbeard called O'Hara sang a song about a girl named Molly in Dublin's fair city, and then one about sweet County Galway. When the lead fiddler called a square dance the folk hastened into formations and the fiddles and banjos struck up a lively tune and the lead fiddler called out the progression of actions and Edward and John who had learned to dance as small boys in Georgia did join in. There followed reels and waltzes and yet more square dancing, which seemed the most popular sort with these folk. In the light of the lanterns the dust raised by dancing feet cast the entirety of the scene in a softened yellow light and the brothers grinned and grinned every time they caught each other's eye as they danced with one smiling girl after another.

When they joined a few of the men for a sip from a jug of corn mash behind one of the wagons, Edward nudged John and said low, "You see that applehaired gal I been squirin? Bedamn if she aint givin me the encouraging eye."

John grinned and said, "I been way too busy mindin that blackhaired filly yonder. See her there—fetchin water for her daddy? Aint she the one?"

Edward affected to scrutinize the brunette and nodded sagely as he stroked his chin. "Well now, brother, I have to admit she aint about half-bad for somebody looks like she's put out a fire or two with her face."

John snatched him around the neck and mock-choked him. "You about the *blindest* son of a bitch!"

Edward laughed as he broke free. "*Me* blind? *I* aint the one thinks she's pretty."

Some of the men nipping from the cider jug were grinning on them, every man of them himself brothered and familiar with brothers' ways. The one nearest them leaned closer and said in a low voice, "I got to agree with this one here"—he indicated John with a nod—"about that crowhaired Jeannie Walsh. She's pret thing, all right. But you boys be careful not to let any these gals' daddies hear ye talkin too familiar about they daughters. Some a these men aint so toleratin of it like others of us."

Edward said, "We weren't meanin any disrespect."

"Say now, mister," John said, "which one's your daughter?"

"Well, now, truth be told," the man said, his grin spreading, "I aint got nary one. It's how come I'm so toleratin."

The brothers joined in his laughter.

They danced and danced. Their hats showed dark bands of sweat and their faces shone and their shirts were plastered to their chests and backs. When the fiddlers and pickers at last put down their instruments and the dancing was done, the girls they'd been dancing with were called away by their fathers. John and Edward stood and watched them go to their wagons. The daddies were waiting on them and both fathers scowled when the girls turned to wave goodnight to the brothers.

They put down their beds under a cottonwood hard by the gurgling creek and lay on their backs and stared up at the three-quarter moon shining through the branches.

After a time John said, "You seen how they looked at us?"

"They was some flirty gals all right."

"Not them. Their damn daddies."

Edward turned and spat off toward the creek. "They just watchin out for their girls," he said. "It's what daddies're spose to do."

"We're bout the best they seen with a damn axe or a saw, either one." John said. "But they know we aint got penny one nor a ounce of dirt to our names. That's why they looked at us like they did. Only reason. They aint about to let their daughters take up with nobody aint got the first bit of property." He propped himself on an elbow and looked at Edward. "It aint but one more good reason we got to get ourselfs a piece a land and work it into somethin any man'll respect. Then we'll see what one among them'll object to his daughter on my arm."

Edward smiled at his brother in the dappled moonlight. "I believe you had you one sip of that jack too much, what I believe."

"You know I'm right."

Edward sighed. "I know it, Johnny. Let's get some sleep."

Just before he fell asleep, Edward heard John say again, "You know I'm right."

They slept till daybreak and by then most of the other families were gone. The brothers took breakfast with the family living in the new cabin. Fatback and grits and sweet fresh cornbread and coffee. And after thanking them for the meal and accepting the family's thanks for their help in the house-raising, they mounted up and hupped their horses onto the western trace and followed their shadows westward.

10

They forded streams and creeks and rivers and made their way through forests so thick they were steeped in twilight at high noon. Eagles sailed from nests in the high pines and redhawks banked slowly over the meadowlands and tall blue herons stepped long-legged along the water shallows. Sharpbilled snakebirds stood on the banks and spread their wings to the afternoon sun. Owls regarded the brothers from bare-branch perches in the closing light of day. A scattering of wolves still roamed these woods and their aching howls carried through the trees. On some nights panthers screeched so near their camp Edward felt the hair rise on his arms. One misty morning they came upon a black bear sow teaching her two cubs to fish in a creek. The sow rose up growling and huge on her back legs with water pouring silver off her indigo fur and the horses

spooked and and the brothers had to fight the reins and then heeled their
mounts galloping down the trail.

On a Sunday morning of soft yellow sunrays angling through the trees
they witnessed a baptism in a misty creek behind a high-steepled white
church. The initiate was a tall man of craggy visage and hair as white as
his collarless shirt. As the faithful sang a hymn of joyful salvation he
pinched his nose shut and was tipped backwards by a pair of burly men
supporting him on either side and he was submerged entirely as the
preacher intoned words of purification. When he was pulled back up,
gasping and spluttering, a woman a few feet from the brothers leaned
toward a friend at her side and said loud enough for Edward and John
to hear, "I kindly pity them fish in the crick. They're like to choke to
death on the sins washed off *that* old rascal!" She caught sight of the
brothers' grins and blushed furiously for a moment before smiling back
at them and turning away.

Here and there along the road they found the remains of abandoned
wagons, most of them turned onto their side and picked-over to the axles
and broken up for firewood. Occasionally they came upon the moldered
carcass of a draft animal simmering with maggots. By the roadside one
day they found a yawning trunk from which spilled a variety of clothing,
including a pair of men's coats of the same size so that Edward's hung
a little loosely on his frame but John's fit almost as if it had been tailored
for him. The trunk held also a few frilly pieces of women's undergarments
and a woman's bent hairbrush. The brothers were roused by the feel of
the thin cotton bloomers with the lace edges and red ribbon ties. They
speculated wildly about its owner and how the trunk had come to be left
trailside with such particularly private dainties exposed to the passing
world. The underwear conjured a host of carnal notions and their night
was restless with concupiscent yearning.

Next day they turned south on the Biloxi road and entered the town
late in the afternoon and made inquiries at a livery. They were directed
to the western skirt of town where there stood a fine large three-storied
house shaded by live oaks and within view of a white stretch of Gulf
beach. The trees were dripping with Spanish moss, the air hazy with
amber sunlight.

The proprietress was a Mrs. Clark, a woman of middle years and aristocratic mien who welcomed the brothers graciously but informed them
that armament was strictly forbidden in the house and told them they
would have to leave their guns and knives with their outfits in care of

the stablemen. She permitted them to take a drink in the parlor while they looked over the girls and made their selection but then insisted they avail themselves of the bathtubs in the rear of the house before the girls could escort them upstairs. John grumbled that the place sure had a lot of rules but the brothers did as she asked.

They sported merrily in adjoining rooms until gentle rappings on the doors signaled an end to the entertainment or a call for additional payment if they wished to continue their lark. The brothers poked their hard pale torsos into the hallway and exchanged grins and said why not. John paid the floorwoman for another go and she provided fresh towels and they traded girls who ran past each other in the hall in giggling nakedness. Their lickerish roister lasted through the night. By dawn they had each had a turn with the same six girls and they limped down the stairs like battle casualties and hobbled out to the stable and carefully mounted up. They had spent all but their last three dollars and Edward used one of those for a bottle of bourbon to take with them. Every girl of the house stood out on the verandah with Mrs. Clark and blew kisses to them and called them champions and the brothers grinned proudly. Mrs. Clark told them of a house in Nacogdoches, Texas, under the proprietorship of her widowed sister, one Mrs. Flora Bannion, and recommended its services to them should they ever visit that lively town. As the brothers rode away the girls waved goodbye and called for them to come back soon.

That night they sat around their campfire and passed the bottle between them in silent contentment for a while. When the bottle was a third gone they began to talk wistfully about the wonderful time they'd had. When its level dropped below the halfway point they began to compare the various attributes of the different girls. They agreed that Jolene's breasts were the best shaped and Sue Ellen's nipples the longest and Belinda's face the prettiest, that Rose May's legs were the most beautiful and Cora's belly for sure the most sweetly rounded and Marcie's lips the most kissable and Belinda's mouth the most talented. But when Edward said there was no question Sue Ellen had the best rump John disagreed and said anybody with a pair of eyes could see that the prettiest rear end in the place was Cora's.

Edward said anybody who thought Cora had a prettier rear than Sue Ellen couldn't tell a woman's ass from a sack of yams. John said Edward might or might not know something about yams but he sure as hell didn't know a thing about women's asses and come to think of it he didn't know all that much about teats either since it was plain as day that the prettiest ones were Belinda's. He'd only agreed about Jolene to be polite but he was damned if he cared to be polite to somebody so ignorant about women's asses. Truth be told, John said, Belinda's mouth wasn't near so expert as Cora's either.

Well if the goddamn truth be told, Edward said, he didn't agree with *any* of John's choices and had only agreed because the Good Book said we ought be kindly toward the feebleminded and anybody who believed Cora had the prettiest ass of the bunch had to as feebleminded as it was possible to be and still know how to breathe in and out.

John said Edward knew as much about the Good Book as he knew about women, which was absolutely nothing.

They persisted in this dialogue until the bottle was empty and their lines of reasoning were thoroughly entangled and they had trouble remembering which girls they thought superior in which respects. When they finally rolled up in their blankets Edward said he couldn't understand it but he was feeling even ranker right this minute than he had the night before.

"Here my poor ole peter's about skinned bloody and my balls feel like some mule stepped on them and *all* I can think about is being pressed up against a nekkid girl."

John said he knew what he meant and wasn't it a shame a man couldn't store up the satisfaction he got from a good humping so he could have it handy to draw from in lonely times. "You know, the way a squirrel saves up nuts for the winter."

Edward said that was about the looniest goddamn notion he had ever heard of and asked John how long he had been suffering from such mental affliction. John's response was a loud wet snore. A moment later Edward too was asleep.

He dreamt of the girls in the Biloxi house. He saw himself now with Jolene, now with Marcie, now with Cora and Sue Ellen and Rose May all together and writhing happily on the bed. Suddenly his heart jumped at the sight of Daddyjack sitting on the side of the bed in his bloody pants and running his hands over the girls' nakedness and grinning widely. The girls were laughing and one of them ran her thumb around the rim of his empty eyesocket and the others took turns fondling his crotch and blood seeped between their grasping fingers. Daddyjack grimaced and clutched at his mutilated privates and looked at Edward who was also feeling sharp pain between his legs. "Hurts like fury don't it?" Daddyjack said. Edward awoke and loosened the crotch of his trousers which had been binding his sore erection. He had dreamed of Daddyjack nearly every night since leaving Florida.

11

They occasionally came across pilgrim families on the trace and traded venison for coffee or cattail bread or ears of sweet corn. They bathed in rivers and washed their clothes and watched brown otters splashing in the water and chasing each other on the banks. They dozed naked in the sun while the clothes dried and the horses and the mule cropped contentedly in the long grass.

"I don't know how come we didn't start livin like this long before now," Edward said drowsily at the fireside one evening as he lay on his side and stared into the flames.

"Cause we hadn't kilt Daddyjack before now," John said flatly without looking at him. He had been moody and closemouthed all evening and was sitting crosslegged and poking at the fire with a stick. His face was shadowed by his hat.

Neither of them said anything more that night, but for the first time Edward wondered if John too had dreams of Daddyjack, and he decided that yes, very likely he did.

12

They rode under bright sunwashed skies. They rode through oak groves hung nearly to the ground with green-gray tendrils of Spanish moss that looked like hair of the dead, the hair of great witches whose forest it might have been. They rode through fields of pale grass that brushed their horses' bellies. For most of a day they rode through clouds of burgundy dragonflies which folk of the region called skeeterhawks and whose abrupt shifts in speed and direction seemed to violate all laws of nature and none did alight on them. Crows squalled from the high pines, mockingbirds shrilled from the brush. Fording a wide slow creek they caught the unmistakably malodorous scent of a cottonmouth, the smell so strong they knew it rose off an entire nest and the horses breathed it as well and riders and mounts all looked wildly about but saw no snakes and the brothers hupped the horses splashing across the creek and up onto the other bank and away from that fearsome stink.

On yet another afternoon they dismounted at a creek to refill their canteens and had no sooner stepped down from the saddle than a huge boar came crashing out of the brake and charged at them. The frighted horses broke away and so startled was Edward that he lost his footing and went headlong into the creek as the boar came at him with its sharp tusks forward. The hog ran to the edge of the bank and veered around and spied John standing agape and went for him. John jumped up and grabbed an oak branch and hugged himself fast to it with arms and legs, the branch some seven feet above ground and perhaps half that distance above the snorting boar's upturned tusks. Then Edward's longrifle cracked and John heard the ball smack into the boar's side. The hog staggered and turned and charged again at Edward who stood sopping in his clothes and now snatched up John's rifle and aimed and fired and the ball struck the animal in the face and its front legs gave way and it tumbled to a heap at Edward's feet and there shrieked and kicked wildly until Edward fired a pistol round directly between its ears and killed it.

John dropped to his feet from the branch and laughed. "Hoo! The look on your face when you seen that pig comin out the bushes! And the *splash!*" He threw his hands up wide to recreate the toss of water when Edward fell in the creek. His walk was staggered for all his hard laughter.

"That wasnt near as funny as the sight of you hoppin up on that tree limb, tell you that. I didn't shoot that sumbitch you'da been up there all damn night, been there till you fell off and he'd of stuck you good then." But Edward's grin was weak. He knew he'd cut the more ridiculous figure. He knelt beside the boar and affected to study it intently until John drew closer, still laughing, and then Edward sprang up and caught him in a bear hug and lifted him off the ground and lumbered with him toward the creek. John saw what he had in mind and struggled fiercely to free himself but Edward managed to stagger to the bank with John tight in his embrace and he let a maniacal laugh as he lunged over the bank edge and they went tumbling into the water. They came up spluttering and grappling and now one of them would shove the other's head underwater for a moment before the other slipped free and assumed the advantage and thus did they dunk each other a half-dozen times each until they called the water wrestling match a draw and crawled up on the bank, coughing and cursing and laughing. Gasping for breath, John struggled to say, "But you *really* ought of seen . . . how you looked when—" and

Edward grabbed him in a headlock and they continued in their wrestling in the creekside grass until the sun was almost down to the trees and both of them were exhausted.

While John butchered the boar in the evening twilight Edward went in search of the horses and found them grazing in a pasture a quarter-mile farther along the trace. They roasted the pig on a spit and the haunches proved stringy but the backribs were tasty and the brothers gorged themselves to greasy satisfaction.

The next afternoon they came on a camp meeting in a wide meadow at the edge of the forest. There looked to be nearly three hundred people attending—men and women, children and oldsters—and the brothers had heard their raise of voices for nearly half-an-hour before the camp hove into view. The day was cloudless and sultry and they reined up behind the crowd and sat their horses in the shade of the trees and watched a preacher in farmer's clothes declaim from an elevated plank pulpit set on the far side of the meadow. He patted at his face with a balled bandanna and his strained voice carried faintly but audibly at this distance. He was speaking of the countless blessings of the Christian Way, the rewards of the Life of Virtue, and his audience listened and nodded and punctuated his pauses with a chorus of "Amen."

Now the preacher bade "God bless you" to the multitude and stepped down and was replaced by another minister, this one looking the part, dressed as he was in black suit and black string tie and a widebrimmed black hat under which black hair hung to his shoulders. For a long moment he stood looking out at the crowd without speaking, leaning on the podium as though he might leap over it and into the field of folk. In the midst of this sweltering summer day that had men mopping steadily at their brows and the ladies fanning themselves without pause, he seemed to stand cool and dry.

And now he began to address the brethren about the wages of sin, which were not only death but the everlasting tortures of hell, the horrifying punishments that were the destined lot of lost souls. He started out slowly and speaking so low that the brothers could barely make out his words at the rear of the crowd. But his voice rose as he warmed to his theme, rose and hardened and assumed the pounding stentorian tone of ordained authority. He spoke of roaring hellfire and sulfurous smoke and pains beyond imagination, beyond all nightmare. Spoke of horned and cloven-footed demons with thorned whips, demons whose aspects and essence defied all rational description and whose eternal delight it was to evoke the rupturing screams of the damned. Demons whose laughter was of the Devil's madhouse and mingled with the incessant wails of the condemned and rang without pause off Hell's burning walls. He spoke of smells that made the rankest jakes and the odors of the rotting dead seem the stuff of flower gardens by comparison, of stenches beyond any foulness ever known to human breath. He conjured one horrifying vision after another and the crowd had early on begun to moan in terror and self-pity and now some among them were weeping openly and some sobbing in their visions of what lay for them beyond the grave if they did not now act to ensure their soul's salvation. And now some among them began to howl and roll their eyes and shudder convulsively as the preacher's terrifying proclamations carried across the meadow and even as John and Edward exchanged uncertain grins their horses began to stamp and shy as they sensed the growing fear and madness around them and the brothers were obliged to rein the animals tighter and speak sooth-ingly into their ear. In another moment the mass of the faithful was taken with jerking convulsions and some fell to the ground and rolled about and all of them moaning and praying loudly to Jesus to save their damned souls. And still the preacher bellowed his perditions. The horses now so spooked they fought against the reins and themselves seemed to be af-flicted with the same jerking convulsions of terrified ecstasy that engirt the crowd.

"Damn this!" John yelled at Edward. "Let's go!"

They reined their mounts around and dug their heels into their flanks and the horses in a single motion rocked back on their haunches and shot forward as if their tails were afire. They didn't slow from a gallop until they were two miles down the trace and even then the mounts preferred to pace at a nervous can'ter than settle to a walk.

John said he hadn't ever seen anything like that before and wouldn't care if he never did again. Edward shook the sweat out of his hat and said he wasn't too taken with it either.

"Why you reckon they-all got afflicted like that?" John said.

Edward said he didn't know. Then said: "Could be they just real hard believers."

"Believers?" John said. "Believers a *what?*"

Edward shrugged and now his mount seemed easier about being reined down to a walk.

John slowed his horse and fell back alongside his brother. "What could somebody believe that'd make him do like they was doin?"

Edward looked at him and shrugged again. "I don't know. What-all they been told, I guess."

"*All* them people believe somethin just cause they been told it?"

"I can't think a no other reason for it."

"Well, damn if ever *I* want to believe *anything* that much."

Edward grinned. "*I* believe we aint got too much worry on that account."

They looked at each other a moment as if each was suddenly seeing something of himself in the other. And then they laughed and rode on.

13

One late afternoon of lacy pink clouds they forded the Wolf River near a small town from which came such a clamor the brothers thought a celebration in progress. They chucked their mounts toward the settlement and soon spied a raucous crowd of about a hundred people gathered around a large live oak at the edge of town. A pack of dogs ran about in high excitement, barking and yipping, locking up in snarling skirmishes broken up by the kicks of laughing, cursing men.

As the brothers drew closer they saw the noosed end of a rope sail over a lower branch of the oak tree and jiggle down slackly to waiting hands. A moment later the rope went taut and the assembly roared as a barechested Negro with his hands tied behind him ascended into view above the spectators' heads, his neck stretching to unbelievable length under the strangling noose, his legs kicking madly, his eyes as big as eggs and his tongue bulging and the front of his beige pants staining with urine.

The rope suddenly slackened and the Negro dropped hard to the ground and the crowd cheered lustily as some of the men rushed forward and kicked him and small boys hit him with sticks and women spat at him and the dogs bit at his legs. Then the rope stiffened with a quiver and jerked the Negro to his feet like an immense marionette and again hauled him up in the air and stones arced out of the mob and glanced off his head and now his kicking legs were hampered by his trousers which had been pulled down to his shins to expose his private parts.

A tall chinless man in a stovepipe hat stepped forward and reached up and grasped the Negro's dangling genitals in one big hand and stretched them out and with a single smooth stroke of a straight razor neatly sliced them away. Blood jumped from the wound and ran bright red down the

Negro's black legs and the spectators howled. The tall man tossed the severed parts into the pack of dogs and there was a fierce brief fray among them and one hound tore away the scrotum and gulped it down and another raced through the laughing crowd with the tip of the dark phallus jutting from its jaws and the other dogs on his heels.

Again the rope went slack and the hanged man dropped hard to the ground. The noose was loosened and readjusted on his swollen misshapen neck and water was flung into his battered face and the mob crowed with delight as the word rippled through the throng: "He's alive yet!"

The brothers exchanged wide-eyed looks. Edward leaned down in the saddle and asked a man standing close by, "Say mister, what'd that nigger *do*, anyhow?"

The man looked up sharply and squinted at him and then at John. "Somethin he damn sure wisht he hadn't!" Several men and women within earshot laughed heartily.

Now the Negro's pants were pulled off his feet and he was doused with lamp oil and again the noose was tightened and again he was hauled into the air. The man in the stovepipe hat struck a match that sparked sulfurously and put it to the black man's bloody and oil-sheened legs and in an instant he was entorched. His legs churned wildly as though they might gain purchase on the air itself and bear him away from this horror. He was screaming through the strangling noose loudly enough to be heard above the bellowing mob and Edward had never heard such a scream from the mouth of man, could never have imagined the sound.

The flames rushed up to engulf the Negro's head and his shivering shrieks rose higher and he convulsed and spun like a great dark fish on a line and now the ropes binding his hands fell away in flames and his arms flailed and streamed fire and then quite abruptly his hands fell and his screaming ceased and he hung limp and was dead.

The corpse continued to burn. The roasting flesh crackled and bubbled and dripped and now the crowd caught the horrid stench and women clamped kerchiefs to their faces and hurriedly pulled their children away. The brothers looked at each other and John said softly, *"Sweet baby Jesus!"*

The fire licked up along the noose knot and the rope abruptly came apart and the remains fell to the ground in a great burst of sparks and smoldering pieces and some of the spectators cheered and some guffawed and a few women shrieked, some in fright perhaps, some in exultation.

Now the man in the stovepipe hat started back toward the town and he was hastily followed by a sunbonneted woman and a half-dozen boys and girls of varying ages and all of them marked by their father's lack of chin. Within minutes of his departing the rest of the crowd dispersed. Besides the brothers the only ones to linger were a handful of boys and a pair of men wearing pistols and neckties and aloof looks of authority as they leaned against the tree trunk and smoked their pipes and conversed quietly. The boys closed around the charred corpse and pointed out various aspects of it to each other and elbowed one another and laughed. One of them kicked the dead man's leg and knocked loose a crisped piece of what had so recently been living flesh and the boys all laughed louder. One of the men at the tree said, "That's enough now you boys, git along," and one of them muttered something under his breath to the others and the man straightened up with a sharp look and the boys raced away trailing peals of laughter.

The brothers looked upon the Negro's mortal residue a moment longer and then reined their horses around and rode on.

14

They hankered for New Orleans—Dixie City, so called since the U. S. purchase of Louisiana, when New Orleans banks issued ten-dollar notes printed with an English "Ten" on one side and a French "Dix" on the other. The Americans pronounced the French word in their own fashion and more often called the bill a "dixie," and the word quickly came to refer to the town itself. The brothers had heard about Dixie City's wicked pleasures and were eager to sample them for themselves. But such pleasures would come dear and they had spent their last six bits on a jug of whiskey proffered by a peddler they met on the trace. So they took work at a timbercamp just east of the Pearl River to replenish their empty purse.

They felled and trimmed cypress and sledded the logs to the river where some were lashed together in rafts to be towed and some loaded on broadhorns or keelboats, depending on the timber's destination and the waterways that must be navigated to get there. They worked hard the day long and put aside most of their earnings, but they alloted a little of their money each payday as a stake for Edward, the better gambler of the two, so he could sit in on one of the half-dozen poker games held every Saturday night in the crew barracks. Over the next few weeks he came out a few dollars ahead at the end of each of game, but there were too many sharps for him to win consistently.

Then one Saturday evening his luck ran riot and within an hour he'd won more than forty dollars. Whereupon a big Swede named Larsson accused him of cheating. As they stalked outside to settle the matter, stripping off their shirts as they went, the betting on the fight was clamorous. Because the Swede outweighed Edward by thirty pounds and stood a head taller, John had easily got three-to-one odds on his brother.

They fought in the torchlit clearing in front of the barracks, ringed about by the raucous timberjacks calling for blood, for maiming. For all his size and strength Larsson was like most timberjacks awkward and clumsy of foot. Edward was quick on his feet and fast with his hands and could punch with the force of a much larger man. He repeatedly sidestepped the Swede's lumbering charges and nimbly dodged his great roundhouse swings and countered with flurries that soon made raw butchery of Larsson's broad furious face. There were outraged cries of "Ringer!" from many in the crowd who had bet big on the Swede. After nearly fifteen minutes of mostly missing with his wild swings and being battered by Edward's sharp counterpunches, the Swede howled in frustration and charged at him with wide-open arms and caught him up in a bearhug and lifted him off his feet and bit off the top of his right ear.

Edward yelped and brought his knee up hard between Larsson's legs and the Swede's eyes bulged and his grip loosened and Edward butted him square in the face and the Swede released him and staggered back on wobbly legs with blood pouring from his nose. Edward then hit Larsson a terrific roundhouse on the jaw and sent him sprawling. Then rushed in and kicked him in the head again and again and had to be restrained by a clutch of cooler heads before he killed him.

John won more than seventy dollars in the betting. He pounded Edward's sore back in jubilation until Edward told him to stop it or he'd break his damned arm. On the following morning Edward's scalloped ear was swollen and caked with dried blood and his back and ribs felt as if he'd fallen out of a tree. But they now had plenty of money and were set to go to Dixie City. They sold the mule to a camp foreman and hired on as polemen on an antique and much-modified keelboat bound downriver with a load of cypress timber and a half-dozen milk cows. They put their horses aboard in the cowpen and on a cool early November sunrise cast loose for New Orleans.

15

They rode the Pearl's lazy current down to the delta, occasionally putting in at a river village for a big feed and a night of barndancing and scrapping with the local bullies. One late night on the river all heaven came ablaze with falling stars. "The Leonids," the captain said. The grizzled crew gasped and pointed like children at a fireworks show. Barrages of comets streaked like burning cannonballs and lit the roof of the world in flames. The brothers gaped.

They took on supplies one early afternoon at a riverside hamlet where a fair was in progress within view of the dock. The keelboat captain gave permission for his crew to attend but warned them he'd brook no reports from the locals of fighting or ill behavior toward the women of the town.

"We'll be in Dixie soon enough and ye can play the slap and tickle all ye want with the sportin ladies there. But here ye best keep it in your pants and be leaving your fists loose too. I have friends living here and I'll not have them bullied nor their girls bothered."

The fair was a small enterprise but a lively one. There were lines of tables whereat ladies exhibited their best quiltwork and men their wood carvings, where women sold servings of their best pies and cakes, bowls of their best stews, small sacks of their sweetest candies. There were pens for stock judgings and prizes awarded for the best hog, the finest steer, the most productive milkcow, the best-laying hen, the loudest cockiest rooster.

The largest tent was that of a traveling show that had but recently arrived in town and attached itself to the fair. A man in a derby hat and a red-and-white striped vest stood at the entrance flap and announced, "Step right up, gents, step right up and prepare yourselves to see some of the strangest sights ye'll ever see. Marvels and curiosities of nature, aye! And all the more amazing for being true, every one of them, for there's nought more amazing than the truth, don't you know?" The brothers looked at each other and shrugged and then paid the ten-cent admission and went inside.

The tent had been partitioned into two rooms by a high folding divider extended from the front wall to the rear. In the first room the brothers saw a green-caped man on a dais eat fire. He shoved the flaming end of a rod deep into his throat and held it there for several impossible seconds and then withdrew it still aflame and brandished it with a grin and everyone applauded. He held the flaming rod out to one of the keelboatmen and asked if he'd like a taste and the boatman stepped back and said, "*Hell*, no!" and the crowd around him laughed. Then another man took the fire-eater's place on the dais and this one carried a small sword with a bright thin three-foot blade and he held up a sheet of paper and neatly sliced it in two to show the sharpness of the blade's edge. Then he put his head back and slid the length of the blade down his throat and as it disappeared into his mouth the spectators gasped. And when he extracted the blade and they saw not a drop of blood on it they clapped and cheered and whistled in awe.

John leaned towards Edward and whispered, "Damn, it's some people'll put *any* damn thing in they mouth, aint it?"

As if to prove exactly how correct John was, the next performer to ascend the dais was a tall thin man with bloodshot eyes and bad sores on his face who pulled a garter snake from his coat pocket and held its wriggling form up high for all to see. In a single swift motion he brought the snake to his mouth and bit off its head and the tent fell absolutely silent as the remaining portion of snake lashed wildly and wrapped itself about the man's arm like an ancient Egyptian armband. The man then spat the head arcing into the air and the spectators jumped aside to let it fall clear in the midst of them. And then burst into the loudest cheers and applause yet.

The brothers heard a man behind them tell another that he's once seen a man in Nashville bite the head off a damn chicken and then choke to death on it while the crowd was giving him what was probably the biggest hand he'd ever got in his life.

And now there came onto the dais a brief parade of freaks. A fellow called the Rotting Man who was a biped festering sore. His nose and lips had rotted away and open sores covered his shirtless chest and ran with pus and the man indeed did stink like rotting meat. The Alligator Man had a normal-looking head and feet but was covered from neck to knee-caps with skin as thick and rough as gator hide. Then came a woman with a beard as bushy as any man's, and a tall sad-faced woman with a third teat about the size of a boy's fist between her two normal ones. And finally a little redhaired boy of about six who had eight fingers on one hand and nine on the other and no toes at all but for the big one on his right foot. Edward thought the boy had the saddest eyes he'd ever seen. Somebody standing close by the brothers remarked aloud that it looked like the boy's toes must've slid up some kind of way to his hands, and another said maybe his momma bounced him around too much before he was born. Both men laughed and boy looked at them with his sad eyes and the freaks all glared at them in the only show of awareness they had made toward their audience. The Alligator Man put an arm around the redhead boy and led him off the dais and out through a rear flap in the tent and the other freaks followed them away.

Edward marveled at the Alligator Man's gesture and the freaks' display of injured pride, at the seeming comradeship of outcasts. For a fleeting and almost frightening instant he felt he should go with them, felt it in a way he could never have explained, yet felt it as surely as he did his beating heart. He looked at John and saw him staring after the departing freaks too. Then John cut his eyes to him and Edward felt an inexplicable sensation of being outside the world but for his brother and he knew somehow that John was feeling the same thing. The brothers showed their teeth at one another. John feinted a punch and Edward feinted a counter and they laughed and punched each other on the shoulder and went into the other room.

Here were exhibits both living and preserved. Each in its own cage were a snapping turtle with two heads, a bulldog bitch with only one eye and solid bone and fur where the other should have been, a three-legged duck, a rattlesnake with two tails and each tail with its own set of rattles, an albino horny toad white as milk. There was also a pair of long benches on which stood rows of glass containers, some no bigger than a canning jar, some the size of a pony keg, and each held some human body part preserved in whiskey, the smell of which was strong in the tent. Several of the jars contained eyeballs. John found himself entranced by a jar holding a single eye as light-blue as summer sky. And then Edward was beside him and looking at the eye too and whispering, "That's just exactly the color of Maggie's." John looked at him and Edward's brow knit and he said, *"What?"* and John was surprised to realize he was glaring at his brother. He shrugged and looked away.

"That there's the eye of a girl stabbed to death by parties unknown," somebody behind them said and they turned to see the derbied man who had been attending the tent door. "That's what the feller said who sold it to me. Feller had no idear what happened to her other eye. Did you boys know that a person's eye will hold a picture of the last thing it sees before death? It's a true fact. You look real close into that eye and you might can see the face of the man what kilt her. Can be hard to see it, but it's there, all right. Looked in there real hard myself and if my own eyes aint tricking me I do believe the feller had a full beard and wore a muleskinner hat. Hard to see clearly though, so I figure she mighta had her eyes pret near half-closed while she was dying."

Edward snorted in derision and moved on to look at a pair of green eyes in another jar and the derbied man shrugged and followed after, saying that *those* belonged to a fine New Orleans lady who'd drowned herself in the Mississippi when she learned her beau, even as he was en route to her on a steamer, had been killed when a boiler exploded. John lingered at the blue eye and felt a great urge to bend down and peer closely into it. But he was as much afraid of what he might see there as he was loathe to have Edward laugh at him for a fool, and so he went instead to look on with his brother at a pair of eyes nearly blood-red with black pupils so wide only the barest rim of brown iris showed. The derbied man said they were of a convicted murderer who'd gone to the gallows swearing he was innocent.

They came to a line of larger jars containing little babies. One wasn't fully formed and had webbing between its tiny fingers and a lump of flesh between its legs and it was hard to say whether it would have been a boy or a girl. Another was a normal-looking baby boy but for the ragged hole in its belly and back. The derbied man said the child was about ready to be born when his daddy who was a hat-maker went crazy one day and shot his wife twice, once in the head, once in the belly, the second shot naturally killing the baby too.

There were containers with fingers and ears and tongues, some with male appendages. One jar contained a foot which the derbied man said he bought from a fellow in the north country. The man had taken an arrow just above the ankle and the wound got infected so bad his only choice was to die or cut off the lower half of his leg, which he did. "He thought to give that foot a decent Christian burial," the derbied man said, "but he figured if he did that he'd really and truly have one foot in the grave, and it give him the chills to think on it. But he didn't want to go around with the foot in his saddle wallet, either, knowing that soon's as the thaw came it would go to rot. I'm proud to say I give him a good solution to his problem. I told him it's be a lot better fate for that foot to travel around in my wagon. He sold it to me in a wink when I told him that so long as that foot stays in that jar of whiskey, he'll always have one foot *out* of the grave, even after the rest a him's dead and buried." The man laughed with his head back and mouth wide, exposing his mostly broken black-and-yellow teeth.

They came out of the tent in time to hear the call for final entries in the shooting contest. Standing shots at a plank target set againt a tree at a distance of fifty yards for the prize of a steer. In addition to more than a dozen of the locals, several of the keelboaters had signed up to shoot. At Edward's insistence John joined the competition too. He won the shoot handily and then sold the steer at bargain price to the first man to make him an offer.

16

They glided through the pass and into the open water of Lake Borgne under a bright morning sun. Pelicans crowned yellow and white banked and plunged into shimmering schools of mullet and resurfaced with their baggy mandibles pulsing with fish. The crewmen poled easily across the lake and then through a connection of canals, and on an early Sunday afternoon marked by brilliant blue sky and a scattering of high clouds as white as ginned cotton they entered the Mississippi.

It was the brothers' first look at the great river the boatmen called the Old Man. They stared dumbly at its immensity. Craft of every description plied the wide reach of its muddy surface. Steamboats the size of city buildings poured enormous plumes of black smoke from their stacks as their huge wheels churned the water white. There were tall-masted schooners and handsome sloops and sleek lighters and old flatboats and makeshift rafts and here and there a skiff hardly big enough to hold a pair of boys.

The crew laid shoulder to the poles to advance the boat against the current. As they rounded a bend the river traffic grew even more congested and the Vieux Carré hove into view. Whistles shrilled and bells jangled and horns blew long and hoarsely. They poled toward the cargo docks beyond the Place d'Armes, the weathered drill field marking the heart of the Old Quarter. The boat swayed in the wake of a passing sternheeler and every blast of the big boat's horns rippled up the brothers' spines. Music and shouting and laughter carried out from the Quarter. The air was enlaced with a mix of exotic smells.

"Take a good breath there, lads," a redhaired boatman named Keeler said as they leaned hard on their poles and paced toward the stern. His big chest broadened as he inhaled long and deep. "Can ye smell it? I don't mean the cookpot stuff, but what's just under it. A bit like warm buttered shrimp set amongst fresh roses. That's Narlens pussy on the air, boys. Dixie City gash. The finest on God's good earth."

They worked the boat into the cargo moorings at Tchoupitoulas Street and there they tied up. The brothers helped to unload the vessel and then walked their horses over to a livery across the street where they put up the animals and stored their outfits and arms except for their bootknives and the snaphandle which Edward kept in his pocket. They stripped to the waist and washed up at a pump and took their coats from their bedrolls and were brushing them with damp cloths when Keeler strode up and said, "Step lively, lads. It's a fine frolic we'll have, aye!" He had put on a clean shirt and river jacket and slicked down his hair. With him was a lean and looselimbed mate named Allenbeck.

They intended to go directly to a fine Old Quarter bordello of Keeler's highest recommendation, a house well-stocked with prime high-yellow whores, but Allenbeck insisted they stop in at a tavern for a quick nip to fortify themselves for the walk to the Quarter and the rest of them said why not.

Before they got halfway down Tchoupitoulas Street they had been in four different honky-tonks and two fights. The first fight started when Allenbeck began crowing that he was kin to the snapping turtle and weaned by a momma wolf and could out-fight, out-fuck, out-dance and out-drink any man on two legs on either side of the Mississippi. A barrel-shaped muleskinner stepped up and said, "Oh yeah?" and knocked out a front tooth with the first punch. Allenbeck jumped up and let a high-pitched battle cry and in an instant they were rolling and grappling on the floor and the drover sank his teeth into Allenbeck's shoulder and Allenbeck was clawing for his eyes to try to gouge them out and Keeler said it was time to move on and hammered the drover on the head with a heavy beer mug in order to dislodge him from Allenbeck's shoulder. They grabbed Allenbeck off the floor and the four of them scrambled out of there. The next fight was between Keeler and a steamboat stoker, and a Keeler punch sent the stoker backpedaling through the door of a gaming room to crash into and overturn a poker table laden with money. So clamorous was the ensuing donnybrook that it drew spectators and participants from a block away. The brothers and the boatmen slipped away through a side exit and ducked into a tavern two doors down and laughed heartily over steins of beer and glasses of Monongahela rye as the smash and roar of the fight echoed outside in the street.

The sun was red and low when they finally strolled into the teeming Quarter and past a pair of city constables who gave them a wary eye.

The night air was piquant with cayenne and perfume, woven with the undersmells of sweat and swamp rot. An empty pillory stood before the Cabildo on Chartres Street and Keeler said no white man had stood in it in the last twenty years but niggers still sometimes found themselves pinioned in it by their hands and neck with a sign on their backs to tell the passing world the nature of their crime. While Keeler bought a fresh bottle of rye in a tavern, Edward stepped into an arms shoppe and purchased a pouch of .44 balls and attached it to his belt.

Although the city had by now been American for more than forty years, the Quarter's architecture remained chiefly Spanish and its character distinctly French. The smooth locutions of French idiom entwined everywhere with the harder growl of English, the rasp and hiss of Spanish, the grunts and gutturals of tongues so alien they seemed not of this world. "It's the thing I hate about this town," Allenbeck said. "All these fucken foreigners and their fucken babble." To the brothers the city was in many ways reminiscent of Pensacola, only bigger and louder and more Negroid.

The house to which Keeler led them was on Orleans Street. As they drew near it they heard a frenzied pounding of primitive drums and spied a mass of people gathered in a large open area a little farther along on the other side of the street. "Congo Square," Keeler said. "The city lets the niggers get together here every Sunday and do their voodoo jigs from back in Africa. Used to be they had to do it in secret, but the dancing gets them all worked up, don't you know, and on dance nights they'd end up fighting and fucking in public all over town. Easier to keep them in control if they're all in one place."

The brothers wanted to have a look, so the four of them crossed the street and shouldered their way to the front of the crowd and only narrowly avoided fights with those who objected to their pushing. The crowd was chiefly male, though some of the better-dressed men women on their arms. There were dozens of dancers in the center of the square, men and women both, whirling and jumping to the beat of the drums, falling to their knees and leaping up again and flailing wildly, chanting in unintelligible tongues, eyes wide, teeth bared. Spectators swayed to the drumbeat and directed each other's attention to this dancer or that one.

"Hey boys, lookit *there*," Allenbeck said, nodding toward a woman the color of raw honey dancing nearby between two muscular barechested men as black as coal and pouring sweat. The woman was statuesquely beautiful, tall and narrow-waisted, with full breasts and rounded hips and rump. She was obviously naked under a thin white shift that clung wetly to her skin, to her long thighs and cloven swell of buttocks and nipples like chunks of coal. Edward's pulse quickened as he watched the woman drop to her knees with her head thrown back and eyes closed and long hair tossing. She spread her legs wide and her hips were thrusting with wild urgency to the tempo of the drums. She ran her hands up her gleaming thighs and the hem of the shift rode to her hips and she slipped a hand under the bunched dress and stroked herself hard and her lips drew back on her parted teeth and her other hand went to her breast and pinched the jutting nipple. One of the dancing men positioned himself directly before her with his hips swaying and she put a hand to his manhood bulging starkly in his tight pants and he snatched her to her feet and dug his long fingers into her buttocks and pulled her tightly against him and they writhed loin to loin and the onlookers whistled and howled.

Edward could not distinguish between the pounding of the drums and the beat of his own blood. His throat felt tight, his genitals heavy and swollen. He turned to Keeler and said, "Let's get in that house." Even his tongue felt thickened. Keeler laughed and said, "I'm right ready meself, lad." John was grinning like a dog, his eyes aglitter.

The crowd had deepened around them and as they shoved their way out of it Allenbeck bumped hard against some hardcase and there was a brief exchange of blows. Then they were across the street and down the block and in the parlor of Miss Melanie's House of Languor.

Minutes later Edward was in a small dimly lighted room with a young quadroon girl of spectacular physique whose lips were pulled into a permanently sardonic smile by the white scar across the right side of her mouth. She fixed a look on his mutilated ear for a moment but made no remark on it. She slipped off her chemise and stood naked before him on smooth long legs, her breasts full and dark-nippled. His trousers had not yet cleared his knees when his ejaculate spurted across three feet of space and spattered her mocha belly. The startled girl burst into laughter and said, "*Hooo!* You the *readiest* boy I ever did see!"

It was house policy that once a man delivered his load he had received due service, and if he wanted another go he had to pay again. Edward dug the money from his belt purse and handed it to the smiling girl and she relayed it to the floorwoman patrolling the hall. She then helped him off with his boots and pants and drew him into bed and gently pushed him on his back and mounted him. He started to protest that this was no way for a man to fuck but she bent forward and put a nipple to his mouth and began slowly rotating her hips and Edward ceased all complaint. Two glorious minutes later he came like a trace chain was being yanked through his cock. The girl held him close and stroked his hair and called him a sweet baby.

Suddenly there came a thunderous boom that rattled the window shutters and Edward bolted upright. The girl giggled and pulled him back to her breast and said he surely was new to New Orleans if he didn't know that was the curfew cannon that fired every night as the order for slaves to get home.

17

A half-hour later they were back on the street and passing the bottle of Nongela among them and telling each other about the wonderful girls they'd been with. Edward asked John how his girl had been and his brother rolled his eyes and grinned widely. Keeler kept saying, "I *tole* you boys it's a fine house, didn't I? Didn't I tell you?" and they all kept saying yes he surely did tell them, yes indeed.

They made their loud happy way over to Canal Street and bought a fresh bottle of Nongela at a tavern and headed west and got lost and all of them cursed Keeler who was supposed to know his way around the town. On Poydras he regained his bearings and led them along South Liberty and even from the far side of the Protestant cemetery they could now hear the timbre of unchecked revelry and smell whiskey and perfume on the night air. Past the cemetery they turned onto Girod Street and entered The Swamp, the most notorious strip of saloons and brothels and gambling dens in the whole notorious town.

"It's any kind of fun ye want here, lads," Keeler told them, shouting to be heard above the din of music and laughter and cursing and threats. "But hereabout they'll slit your throat for the penny in your pocket and that's no lie. It's a dozen killings a week at the least, so keep your wits about. The police won't come round here and for damn good reason. They'll likely put a torch to the whole place one day."

In a public house abounding with unidentifiable reeks and the clatter of dishware they ate a supper of sausage and peppers with red beans and rice. Having done with their meal they repaired to The Hole World Hotel, a sprawling two-story edifice a little farther down the street. It was the sort of hotel, Keeler said, where a man could buy damn near anything he could think to want. "If they aint got it," Keeler said, "they'll send somebody out to steal it for you. For a price, naturally.''

The place was packed, hazed with pipe and cigar smoke, raucous with laughter and bellowed conversation, with squealing fiddles and plinky piano music, with singing and strident argument and the calls of card dealers. On a narrow stage along the wall opposite the bar a sextet of girls in red velvet dresses danced and kicked their legs high to show their frilly white bloomers and each time they turned and thrust their derrieres at the audience and yanked their skirts up over their rumps they inspired whoops and whistles and were showered with coins.

"French dancing!" Keeler shouted, nudging Edward with an elbow. "Aint it fine!"

They pushed through to a rude plank bar and ordered glasses of Nongela and tankards of beer. "Say now, lookit yonder!" John said. He directed their attention to a nearby table on which lay a muttonchopped man with a horribly mutilated face. Even from where they stood they could tell he was dead. The barkeep told them the fellow had been caught trying to switch dice at the table and then taken outside to be taught a lesson.

"Poor fella didn't, ah, survive his moral instruction, you might say," the barkeep said with a smile. "Right cheeky bastard. Said he wasn't doing anything the house wasn't. 'Got to cheat when you play with cheaters,' he said. He'll lay on that table as a warning to other tinhorns till somebody takes his place or he starts smelling too bad to put up with and then they'll take and throw him in the river. It's almost always somebody on that table, you bet." He explained that the house ran the craps, faro, blackjack, and roulette games, but the poker tables belonged to the players.

When Allenbeck asked if the place had girls the barkeep laughed. "Does the river have catfish, why don't ye ask?" He pointed to a pair of curtained doors in the rear of the room. "The one on the left's the kitchen, see, so unless you're wanting to fuck a bowl of beans it's the one on the right ye want to go through. It's a little foyer, like, and a fella sitting there. You pay the gent and he'll send ye on up to the good mother upstairs. If you like them special young it's the stairway to paradise. You won't find them younger than they got here unless you rob the cradle and that's the God's truth. There's one seventeen and she's a crone, practically. Most aint but fifteen. Hear tell they got two in the other day and neither one yet thirteen years old. I've not had the chance to check them out meself. Had a fella here a while ago saying 'Twelve!' like it's a bit too young for it, but I figure it's like the Mexicanos say: If they're old enough to bleed they're old enough to butcher."

John said he was of a mind to do a little butchering himself right about now but Edward and Keeler were in more of a mood to try their luck at the card tables. John and Allenbeck chided them for limp-dick weaklings and set off across the crowded room.

Edward watched his brother wend his way through the haze toward the curtained door and grinned after him. "I swear, he must have him a hickory dick," he said to Keeler. "Me, I *still* aint recovered from that yellow gal."

"Some fellas can't get enough of the bearded oyster, that's true enough," Keeler said. "I do love it meself as the Good Lord knows, but a man needs other diversion, begad, or he'll go soft in the brain sure."

They ordered another bucket of beer and agreed to split their winnings and then found a poker game with two open seats and sat down to it.

III

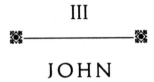

JOHN

1

In the foyer behind the curtained door a man in gartered sleeves sat at a small table in the niche under the stairway, talking to a man in a bowler hat who sat astraddle a reversed straightback chair, smoking a cigar and massaging his knuckles. He wore a pistol on his belt. At the foot of the staircase behind him was a doorway into the alley.

The garter-sleeved man was the teller. He patted the tabletop and said, "It'll cost you two solid dollars, boys." The bowlered man scrutinized them as they paid. The gartered man asked their preferences and Allenbeck said he was in the mood for a redhead. From a wicker basket holding a variety of poker chips the teller extracted a white one with the number four painted on it and handed it to him. "Give this to the niggerwoman upstairs," he said. Allenbeck winked at John and took the steps two at a time.

John wanted a quadroon but was told all three were busy and likely to stay that way a while, so he asked for a blonde but both of them were occupied too. The teller suggested a Chinese girl, a Celestial darling fresh off the boat and only just turned thirteen years old, a virgin, practically. For such freshness he would only have to pay one more dollar. John handed it over and was given a blue chip bearing the number thirteen.

"I'll hold that there bootknife till ye come back down," the bowlered man said. John met the man's eyes. The bowlered man grinned and shrugged. "You aint got to give it to me, boy, but it aint goin upstairs." John slipped the knife out of his boot and laid it on the table. Without taking his eyes off him the man said, "Thank ye kindly."

On the upper landing a hugely fat and yellow-eyed Negress sat in a wide rocking chair flanked by a low wooden box holding a collection of poker chips. She took John's and glanced at it. "Room number eight," she said. "Lass on the leff." She tossed the chip into the box and gestured through the open door into the narrow and dimly lighted hallway flanked by numbered doors on either side.

The hall lay empty but the thin doors hardly muffled the moans and curses of men in the wallows of passion. A pair of shutters that opened onto a balcony at the end of the hall was closed against the clamor in the street below. Passing the second set of doors he heard Allenbeck's voice from the room on the right, number fifteen: "*Easy*, dammit! Suck it *gentle*, you red bitch!"

Halfway down the hall the door to number twelve abruptly swung open and a glowering fat man wearing only his trousers and boots stepped out muttering, "Goddamn little cunt!" He called, "Hey, auntie!" and John glanced back to see the black woman lean forward in her rocker and peer in at them. The fat man beckoned her and said, "Get on over here and see about this, goddamnit!"

As he passed the open door of number twelve John glanced in the room and saw a girl lying on her back on the narrow bed with her eyes closed and her short green satin chemise up high on her hips and exposing the patch of blonde hair between her legs. He took two more paces and stopped and came back and looked in again and saw that it was his sister Maggie.

He looked down the hall at the Negress who was still in her rocker and was tucking a fresh chaw in her jaw and appeared in no hurry to come see what the fat man wanted. The door to number four opened and a man in a goatee came out and adjusted his coat and planter's hat looked at them and then strode down the hall. The Negress was on her feet now and stepped into the hallway and then she backed out again to give the man room to go by her.

John's breath was lodged in his throat. He looked back into the room and told himself he was wrong, it wasn't her, could not be her. But he knew it was.

The fat man looked at him and said, "Little bitch. I get in there and ask her does she want a drink. She was fairly wall-eyed already, so I shoulda known better, but she says sure, so I hand her my pint of rum that's near half-full and turn around to hang up my coat and shirt and I hear her bubbling that bottle like a sawmill nigger. I mean she *drained* it, friend. Not five seconds and it was *gone*. I said, 'What the *hell* you doing, little girl?' and she gives this shit-face grin and her eyes roll up in her head and she falls on the bed. I like to thought she was dead but the little bitch's only drunkern hell is all. If these bastards think I'm paying to hump some passed-out little dipso cunt who drank all my hooch they best think again."

She lied, John thought. *She lied, she lied, our lying goddamned crazy mother.*

"Listen, friend," he said to the fat man, "I'll trade you. You can have mine in number eight. She's a three-dollar special, a Celestial, thirteen years old, practically a virgin, they say. Me, I *like* it when they're out cold." It was the only explanation that leapt to mind. His heart was racing, his mouth dry. He wondered what he thought he was going to do.

"What you want?" the black woman said as she came up to them.

The fat man looked askance at John. "You *like* them passed out? Shit, son, that's like humping the dead. It aint no fun in *that.*"

"It's what I like. Look here, mister, I'll throw in a dollar for the deal." He dug out a silver dollar and handed it to the fat man, thinking that if he did not accept it he would offer him all of the rest of the money he had, about four dollars. And if the fat man still refused he would stomp the son of a bitch to pudding.

"Why you all standin here for?" the Negro woman said.

The fat man held the dollar like a poker chip he was not sure he wanted to bet. "You must got a hell of a hankering, son." He took a look down the hall toward number six. "A Chinee girl, you say?" He looked at the dollar in his palm again and smiled and put it in his pocket and said, "Deal."

"What you mens *doin?*" the Negro woman said. "Caint be goin from one room to another. Aint allowed."

The fat man went back in the room aThat's all we do in this fuckinhes and came out and said to her, "You just get back to your chair, auntie, and mind your own damn business." He walked over to number eight and went in and shut the door behind him.

"*Is* my business," the Negress said, looking hard at the door and then at John.

John stepped into number twelve and started to close the door but the big woman easily held it open with one hand and peered around him at the girl on the bed. "That girl be drunk *again?* Mista Boland gone whip her ass good."

"Listen, dammit, I don't care she's drunk," John said. "Just let us be." He was ready to punch her if she did not release the door.

"We see bout this," she said and lumbered off toward the landing.

John shut the door and stepped over to the bed and looked down at Maggie. She was breathing through her mouth and smelled like she'd been pickled in rum. He touched her face gently, marveling at the reality of her. He stroked her powdered cheek and saw that under the powder a cheekbone was lightly blued with a bruise. There was a small fresh scab in the corner of her mouth and a front tooth had been chipped. Her legs showed a few yellowed bruises. Her pubic hair was neatly trimmed. He stood there for a long moment staring at the compact lips of her vulva before becoming aware of his arousal and flushing hotly and quickly tugging down the hem of her shimmy to cover her sex.

His mind spun. He had no idea what to do. The front balcony was a good fifteen feet above the sidewalk. He could make the drop himself but never with Maggie in his arms. He could go downstairs and get Edward but then how would—

Bootheels came thumping down the hall. He went to the door just as the man in the bowler hat strode up, his face as tight as the fists at his side. He still wore the pistol on his belt. Behind him came the big Negress.

"What the *hell* are you—" the man started to say, and John interjected, "Listen, mister, she's bad hurt! Somebody done stuck a blade in her gut! She needs help real bad!"

The bowlered man shifted his eyes to the girl in the room and in that instant John drove an elbow into his face with all his weight behind it and nearly lost his own balance as the man's head snapped back against the doorjamb with a loud crack and his legs went out from under him and he sat down hard and his bowler rolled away. John snatched the pistol from the man's belt and jumped back and pointed the gun at the black woman who had turned and started for the stairs and said, "Stand fast, mammy." The pistol was a fancy silver-mounted Kentucky dueling model and its .54 caliber ball was capable of removing a sizable portion of her head.

The Negress turned and folded her arms over her great bosom and stared at some point just to the side of him. "I aint studying nothin or nobody," she said.

The man on the floor moaned and gingerly fingered his face. Blood streamed from his mouth and ran down his arm and crimsoned his white sleeve. He worked his tongue slowly in his mouth and let two teeth drop to the floor in a bloody web of spit, then looked up at John and said, "Bruck ma yaw sumbish."

He braced himself against the jamb and started to get to his feet and John clubbed him with the pistol barrel behind the ear and the man crumpled without a sound and lay dead still. John took the man's purse and looped it onto his own belt and then swiftly searched him for his bootknife but it was not on him. The door to number three opened and a man poked out his head. John showed him the pistol and the man's head vanished and the door slammed shut.

"Pull him in here," John said, gesturing for the woman to drag the man into the room. The Negress did it, laboring as much to squeeze her own bulk through the door. She seemed to fill the room. John sat on the bed and told her to put Maggie over his left shoulder and the big woman draped the girl over him facedown like a sack of flour. John stood up with Maggie's arms and hair hanging down his back and her legs dangling against his chest. He held her against him with his free hand tight on her exposed ass and jostled her, shifting her weight to set it more securely. He told the woman to pull the Maggie's shimmy down but the garment wasn't long enough to cover the girl's bare buttocks completely and so he ordered her to remove the shirt from the man on the floor and wrap it about the girl's waist. She did it and then John told her to sit down and stay put if she knew what was good for her.

He was hoping for Allenbeck's help but when he got to number fifteen the door was open and a redhaired girl sat naked and alone on the bed. She gaped at him dumbly and put her hands over her breasts. A door opened down the hall behind him and a fully dressed man stepped out and glanced from the girl on his shoulder to the pistol in his hand and quickly retreated into the room.

He felt Maggie's belly spasm against his shoulder as she retched and warm vomit ran down the back of his pants leg and he heard it splatter on the floor and smelled its acrid stink. He shifted her weight once again and went out onto the landing. The music and babble from the front room seemed louder now, but even through the din he could hear laughter and voices from the niche below the stairs. The alley door at the bottom of the stairway seemed vastly distant. He was midway down the stairs when a laughing man came into view and looked up and saw John pointing the pistol at him and his laughter caught in his throat.

"What, Stevie?" a voice asked. "Big Bertha looking down mean at you?"

The garter-sleeved teller and a lean and mustached man with a pistol at his waist appeared beside the man named Stevie, both of them smiling, and then they saw John on the stairs and lost their smiles.

He aimed squarely at the armed man's face and said, "Hands behind your neck, friend. I mean quick." The man glowered, hesitated, and then complied. John kept the pistol on him as he descended the rest of the stairs and told the man named Stevie to turn around and put his face to the wall and lace his fingers behind his neck. To the teller he said, "Take your friend's pistol there and tuck it in my belt and be quick and careful about it."

The mustached man stepped back from the teller as if to deny him the weapon. John stepped forward and backhanded him across the face with the pistol barrel. The man dropped to his knees with both hands over his broken nose and blood running through his fingers. John readjusted Maggie's weight on his shoulder and said, "Do it." The teller took the pistol from the man and gingerly slipped it into John's belt. It was a fine Kentucky model fitted with a percussion lock.

A man came in through the curtained door from the front room and looked at each of them in turn and put his hands up without a word.

John told the teller to open the alleyway door, then ordered them all to get down on the floor and sit on their hands. When the mustached man took his hands from his nose the blood gushed over his mouth and chin and onto his shirt. His eyes were pouring tears and flaming with pain and hatred.

"I'll shoot the first sonofabitch who sticks his head out this door," John said. He backed out into the alley and kicked the door shut.

2

The near end of the alleyway abutted the brightly lighted street in front of The Hole World Hotel and throngs of people were passing by. He hastened toward the darkness in the other direction, his heart pounding, his ears straining for cries of alarm and shouts of pursuers, but all he heard were the sounds of revelry in the street behind him and a low rolling rumble of advancing thunder.

The shadows stirred like living things in the rapidly shifting light of a quarter-moon rushing through gathering storm clouds. He followed the alley across a narrow lane without even glancing toward the voice that called, "Four bits for your package, cap'n," or at the men who laughed in response. Now the alley wound behind clusters of lightless buildings and rows of double-storied derelict warehouses and the moon abruptly disappeared in a scud of heavy clouds and in the enveloping blackness he almost walked into a stone wall. For an anguished moment he thought he was in a cul-de-sac and would have to retrace his steps and then he realized the alley branched to the right and left. He could not get his bearings and felt thoroughly lost and was certain a posse was closing on his heels like silent tracking hounds. Then a steamboat horn groaned hoarsely from somewhere off to his right. He cursed himself for a panicky fool and set out toward the sounds of the river traffic. He bore toward the horns and bells and whistles, wending a crooked course through the dark back-alley world of vague shapes and impenetrable shadows. There came a longer and closer roll of thunder. He made his way through washes of litter, stumbling on chunks of brick and discarded lumber, bumping into broken crates. He waded through layers of slippery reeking garbage. Chittering rats scurried over his boots. A dog growled in the darkness. He felt eyes watching from the deepest recesses, heard muffled coughs in the shadows, muttered curses, startled gasps. Passing by an adjoining alley he heard the urgent pantings of sexual coupling.

The alley was suddenly lit brightly white by a shimmering flash of lightning and the ghostly instant revealed a black woman naked but for her shirt sprawled on a heap of refuse, her teeth bared in a rictus under the rats feeding on her eyes. And then the world was black again and an explosive blast of thunder staggered him so that Maggie almost slipped from his grasp.

Scattered raindrops began to fall as he emerged from the alley on a street fronting the river. He slipped the pistol under his coat and into his belt, next to the gun he'd gotten from the mustached man. He was surprised by the ache in his hand, so tightly had he been gripping the weapon. He stood there pondering, raindrops smacking on his hat brim. The thing to do was get off the streets until Maggie regained her senses, then make their way to the livery at the Tchoupitoulas docks where they'd stored their outfits and wait for Edward to show up or find him already there.

Lightning flared and thunder cracked and now the wind picked up. Men hurried to ships moored at the wharves or to taverns along the street. He thought he spied a hotel sign down the street to his left and so he headed that way. A pair of men in the loose shirts of rivermen were about to enter a saloon but paused at the door to watch him pass by. He became aware that the shirt around Maggie's hips had slipped down to expose most of her ass and he pushed it back in place. He heard the sailors fall in behind him. "Looks well bored with his company, don't she now?" one said, and the other lewdly laughed. John drew a pistol and turned and pointed it at them and they stopped short. "That's all right then, bucko," one said, raising his hands in a gesture of wanting no trouble. They turned back to the saloon and gave him a grinning rearward glance and went inside.

Midway down the block an overhanging sign swaying and creaking in the wind announced The Mermaid Hotel, a small and shabby two-floor establishment whose grimy front window bore the faded pronouncement, SPIRITS—FOOD—ROOMS. He entered a nearly deserted taproom as the rain suddenly swept up the street in a torrent. Except for a man sleeping with his head on a tabletop, there was no one in sight but two men rolling dice at the bar. One of them was bearded and clothed in the manner of a riverman and the other was the boniface and said yes, he had a room for the night. One dollar. The men's eyes roved boldly over Maggie's bare legs.

"That your parrot?" the bearded man asked with a grin.

"My sister. She's sick."

The bearded man laughed and gave a broad wink. "Right you are, boy. I've had me some pretty sisters with the rumhead sickness a time or two meself."

"She *is* my sister," John said. The bearded man smiled broadly and nodded and said, "Well now, course she is."

The room was upstairs, one of six in a narrow hallway lighted dimly by a wall-mounted lamp. The hall resounded with erratic snores and was ripe with the malodors of unclean men. The innkeeper led him to the room and went in first and lit the oil lamp on a small bedside table that also held a washbasin and a pitcher of water. A small brass bed with a stained pungent mattress was the only other furnishing in the room. The lamp flame fluttered in the glass, jumping to the breeze blowing through a door open onto a narrow balcony overlooking an alley. The boniface closed the door shutters against the spray of rain. John stooped and angled his shoulders to let Maggie slide off onto the bed. He nearly cried out at the relief to his cramped muscles. The shirt had fallen free of the girl's hips again and the boniface's bright eyes were fastened on her exposed pudendum. John pulled down the hem of her shimmy and the man smiled at him and shrugged and left.

Her breathing was deep and regular but she made no response when he sat on the edge of the bed and shook her by the shoulders and gently slapped her cheeks. He'd never seen anyone so insensibly drunk, not even Daddyjack. He soaked the shirt in the water basin and washed the streaks of vomit off her face and arms. Her damp hair looked dull and felt greasy and he recalled that she had always prided herself on her cleanliness and the sheen of her gold hair most of all.

He shook her again and her breasts jiggled freely under the thin shimmy. He stared at them. Then looked over his shoulder at the door. Then gingerly touched one. Pressed it lightly. Felt of its firm softness. His blood thumped in his throat and his chest tightened. For years he had harbored such shameful secret yearnings. . . .

Sweet Jesus! He jumped up from the bed covered her legs with the damp shirt. *You rotten son of a bitch! What in hell's wrong with you!* He was suddenly desperate for a drink. He went to the door and looked out into the dim hallway. Snores and farts and sleep babblings from the other rooms. The door had a swivel latch on the inside but there was no lock on its outer side. He closed the door behind him and went to the end of the hall and peered over the landing rail and saw the bearded man and the boniface still at the bar and no one else about.

He went downstairs and asked for a bottle of Nongela. A look passed between the boniface and the bearded man but he made nothing of it.

The boniface said he had to get the Nongela from the storeroom in the rear and suggested that John take some food back upstairs with him. "She's like to be hungry when she wake up," he said. "They love you forever if you feed them. I can have my scullery boy to lay out a plate of bread and cheese."

It occurred to John that Maggie might not have eaten for some time and some food at hand when she came around would be a good idea if she wasn't too hungover to eat. From this end of the bar he could easily keep watch on the stairs while the plate was made ready. "All right," he said.

The boniface said fine, he'd be right back, and he poured John a large glass of whiskey on the house to sip at while he waited. The bearded man said it didn't look like the rain was going to let up anytime soon so he might as well quit waiting and just get on back to his boat and to hell with getting soaked. He tossed off his drink and said so long and set out the front door into the downpour.

The rain struck like flung gravel against the front window and thunder quavered through the wooden counter under his elbows and the air was sharp with the smell of lightning. He drank the whiskey and watched the stairs and the minutes passed and then he remembered the balcony outside the room's shuttered door and wondered if it ran the length of the building and maybe even all the way around it.

He spun off the stool so fast it twirled on one leg before toppling and he took the stairs three at a time and had a pistol in his hand and then recovered sufficient presence of mind to come up on the door quietly, the crash and drum of the storm covering the creak of the floor under his boots. He paused at the door and pushed it gently but it held fast. He cocked the pistol and stepped back and then kicked the door hard with his bootsole and the latch snapped loudly and he rushed into the room and there the sons of bitches were.

In the quavering light of the oil lamp the rain-drenched boniface stood slack-mouthed just inside the open shutters with his fingers at the buttons of his pants. The bearded man was between Maggie's wishboned legs with his soaked shirt plastered to his back and his pants bunched around his booted feet and his pale ass driving hard and he gaped big-eyed over his shoulder at John and stopped humping and raised up on all fours as the boniface whirled and darted out the open shutters and ran away along the balcony.

John thrust the pistol within inches of the bearded man's face and pulled the trigger and the flint sparked but the gun did not fire. He threw it aside and grabbed for the other pistol under his coat but the man lunged and caught him by the shirtfront and the second pistol slipped from John's grasp as they tumbled to the floor in a snarling embrace. Though hindered by his pants tangled about his ankles the man rolled on top of John and got both hands on his throat and began strangling him with red-eyed fury. John worked his hand between them and found the bearded man's bare balls and clenched his fingers around them with all his might and yanked hard and felt the scrotum rip free and blood rush hotly over his fist.

The man screamed. His hands left John's throat and he fell on his side and clutched his torn nutsack. John scrambled to his knees and caught him by the hair and shoved his head back and punched him in the Adam's apple and the man's face instantly purpled and he gagged horrifically. John stood and grabbed him by the collar with both hands and dragged him out onto the balcony and into the pouring rain and pulled him to his feet and shoved him over the railing.

The man fell into the darkness without sound and struck the muddy ground with a dull splash. Heaving for breath, John leaned over the rail but could not see him in the blackness below until a shimmering blue flash of lightning showed him lying on his belly with his face half-buried in the mud and his bare ass gleaming and his legs crossed at the ankles where his trousers were twisted round them. Then the alley went black again and John wanted to spit down into it but his bruised throat could not hawk up saliva. To swallow was torture. He stood at the rail and let the rain wash the blood off his hands. In the next flare of lightning he caught a glimpse of the drain pipe running down along the corner of the building, the pipe the bastards had shinnied up.

3

He staggered back into the room and closed the shutters. The floor was slick with blood. He retrieved the percussion pistol and went to the open doorway and saw that the hall was still deserted. The snores persisted, the sporadic mumblings of sleeptalk. He supposed that screams and the sounds of fracas were so commonplace at The Mermaid Hotel as to rarely attract notice. He closed the door and checked the flintlock and saw that the primer powder was wet. The percussion pistol was still nicely dry.

Maggie was yet unconscious, spreadlegged on her back, her blonde pubic patch glistening, her shimmy bunched above her breasts. Her nakedness seemed profound. Had he not seen it with his own eyes he would not have believed a woman could be so drunk that she was unaware of being ravished. He gazed on her for a long moment before hastily pushing her legs together and again readjusting the shimmy and covering her thighs with the shirt.

He dismissed the idea of putting her back on his shoulder and going in search of another hotel. If the boniface wanted to even the score for his friend in the alley it would be best to stay put and make the man come to him rather than try to get out of the place while carrying Maggie. Even if the boniface recruited confederates, he knew John was armed. They'd not be likely to rush into the room and risk a ball in the teeth.

He felt a rushing sense of elation that he could not have explained to anyone. He damn sure had a tale to tell Edward. *And where the hell were you while I was busy savin our sister's hide is what I want to know.*

He cleared off the small table and set the lamp beside the bed and then braced the table firmly against the door. He balanced the basin and pitcher at the edge of it so that any jar of the door would topple them to the floor in warning. He took off his sopping coat and shirt and wrung them and put the shirt back on and hung the coat on the bedpost to dry as best it could. Then he got in the bed and sat facing the door and with his back against the wall, the cap pistol in his hand and his leg against Maggie's flank. The front of his pants was damp and stained with blood. He wanted to take off his boots for comfort but felt readier for trouble with them on. A minute later he thought to blow out the lamp to give himself cover of darkness and make a better target of anyone who might suddenly open the door and frame himself against the light of the hallway.

For the next hour he sat keenly vigilant, his eyes fully adjusted now to the darkness. Lightning sporadically flickered blue-white against the shutter louvers. He heard nothing other than the relentless splash and rumble of the storm. He now felt certain that the boniface would not pursue the fight. He had also become intensely conscious of Maggie's pressing warmth. He tried to think of other things, of the sights he'd seen between Florida and New Orleans, of his first view of the Mississippi, of anything but Maggie lying beside him in near nakedness. But the harder he tried to ignore the feel of her flesh against his leg the keener his awareness of it.

He looked at the shadowed shape of her, at the easy rise and fall of her breasts. He spoke her name and patted her cheek and gently shook her shoulder. She groaned lowly and rolled onto her side facing away from him and the shirt fell away from her legs and her bare buttocks snugged against his hip. He said her name again and stroked her hair but she did not move nor alter her breathing. He put his hand over her breast. Caressed it through the smooth satin. Felt the nipple draw tight. He startled himself with his moan.

How many times back in Florida had he sneaked up to the river on warm days when she went there to bathe and watched as she splashed naked in the shallows and lathered her breasts and fingered their pink tips and stood in the thigh-deep water with her eyes closed and slowly soaped herself between her legs? She wasn't yet thirteen years old the first time he spied on her but he could never afterward be near her without wanting to put hands to her. He had ached to touch her, kiss her, to fondle her little breasts and stroke her pretty legs. To put his face in her hair and rub his cheek on her belly. To kiss her blonde sex.

His self-loathing had nearly consumed him. Only the lowest, sorriest, most worthless son of a bitch on two feet could ever look on his own sister that way, could have such damnable hankerings as his. In the early months of watching her from the bushes with his throbbing cock in his hand his disgust with himself was so great he thought of hanging himself from a stable rafter. He'd pin a note to his chest: "Not fit to live another day." But over time he'd learned to accommodate his self-disgust by simply enduring it to the point of familiarity. Yet he'd sworn to himself he would never touch her in any such way as he yearned to. Would never behave toward her as anything but a good brother. Would look out for her and protect her as a good brother should.

Liar! Goddamn dirty liar! You're as much a liar as your goddamned mother. It's the same low blood in both you, low and mean and not worth a rat-damn.

He laid the pistol by and turned on his side and ran a hand over her hip and caressed her bare rump. He insinuated his fingers between her legs and felt of the fuzzy nestling warmth there, and now the sudden slickness. The ripe smell of her sex closed over him like a net. His erection pulsed painfully in the stricture of his trousers. He cursed himself under his breath and unbuckled his belt, undid his buttons, shoved his pants off his hips. His phallus bobbed free, aching to its roots.

No, goddamnit, don't! DON'T, you bastard you damned bastard. . . .

He might as well have commanded the storm to cease banging at the shutters. He moaned as he entered her from behind, sliding in smoothly and deep, pulling her tightly against him and almost immediately spasming, crying out as if spilling the devil's own milk. . . .

He clung to her for a time, stupefied with horror.

Then extracted himself and hoisted his pants and buckled his belt and sat up against the wall. She stirred and mumbled slurringly and rolled over and snuggled into him with an arm over his hips.

For a time he sat unmoving, feeling the rhythm of her deep respiration against his leg, his own breath raw and tight in his throat.

God damn me.

It was his only thought. *God damn me.*

4

He had no idea how long he'd been dozing when he opened his eyes in the dark and immediately felt the difference in the way she was breathing and knew she was awake. He stared down at the dark shape of her and his heart jumped as she abruptly pulled away from him and said in a strangled voice, "Who're you? *Who?"*

"Don't be scared." It was all he could think to say. The effort of speech pained his throat.

"Who *are* you?" Her voice had a hysterical edge. "Where *is* this? *Where?"*

"Hold on a minute, just hold on." He reached down and groped alongside the bed and found the lamp and brought it up and dug a box of matches from his pocket and struck four duds before one flamed. He lifted the glass and lit the wick and the room was cast in weak yellow light.

She was huddled at the foot of the bed, staring at him, arms crossed tightly over her breasts, legs folded under her. Her face was puffed and her eyes red and wide and uncomprehending.

"It's me, Maggie. Johnny."

Her brow knit as if she'd been asked a strange question.

"Johnny," he repeated. "Your *brother."* He held the lamp closer to himself.

Her eyes roved over his face, searched his eyes intently, lingered at his mouth. "Johnny," she said dully. She abruptly put her thumbnail between her teeth and bit on it and immediately pulled it away again and folded her arms tightly once more. Her eyes were on him but somehow did not seem to be truly *looking* at him.

"Maggie, don't you *recognize* me?" The look in her eyes was frightening. "I'm your brother, goddamnit. Johnny, I'm *Johnny."*

And then she said "*Johnny*," almost as an exhalation. And smiled.

His heart leaped. "*Yes!* Oh Jesus, Maggie, I thought . . . *we* thought you were. . . . She said . . . momma, I mean . . . she said—" He stopped short at her sudden laughter. It was hollow and toneless, as unnatural as the awkward set of her smile and the vague focus of her gaze.

"She said he *killed* you," she said, smiling unnaturally, crookedly. "She said he killed *both* you all is what she said."

"Maggie—"

"No, no, she did, she did!" Now her eyes widened and then she leaned toward him and said in a breathless rushing whisper, "She used to talk to me when nobody else was about. She told me he was crazy and beat her awful all the time and was going to kill her and so she was going to run away and did I want to go and I said yes, yes, yes, and she said for me to sneak out at night and take his horse and wait at the place upriver where me and her used to go to get mussels and not to move from there no matter what till she showed up. I took some food and matches and stuff and waited and waited for I don't know how many days. I was so awful scared at night. I was sure a painter would eat me, or a gator. Finally I couldn't just wait anymore and I started back to home. Then I saw smoke from over where the house was and I could hear him yellin way off somewhere, yellin and cussin. I was too scared to go look so I went back to where I was spose to wait and I waited and waited I don't know how long. And then I heard a shot and then another one and I was so scared. And then she finally showed up and she was all beat up and her dress was all tore and she had Foots and Remus and she . . . she told me . . ."

Her look seemed to fix upon him clearly for a brief moment and she put her fingers to her mouth.

"What happened?" he asked gently. She looked all around the room. "After she showed up," he said. "What did you all do then?"

She turned her vacant eyes back toward him and her fingers moved down to her breast. "She said he *killed* you. Both you. Said you went lookin for me and when you got back you all got in a argument and he shot you the both dead. She said we had to get away quick before he found us and killed us too. We rode and we rode. We slept in the woods. She had this big butcher knife. She made me wait in the woods outside Mobile while she went in town and sold one of the mules and then we could pay to sleep in a inn ever now and then and buy us some food.

But mostly we slept in the woods. Ever time we saw somebody comin down the trace we got off into the bushes and hid."

Now her eyes widened fearfully at some vision in her head and her rasping whisper dropped lower still and he had to lean forward to catch what she was saying. "In Missippi these men come on us in the woods, these three men. He had a number twelve on his eye, the biggest one did. He grabbed her by the arm and she cut at him with the butcher knife and he twisted her hand and her arm cracked just like a stick. He laughed at her and pulled her down on the ground and pushed up her skirt and did it to her. This other one who smelled like dead fish, he did it to me and I hollered it hurt so bad. Then the other one who looked part nigger did it to me. Then the biggest one. He hurt the worst of all. I thought I'd die. She kept tellin me not to cry, not to give em the satisfaction, and all the while they're takin turns on her too. When they finally quit I couldn't stand up. I was all bloody. It felt like I was all tore up inside."

As she spoke she was rocking slightly and cupping her sex with both hands as if holding to a wound, her eyes wide with the envisioned memory. John felt as if his chest might burst with his rage.

"Her hand was twisted funny and all swollen but she never did cry, she never did. They were drinkin and laughin and said they were goin to sell us to a whoreman in Narlens. They put a rope round her neck like a dog and tied me sittin up against a tree. I musta fell asleep cause next thing I knew it was nearly daylight and the one looked part nigger was layin on his back with his pants around his knees. His throat was cut open and the ground was dark red all around his head and between his legs where she'd cut off his thing. The rope leash was layin there and she was long gone on the best one of their horses. Nobody never heard nothin. The other two cussed a blue streak when they saw what happened and I started to cry cause she'd left me behind. The fishy one started kickin me and cussin me and the big one told him to stop or I wouldn't be worth nothin in Narlens. But he kept on and said he was gonna make me pay for what she done to Larry who I guess was the the nigger one. The big one grabbed him away from me and they started fightin. The big one got the fishy one around the head and twisted it and you could hear his neckbone when it bust."

"*Damn* him!" John said. "I wish *I'd* killed him, Maggie, I do! The other ones too—all the sonsabitches!" And he thought: *Listen to you, you no-good piece of filth.*

She looked at him narrowly and then rubbed her eyes hard with her fingertips. And then went on, less hurriedly now, her eyes fixed on the space of bed between them. "We rode all day ever day and he said he wouldn't put his thing in me no more so I could heal up down there and he could get more money for me. But ever night he made me . . . made me, you know, put my mouth on him. At first I about choked, but after awhile I got so I could do it all right except when he'd let go and I felt like I was drowning. He—" John punched the mattress between them with such sudden ferocity she flinched and gave him a puzzled look. And then she went on: "He give me whiskey. Said it'd make everything easier. The first time, I drunk it down quick just like I'd seen him do and it came right back up through my nose and burned so bad I couldn't see for the tears. He thought it was real funny. He showed me how to drink it in little bitty sips till I got used to it. He had me drink with him ever night when we made camp, and after a while I guess I got to like the way it burned its way down to my belly and made my lips get all numb and not care about nothin. He'd laugh when I got so I couldn't walk straight. Sometimes he played on his mouth organ and I'd dance all around the fire." She paused again, still staring into the space between them, and seemed to smile slightly. "One night I took off all my clothes while I was dancin and he clapped like he was at a show and called me darlin and kissed me on my mouth for the very first time."

Now she looked up and past him and her face darkened and her words came faster. "When we got to Narlens and he sold me to Boland for one hundred dollars. Told me he was gonna miss me awful bad and he kissed me goodbye. I was so surprised and all confused because right away I missed him so much I couldn't hardly breathe. I come to feel like nobody could hurt me when I was with him. When he left I cried and I cried till Boland took a strop to me to make me quit."

She brushed brusquely at her tears as if they were pestering flies. She stared fuzzily at him for a moment, then showed a twisted smile and said, "Say, you aint got maybe a little somethin to drink?"

He looked at her for a long moment, unable to find words to tell her what he was feeling. "No. Wish to hell I did."

She yawned hugely and swayed and caught hold of the bedpost. "Jesus," she said tiredly. She stretched out beside him and accommodated herself, nestling her blonde head on his chest.

"What was his name?" John asked. "The one who sold you like you was some slave girl on the block."

Her words were muffled against his shirt. "Twelve. Big ole twelve on his eye. . . ." And then she was asleep.

His own fatigue weighed heavily on his burning eyes and he lowered the lamp to the floor and settled himself supinely and readjusted Maggie's head to the hollow of his shoulder. The thunder was now a distant growling and the lightning had ceased flashing against the shutters and the rain had eased to a light patter.

Don't think on it. Think of how you found her and got her away from there. Think of how she's all right. She's all right because you did good. Don't think on the other. Things just happen sometimes. Aint nobody's fault. Things just happen. She anyhow don't even know. Nobody knows. Nobody but you. Leave it be and don't think on it, you no-good rotten son of a whore bitch. . . .

5

In the gray dawn the door burst inward and sundered the little table and sent the basin and pitcher clattering across the floor and a trio of city constables rushed into the room. Maggie sprang from the bed with a shriek and ran smack into the clutch of the boniface standing at the door. John groped wildly for the pistol as he came off the bed but it slipped away from him as the lead man struck him with a truncheon. He took the blow on the shoulder and countered with a punch to the man's throat. But now one of his arms was seized and he was hit hard on the ear and he saw stars and his knees went loose and as he staggered backward he caught a glimpse of the boniface doubled over in the doorway with his hands at his crotch and Maggie vanishing into the hall. The man gripping John's arm had him by the hair as well and was shouting at him in French and John punched him full in the mouth an instant before a rifle buttplate drove into his face and his nose went numb and he fell on his ass and boots kicked at him and he clubbed at a knee with the heel of his fist and then white light flashed in his head and the fight was done.

6

He came to consciousness on the floor of an iron-barred prison wagon clattering over the cobblestones. Pain pounded in his skull with each heartbeat. The benches on either side of the cage were full of men in manacles, and the few who glanced his way did so without curiosity. He became aware of the chains on his own wrists and of the press and weight of other men sprawled on the floor with him. The pain of his head flared redly as he sat up. He had to struggle to free his leg from under a large, reeking, unconscious man who was naked but for his shirt and socks. On one of the benches sat a man who was completely naked, covering his hairy privates with his hands and looking chagrined. He gingerly felt his nose and winced at its bloated tenderness. He probed the back of his head and felt a raised and tender mass under a sticky mat of hair. His fingers came away bloody and now he saw that his hand was swollen and imprinted with teeth. A man on a bench chuckled and then looked away when John glared at him.

The sun was risen just above the rooftops and blazed brightly in a cloudless sky, but the chill of encroaching winter was in the air. One of the constables rode seated at the rear of the wagon, just outside the cage, and John recognized him as the one who'd hit him with the truncheon. Two more policemen rode up front in the wagon seat, one of them driving the yoke of oxen, the other the officer in charge. When the officer turned to say something to the driver, John saw the bruised and bloated lips of the one he'd punched in the mouth.

When they arrived at the city prison they were led from the wagon in their clanking chains into a dimly lighted passageway and they passed under a huge portcullis of heavy lumber and into a bare yard surrounded by high stone walls manned by armed guards. There they had their manacles removed as they were processed into the prison ledgers and then they were ordered through a set of double iron gates into the prison block and the gates thundered shut behind them.

Nearly two weeks passed before he was taken before a judge who asked how he pleaded to the charges of theft, assault, and intent to commit murder. Not guilty John said. He scanned the sparse courtroom crowd but did not see Edward among it.

The officer in charge of the arrest testified that on the night in question he and his deputies had been summoned to the Mermaid Hotel by the proprietor, who told them that he and some friends had found a man lying in the alleyway behind the hotel as they were returning from an evening on the town. By the proprietor's account, the victim was a guest of the hotel named Gaspar Smith. He had been barely conscious but able to tell them he'd been attacked by the defendant, also a guest of the hotel, after an argument over a fille de joie. The defendant had been about to take the girl into his room when Smith happened into the hallway and offered her a better price. A fight ensued and the defendant mutilated Smith horribly in his manly parts and then attempted to kill him by throwing him from the second-floor balcony of his room. The proprietor and some friends had conveyed the victim to the nearest surgeon and then called upon the constabulary. When the officers went to the defendant's room to arrest him he resisted and had to be subdued by main strength. There had been a girl in the room, yes, but she absconded during the struggle with the defendant. The proprietor had identified her to them as a young prostitute often seen plying her trade along the riverfront streets. And yes, they had gone to interview the victim in the lodging house where he was recovering from his terrible wound as well as a broken leg. He proved to be one Gaspar Surtee, a known thief who had several times served brief sentences in the city prison. M. Surtee would not, however, be present to testify in court. Two days previous he had gotten in a fight with a fellow resident at the lodging house and the other man had beaten Surtee to death with his own crutch.

The bowler-hatted man—whose name was Joseph Barbato and whose speech was yet so severely hindered by his broken jaw that he was obliged to write down his answers to the court's questions—and the mustached man, whose name was Willard Moss and whose nose now angled decidedly to one side, both testified that earlier on the evening in question John had not only robbed them of their pistols and money but had viciously assaulted them as well. Their stories were corroborated by the teller who'd worn garter sleeves that night and gave his name in court as Harris Wilson.

Testifying in his turn John called his accusers liars and explained how he had rescued his sister from the brothel in The Hole World Hotel. The court listened to him intently until he was finished. Then the prosecutor turned to the judge and spoke briefly in French. The judge nodded and then turned to John and asked him why his sister was not present to testify on his behalf. John said it was as the constable had told them, she'd run away while he was being arrested, and he had no idea where she might have gone. The judge eyed him narrowly and then turned to the prosecutor who arched his brow and shrugged.

John glanced from one to the other and hurriedly said that even if he couldn't prove that Surtee had been attacking his sister, the constable himself had said that Surtee was a known thief, and since no one questioned that Surtee had been thrown from the balcony of John's room, the least that could be reckoned about the man's presence there was that he was set on thievery. Surely a man was within his rights in attacking a thief he found in his quarters.

The judge raised an eyebrow and turned to the prosecutor, who clasped his hands behind him and fixed his gaze on the floor at his feet The judge regarded John solemnly for a moment and then leaned back and looked up at the ceiling and pursed his lips and drummed his fingers on the bench. Then he sighed heavily and looked down at John again and pronounced him guilty of petty theft and minor assault and sentenced him to three months in the city prison.

7

In the sameness of his days the time passed slowly. He worked and ate and slept and dreamt. Dreamt of Daddyjack pointing at him in accusation. Of his mother standing over Daddyjack's dead body and laughing down at him. Of his brother walking along dark cobblestone streets with a pistol in each hand, calling his name in the shadows. Of Maggie dancing and swirling her skirt and showing off her pretty legs. Of her sitting on the porch with her heels up on the railing and himself sitting on the steps below and sneaking glances up under her dress and her catching him at it and smiling and letting him look. Dreamt of hiding in the bushes and watching her bathe in the river shallows. Of watching her kneeling at a log on the riverbank and being humped from behind by a bearded stranger who in the next instant was Daddyjack. Dreamt of the courtroom of his conviction where the judge was now Daddyjack as well, fresh scrubbed and robed in black and blackpatched over his missing eye and looking down on him not unkindly. Saying, "I aint forgivin you now or later, boy, you know I aint, but ye best remember what-all I taught ye if ye gone have any honor about yeself at all. Remember: you can die hangdog or with a ready dick. It's all the real choice a man got in the world."

The block he'd been assigned to was roused before daybreak every morning and fed a breakfast of bread and molasses and coffee before being manacled by the ankle, two men to a chain, and taken out and put aboard a prison wagon. Every day they were driven to a different part of the city and put to work cleaning the streets and alleyways and ditches. They were prohibited from speaking to one another as they shuffled along in pairs, their leg chains rattling, one man of every pair wielding a spade and the other carrying the canvas collection sack, the bored guards trailing behind with shotguns in the crooks of their arms. They daily filled the sacks with all manner of refuse, with offal, with dead dogs and cats, with rotted meats and produce. Sometimes they found a dead baby in the alleyway garbage, and whether the infant had been discarded dead or alive none would ever know.

Most of the local residents scarce took note of them, so commonplace were the prisoner collection crews. Occasionally a bevy of girls just come of age might happen by, nudging each other and giggling behind their hands and blushing furiously at the prisoners' salacious leers and broad winks. Packs of schoolboys taunted them and sometimes made a game of dashing up in a crouch to touch their leg chains and dart away again. One day a boy ran up to touch the chain manacling John to a hardbark graybeard with a "T" branded on one cheekbone and the graybeard spat expertly between his teeth and hit the boy square in the eye and all the convicts laughed to see the kid scamper away with a wail. "What ye damn well get!" one of the guards called after him.

The graybeard's name was Lucas Malone. John ofttimes found himself manacled to him for the day's work. Malone was more likely than most to violate the rule of silence whenever the guards were beyond whispering range—remarking salaciously on the attributes of one or another of the females to pass on the street, making jokes about the guards, sometimes simply cursing the weather, the early mornings now so cold their hands and feet ached, some days so windy it seemed their ears might freeze and break off.

John's acquaintance with Lucas Malone was further fostered by their proximity in the prison block where they held claim to adjoining pallets at one end of their long narrow cell. On his first night in the cell John discovered that the length of the floor was askew and every spill of a slop bucket or errant portion of piss ran down the stone floor to the lower end of the room. A hierarchy had therefore been established whereby the toughest inmates had their pallets at the higher and cleaner end of the cell and the weakest had to endure life at the filthy nether level. At the time of John's arrival the higher floor was held by Lucas Malone and an inmate named Hod Pickett, but after one night of sleeping in the soaking reek of the low end of the cell John went to the other end and carefully looked from grinning Lucas Malone to slit-eyed Hod Pickett before deciding that any graybeard who had been able to hold his claim to the highest portion of floor against all challengers must be uncommonly ferocious, and so he challenged Hod Pickett instead. Fifteen minutes later one of his eyes was badly swollen and his lips were bloated hugely and his knuckles were puffed to the size of bird's eggs. But Pickett was unconscious and had to dragged to the other end of the floor along with his pallet and would not be able to see clearly through either eye for days to come nor to take a deep breath for the pain of his broken ribs and it would be weeks before he could again swallow properly or talk coherently for the punches John had landed to his throat. Lucas Malone had helped John arrange a pallet adjacent to his own, chuckling the while and remarking: "Bedamn, boy, if you aint but a wildcat. I guess the only way I'da whupped you is to kill you."

John learned that Lucas had lived the greater part of his life in various highcountry regions of his native Tennessee and had made his way chiefly by working other men's land. He was vague about his legal troubles back home except to say he'd had a few. He did admit to departing the state posthaste following a poker game in which a fifth king mysteriously appeared in the deck to turn tempers nasty and a man ended up dead on the floor.

"All I ever hankered for was a grubstake to buy me a plot of land to work for meself," he told John. " I kept hearin Texas was the place for prime land at a cheap price and that's where I was headed when I got thowed here."

He'd come down on a flatboat from Memphis and immediately on landing in Dixie booked his passage on a steamer to Galveston. But the boat would not be shipping for another three hours and so he decided on a stroll through the Quarter. He'd not been in town an hour when he stood confronted on the sidewalk by an outraged man at whose wife Lucas had boldly winked as they'd passed on the sidewalk. The man's suit and high hat looked expensive, as did the wife's lacy dress and parasol. A crowd of onlookers quickly gathered as Lucas rejoined that if the fellow didn't want anybody winking at his wife he ought instruct her not to smile so invitingly at strangers as she had at him. When the furious fellow raised his cane as if he would strike him, Lucas punched him on the jaw and sent him sprawling. The man's head hit hard on a cobble and he was unconscious for five days before he came out of it. The pending murder charge was put aside and Lucas drew six months in the city prison for major battery. He was due for release but two weeks before John.

For his part John told Lucas Malone that he and his brother had been heading for Texas to seek their fortune but got separated on their arrival in Dixie City. When he was searching for Edward in the Old Quarter one night he was attacked by a pair of robbers. When the constables showed up to break up the fight the two thieves charged that John had earlier that evening stolen their pistols from behind the bar in a tavern and they had simply been trying to get the guns back. The constables seemed familiar with the robbers. John swore he saw winks of complicity pass between them. Lucas Malone shook his head in commiseration and said it was a damn shame that so often in this world the innocent suffered while the guilty ran free. And then they grinned hard at each other.

They became friends over the following weeks, though John never spoke of his family save sparingly of Edward, and Lucas Malone revealed none of his past but for entertaining accounts of sexual trysts with mountain girls and epic brawls with rivermen. A few days before he was due to be released, Lucas suggested they make their way to Texas together.

"Might could be your brother's headed there already and ye'll find each other," he said. " But I hear tell the road to yonder's bad with highwaymen. A compny of two's less likely to get waylaid than a man alone. I'll wait for ye to be let go and we'll set out together. What say?"

John said fine with him. Lucas said he'd be waiting for him at the Red Cat Tavern, which stood in an alleyway off the west side of the Place d'Armes, at six o'clock on the evening of the day he was let out. John said he'd be there.

8

Two weeks later he was restored the thirteen dollars he'd had in possession on his arrest and turned out into a gray day blustering with a norther. The trees shook under low-scudding clouds and shop signs clattered on their chains above the sidewalks. He tugged down his hat and dug his hands in his pockets and trudged through a razorous wind and entered the first gun shop he came upon. A half-hour later he was again striding through the icy wind, a charged .54 caliber flintlock pistol tucked in his waistband under his jacket flap, the piece guaranteed against malfunction by the Acadian smitty or his money back. Thus prepared did he arrive at the alleyway door of The Hole World Hotel.

Holding the pistol ready under his jacket he slowly pushed open the door and entered the little foyer and saw no one. He eased forward until he could see under the stairway niche and found the little table unattended. The low volume of laughter and conversation from the main room bespoke few patrons at this early hour. He ascended the stairs slowly and was two steps from the upper landing where the rocking chair stood empty when the big Negress came out of the hallway and saw him. She stood fast and shook her head slowly in resignation of ever understanding the folly of the human heart.

He stepped up close to her, the pistol still hidden, and whispered, "She in the same room?"

The Negress' smile was small and sad. "You boy," she said.

John brought out the gun. "I aint foolin any moren last time, auntie. Where's she at?"

The door of one of the near rooms opened and the man named Harris Wilson, he who had worn the sleeve garters that night, came out into the hallway, tucking his shirt into his pants and hiking his suspenders onto his shoulders. He shut the door and turned to the hallway door and saw the pistol pointed at his face from three feet away and he went absolutely still.

"Where's she at?" John said.

The man blinked into the muzzle of the gun. "Where's *who?*" And now looked from the pistol to its holder and saw John and said, "Oh," as recognition showed in his eyes. "That girl, you mean, the one you taken away. Hell boy, *she* didn't never come back here."

"Not on her own, I wouldnt reckon," John said. He cocked the pistol.

The man's eyes went wider and he put up his palms as if he might fend the bullet. "Listen now—*listen*! She aint here, I *swear* she aint!" The fear in his face was stark. John thought he might be remembering his false testimony in court.

"Let's have us a look," John said. He gestured for the Negress to precede them into the hallway. "You open up ever door, mister," he said. "Open it up and stand there and I'll have a look over your shoulder. If that bowler-hat sonofabitch is takin his pleasure in one of these rooms like you just were, I aint about to stand square in a doorway and make a target for him." He pushed the man ahead of him to the first door on the right, number 16.

"Bowler hat?" the man named Wilson said. "You meaning Barbato? Shit boy, he's *dead*." He glanced back at John. "I aint lying. He stepped out to take a piss one night and didn't come back. Coupla days later they found him floating in the cattails downriver with the garfish feeding on him. Somebody'd cut his throat is what happened."

"Damn shame," John said. "I was hopin to do it myself. Open the door."

"I want you to know, son," the man said, "he said he'd kill me if I didn't say like he wanted me to in that courtroom. It's the only reason I—"

"Open that door."

The man quietly opened the door to reveal a naked mulatto whore standing beside the bed who looked out at them with neither surprise nor curiosity. Wilson closed the door and they moved on to the next one. They looked in every room and nine of them were empty and only in four of them were the girls within at work and none of them was Maggie. Three of the men were so engrossed in their pleasure they were not even aware of their brief audience at the open door. The fourth glared at them from over the head of the girl ministering to him with her mouth and said, "What the hell?" and Wilson quickly shut the door again. The idle girls in the other rooms looked out at them as if they'd been staring at the door since before it opened and would continue staring after it closed again, would go on staring until the next patron came in to have his pleasure.

"The other girls be here by five o'clock," Wilson said, "if you be wanting to see them too."

He knew she would not be among them. Knew now they hadn't caught her and she was most likely long gone. He slipped the pistol in his belt and headed for the stairway.

Wilson and the Negress stood on the landing and watched him go down. "I known a thousand young fellas thought they in love with a whore," Wilson called after him, "and it's about the most pitiful thing in the world, if you pardon me saying so. Hell boy, it's no telling where she be. Texas maybe. It's lots of girls going to Texas cause the army's there and it aint a whore alive don't believe but the army'll make her rich."

At the livery on Tchoupitoulas where he and Edward had put up their horses and stored their longarms and possibles he found nothing belonging to either him or his brother. The stablebuck recalled nobody named Edward Little nor fitting John's description of him, nor was he holding any messages for anybody named John. He said the boy who worked the place at night would be in after supper if he wanted to ask him about it.

But he did not want to wait all day for a boy who wasn't likely to know anything about Edward either.

He made his slow way to the Place d'Armes, holding his jacket close around him, the icy wind cutting his cheeks and stinging his eyes. In this town full of people and loud talk, full of laughter and music and the smells of good cooking, he felt alone and adrift. If Edward had left town he surely would have pushed on to Texas, as Lucas said. And maybe that Wilson sonofabitch was right and Maggie had gone to Texas too. But what if one of them was still in town? What if they both were? He looked all about him as if he might spy one or the other walking along the cold windy streets. He checked an impulse to howl.

The early evening darkness was closing fast as he arrived at the Place d'Armes and entered the warm and smoky confines of the Red Cat Tavern and breathed of its redolence of spirits and pickled foods. The place was raucous with shouted conversation and the toot-clink-and-twang of a skiffle band. He heard the voice of Lucas Malone calling, "Johnny boy! Here!" and spotted the graybeard at the bar. He felt himself grinning as he made his way through the crowd and toward the brighteyed old rascal. "Welcome to the free world, lad!" Lucas yelled as they clapped each other on the shoulder.

Lucas called to the barkeeper for a cup and poured out a drink from his jug and pushed the cup to John. "Drink up, boy! Ye got a ways to catch up to me!" He made the happy claim of having been drunk for the entire two weeks since his release from the city prison. He swung the rum jug by its fingerhole handle up onto the crook of his upraised arm in the manner of a riverman and tilted his elbow upward to take a deep draught. John gulped down his drink and Lucas poured him another.

The talk in the tavern was mostly of war and the talk was loudly eager. As they put down one drink after another John came to learn that Texas had been annexed at the end of December and that the U. S. had claimed its southern border at the Río Grande, where the Texas Republic had for the last ten years said its border was. But the Mexicans said the U. S. be damned. They insisted as they always had that the border was more than a hundred miles north at the Río Nueces. President James Knox Polk had likely figured that would be the Mexicans' attitude and was probably glad to hear it. Everybody knew Mr. Polk was set on expanding America's western border to the continent's western reach and was therefore out to acquire every foot of Mexican soil that lay between Texas and the Pacific. It seemed of little matter to him whether he bought that property with dollars or took it in blood through a war inspired by the border dispute. His ambition was widely shared by his countrymen. One New York magazine editorial had quite recently claimed that it was America's "manifest destiny," its divinely sanctioned mission, to establish American sovereignty from sea to shining sea. Back in midsummer Mr. Polk had sent General Zachary Taylor down to the mouth of the Nueces at Corpus Christi with almost four thousand regulars, over half the U. S. Army. Now here it was February and there they still were. But the rumor was everywhere that Old Zack had gotten his orders to move down to the Río Grande and would any day now start marching south.

"And we're gone be right there with Old Rough and Ready when he do, by God!" This last bellowed by a drunk sergeant in the company of a tableful of comrades sitting near the bar. They were the loudest patrons in the Red Cat, crowing without pause of the thrashing they intended to give the Mexicans, the glory they would reap for self and country, the honor they would every man of them carry back home. Even through the haze of rum now swirling round his head John was aware of Lucas's frequent sidelong glares at the boasting bigmouths. And now one of the soldiers took notice of Malone's hard look and said something to a large comrade at his side who then looked over at Lucas with narrowed eyes. The graybeard looked at them each in turn and spat disdainfully on the floor. At that moment John realized how much he was himself aching for a fight. As the two soldiers stood and advanced on them with aspects of ready malice he felt his spirits rise.

"Say now, grandpa," the bigger one started to say, "who the hell you—"

Lucas' punch sent him running backwards to crash into his fellows' table and upset it as he fell to the floor.

John kicked the other soldier in the balls and as the soldier bent forward with his hands at his crotch he drove a knee in his face and felt the man's nose give way with a satisfying crunch.

Now the rest of the soldiers came at them in a rush and some of the patrons fled the tavern and raised a hue and cry on the street as Lucas snatched up a stool and swung it two-handed against a soldier's head and the man dropped like a sack of feed and John went down under a snarling knot of cursing punching kicking soldiers and there came the high piercing shrill of a whistle as he felt his fingers digging into a screaming man's eyes and tasted blood from the ear between his teeth and then sparks were bursting in his head and then he saw and felt nothing more.

9

He woke to the pain of a jaw that felt somehow offset but he could bear the pain of working it and so knew it was not broken. His ribs ached with every breath. He was sitting against the wall of a narrow room with a malodorous muddy floor and a heavy portal whose small barred window was gray with dawnlight. It wasn't the city prison but it was without question a cell and his heart sagged with the realization that he was once again in jail.

A groan from the shadowed floor beside him. The effort of turning his head sent grinding pain through his neck. It was Lucas Malone stirring, groaning again, sitting up with the slow careful movements of an aged man. He looked at John with blackened bloodshot eyes as he worked his tongue carefully in his mouth and gingerly inserted two fingers and withdrew a tooth. He gazed upon it with a miserable grimace and John saw the new gap in his top row of teeth.

The room held three other men, two of them sprawled unconscious, the other sitting close by Lucas and looking at them with no trace of interest. There now came a loud rattling at the heavy wooden door and a lock clacked free and the door swung open to reveal a sprucely uniformed army sergeant who filled the doorway and stood scowling upon Lucas and John.

"You sorry bastards are in the garrison stockade," the sergeant said in a rasp. "Two of them you busted up last night are recruits just yesterday got here from Fort Jessup. One's lost an eye and the othern's brains are leaking out his busted skull. He's like to die before the day's done. He do, and both you'll be charged with murder, since it's no telling which a you did the busting." John and Lucas exchanged hangdog looks.

"Now hear me good," the sergeant said, "cause I aint saying this but once. I don't give a fiddler's fuck about either a you anymoren I do about them stupid shitheads you done ruint, but you bastards put me two men shy of my quota for the boat to Texas and I'll be goddamned if my ass is gonna get chewed because of it. So mark me now. I can hand ye over to the city prison till you stand trial and get sent to some penal camp in the swamps for the next twenty years where ye belong—or you can sign up to take them two's place and be off to Texas this afternoon. You fuckers like to fight, let's see you fight the fucken Mexicans. Now then, I'll ask ye but once: what's it to be?"

The man beside Lucas started to rise, saying, "Hell with these snip-jacks, *I'll* take the army over a damn prison camp."

Lucas Malone caught him by the collar and jerked him back and his head hit the wall with a solid thunk and he crumpled and lay still. Lucas stood up and looked down at John. "What the hell, Johnny lad. Army's a sight bettern prison for damn sure."

John hesitated but a moment before shrugging and putting up his hand. Lucas took it and pulled him to his feet and they grinned crookedly into each other's battered face.

"All right, then," the sergeant rasped. "Come along."

They signed the standard certificate of enlistment for a five-year term of service:

I ＿＿＿＿＿＿ DO SOLEMNLY SWEAR, THAT I WILL BEAR TRUE FAITH AND ALLEGIANCE TO THE UNITED STATES OF AMERICA, AND THAT I WILL OBSERVE AND OBEY THE ORDERS OF THE PRESIDENT OF THE UNITED STATES, AND THE ORDER OF THE OFFICIALS APPOINTED OVER ME, ACCORDING TO THE RULES AND ARTICLES OF WAR.

The sergeant added the requisite notation on the certificate that he had personally inspected the above named recruit prior to the application of his signature and found him "entirely sober when enlisted." He then took them before a rheumy-eyed surgeon just roused from sleep whose breath even at a distance of half the room was a miasma of whiskey and whose gaze wavered once over each of them before he signed their enlistment forms in attestation that he had carefully examined each recruit and that "in my opinion he is free from all bodily defects and mental infirmity that would in any way disqualify him from performing the duties of a soldier."

10

By noon of that day they were outfitted in new uniforms and carrying Jaeger rifles slung on their shoulders. They accompanied the sergeant and a half-dozen other recruits, a couple of whom looked younger even than John, to a public house down the street where the sergeant bought the first round in honor of their new membership in the United States Army.

His name was Lawrence and he proved an amiable drunk. In his cups he professed to be a veteran of San Jacinto and regaled them with tales of their great rout of Santa Ana's army and the slaughter they wrought in vengeance for the Alamo and Goliad.

"We kilt a thousand of them greasy sumbitches in twenty minutes," he said. "They was down on they knees saying 'Me no Alamo! Me no Alamo!' Hell, we just run our bayonets through they lying mouths. Some a the boys took to docking ears and noses and just generally cut em up a goodly bit. They was hacked-up Mexicans everwhere you looked. Some said you could hear the flies from a mile away. Course it wasn't none of us about to bury them stinking halfbreeds and so after a coupla days the smell got so rank Houston had us to move the camp upwind of it. When the war comes I expect you boys'll kill a good many more since you'll be down there where's there's a good many more of the sumbitches to kill."

There were exclamations among the recruits of "You damn right!" and "Watch *me* how many I put down!" Not a man among them had a doubt that war was imminent, and they toasted the sergeant and told each other the soldiering life was the best there was. Sergeant Lawrence smiled and said they might want to reserve judgment on the soldiering life till they'd seen the elephant for themselves.

"*Elephant?*" a young recruit said, eyes rolling with drink. "Jiminy! Is Mexico got *elephants?*"

The sergeant smiled and said, "I hear tell it's some there." Most of them had come to know the vogue phrase "to see the elephant" as a reference to novel adventure, especially one that failed to live up to expectations, and John and Lucas joined in the general ridicule of the boy's ignorance.

Sergeant Lawrence now suggested they take advantage of the cathouse upstairs while they had the chance. "I hear tell Mexicaner poon is right nice stuff, but it's like to be a while afore you boys get ye a chance at it."

They had not known of the brothel upstairs and were all of them hurrying for the stairs even as Lawrence was still talking.

John's girl was a pretty blackhaired Cajun missing a front tooth. She had a heavy accent and the thickest pubic bush he'd ever seen. He relished the springy feel of it under his hand, against his belly. Her taste was of riverwater and he couldn't get enough of fondling her breasts and the swells of her hips and buttocks, kissing her, tonguing her thick nipples.

She was a goodhearted girl who had not long been in the business and she smiled on his hunger and said she guessed it'd been a while, huh. When he entered her for the second time she giggled and clutched him to her and said nothing about having to pay again.

That afternoon Lawrence led them down the docks to a waiting steamboat where some forty other recruits were already on board and hooting at them to hurry along, goddamn it. Sergeant Lawrence got them aboard and waved farewell from the dock as lines were cast and whistles shrieked and the steamer set out downriver under thick plumes of purple smoke arcing from its stacks.

They entered the open gulf under a brilliant blue sky full of screeching white seagulls. "Well old son," Lucas said, staring back at the receding delta, "I reckon we off to see the elephant, sure enough."

11

In command of the party of recruits was one Lieutenant Stottlemeyer who generally kept to his quarters and left the troops' daily training to a Sergeant Frome. Frome roused the men every morning before daybreak and as soon as they had done with their mess he put them out on deck to drill the morning long as the dark shoreline slowly and easily lifted and fell on the north horizon. Occasionally a man broke ranks to run to the rail and cast up his breakfast to the sea. The early part of each afternoon was given over to washing clothes and cleaning gear, to learning military organization and regulations and general orders and the chain of command. Then came rifle practice off the stern. They shot at bottles and tins bobbing in the steamer's wake and they made bets and John won most of them. He gained quick reputation as the deadeye on board. Following the shooting session the men were put to cleaning their rifles and then ordered into formation and Lt. Stottlemeyer would come out to make his afternoon weapons inspection. That done, the day's duties were at an end but for those assigned to the night guard. Each day's posting of the guard roster met with grumbling from those whose names were on it, and no one grumbled louder than Lucas Malone.

"What in the hell we guardin *against?*" he carped. "We're out on the damn *ocean*, for the love of Jesus! Anybody really think some Mexican's gonna swim out here to this boat and sneak aboard and cut your throat in the middle of the night? Bad enough we spend ever damn morning marchin around like we gonna *impress* the Mexicans to death, but this guardin against nothin but the seagulls aint but a lot of stuff, you ask me.''

To which Sergeant Frome would invariably respond: "Aint nobody askin you, Malone. And you best get holt a that loose tongue.''

To which Lucas Malone's invariable response would be to wait until Frome turned his back and then stick out his tongue and pinch it between two fingers and cross his eyes and give a twisted lefthanded salute. The other recruits would burst out laughing and Frome would whirl about to see Lucas affecting to study his fingernails.

John thought he himself might be the only man on board who liked guard duty in the dead of the night. He liked being alone on deck when the passing sea was silverish purple under the moon and the sky was a riot of stars. Every now and then some large swimming thing broke the surface hard by the ship and trailed a greenyellow fire. The only sounds were of the paddles churning through the water and the stays humming in the saltwind. Since his first look at the ocean back in Pensacola he had wondered if he were perhaps a seafarer at heart. In these solitary hours of watching the night sea rolling by he thought he surely was

Two weeks out of New Orleans they were struck by a norther that blacked the sky for the next two days and raised eight-foot swells the color of lead. The steamboat rose and dropped and the wind howled in the craft's every crevice. Waves burst white over the decks. Most of the troop became seasick at the boat's first marked undulations and by the end of the storm's first day the whole vessel reeked of vomit. Like most of the other recruits Lucas Malone kept to quarters with his head hanging over the edge of his bunk and sporadically added to the coat of puke on the deck. Even some of the crewmen were unable to keep food on their roiled stomachs. Among the recruits only John and a fellow named Jimmy Zane who'd been a lighter crewman along the Mississippi coast were not bothered by the steamer's relentless pitch and roll. They went topside and clung to the rail and hollered with delight as the seaspray stung their faces and the wind tossed their hair wild. They then went below to the galley laughing and shivering in their dripping clothes to warm themselves with cups of hot coffee.

12

On a bright clear morning a week later they were anchored outside the shallows of Corpus Christi Bay and across from the wide sandy bight where lay the mouth of the Nueces River. Even before they'd come around the barrier islands and hove into view of the mainland they'd seen the dust and smoke rising off the seven-month-old encampment of General Zachary Taylor's army of 3,500 men. Beyond the camp lay the town of Corpus Christi itself, whose population had swelled from 2,000 before the arrival of the army to tens of thousands now. It had become a sprawling enterprise of whiskeysellers, outfitters, thieves, gamblers, whores, sutlers, and troupes of entertainers. And the larger the town had grown the worse had become Taylor's problems with drunkenness and brawling among his troops and a general erosion of discipline in the ranks.

They lowered into lighters to be conveyed across the bay. As they closed in on the river landing they saw that the camp was in high commotion. Work details were busy everywhere, striking tents, loading wagons, hitching them to teams of oxen and mules, lining them in formation, wrangling and saddling horses. The air was clamorous with blatting regimental bands and barking dogs, shrilling horses and bellowing men. The sense was of chaos barely contained. The helmsman laughed at the recruits' excitement and said, "You boys here just in time to get moving with Old Zack to the Río Grande. Second Dragoons done left yesterday."

"The Río Grande!" a recruit said. "Is war been declared?"

"Not yet it aint," the helmsman said with a blacktoothed grin. "But some Mexican shoot you in the head afore it is you gone be just as dead."

They were met at the landing by a personnel officer and his assistants who swiftly processed each man's papers and assigned him to a unit and directed him to one of a handful of waiting company sergeants. John and Lucas and the Mississipian Jimmy Zane were among five assigned to Company A of the Fifth Infantry. They were turned over to a short hardfaced master sergeant named Kaufmann who ordered, "Fall in, goddamnit, and follow me."

He led them through the dusty hubbub of the massive but orderly process of an army readying itself to march a long way. They wended through a maze of tents still standing and around groups of soldiers tending to their equipment who hooted at them and called "New fish!" at their passing. At the perimeter of the officers' billets Master Sergeant Kaufmann told them to stay in place and then went to one of the large tents and announced himself and was granted entry. A few yards away in a small roped-off square a hatless soldier stood on a barrel with his hands tied behind him and a handlettered sign hung round his neck. The sign read I AM A JACKASS. Lucas Malone called to him: "Say bucko, what was it ye done to earn youself that place of honor?" The hapless soldier made no response but only stared glumly at his feet.

A minute later Kaufmann reemerged in the company of a young captain whose hat was set at a rakish angle. He stood before them with hands clasped behind him. His boots shone black and his brass buttons gleamed. "I am Captain Merrill," he said, "commanding officer, A Company, Fifth Infantry. I welcome you and have but one thing to say to you and I say it with all possible fervor: Soldier well. We have no place for the man who will not soldier well. We have no tolerance for him, we have no pity. So soldier well and trust in the Lord. That is all. They're yours, Master Sergeant." He turned on his heel and went back in his tent.

John glanced at Lucas Malone who cast up his eyes. Kaufmann barked, "This way!" and ushered them to a supply wagon where they were outfitted with full field packs and powder flasks and pouches of ammunition for the Jaegers. He then led them to A Company's position and introduced a beefy man named Willeford as their platoon sergeant. The platoon was busy packing gear and few men gave them notice.

"Before I turn you over to Sergeant Willeford," Kaufmann said, "I want to make something real clear to all you. Any a you steps one goddamn foot out of line I'll kick your ass black and blue and that's a fucken promise. We gone have a war to fight real soon and we got no goddamn time for foolishness. Do what you're told and do it smartly. I got no use for peckerwoods aint able to be a proper soldier."

Jimmy Zane leaned over to John with a small grin and whispered, "Kiss my ass if it aint one damn bossman or another making threats at us."

Kaufmann heard him. He stepped up to him and because Jimmy Zane was almost as short as he was he did not have to crane his neck as he usually did when he was face-to-face with a man. "I guess you don't hear too good," he said. "Or maybe you just can't be bothered to pay attention."

Jimmy Zane smiled lazily. "I hear all right," he said.

Kaufmann drove his knee up hard between Jimmy Zane's legs. The recruit's eyes bugged and his mouth fell open and Kaufmann punched him in the stomach with his whole shoulder behind the blow. Jimmy

Zane's slung rifle slipped from his shoulder as he fell to all fours. His face turned darkly purpled he could not breathe. The rest of the platoon had quickly gathered about with faces avid for a violent entertainment.

Willeford stepped between Kaufmann and Jimmy Zane and said, "Hold on, Bill, it's enough. Christ, he's new fish, he didn't know no better. You taught him plenty just now."

Jimmy Zane was at last able to pull in a breath and he promptly vomited. Kaufmann pushed Willeford aside and squatted beside the gagging recruit and grabbed him by the hair and jerked his head back so he could look him in the face. Jimmy Zane's eyes were bloodshot and tearful. His belly convulsed again and vomit welled from his mouth and ran off his chin.

"Next time I'll go hard on you, boy," Kaufmann told him. "Ye best remember it." He released him and stood and looked at the other new men and said, "That holds for all you. It's warning to you as much as—"

"*Atten*-HUT!" someone shouted, and every man drew stiffly upright but for Jimmy Zane, who remained on hands and knees, still gasping and puking by turns.

"At your ease!" The voice was gravelly and almost bored. John turned and beheld General Zachary Taylor, Old Rough and Ready himself. He knew him on the instant, this famous hero of the Florida Indian wars, had seen his ink-drawn likeness in myriad newspapers, on posters in New Orleans. Gray and weathered he was, with a face that looked hard enough to blunt a hatchet, wearing his farmer's outfit of straw hat, checked gingham coat, pants of dirty burlap. He was mounted sidesaddle on Old Whitey—the horse's name known to every man in camp—and flanked by a coterie of a half-dozen officers. He leaned forward and spat a streak of tobacco, then nodded at Jimmy Zane and said, "What's troubling that man, Master Sergeant?"

Kaufmann stepped forward and saluted smartly. "Naught but a dose of discipline, General. Man was insubordinate. He's new fish, sir, but it aint no excuse."

Taylor regarded Kaufmann carefully and slowly nodded. He looked at Jimmy Zane now gaining his feet. "Son," he said gently, "look up here." Jimmy Zane lifted his red eyes and wiped vomit from his chin with his sleeve.

"Now boy, you look to have a proper wit," Taylor said. "So I reckon you'll understand me when I say there's damn good reason for a chain of command and only a purebred fool tries to rattle it. An army without discipline is no more than a mob, and mobs don't win wars. Follow orders, son. Follow orders and do your duty. I know you'll make us proud." He put the white horse forward and the other officers heeled their mounts after him.

Kaufmann looked hard at Jimmy Zane and pointed a finger at him in final warning and then turned and strode away. As the crowd of spectators broke up, a corporal called out to Jimmy Zane, "Welcome to the Yoo-nited States Army, new fish," and several soldiers laughed.

Watching Kaufmann go, John said, "I believe somebody ought beat down that little bullying bastard."

Lucas said, "I'd like to be that somebody, what I believe."

13

Working alongside their new comrades that afternoon they found it was as the young volunteers in Baton Rogue had said: there were men in this army whose English they could barely understand, men who spoke the language not at all and could understand none of it save basic military commands. The English spoken in the ranks was tangled in a dozen accents. The brogue of Eire was commonplace. The ranks abounded with Irishmen fled from the Famine and landed among a people who loathed them for immigrant Catholic rabble and posted signs on their establishment doors: "No dogs or Irish allowed." In Boston and Philadelphia and Saint Louis, Catholic churches had been burned in riotous protest against the waves of papist potatoheads washing up on American shores. Only the army offered the newly arrived Irishman a ready place, as it did other foreigners as well—Germans mostly, some French, a few Swedes and Dutchmen, and men whose place of origin and native tongue would ever remain a mystery. Some of these immigrants knew only the soldier's trade and would have come to the ranks in any case, but most had no trade at all and enlisted solely of economic need. Naturally their patriotism was held suspect and they were often found wanting by their native-born Protestant officers. And so naturally they suffered the greatest portion of punishments. And so naturally they were many of them embittered.

As they busily struck and rolled tents Jimmy Zane's muttered curses about Kaufmann met with derision from his new platoon mates. "Shitfire," a soldier from Kentucky said, "that warnt nary punishment. I knew a feller in the Second Infantry was made to sit astraddle a sawhorse with his hands tied behind him and a twenty-pound weight hung on each foot. Made to sit like that for twelve hours. Said his balls and asshole ached for a month after. Said ever time he took a piss it stood him on his toes. Know what for he got punished thataway? Laughing. He laughed during roll call."

Another told of punching a sergeant who'd kicked him for being slow to rise from his bunk one morning. As punishment he was fined six months' pay and made to carry a thirty-pound iron ball everywhere he went for the next two months. "It was chained round me waist, it was, so I couldnt set the bloody thing down for a fucking minute except I sat on the ground and laid it beside me. It was a job to take a piss, I tell ye. Had to do it on me knees. End of the day me back was sore as a whore's with the holding of it. It give me arms like Hercules and the back of an old man, it did. Hell, a knee in the walnuts is nothing to carrying that iron ball for two goddamn months."

"You think that is fucking punish?" a soldier with a heavy Prussian accent asked him. "Look to here what happens for *I* hit a sergeant." He stripped off his shirt and exposed a back crosshatched with pink ropy scars left of a flogging endured more than a year before. "This is twenty lash," he said. "I seen some have forty. Fifty. I seen some die."

"Why'd you hit him?" a young recruit asked.

The Prussian looked at him as a parent upon a slow-witted child. "Because he is deserving it is why."

A private named O'Malley showed them his outsized thumb knuckles, the consequence of being hoisted to his tiptoes by his bound thumbs and let to hang that way for two hours with a gag in his mouth. "Most times they'll do ye by the wrists and then it aint so bad," he said. Someone asked what he'd done to get that punishment and he said he couldn't quite remember. "I was bloody drunk at the time but I have a wee recollection of some son of a bitch calling me a damned Catholic cannibal."

They heard too all about the "yoke," an iron collar weighing eight pounds and fitted with three prongs, each a foot long. "After the first coupla hours it feels like your neckbone's about broke," said a soldier bearing a "T" brand under one eye. "And just try sleeping with one a them things round you neck."

Commonplace was the buck and gag, whereby the malefactor was made to sit on the ground with his heels drawn up against his buttocks and his hands tied together around his knees and a stout stick positioned under his knees and over his arms and a gag placed snugly in his mouth.

One among them told of being bucked and gagged on the same long pole with three friends for an entire day and night in near-freezing weather. They were guilty of failing to return to camp at the end of an evening's pass and then coming in drunk the next morning. "When they finally set us loose from that buck we couldn't hardly stand up. I thought my back would be crooked the rest of my days. I thought my hands would hang to my knees forever. And sitting on that cold ground gave me a pile the size a your thumb, I aint lying."

"You see now, new fish," a soldier said to Jimmy Zane, "that wasn't hardly *punishment* ye got from Kaufmann. The sarge just wanted your attention is all."

14

They were on the move before daybreak in the rising dust of hundreds of wagons and draft animals and thousands of marching feet. The bands blared "Hail Columbia" and "Yankee Doodle" and "The Star-Spangled Banner." The infantry sergeants sang cadence and Mexican muleteers cracked their whips and exhorted their teams in profane Spanish amid the rumble of hooves and clatter of wheels, the rattle of armament and harness rings. They followed the Nueces westward, away from the coastal marshlands and out to the firmer ground of the prairie and there made their turn south. Mexican sheepherders fifteen miles downcountry felt the ground quiver under their feet and spied the dust raised by the coming of the Yankee killing machine and made swift signs of the cross.

The first few days were clear and mild, the evenings pleasant. John saw his first armadillo and Lucas snatched it up by the tail and they marveled to discover that although its back was armor-plated its belly was softly furry. In exchange for a portion of it for himself a Mexican drover that evening dressed it and roasted it on a spit and basted it with a chile sauce and John and Lucas agreed it tasted somewhat like pork but was more savory. The army fed too on the wild cattle ranging in the brush and though its meat was found tough and stringy it was yet beef and the men were grateful for it. At night the line of campfires stretched for miles under a black-silk sky spangled with stars. The melodies of the regimental bands carried through the camps. The generals' Negroes entertained with banjos and bones and dancing and singing. Especially popular was their rendition of "The Rose of Alabama."

They learned now, John and Lucas, that there were women traveling
with the supply train. Camp women they were called. They did some of
the cooking and most of the laundering and all of the nursing and made
themselves useful in sundry other ways. All of them had husbands in the
ranks because regulations permitted only soldiers' wives to accompany
the entourage. According to Sergeant Willeford most of them were devoted wives willing to work for the army simply to be near their husbands.
But some were outright whores as profit-minded as the enterprising soldiers they'd married strictly for the sake of business. When these soldiers
went to visit their spouse at the supply train in the evenings they took
with them several comrades eager to pay two dollars each for ten private
minutes with the accommodating wife. "Most popular supply in camp,
don't you know?" said Willeford. According to him, Old Zack and his
officers had known of this thriving enterprise the whole while it existed
at Corpus Christi and saw no reason not to let it accompany the army to
the Río Grande. They approved of it on the principle that it was good
for morale. "And they mean they own morale as much as anybody
else's," Willeford said. "What I hear, the general's always Rough and
Ready to have a visit from Mrs. Borginnis in his tent."

His reference was to Sarah Borginnis, wife to a sergeant of the Seventh
Infantry and known throughout Taylor's army as The Great Western
because like the famous transatlantic steamship of that name she was a
wonder to behold. She was said to be on her fourth husband and was
renowned for her cavalier attitude toward conjugal fidelity. She was par-
tial to soldiers and never hesitant to bestow her favors on any she took
fancy to, and Willeford's claim that Old Zack himself was one of her
predilects was a favorite rumor of the Army of Occupation. Yet she never
took money in exchange for her affections, and her legion of admirers
would thrash any man who called her a prostitute. Not that she required
any man's protection. She stood over six feet tall and was reputedly strong
as a mule. Just a few days previous and in front of a dozen witnesses she
had punched a civilian wrangler unconscious for his loud complaint that
her jackrabbit stew was so godawful it could be a Mexican secret weapon
to poison every American in the ranks. The Great Western, it was said,
had a damn fine sense of humor about everything except her cooking.

John got his first look at her one night when she came to the Fifth
Infantry camp to deliver a fresh load of laundry and was greeted with
rousing cheers. She was darkhaired and alluringly configured with a narrow waist between rounded hips and ample bosom and her mouth was

wide and sensual and quick to pucker in a kissing gesture in response to the soldiers' hallos. Her face might have been pretty but for a dark scar across her chin and another that traversed her right brow in a thin white line to the corner of her eye and held the lid slightly closed. The muscles of her forearms stood like cords under the rolled sleeves of her shirt and her hands were large and rough-knuckled. She accepted a fresh pipe of tobacco from one of the soldiers and John stood leaning against a wagon several yards removed and watched her smoke and banter with the group of riflemen. At one point she caught him looking at her and smiled and winked and he felt himself flush and turned away. He heard her laughter and cursed himself for a damn fool and looked her way again but she was now taking leave of her admirers, waving and saying so long. Then she caught his stare and winked again and was gone.

They moved steadily downcountry on the Camino del Arroyo Colorado. The land had gone flatter still, softer of sand. The trees were fewer and the chaparral thicker. The sun was relentless. Each passing day Lucas Malone glared at the barren countryside and cursed the name of every man in Tennessee who'd told him of Texas's fertile wonder. They pressed through a sandstorm that blew without pause for most of a day. Their eyes were raw and their lips cracked and the backs of their necks sunburned and peeling. Tempers got short and raw. Fistfights broke out round the night fires and the scrappers were bucked and gagged till dawn. They went more than two days without coming on water and their barrels were near exhausted when they at last arrived at a muddy creek and replenished themselves. They slew dozens of rattlesnakes every day. They were stung in the night by spiders and scorpions. A man bitten by a tarantula went into a spastic delirium and had to be tied with ropes and put in a wagon until he at last regained his senses. Their fingers and lips were stung swollen by the tiny spines of the prickly pear's sweet red fruit. There was much muttered cursing in the ranks about the meanness of the country.

They were six days from the Río Grande the next time he saw her. He was sitting in a fireside poker game with four other men of the company, including a tall copperhaired one they called Jack who was winning the biggest hands. John was a dollar ahead when the Borginnis woman showed up with another delivery of laundry and again stayed to chat awhile with some of the men over a pipe. He was watching her and did not hear the call for cards. The fellow called Jack was dealing, and in irritation he leaned over and lightly rapped John on the head with his knuckles and said loudly, "Wake up, boy! You'll not be finding any cards in yonder teats now, will ye?'

The Borginnis woman looked their way and laughed and John felt a surge of furious embarrassment. He abruptly kicked the dealer in the chest with the heel of his foot and toppled him backward. Both of them jumped to their feet and stripped off their shirts and squared off. A loose and raucous ring of spectators immediately formed about them, some in the crowd brandishing flaming chunks of firewood to better illuminate the fight. Bets were called and taken and still more soldiers were running over from neighboring camps as the first punches flew.

Jack the dealer was muscular and lithe as a gymnast, fast and bigfisted. In his fury John swung wildly, missing with roundhouses, and then suddenly saw stars and went sprawling. The surrounding crowd whirled about him like a firelit carousel and he heard cheering and exhortations and tasted blood. He scrambled dizzily to his feet and the dealer came at him again, shoulders hunched and fists pumping, smacking into his arms and shoulders and forehead, driving him back into the crowd that parted for them, closed around them, followed after them yelling for blood.

The dealer was a smooth and practiced pugilist and was carrying his hands lower now, so confident was he. He jabbed to the eyes, hooked to the ribs, crossed to the head. The punches struck sparks in John's head and he backpedaled and counterpunched awkwardly as he tried to clear his vision. Some in the crowd exhorted, "Hit him, new fish! Hit him, goddamnit!" But the cheers were chiefly for the dealer and somebody hollered, "Don't be toying with the lad, Jack! Put him down and be done with it!" The crowd laughed and Jack the dealer grinned widely and landed a quick left-right to John's head.

Now came the Borginnis voice clearly and loud—"Handsome Jack darlin! I'll be treating the winner to a fine time, I will!"—and the crowd cheered its approval. Handsome Jack's eyes flicked sidelong in the direction of her voice, and in that instant John hit him a solid right to the neck and a left to the jaw that staggered him. And then the two were toe-to-toe and slugging with both fists and blood flew off their mouths and eyes and the onlookers were raging for them to kill each other.

But now a guard detail with fixed bayonets came running to break the crowd apart. The officer in charge was one Captain Johns who swatted at the combatants with his saber to separate them and he gashed Handsome Jack's head and sliced open John's cheek to the bone and they let off punching each other and turned on him. Captain Johns blanched and backed away and commanded, "Stand fast, Riley, damn your eyes!"

But Handsome Jack Riley came on with blood streaming from his hair and John saw murder in his face. The captain slashed at Riley and cut his fending hand and then fumbled for the pistol in his belt but John lunged and seized his arm and grabbed away the gun as Riley wrested the saber from him and the disarmed captain staggered backward and fell. Riley stepped toward him with the saber poised to run him through but just then a trio of guards with brandished bayonets rushed between him and the fallen officer. The sergeant-at-arms ordered them to drop the weapons or die where they stood. John let the pistol drop. but Riley seemed to debate the order for a moment before breaking the blade over his knee and contemptuously tossing the pieces aside.

They spent the night gagged and bucked to the same pole on a flatwagon placed in the very center of the encampment where they would be on full display to everyone at reveille. At the moment the camp was asleep but for the guards walking their posts and the tall shadowy figure that now approached the flatwagon and was halted by a guard who stepped out of the shadows nearby. The figure leaned in to the guard and their silhouetted faces seemed to meld together for a moment and John heard an unintelligible whisper and the guard hissed, "All *right*, dammit! But only for a minute. And stay low!" He walked off into the farther shadows and the other figure climbed up on the flatbed and crouched before them and they saw it was The Great Western. They could not see her eyes in the shadow of her hatbrim but her grin was wide and white in the light of the quarter moon.

"I known you for a hellion, Handsome Jack Riley," she whispered, putting a hand to his face, "and I've loved you for your bold ways. But now"—and she turned to John—"who is this other fearless rascal here, I want to know?" He flinched when her fingers touched the wound on his cheek that yet seeped blood through the surgeon's stitches. She dabbed at the blood beads with the hem of her skirt and kissed the cut and said, "You'll carry this scar to the grave, you will," and then gently kissed him on the upper lip just above his gag. She mopped at Riley's bleeding scalp and kissed him too and stroked his face with one hand and John's with the other. "You two aint scared of neither Saint Peter nor Old Nick, are ye? Look at ye! Look at them *eyes* on ye both!"

Her breath had quickened and now her fingers left their faces and John felt her hand between his legs and he was instantly engorged. She grinned hugely at him and then at Riley. "You two rascals! You'll go to hell itself with a hard-on, won't ye?'' She fumbled with his trouser buttons and released his erection and then attended to Riley for a moment and then she had a hand on them both and was grinning from one to the other and she hadn't stroked him a dozen times before John grunted into his gag and gushed hotly over her hand. She giggled like a girl and leaned to him and kissed his upper lip and then a moment later Riley groaned in his release and she kissed him too. She dried her hands on her dress and rebuttoned their trousers. Then she gently touched their faces again and whispered, "You *two!*" And then she was gone.

For a minute they sat unmoving. John thought he might have imagined the whole thing. He thought he might be addled from Riley's punches or the sword gash on his face. Now Riley made a snuffling sound and John turned and saw Handsome Jack staring at him with bright wet eyes and for a moment he thought Riley might be strangling on his gag, or was perhaps crying. And then he knew it was neither. Handsome Jack Riley was laughing. Laughing into his gag. John tried to say, "You're a crazy son of a bitch" but it came out sounding like "Ooo-*ayhee*-un-ick" and Riley snuffled more loudly still and the tears spilled down his face. And then John too was snuffling with laughter and feeling his eyes fill hotly and having trouble breathing around the gag for the mucus flooding his nose, and they were both like that, laughing into their gags and weeping with mirth until their bellies ached and their eyes were burning and they thought they would choke to death on their laughter.

15

By midmorning of the following day they'd been tried and convicted and sentenced to forfeiture in pay—three months' pay for John, five for Riley—and to carry a thirty-pound ball and chain for the next twenty-five days. They were furthermore prohibited from speaking to anyone for the remaining six days of the march and were firmly gagged to ensure they did not. Riley's extra fine was levied against his destruction of United States Army property in the form of Captain Johns's saber. Their punishment could have been much worse, but because neither man had actually struck Captain Johns, and since there were dozens of witnesses ready to testify that Johns had bloodied both of the accused with his saber and they had simply been trying to defend themselves, and since Captain Johns had wide reputation as a harsh disciplinarian, the adjudicating officer, Colonel Belknap of the Eighth Infantry, decided that there had been no assault on the captain but only a gross insubordination toward him.

The ball each carried was attached to an ankle by a four-foot chain. They carried it first under one arm and then under the other as they marched along, shifting their slung rifle to the opposite shoulder each time, pouring sweat with the lugging of the extra weight under the broiling sun. They were made to march at the rearmost of the company where the raised dust was thickest and breathing was even more difficult than already rendered by their gags. Sweat ran off their battered faces in muddy rivulets and soaked their gags and they tasted dirt and their own raw exudates. They were careful not to look each other's way too often because each time they did they started laughing and choking.

Only at mealtimes were their gags removed, and then a guard was posted over them to enforce silence between them as they ate. Once, when the noon meal guard drifted away a few yards to borrow tobacco from a passing friend, Riley hissed at John to get his attention and then whispered, "What's your name, lad?"

John told him. Riley said, "I'm John too. John Riley. But they mostly call me Jack."

"*Handsome* Jack, what I hear," John said. His smile pained his face and felt thick and twisted.

Riley grinned awkwardly and put fingers to his own swollen face. "I aint feeling so terrible handsome this moment, no thanks to you."

"You'll get no apology from me, damn ye. These lumps on my face are *your* doing."

Riley chuckled. "The lumps aint nothing to that cut on ye cheek. At least mine's in my hair, I can hide it under a hat."

"That son of a bitch."

"Aye. It's no proper way to treat men like us. The fools ought to give me a command, not be chaining me to a damn cannonball."

"Maybe Old Zack will see the error of his ways and make you a company commander tomorrow," John said.

"It wouldn't be the most foolish order he ever gave," Riley said. "I was a sergeant, you know. One day this lieutenant fresh as a shavetail mule and twice as ignorant tries telling me the best way to set up a six-pounder gun. Me! I'd already forgot more about artillery than that wet-ears will ever know. Anyhow, one thing led to another and he calls me an arrogant Mick, he does. Well then, he tripped somehow and fell in the mud in his spanking new uniform, don't you know, and didn't everybody laugh at him. Next thing you know it's me that's blamed for the fool's clumsiness and there go my stripes." He spat to the side as if ridding his mouth of a bad taste.

"I tell ye, Johnny, I hate these sonsabitches. Back in Michigan I thought I was joining an army what knew the true worth of a man, an army where a man could make a life's work for himself, sure. Jesus, what a fool! All these bastards see is me Irish. It's what they see in you too. I doubt ye be from the sod yourself, but tell me, where's your da hail from, eh?"

"County Cork he always said."

"Aye, sweet County Cork, I know it well. I should have guessed it, for it's in your bearing, tis. I tell ye, Johnny, they know ye for the Irish rogue you are, no matter you don't sound it. And they'll keep ye down for it, they will."

Riley's tone was offhand but John sensed the fury that underlay it. And sensed too the truth of what he said.

Now Riley smiled. "But how about that big bold Sarah now? Aint she a prize?"

"She do know how to boost a man's spirit in his time of sufferin," John said.

"Spirit? Hell, man, it wasn't me *spirit* she boosted!"

They snorted and tried to stifle their laughter. The guard heard them and hurried back and told them to shut up. They fell to their bowls with their spoons but every time they traded glances one or the other would laugh abruptly and spray a mouthful of beans.

IV

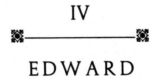

EDWARD

1

Two hours after John disappeared through the curtained door at the rear of the gaming room in The Hole World Hotel, Edward was still at the stud table. He had won $122, most of it in gold and silver specie, some of it in the paper issue of various states and of doubtful value except to whichever parties agreed to transact with it. He'd won too a silver pocketwatch and chain, a gold-capped incisor, and a finely honed bowie knife a filibuster down on his luck had put up in lieu of a five-dollar raise after running out of money.

And he had won a packet of five daguerreotypes. A buckskinned gray-beard with a fierce consumptive cough had put up the packet as the equivalent of Edward's one-dollar raise. The pot held over twenty dollars and Edward and the graybeard were the only ones left in the hand but the old man was out of money and desperate to make the call.

"What's this?" Edward said when the graybeard tossed the packet in the pot. The old man told him to open it up and have a look. Edward untied the ribbon and opened the flap and his breath caught at the sight of the top photograph, grimy and much smudged, which showed a wholly naked young woman lying on her side with her back to the camera and smiling over her shoulder. Edward looked and looked at her full round buttocks.

The graybeard laughed and had a coughing fit, then managed to get out, "It aint no drawings, boy. That there's the real thing, by Jesus."

Edward had never before laid eye on a photograph. The reality of the girl was stunning. He cleared his throat and swallowed hard and looked the rest of the pictures. He saw the same smiling woman reclining on her back with legs apart and knees raised and one hand between her legs on her great hairy nexus and the other over a breast. Saw another completely naked young woman of fairer face and lighter hair recumbent on her left side and with her right leg raised straight up in the air as gracefully as a gymnast's to expose her vulva fully to the camera's infallible memory. Saw a side view of this same woman kneeling and grinning into the camera as she gripped the erect phallus of a standing man visible but from the shoulders downward. And this same woman kneeling before perhaps the same man with her eyes closed and both hands around his erection and her mouth over its glans.

"Yeeow! It's one a them Frenchy picture cards!" the man to Edward's right said, leaning over in his chair to have a look.

The graybeard leaned over the table and snatched the photographs from Edward. "I said have a look, boy, not do no memorizing!" He coughed harshly and pimpled the tabletop with pink spittle. "They worth plenty more than a damn dollar. Twenty dollars be more like it. But I aint looking to let ye buy the pot by raising ye and letting ye raise me right back again. I'll say them pitures are worth a dollar and call ye right here and now."

The other men at the table clamored to have a look but the graybeard told them to go to hell as he carefully replaced the photographs in the packet.

Edward yearned for the pictures but affected only the barest interest. He pursed his lips and shrugged indifferently and said all right, he'd allow them as a dollar. The graybeard grinned and tossed the packet in the pot and called him and turned up a ten as his hole card to go with the two tens he had showing. But Edward showed three jacks and the old lunger had such a violent fit of coughing his face turned purple and it seemed the veins in his forehead might burst. Edward took the photographs off the table and put them inside his shirt.

Keeler had lost all his money in the first twenty minutes of play and had since been standing at the bar, drinking and half-listening to Allenbeck belabor the details of his episode with the redhead whore upstairs. Allenbeck was directing his narrative as much to the barkeep across the counter, but the barkeep's trade had over the years made him privy to more tales of erotica than he cared to listen to anymore, and he barely attended the riverman's account as he cursorily rinsed beer mugs. Keeler kept a close eye on the game's progress and smiled broadly every time Edward pulled in a pot, since by agreement he was entitled to half of Edward's winnings. No other player now at the table had been there when Edward joined the game.

The din of conversation and laughter now dipped noticeably and much of the room's attention turned toward the front of the room. Edward looked to the doors and saw a band of a half-dozen men who stood there and glanced about the big room with expressions of amused disdain. Two of the men were uniformed U.S. Army officers but the unmistakable leader of the group was a man with an imperial beard and black hair to his shoulders, resplendent in a suit of green broadcloth and matching cape, a wide-brimmed hat with a gray plume, a white stock around his throat, a lace handkerchief dangling from his sleeve. His gloved hand held a silver flask and now he took a drink from it but made no offer to his fellows. The other three were all young men in identical black jackets, white silk shirts, red scarves that hung to their knees, and high boots shined to gloss. They wore rapiers and flintlock pistols on their belts. The man in the green suit said something sidelong to the others and they all laughed loudly, and then he turned and went out and they followed after.

"Who was *that?*" Edward asked the player to his right, a sallow ragged man named Desmond whose bearing and diction bespoke a past in which he had occupied higher station than his present.

"That, my boy," Desmond said, "was Marcel DeQuince, one of the city's supreme maitres d'armes. Perhaps the great Pépé Lulla is more adept with a broadsword, but not even Gilbert Rosiere himself is his equal with a rapier. They are rather a rogue royalty in this town, the maitres d'armes."

"What's a matter darms?" Edward asked.

"*Maitre d'armes*, young man, *maitre* d'armes. A master of arms. Rapier, dirk, broadsword, pistol, any weapon meant for the hand of man. De-Quince has killed some six or seven men in duels these past two years. So they say. Say he's making a fortune teaching American officers to fence with sabers. I expect they're set on giving a heroic account of themselves dueling the Mexicans in Montezuma's fabled halls. Those other fellows were his students as well. You can always tell them by those red scarves."

Edward wanted to ask who Montezuma was but he was smarting from Desmond's correction of his pronunciation and did not want to further display his ignorance.

He folded after the third card on the next two hands, then got into a betting war with Desmond and a paddlewheeler cook after the last face-up card was dealt. The pot swelled to thirty-seven dollars before the cook called and Edward showed a full house of nines over deuces to take the hand. "Kee-rist!" the cook said, and shoved his cards away. Desmond sighed and gently threw in his cards.

Edward had been sipping beer since sitting down to the game and now told the table he was going to take a piss and to not let anybody fill his chair while he was gone.

"Hell, boy, why bother to go outside?" said a man with raw sores on his face who'd been in the game for over an hour and had been losing steadily. "You kindly been pissin on *us* all night."

Edward laughed and slipped the sheathless bowie into his belt, marveling at the huge weapon's balance, at its comforting heft. He put the folding money in his shirt pocket and scooped up the specie and the gold tooth and the pocketwatch and stuffed it all in his purse, then took his beer bucket to the bar and told the barkeep to fill it.

Keeler was grinning crookedly. "We doing real good, eh?"

Edward gave him a look and smiled. "Yeah, *we* doin just fine." He looked around as he handed Keeler the purse and said, "Hold this while I go out and water the flowers. Where's Johnny at?"

"Aint seed hair of him since he went up to sample the fillies. Probly still at it. Wish this one here was still up there too so I wouldn't have to keep hearing about how he did this and that and the other with some gleety redhead. He's bout paralyzed my ears with his bullshit."

Allenbeck made a rude hand gesture at Keeler. "Aint bullshit and she aint gleety. You just too old to cut into the hair pie but once a week anymore, grandpa."

Keeler put his face up close to Allenbeck's and scrutinized his features intently. "You know, I just might *be* your grandpa. I believe I knew your grandma real well."

"You gutterborn bastard," Allenbeck said. "Everbody on the river knows your *momma*."

The friends exchanged such dire insults regularly and were still at it as Edward went out the front doors. Lightning quivered to the south and thunder rolled lowly from the Gulf. The sky was crowded with heavy cloud. In the dim light of the streetlamp a pair of oxcarts loaded with cypress planks were rumbling past, one behind the other. From the other side of the wagons came voices and a staccato metallic clash but Edward's straining bladder would brook no further delay and he hastened around the corner of the building, unbuttoning as he went. The jakes stood in the alley but only a man desperate in his bowels would do his business in the dark and miasmic foetor of its rotted and ratcrawling confines. The pissers simply let fly against the side of the building as Edward now did, being careful how he set his feet in the slickness of the urine-sopped mud.

Emerging from the alleyway he saw a small crowd looking on as DeQuince's two officer students crossed sabers in the street, shuffling to and fro, thrusting and parrying as the master stood by and observed them, sipping from his flask. Abruptly he barked, "Non!" and the swordsmen stepped back from each other and gave him full attention.

DeQuince handed the flask to a red-scarved student and gestured for one of the officers to come to him. He took the soldier's saber and softly discussed with him some point of technique and then he stepped out to face the other officer and said, "En garde."

The officer saluted with his blade and assumed the ready position. The maitre d'armes' own garde posture was languid, the saber drooping loosely in his upraised right hand, his left hand on his hip almost girlishly. He seemed bored. He showed a small smile and asked something and the officer nodded curtly and worked his fingers tightly on the hilt and his aspect was utterly serious. Thus poised, the officer began circling DeQuince slowly. The master moved with him as smoothly as if the ground itself were revolving under him, smiling easily. And then he yawned hugely and the onlookers laughed. Even in the streetlight's weak illumination Edward could see the flush on the officer's face and the angry tightening of his lips. The officer thrust and DeQuince parried with the barest flick of wrist and no change of posture or expression whatever. He made a remark in French that drew laughter from the other students and the officer flushed more deeply still. Another intent thrust glanced off another casual parry.

The officer feinted and DeQuince laughed aloud and the soldier's face clenched in fury. He lunged in a thrust meant to skewer DeQuince's heart but the master sidestepped easily and his brightly blurred blade entwined itself around the officer's saber and snatched it from his hand and sent it arcing through the air, turning end over end. The spectators were applauding as the sword clattered to the ground at Edward's feet.

As the officer stalked over to retrieve his weapon Edward bent to pick it up with the intention of handing it to him but before his fingers touched the hilt the soldier roughly shoved him aside and snarled, "Get away, you damned river trash," and stooped for the saber himself.

Reacting without thought Edward backhanded him in the side of the head with the heel of his fist. The officer staggered sidewise and fell to all fours and Edward kicked him in the stomach, knocking him onto his side, and then kicked him in the mouth, spinning him over on his face. The officer lay still and breathed wetly against the cobblestones.

The crowd stared at Edward in slackjawed silence. He cursed himself for his stupidity as he stood facing them. *It's a bunch a them and you got no gun, you damn fool!* His only arms were his knives—the bootknife, the snaphandle in his pocket, the big bowie flat against his belly.

Now the other officer said, "You snipjack bastard," and went for his pistol but DeQuince slapped his blade against the man's belted flintlock to stay his hand. The officer stared at the maitre d'armes in confusion. DeQuince shook his head and then advanced on Edward with an air of indolence, smiling easily, the saber dangling at his side.

The fallen soldier lay on his pistol and Edward sensed that if he tried for it the maitre d'armes would run him through on the instant. DeQuince closed to within easy sword thrust and there paused, his smile remote, his eyes as devoid of malice as of warmth, bored eyes, indifferent to whether they looked upon rain or blood or sparkling wine. Edward had not seen eyes like them before.

DeQuince addressed him softly in French. Edward shrugged. The master at arms smiled and tilted his head and looked at him with slitted eyes as if trying to see him in clearer focus, then spoke again, more loudly, and the onlookers all laughed.

"'He had no call to put hand to me," Edward said. He did not know if the maitre d'armes spoke English. The bowie in his belt felt far from his hand.

DeQuince again spoke in French and the rising inflection of his words suggested he was making inquiry. Edward shrugged and said, "Shit, I don't talk Frenchman." The master of arms pulled a mock-serious face and shrugged hugely in exaggerated mimicry and the spectators laughed. A rush of anger burned Edward's ears. He turned his head and spat and in the same moment DeQuince's saber flashed up and flicked away the top button of his shirt. The crowd laughed more loudly yet. Edward backed up a step and without seeming to move at all DeQuince kept the same distance between them. The saber tip rested lightly on Edward's chest just under the second button.

Edward raised his hand to push the saber away and in a move faster than the eye DeQuince slapped his wrist with the flat of the blade and with a backhand flick took away the second button and the sword tip now dimpled the cloth under the third. Again Edward backed up a step and DeQuince moved with him as effortless as shadow. The crowd applauded.

"You son of a bitch," Edward said through his teeth. With the barest sidelong turn of his head DeQuince said something loudly and pricked the crowd to laughter again. He flicked away the third button and the saber tip dropped to the fourth.

Something batted the plume in DeQuince's hat as it sailed past his head and shattered on a wall. A bottle flung by Keeler who stood drunkenly grinning from the entrance of The Hole World Hotel with Allenbeck swaying alongside him and yelling, "Hey, you fucken monsewer bastard, try that on me why doncha!"

In the instant DeQuince's eyes cut to the saloon doors Edward snatched the saber blade tightly with his left hand and ignored its burning incision into his palm as DeQuince's hold on the hilt tightened reflexively and Edward yanked the blade sidewise and pulled him off balance and the bowie was now in Edward's right hand and he thrust it to the hilt in DeQuince's belly.

The master of arms' eyes went very wide and white and were not at all bored now and his lips puckered as if for a kiss. Blood gloved Edward's hand as he shoved down hard on the haft and the razorous blade slid easily through gut and organs and gristle and struck bone and he leaned harder into the knife to cut through it and the blade sliced through DeQuince's crotch and came free in a great hot rush of entrails. He released the saber and jumped back and DeQuince stood wavering and staring down horrified at his viscera unraveling to his feet with a soft hiss and he sank to his knees and fell forward into the spilled ruin of his life.

For an instant everyone stood in mute tableau—and then Edward turned and ran. He heard behind him Allenbeck's shrill battle cry and then a pistolshot and a yelp and he turned the corner as more shots cracked one behind the other and a round ricocheted off a wall behind him. He ran the length of several dimly-lighted blocks as people jumped aside of his headlong flight. He turned into an alley and in the blackness crashed into a pile of broken crates and fell and scrambled up again and dashed out onto a high-curbed cobbled street and recognized it and knew now where he was and where the river lay and he headed that way but not directly, instead threading his way through alleys and narrow back lanes, not running now but moving fast along the shadows close to the walls, hearing no sounds of pursuit. He rounded yet another corner and a knot of men on the walkway before him was passing a bottle among themselves and they saw him coming and broke clear of his way and he realized that he still had the bowie in his bloodstained hand and his pants were sopped with DeQuince's blood and his left hand was dripping red from the gash opened by the saber blade and his aspect was surely demonic.

By this roundabout route he arrived at Tchoupitoulas Street and made directly for the dark end of the block and the livery where they'd housed their outfits. The bowie was now under his coat and his bleeding hand balled tight in his coat pocket. He attempted an air of casualness wholly unnecessary on that roistering street where he was twice obliged to step over men on the sidewalk who lay dead or insensible with drink, who could say which, to the utter disregard of the passing world.

The livery boy went bigeyed at the sight of him but hastened to follow orders and saddled his mount while Edward checked the loads in his rifle and pistol and then bound his hand tightly and scribbled a note to John saying he'd wait on him at Mrs. Bannion's house in Nacogdoches. He pondered a moment, then thoroughly blacked over the names of both town and madam and wrote "at Aunt Flora's in N.," since there was no telling who might get a gander at the note. He slipped it in with John's possibles and gave the boy two bits to tell John the same message if he happened to see him.

The boy gave him directions for the quickest route to the western road and Edward thanked him and rode off into the night as the sky lit white with lightning as thunder blasted and the rain came crashing down.

2

Two days west of Dixie City there struck a hard norther. The trees and bushes shook in the icy wind and then frosted white . The land went hazy and blue with cold. Breath plumed palely from horse and rider. Edward's thin jacket and slicker were of little effect. His ears rang with the cold, his fingers cramped, his feet ached to the marrow. He draped the reins loosely round the saddlehorn and hugged himself tightly and let the horse follow the trail.

He made camp early that evening and built two large fires and though he'd not eaten since morning when he'd killed a rabbit for breakfast his appetite was blunted by the cold. He let the lee fire die out and spread a layer of dirt over the smoldering ground and there made his bed. He recharged the other fire and with the heat of it wafting over him he wrapped himself in his blanket and went to sleep. Two hours later he woke in frozen darkness with all muscles stiff against the icy night. He blew on the coals and fed them kindling and revived the flames and huddled so near to them that next thing he knew he was afire.

He jumped up yelling and beating at his smoking coat with both hands and so frighted his horse it pulled free of its loose tether and bolted away into the dark. He finally thought to take off the coat and beat it on the ground to extinguish it. A large charred patch on its left flap was burned through in spots about the size of silver dollars. His shirt had burned too and he was blistered at midchest. He scraped frost from a willow branch with the edge of his hand and pressed it to the burn and flinched and muttered curses the while.

He put the coat back on and buttoned it to the neck and turned up the collar and put on the slicker and wrapped a bandanna round his head so that it covered his ears. Then pulled his hat low and picked up his rifle and set out in search of the horse. He gave up after an hour of calling into the freezing nightwind. He'd lost all feeling in fingers and nose. He went back to the fire and built it up again and kept a careful distance from the windtossed flames and popping sparks. After warming his hands and feet somewhat he again wrapped himself in the blanket and slept fitfully the short rest of the night. When he awoke just before dawn the wind had abated and the horse stood at the campfire embers with its head lowered to the last of their heat.

The sun of the following days was dull and tepid, the cold air sharp but fairly still. He passed fields where isolate Negroes or meager families of them walked astoop and picked the scattered remains in cotton fields stripped nearly naked not long before. He spied no game, fed on green tomatoes he found growing alongside an abandoned and roofless shack, a small turtle he shot off a creekside log. The main road lay west-northwest through the pinelands, skirting vast swamps to the south and winding about large and small bodies of water rimmed with high reeds. One late forenoon he hove within sight of a small farm where a family was at work slaughtering hogs. He reined his horse toward the farm and hallooed the folk and was invited to come ahead and rest himself and take dinner with them.

They ate at a roughhewn outdoor table set near a blazing firepit, gorging on fried ham and chitlins, roast ears of corn, huge slabs of sweet potato pie. The patriarch was a broad baggy-eyed man named Ansel Welch who had sired four surviving sons with his first wife before she died of brain fever. Three of those boys had since come of age and moved off and started their own families and only seventeen-year old Benson was still with him. His second wife was twenty-one years his junior. She was quiet and thin and weathered beyond her thirty-three years but hard muscle stood on her arms. She'd been sixteen when they wed and had borne him seven children, only four of whom were yet alive—two more sons and the only two daughters Ansel Welch had ever fathered. He was vastly proud that he had a grandson sixteen years of age as well as a daughter not yet two, and that his wife's belly now bulged with a child due at the end of winter. The elder daughter was called Sharon. She was just turned sixteen and Edward's heart quickened at the sight of her. She was tall and lean and well-breasted. Her freckled cheekbones went rosy under his gaze but she met his eyes boldly.

On learning that Edward was bound for Nacogdoches the farmer claimed he was a friend of Sam Houston. "I'm damn proud to say I know the man. He done more than anybody to make Texas a republic the last ten years and I figure he'll easy be elected governor or leastways a senator now the Texians are finally joined the Union. Course now, they sayin the damned Mexicans don't like it a bit, seein as they aint never quit believin Texas still belongs to them. They say it's lots of war talk in Mexico and Washington both, lots of it."

A little over thirty years ago, the farmer said, he and Sam Houston had fought together under Andy Jackson at the battle of Horseshoe Bend. "I was twenty-three-year old and part of Andy's militia and Sam was a youngster lieutenant in the regular army outfit that joined us for the fight against the renegade Creeks. Red Sticks. Meanest red niggers east of the Mississippi. Just six months previous they murdered five hundred white folk at Fort Mims. Defiled them in ways I can't say in front of my wife and girls, but I mean to tell ye, we were hankerin after them devils bad. I know for a fact it was a thousand of them at Horseshoe Bend cause after it was over Andy had us cut the nose off ever dead Injun and count them out in a pile. We tried to feed them noses to the dogs but the curs just turned away and wouldnt eat of that Injun meat, not even that we roasted. We anyhow made the south of Alabama safe for Christian folk is what we did."

He brandished a hand on which the two fingers next the pinky were but stubs. "It's some of us paid a price for it. Arrows hissin through the air thick as bats lettin out of a cave at dusk and one a them took both these fingers neat as you please. Didn't hardly bleed much. I was luckiern Sam. He took a arrow in the balls and they just poured blood. But he got somebody to yank it out and doctorfy him and he went right back to the fightin. Got hisself shot all to hell. He was so bad off we laid him out with the dead to be buried next day but damn if he still wasn't breathin in the morning. Old Hickory hisself had a look at him and couldn't believe he was still alive. Bedamn if that hardbarked sumbuck didn't pull through and end up President of Texas."

When dinner was done the family went back to work. Edward had been taught the ways of hog killing by Daddyjack, and Welch accepted his offer to lend a hand. While the two younger boys busied themselves washing out hog guts to be used for sausage casing, Edward and the Benson boy threw slops in a trough and when the pigs lined up to feed at it Welch stepped up behind each one in turn and struck it square between the eyes with the flat of an ax, dropping each pig dead with one expert swing. Edward slashed the felled pigs' throats with the bowie to bleed them and the blood gushed out and made red mud of the ground. Benson jabbed strong sharp-pointed sticks through the pigs' heel strings and they dragged the animals by these sticks to big tubs of water seething over fires set in holes so that the tub rims were about even with the ground. They shoved the pigs into the tubs and scalded them till the hides could easily be scraped clean of all bristle. Then they hung the carcasses from a tree branch by the heels and gutted them. They washed each carcass out good and scraped it of fat and butchered it and hung the hams and middlings in the smokehouse. The mother and elder daughter would fry most of the fat into crisp cracklins to be mixed with cornpone and what they didn't fry they would render into lard or boil into soap.

At the end of the day the men's clothes were stiff with gore and the chilly air was ripe with pig blood. They washed up at the creek and Benson traded Edward a clean pair of pants and shirt for his bloody ones. They were a fair fit but for being a tad short at the wrists and ankles. They supped on pork ribs and baked yams and corn and the Sharon girl's peach cobbler. Every time Edward and the girl looked each other's way she flushed and he felt heat in his own face. Her eyes were green and bright with mischief. The mother caught their looks and scowled darkly and the girl gave back a tight-lipped look of defiance. The farmer seemed entirely oblivious to all the ocular byplay. Edward deftly avoided the mother's scolding stares by ducking his head to his cobbler and coffee. He wondered at the girl's boldness and tried to imagine what she looked like without her clothes.

The temperature had dropped with the sun and the night was near freezing. Welch offered to have his wife lay out a pallet for him on the floor next the fireplace but Edward declined with the explanation that he would be riding out well before first light and did not want to disturb the house with his stirrings. The farmer remonstrated mildly and the woman packed a bundle of food for him to take. Welch escorted him out to the barn with lantern in hand and stood by while Edward made a comfortable bed of straw next to the stall that held his horse.

"When you get acrost the Sabine into Texas," he advised Edward, "keep to the northwest trace. It'll carry you direct to a spur of the Nacogdoches Road."

Edward thanked him for his hospitality and the farmer thanked him for his help. They bid one another goodnight and farewell and Welch left the lantern with him and headed back to the house.

In his dream he saw himself shivering in his sleep in a vast and rocky wasteland under a sunless sky red as blood. Beside him lay the skeletal remains of a horse and in his sleep he could hear the cold wind whistling through the pale ribcradle. And now the whistling came from Daddyjack who hove up from behind a low sandrise and came shuffling toward him with tattered clothes aflutter and eyesocket gaping and blackrimmed with blood. Edward now woke inside the dream and watched his cadaverous father's advance and shivered as much with fear as with the cold. Daddyjack squatted beside him and showed a yellow grin. He smelled powerfully of horseshit. His single eye roved over Edward's face like some fierce animal pacing in a cage Then he replaced his hat and stood up and walked off whistling into the emptiness and sank from sight into the next depression.

He was truly awake now and heard the wind whistling in the cracks of the walls. A bright narrow strip of moonlight showed where the barn door was open slightly and the lower end of that strip was dark where somebody stood.

"Are ye woke?" the Sharon girl whispered.

The door opened wider and she slipped inside and shut it behind her. In the weak light admitted by the single small window on the far wall he could make out her shadowy form. He heard her stamp her feet against the cold.

"I brung you a blanket," she said softly. "It's so cold."

He sat up and took a box of matches from his jacket and broke one off the block and struck it against the stall post. In the sudden sulfurous flare of blue-yellow light he saw a steaming pile of horse droppings at the edge of the stall and then saw her standing just inside the door with the cowl of her cloak pulled over her head. She was hugging a folded blanket to her chest and in the glow of the matchfire her eyes widened and she hissed, "No light!" and he snuffed the lucifer between his fingers.

For a moment there was only the sound of their breathing. His heart thumped in his throat. Her boldness at once alarmed and excited him. He heard her feet moving through the straw and the blanket she brought fell open with a soft sound. She spread it over his own blanket that yet covered his legs. He felt her weight settle beside him and her seated silhouette was clearer now but he could not distinguish her features.

"Hardly nobody ever comes by here," she said, her voice so low he could barely make out her words. She appeared to remove the cloak and now was doing something with the front of her dress. "The world's way out yonder and I aint *never* gonna see a bit of it nor get to know anybody much in it. I know I aint. Momma was the age I am now when she married and I don't reckon she saw much before she said 'I do,' but I know for a fact she aint seen much but a day's work ever since." She seemed to shrug and her form became somehow paler and he suddenly realized she had made herself naked to the waist. She stood now and fumbled with the dress bunched at her hips.

She continued in her whispered plaint as she undressed but he wasn't listening. He was thinking of tales he'd heard in the Pearl River timbercamp about how fathers looking to marry off a daughter sometimes arranged for just such a situation as this. As soon as the unsuspecting fellow and the sweet thing got their clothes off, the father would barge in with a shotgun and give the jughead no choice but to marry the girl or get his useless brains blown out. But even if this one wasn't up to any such trick, her father might wake anyway to find her absent from her bed in the dark of the night and the first place he'd look for her would surely be in the barn where the passing stranger lay. And he'd as likely come with a gun and not be of a mind to offer him any choice at all. But he remembered too Daddyjack's adage that life's truest pleasures were full of risk and that's what made them special. Watching her vague silhouette step out of the dress and drape it over a stall rail, he reached out and pulled his rifle closer and then slipped his hand under his saddle that he was using for a pillow and withdrew his pistol and bowie and set them readier to hand.

She knelt beside him and he could sense she was shivering and could smell her warm nakedness on the cold air. He reached out and touched her hair. She brought her hand up to his and squeezed it. His other hand went to her breast and she gasped and flinched at his cold fingers and brought them to her mouth and exhaled forcefully on them several times and then placed them back on her breast and whispered, "That's some better." The nipple against his thumb was thick and erect. His night vision had sharpened now and he could vaguely distinguish the freckles on her pale breasts. He stood and quickly shed his pants and they scrambled under the blankets and smothered their yelps and giggles as they laid cold touches to each other. Soon enough their hands were well warmed and they groped and probed and lapped at one another with lickerish delight.

And then they were coupled and rocking together in the most ancient of human rhythms—but still he kept an ear cocked for the approach of Farmer Welch's paternal wrath. His pleasure was the greater for the danger of possible discovery, though he knew now she was up to no trick. She was but a pretty girl aching with loneliness, feeling her youth and beauty wasting in this backwood as far removed from the city life she pined for as from the moon, distant beyond reckoning from the sights and music and streetlights and throngs of exciting strangers she imagined to bepopulate the metropolis. He suddenly envisioned his sister Maggie slouched on the porch rocker in Florida with her eyes closed and her heels hooked over the railing and him and his brother sitting on the lower steps and looking up the exposed backs of her legs to her white cotton drawers. He was shocked to feel himself harden the more at the memory and he thrust with even greater urgency into the gasping girl.

A moment later he thought he heard something and abruptly ceased his rocking and braced himself on one hand and grabbed up the pistol with the other and listened intently even as he remained embedded in the girl. She listened with him and then clucked her tongue impatiently and whispered, "Aint nobody! They all them sleep like rocks."

"Then how come we whisperin?" he asked, smiling, feeling himself throbbing inside her. He heard the sound again and realized it was a shrub slapping softly on itself in a changed wind.

She locked her hands behind his neck and pulled herself up so her mouth was at his ear and said, "Cause I guess you caint never know for *absolute* sure." She giggled and stuck her tongue in his ear and worked her pelvis hard against him. He growled happily and fell to his rhythm again and ducked his face to her breasts.

At the false dawn some time later she got up and began to dress, slapping Edward's fondling hands from her as she did. Edward grinned in the dark and thought he must be crazy. Her daddy might yet come through those doors with a gun in his hand. Might yet shoot him dead. Unless of course he managed to shoot Welch first. The idea of being forced to shoot Welch slowed his gropings for a moment. He was for a fact violating the daughter of a man who'd done him kindness—and what father wouldn't be obliged to do something about it if he knew? But now the girl was done with the buttons on her dress and gone to the door to open it slightly and put her eye to the gap, and he shrugged off his guilty musings and went to her.

She turned to him and took his face in her hands and kissed him hard and deep, then broke the kiss and took his hands off her hips and held them tightly and smiled at him. "It aint no need to look like somebody's choking you," she said. "You aint beholden."

He opened his mouth without any idea of what he was about to say but she put her hand to his lips to shush him and then quickly kissed him again. "I'll think on you, boy. Now go on, get gone." And with that, she was out the door and vanished in the shadows.

A few minutes later he led his saddled horse out of the barn and mounted up. He glanced toward the house and saw the dark windows and wondered if she was at one of them and watching him. He waved goodbye in case she was. The taste of her stayed on his tongue and the smell of her on his skin well into the next afternoon.

3

The days continued cold but mostly bright and windless, the nights sharp with frost and blasting with stars. He rode slowly, shawled in both his own blanket and the one the Sharon girl had brought to him in the barn and which the mother would surely miss and then figure what became of it and how. He had several times wondered if the woman would let on to Welch, and if she did, if the farmer would hang the girl naked by the wrists from a tree limb and whip her bloody for a whore. The idea angered him sufficiently that he muttered curses and several times considered going back. But each impulse to rein about was followed by the question of what he would do then. Ask her to come with him? The notion was pure-dee loony. Come with him where? And do what? Start a farm? Spend the rest of his days grubbing in the dirt for a living? Her maybe going crazy someday? His daughter maybe taking to lay with passing strangers or to run off with his best horse? His sons maybe one day taking to raise hand to him? Maybe killing him? He spat. Better to burn in lonely hell. Whereupon he thought: *You likely*. And smiled wryly. And hupped the horse on.

The country once more rose to timber. The trees drew closer together and stood higher and layers of pine needle softened the fall of the mare's hooves. He'd long since finished the food the woman had given him. He had not eaten in nearly a day when on a high noon gray with mist he hove onto a rise overlooking a booming river. A short distance northward on the near bank a ferry swayed and tossed at moor on its pulley rope. A sagging cabin on short thick pilings stood close by the landing with smoke winding from its narrow chimney. Edward heeled the mare down the slope.

A freshly painted wooden sign at the ferry landing read: TEXES FERRY 1 DOLLER. The ferryman sat whittling on the porch in a straightback chair tipped back against the wall. Beside him leaned a rusty Kentucky rifle. He was gaptoothed and near bald, shirtless and his longjohn top was grayish black with filth. Even from where he sat the horse at the bottom of the steps Edward could smell him. An odor even more rancid wafted from the house.

"Got a possum stew on the pot," the ferryman said. "If you of a mind for a bowl it's two bits. Want a drink of shine it's nother two bits. Want acrost the river it's like the sign says, a dollar. In coin. Don't take no scrip."

"Mister, I wouldnt pay a dollar to have the Angel Gabriel fly me and my horse across."

The ferryman showed a black-yellow grin. "Thats all right. But you aint findin no ford upstream or down for miles, not with her runnin like she be."

Edward studied the swift river and the densely timbered shore of Texas on the other side. He drank from his canteen and sat the mare and watched the river pass by while the ferryman sat on the porch and watched him. He'd been hungry until he caught the stink of the ferryman's stew.

He heard a horse blow and he looked over toward the woods where a rider was emerging from the trees. The horse was a black of good size but seemed diminished by its rider, a huge blackbearded man holding a shortbarreled rifle across the pommel of a saddle with a horn as wide as a pie plate. He wore a flatbrimmed hat and an open frock coat under which a pair of pistols hung in simple sling holsters. As the rider drew nearer Edward recognized the pistols as revolvers, a type of firearm he'd heard described but never seen until now. Texas Colts they were called, though they were made in the distant land of New Jersey. They lacked trigger guards and carried five rounds and a man might fire them all before having to reload. He had heard tales of frontier rangers killing red savages by the quick dozen in an open country fight with such pistols.

The big man reined up at the sign stating the cost of a ferry ride and appeared to consider it. He chucked his horse over to the cabin and there regarded Edward for a long moment without expression, his eyes touching on Edward's empty hands, on the flintlock pistol and bowie in his belt, the Kentucky longarm in the makeshift saddle scabbard. He turned his attention to the house and looked hard at the dark door and window, then looked at last on the ferryman, who on spying him come out of the woods had picked up his rifle and laid it across his lap and now licked his lips nervously under the big man's gaze.

"Anybody inside?" the big man said. The ferryman shook his head and Edward could see he was too scared to be lying. The huge muzzle of the blackbeard's rifle swiveled slightly and pointed squarely at the ferryman's chest. "Toss it," the big man said as offhandedly as one might tell another the hour of day.

The ferryman pushed the rifle off his lap and it clattered to his feet. The big man looked at it and then back at the ferryman and his eyes narrowed and so the ferryman shoved the rifle hard with his foot and sent it skidding off the porch.

Wielding the short heavy-looking rifle as easily as a pistol the blackbeard brought the barrel up to rest on his shoulder. He peered toward the cabin door and made a face of distaste. "Good Christ. You aiming to *eat* what's making that smell?" The ferryman shrugged and seemed offended despite the circumstances.

The blackbeard looked at Edward again, jutted his chin toward the sign and said, "A dollar for a damned ferry ride seems just about ninety cents too much, wouldn't you say so, boy?"

Edward said he believed the toll was just about a dollar too much and the big man laughed.

"Well, they say generosity is balm for the soul," the big man said. "I believe this feller's greedy soul might be soothed by the generous act of giving us a free crossing."

And thus the ferryman did, politely requesting that the two men walk their horses to the outer end of the ferry in order to ease the weight of the inner end and let it float free. He hauled powerfully on the pulley rope stretching across to the opposite bank and the craft lurched into the river.

It was a heady crossing. The swift current pressed against the ferry's side and bowed the pulley line and the ferry bobbed on the rope like a toy. The horses were white-eyed and stamping and Edward and the blackbeard dismounted and strained against the reins with one hand as they clung tight to the rail with the other and gritted their teeth against the icy riverspray. The ferryman stood easy as a cat. He jabbed a long pole into the river bottom and pulled hard on it hand over hand and propelled the craft along on the pulley ropes. By this laborious process he carried them over the Sabine River and landed them in Texas.

Once ashore and again in the saddle the blackbeard inquired of the ferryman if he didn't feel somewhat atoned for his extortions of the past. The ferryman shrugged and said yes, he guessed he did. The blackbeard shook his head with a rueful sigh and said he didn't believe the man's repentance was sincere. "Maybe a little hardship will help you see the error of your ways. Get off there." The ferrymen disembarked warily. From under his coat the blackbeard withdrew a bowie even larger than Edward's and leaned out in the saddle and slashed through the thick pulley rope. The ferryman sprang to the edge of the bank with a stricken look and watched the craft whirl away on the current. Now the big man put his horse forward and the animal forced the ferryman off the bank and into the rushing water and only a desperate grab of a root jutting from the muddy bankwall kept him from being swept downriver.

"You just hang there awhile and let it wash some of that stink off you," the blackbeard called down to him, and laughed. He winked at Edward and reined his horse about and into the woods.

Edward hupped the sorrel mare forward through the trees and into a small clearing where the man sat his horse and said, "Look here, boy. At this sign here." He gestured for Edward to come up alongside and pointed at the ground next his horse. "What you make of it?"

As Edward drew up beside him and leaned out of the saddle to peer down, the big man's horse sidled and in that instant Edward knew the blow was on its way but felt himself held fast in the moment and then light burst behind his eyes and he did not even feel himself fall.

4

He heard low chuckling and woke to cold darkness and the sensation of his skull being prized apart. He slowly came to perceive that he was on his back, that the moving shadows he looked upon were topmost tree branches rocking in the wind, that the steady chuckling was the run of the river through the reeds. He tried to sit up and heard himself groan at the shuddering blaze of pain in his head and he fell back. When next he opened his eyes the sky was gray above him and he knew he'd again been unconscious for a time. With moaning effort he managed to roll onto his belly and then raised himself on all fours and vomited. After a time he sat back on his heels and put his fingers to the back of his head and gingerly fingered the swelling under his hair and the thick coagulating blood. He felt a rank fool. The only reason he could think of why the man hadn't simply shot him dead was he didn't want to chance scaring off the mare.

He made it to his feet and held tight and gasping to a tree until the quivering in his knees subsided. He was in his stocking feet. He looked about and spied a boot beside a tree trunk and a moment later the top of the other in the weeds. The man had pulled them off to search them. Son of a bitch for damn sure was not new to the trade. At least he'd left the boots. And his coat. Likely figured them too worn to be of worth to anybody with anything to trade. But he'd made off with the knives as well as the firearms and the Janey mare. Edward checked his shirt pocket and was surprised to find the daguerreotypes still there. The bastard must've been too busy checking hiding spots like his boots to search the obvious places. He wished he'd thought to keep his money in his shirt. He pulled on the boots and then spotted his hat askew on a bush. And close by was his extra shirt with the sleeve ripped to the shoulder. And there a spare sock. There the small frypan. But blankets and slicker were gone, the wad of scrip, even the box of matches. He took off his coat and put the torn shirt on over the one he was wearing and then put the coat back on put the sock into his pocket and went to the bush and retrieved his hat.

He stumbled through the brush to the riverbank and found a smooth slope where he could stretch out on his belly and duck his head in the river. The cold water's first touch on the wound made him yell out in shock, but repeated duckings gradually eased the pain to a partially numbed and dully throbbing ache. He drank his fill and felt the better for it. He looked across the river at the ferryman's cabin but saw no sign of anyone there and no smoke from the chimney. He wondered if the man had been carried off by the current or managed to extricate himself.

After a time he stood up and gently put on his hat, tilting it well forward and away from the wound. The morning was hazed and frosty cold and the high pines swayed and hissed in the breeze. He balled his hands in the side pockets of his coat and made his way through the trees and found the trail and set out with his head down against the wind.

There followed now days of wandering through piney woodlands and cypress swamps, hungry, unarmed, horseless. Cold fireless nights of dozing with an ear cocked for footfall or approach of shuffling beast. Some days were warm enough he didn't shiver in his bones. Somewhere early on he took a wrong fork and the trace grew wilder as he proceeded and he knew none had passed by here in a long time. Then he was in dense brush thickets, in grass to his thighs. He found a deer trail and followed it through shadowy forest of mossy oak and pine and stagnant bogs and sloughs. He bore north by west and came at last to a road that took him to an inn at a ford. He bartered one of the daguerreotypes for a full meal and then another for three mugs of beer. The proprietor kept glancing nervously over his shoulder while they bargained, keeping watch for approach of his wife.

At a crossroads one gray evening he was accosted by a pair of highwaymen not much older than himself. The taller one held a large-bored flintlock pistol on him while the other searched his person and found naught but the packet with the remaining three daguerreotypes. His mouth fell open when he saw them. He gave Edward a quick look and kept his back to his partner as he slipped the pictures out of the packet and into his shirt. The robber with the gun asked what he'd found and he said, "Nothin but this here empty paperholder," and turned and showed it to his partner and tossed it aside. He squatted and looked close at Edward's boots which were worn even worse than their own and he laughed and told his partner they'd been fools for calling for this one to stand and deliver. They shared with him the last of their meager ration of jerky and spared him a few matches. But when Edward asked if he might have a look at their pistol the taller one stepped back in quick suspicion and pointed the gun at him from his hip and said he could have all the look he wanted right from where he stood. Edward cursed himself for lack of guile. The highwaymen started down the south trace, warning him over their shoulder that if he tried to follow they'd lay for him and kill him.

He pushed on. Found occasional work at farms in exchange for a meal and a warm place to sleep the night. Split wood, mended fences, dug privy holes. He shoveled manure and fired stumps. He was set on thieving the first gun he saw unattended but every farmer kept his rifle close to hand and there were no pistols to be seen.

At a weed-grown farm where tools were rusting on a sagging cabin porch and there was no sign of any man about, a leanly strong and handsome Negro woman the color of caramel fed him a rabbit stew so savory he nearly moaned aloud on the porch steps where he ate. She stood at the door and watched him the while and her children gaped from behind her skirts. Even through the aroma of the stew he could smell the muskiness of her and he would have liked to put a hand to her to test her inclinations but the cool steadfastness of her eyes made him feel callow and unsure. As he headed back toward the trace he looked to the side of the house and spied a quilted blanket drying on a line strung between a pair of young pines and he trotted over and took it and raced away even though no one called after him.

Wagons passed his quilt-shawled figure on the road in either direction but mostly to the west, travelers who sometimes fed him, sometimes warned him off at gunpoint, sometimes carried him a ways. A rotund Dutchman invited him to take supper with the family at their camp under a creekside oak. Midway through the meal this sharpeyed father caught the look between this tatterdemalion with feral eyes and a man's hands and the thirteen-year-old daughter who was rarely other than sullen toward her daddy. He lunged and swiped her a backhand that unseated her off a stump and sent her supper plate twirling. The mother swooped to the bloodymouthed girl and the Dutchman's longarm muzzle appeared in Edward's face like a magic feat, so fast did the man move. His face brimmed with murder but the woman beseeched him not to shoot the boy as she held the daughter to her bosom. The man let a hissing breath through his teeth and told Edward he had to the count of ten to disappear. Which he did, nearly choking on his rage as he went, striding quickly but refusing to run, his clenched fists aching. He considered circling around and coming up behind the bastard and breaking his head open with a rock or a tree limb but chose not to widow the woman who'd saved his life. Without the Dutchman she and the girl might fare still worse.

His anger writhed in his chest. Bedamn if he would anymore depend on Good Samaritans for his sustenance. He reconnoitered farms from a hidden distance, noted if there were dogs about or anyone with a gun, marked the nearest shrubbery to the chicken coops. He pilfered from cornfields and gardens. Stole a peach pie from the kitchen window where it cooled and gulped the entire thing in an oak grove and burned his mouth and suffered a bellyache for an hour after. Made off with a skinning knife left carelessly on a chopping block. Raced for cover of the woods with a clamorous hen in his grip flailing and shedding feathers as rifle report and curses echoed behind him from the violated coop. He was miles removed from the scene of the crime when he dressed the bird and roasted it on a stick and ate it to the bones.

On frosty nights he built large fires and sat beside them with the blanket over his shoulders and watched the wavering flames under the rising moon and thought about things. He supposed John had already arrived in Nacogdoches and was waiting for him. He smiled at the thought of how his brother would laugh on hearing of his travails. He was sure Johnny loved this country. Texas was everything they'd been told. The pines were tall and thick and plentiful beyond reckoning. Johnny would surely want to get a section of timberland hard by a river and waste no time settling into a life of hewing and sawing and selling. He would likely be quick about building a house and taking a wife and siring sons, Johnny would. Such was the natural yearning of a normal soul. His own lack of such inclination Edward had long accepted as a fault of restless character that might never be remedied. Each evening his gaze did fix on the wide sky to the west burning red as blood.

5

He entered the venerable town of Nacogdoches on a graying afternoon turning chill. Through this Texas gateway passed all manner of desperate men. Here had conspiracies and filibustering expeditions and rebellions been formed. Here had the Republic of Fredonia blazed brief and bright.

He came a shambling specter of ill fortune, his clothes ragged and foul, his boots red with dried mud and coming undone at the soles. He was footsore. His hair hung in tangles under his tattered hat. He carried his blanket rolled under his arm and the skinning knife in his boot top. Yet his spirits were high in anticipation of finding John and his ample poke at Flora Bannion's house and soon enough being clean and newly clothed and washing down a beefsteak with a mug of beer.

He passed by an neat oak-shaded cemetery where a gravedigger left off his labor to regard him. Only his upper torso was visible aboveground and his eyes were hidden in the shadow of his hat. Edward tried to stare him down but the digger leaned on his spade and showed yellow teeth and continued to look after him till he was well down the road.

La Calle del Norte was chock-a-block with wagon traffic and horsemen and people afoot. He was obliged to step nimbly. A dogfight broke out in the middle of the street and a frighted mule kicked at the combatants and sent one yowling away on three legs. A banjo twanged in the darkness of a saloon and a fiddle followed its lead. He stared longingly at the dark door and yearned for a drink. He spied a man reading a newspaper in a chair tilted back against the front of a dry goods store and went over and peered at the front page. The headline was of Mexico and President Polk, the date the seventeenth of January, 1846. He'd been afoot more than a month.

Something about the date nagged at him a moment and then he recalled it as his birthday. He was seventeen years old this day.

He inquired of a clerk sweeping the sidewalk the location of Flora Bannion's house and was directed to turn right at the next street and look for the pink two-story building with a flower garden in front of the porch. "But that old cat can be awful damned particular who she lets in," the clerk said, scanning Edward's tattered aspect. "You'd be better welcome at Sally Longacre's the next block over."

The western sky was afire now and gleamed redly along the rippled clouds. An orange lantern by Flora Bannion's front door was already lighted when Edward arrived at the gate. A pair of laughing men in suits were being admitted and then the door closed behind them. He went up the walkway and onto the wide porch and worked the knocker, an iron cast of a cat in repose. A neatly aproned young Negress opened the door but slightly and looked him over and wrinkled her nose against the smell of him. She said if he was wanting something to eat he could go around to the kitchen door. He said he wanted to speak with John Little if he was on the premises. The black girl said the only man on the premises was Bruno the caretaker who could sure take care of any smelly tramp troublemaker. Edward wanted to slap the cheeky bitch. Well then, he said, he'd like to talk to Flora Bannion. The girl said Miss Flora didn't talk to strangers, least of all tramps and she started to close the door on him and he quickly said he had a message for Flora from her sister Molly in Biloxi. The Negress looked at him suspiciously and then told him to go wait at the kitchen door.

The woman who appeared there was fleshy and pouch-eyed and wore a shiny green dress. Her mouth turned down at the sight of him. She asked what message he'd brought from Molly and he said just that she hoped Flora was doing well and to let her know she was thinking of her. The woman's lips tightened in irritation and she said "Molly never said no such thing in her life. You're just another damned liar looking to be given more than you deserve." She made to shut the door and he hastened to say that he truly had been to Mrs. Clark's house within sight of the beach at Biloxi. He quickly described it and said Mrs. Clark had recommended that he and his brother pay a visit to her sister Flora Bannion's place in Nacogdoches and he had lied about the message because he thought she'd be pleased to hear it and be more likely to talk to him and answer him a question.

She stayed the door and eyed him closely and her expression softened somewhat. "All right, sonny," she said. "Ask."

"I just want to know if my brother's here or been here, is all." He explained that they had got separated in New Orleans but were agreed to meet here and he wondered if John had already showed up in search of him. He described him in detail but the woman shook her head and said no, he hadn't been there, she would have remembered if he had, she had an excellent memory for faces. "But now listen, honey," she said, "you get yourself washed up and burn them awful clothes and dress up clean and come on back, you here?"

He went across the street and ducked his head in a water trough and scratched his festering scalp through his sopping hair and ducked his head again and scrubbed his face with his hands and shook the water off them and put his hat back on. He sat on the edge of the trough and regarded the pink house. If John had been there he would have asked after him and Miss Flora would have remembered. Maybe the stable boy in Dixie City didn't give him the message. Maybe the boy or somebody else stole his possibles and the note secreted among them. Why else wouldn't he be here? Maybe he had some kind of trouble back in New Orleans. Or maybe he ran into trouble after leaving town. There was no way to know. But if he wasn't in trouble and even if he hadn't gotten the message, wouldn't he come looking for him in Nacogdoches? John had been standing right there beside him when Mrs. Clark told about this place.

There was nothing to do but to stay put till John showed up or he didn't.

And if he don't show?

He'll show.

Sure he will. But what if he don't?

Then he guessed he's have to go back and try to find him.

Back was a long way in the other direction.

He envisioned DeQuince lying in his own guts in the sickly yellow light of the streetlamp.

He'd find a rope round his neck back there is what he'd find.

And now he thought that Johnny might likely have found himself a generous girl back in Dixie City or somewhere along the way and was getting topped three times a day and twice that much at night and who could blame him if he wasnt in a hurry to leave off the pleasure? Hell, he likely hadnt had a full sober minute since they last saw each other. There Johhny was, having himself a time and here *he* was, looking like rotten possum on a stick and with no gun nor horse to call his own. He was a damn fool to be worrying about John when he had plenty enough to do just tending to himself.

But there was no denying that not even at any time in the past weeks of wandering alone in the woodlands had he felt as alone as he did at the moment.

After a while he went walking the streets and peering over fences and keeping a sharp eye for unlighted open windows but this was not a town to be careless about invitations to theft. He wandered about and studied the houses and slowed his pace as he went by a prosperous-looking white-washed home with huge brick chimneys at either end and fronted by a deep verandah. A pair of mastiffs on long leather leashes fastened to the step railing showed their teeth in the twilight and growled lowly as he passed.

He took a turn by the old stone fort where a man in manacles was being led inside by two men in uniform. Other heavily armed men stood smoking on the lower portico and ceased their conversation to watch him go by. He felt their eyes on him until he was to the corner of the street and around it.

At the second livery where he made inquiry he struck a bargain and spent the next two hours shoveling out the stalls and forking fresh hay, freshening water troughs, straightening tack on the walls. He was paid a silver half-dollar for his labor and then made his way to a brightly lighted tavern at the end of the street where the stablebuck had told him he could get a good meal for two bits and a fairsized glass of whiskey could be had for the same price.

A half-dozen horses stood at the hitching rails in front of the tavern and as he approached the doors he glanced at the animals and stopped short. Then stepped down off the sidewalk to more closely examine the sorrel mare and saw in the cast of light from within the room that it was the Janey horse all right, though she now carried a good saddle furnished with bedroll and wallets and hung with a canteen and lariat. She twitched her ears and he patted her and said, "Hey girl."

He quickly scanned the other mounts at the rails but none was a black stallion. He eased up to the doors and peeked over them and saw in the well-lighted interior a pair of men conversing with the barkeep at the counter and another man drinking by himself at the far end of the bar. Five men played cards at a table toward the rear of the room. Just inside the door sat a solitary drinker with his head on the table and a glass and half-full bottle in front of him. He did not see the giant blackbeard anywhere in the room.

One of the card players stood up and bid the table goodnight. Edward stepped down beside the mare and when the man came out and mounted a tall blaze he said, "Pardon me, mister, I wonder can you tell me whose horse this is?"

The man settled into the saddle and looked down at him.

"Like to make the owner a offer on her," Edward said.

The man wore a saddlecoat of good cut and a spotless white hat. His horse tossed its head and he settled it with a pat on the neck. "No offense, boy," he said, "but you don't look like you could make the price of a day-old glass of beer. I think you ought know that around here they will hang a horsethief quicker than you can say Sweet Jesus."

"I aint no damn horsethief."

"Course not. But now we're on the subject, there's nobody I'd rather see get his horse stolen than Marcus Loom. If I had an hour to spare I could begin to tell you my low opinion of the son of a bitch."

"Is Marcus Loom whose horse this is? Is he inside there?"

"He is. The rascal with the red necktie and the long mustaches on his liar's face. Luck to ye, lad." He reined the blaze around and hupped it down the street.

Edward took another look into the room and picked out Marcus Loom easily. He wore a thin red necktie and a dark suit and a widebrimmed gambler's hat. He sat with his back to the rear wall and laughed as he dealt out a hand.

Edward looked about and spied a crate leaned against the corner of the building. He stove it with his foot and wrenched free a pine scantling three feet long and over two inches square. He propped it against the wall just outside the entrance and lay his blanket roll beside it and then pushed through the doors. The men at the bar watched him advance directly on the back table and then stand there looking at Marcus Loom while the gambler considered his cards. The other three players looked up at Edward and appeared more curious than disturbed by his looming presence. Only one of them wore a pistol on his hip that he could see.

Marcus Loom tossed out a discard and said, "Dealer takes one," and dealt himself a card. He picked it up and looked at it and carefully fit it into his hand. Then he gently lay the cards face down on the felt and leaned back with one hand under the table and looked up at Edward.

"Sorry to bother you at your game," Edward said, "but I been told it's you been ridin my horse."

Marcus Loom stared at him for a moment as though he'd been addressed in a foreign tongue. Then smiled and said, "Beg pardon, sonny?" He looked at the others and winked. One of them chuckled.

"That sorrel mare out there's mine. She was stole off me back at the Sabine ferry. I been huntin her all over and now I found her and just want you to know I'm takin her back. I reckon the saddle's yours so I'll leave it on the porch."

He turned and headed for the doors and was halfway to them when Marcus Loom said, "Lay hand to that horse, boy, and I'll have you for breakfast." As he went past the drunk asleep at the table he snatched up the whiskey bottle and slipped it into his coat pocket.

He stepped outside and glanced back and saw Marcus Loom coming for the doors with his face clenched tight and a pepperbox pistol in his hand. He picked up the scantling and gripped it tightly in both hands and set himself beside the doors. They flew open and Marcus Loom stepped out with the pistol before him and his eyes on the mare and Edward swung and hit him in the face and the *thonk!* likely carried to the next street. The gambler fell against the door jamb as the pepperbox discharged with a flaring yellow blast and the horses shied against their reins looped on the hitch rail. Marcus Loom sat down hard with his hat askew and his nose pouring blood and Edward brought the scantling down on the crown of his head like he was malleting a stake and the gambler folded over on his side and lay still.

Edward scooped up the heavy-barreled pepperbox and his rolled blanket and took up the mare's reins and quickly stood up into the saddle as the others came spilling through the doors. One of them knelt to see about Marcus Loom and the rest stood looking at Edward sitting the mare with the reins in one hand and the pistol in the other. None brandished a weapon but the barkeep who was holding a short musket and Edward pointed the pepperbox at him and told him to let it fall and he did.

"Damn, Jeff, look there at your horse it's been shot!"

The horse at the mare's right side stood with its head lowered and snuffled wetly and a lanky man who'd been at the card table cursed and glanced up at Edward and then glared down at the unconscious form of Marcus Loom.

The man checking the gambler said, "He'll live. Nose is broke and he's got a knot the size of a apple on his head but he'll live a while yet." He stood and looked at Edward. "Boy, you give him a *thumpin.*"

"He damn well had it comin," Edward said. "You all know he meant to shoot me without another word on the matter."

"You say that there's *your* horse?" someone said.

"Sumbitch who stole her took my whole outfit, down to my bootknife. Big rascal with a beard. Rode a black. Had him a pair of Texas revolvers."

"That's the fella Marcus bought the horse from, right enough," one of the gamblers said. "Just last week over at Dean's Livery. Seen him myself. Bearded and outsized, he was, and rode a black like the boy says." Another man nodded in verification.

"I was gonna leave him the saddle," Edward said, "but since he come for me with a gun I reckon he owes me proper satisfaction. I figure the saddle and this here pistol about makes us even. Tell him if he wants to discuss it he can find me in New Orleans. Tell him ask around for Bill Turner."

He walked the mare backward so as not to turn his back to them and then reined the horse about and put heels to her flanks and lit out down the street and into the night.

6

Horsed and pistoled he felt reprieved. He struck the main road and let the Janey horse have her head till he could no longer see the lights of the town behind him. The waxing half-moon was near its meridian and high over his shoulder and they rode through its ghostly light hard on the heels of their own shadow. He thought then to get off the main road and turned the mare into the high grass and brush and shortly came onto a weedy wagon trace that ran north and south and he rode south for another two hours before at last halting at a cottonwood copse cut through by a swift shallow creek. He loosened the cinch on the mare and let her blow and patted her and whispered to her what a good horse she was. He checked the wallets and found some bundled strips of jerked beef, a rolled clean shirt and a pair of socks, a box of matches, a sheathed Green River knife which he slipped into his boottop. He took the lariat off the saddle and put the horse on a long tether to a tree and let her drink. He got down on his belly on the bank and ducked his head in the chill water and gasped with pleasure. He pulled off his malodorous boots and soaked his feet a while and then put the boots back on. He made no fire and sat leaning against a tree and ate some of the jerky and drank from the whiskey bottle and listened hard but heard only the soft cropping of the mare and a solitary frog croaking in the creek. He'd never tasted better jerky and the whiskey warmed him wonderfully. He laid out his bed under the tree and slept with the pistol in hand. Sometime in the night he was startled awake by the mare's warm breath on his face and he stroked her muzzle and told her she had nothing to fret about.

In the morning light he saw that the pepperbox was a six-barreled .36 caliber Darling and the only uncharged barrel was the one Marcus Loom had fired as he'd fallen. He wanted to shoot the piece for the feel of it but without powder and shot for reloading he decided not to waste a round. He refilled the canteen at the creek and tightened the saddle on the mare and tied down the bedroll behind the cantle and then mounted and hupped the horse southward.

Near noon he came upon a small ranch where the foreman invited him to join him and the hands to dinner. He ate his fill of beefsteak and beans and offered to work the afternoon in exchange for the meal but the foreman wouldn't hear of it. He informed Edward that San Antonio de Bexar lay three days south on the Camino Real. The ride was a little longer, the foreman added, if a man preferred to follow the side trails. But he did not ask why Edward had been traveling off the main road nor did he even ask his name.

He rode the day without seeing another soul until the trees flamed in the evening sun and rang riotous with roosting birds and he spied a campfire in an oak grove just ahead. A chill wind rustled the trees. A pair of oxen grazed on a grassy rise and a covered wagon stood under a high wide oak. A woman worked at a smoking pot hung over the fire and a tall man in black came forward and raised a hand in greeting and Edward hallooed him. The man called out, "Come rest a spell, brother, and take some supper with us."

The man introduced himself as the Reverend Leonard Richardson, founder of the Church of the Blood of Jesus. He bade Edward to set by the fire and take a cup of tea while his wife finished preparing the supper. Edward loosened the cinch on the mare and dropped the reins and let her graze where she stood. The reverend poured tea from a kettle. The woman was thin and angular. Her back was to them as she ladled from the pot into three bowls.

"Smells mighty good," Edward said.

"Turtle stew," the reverend said. "She makes it real fine."

Now the woman turned with a bowl in each hand and in the dim light of the fire Edward thought that she was wearing a mask. But when she came closer to hand him a bowl he saw that she wore a sort of bridle fashioned of thin metal straps tight around her head and fitted with an iron bit that pulled hard into her mouth between her teeth and held the tongue fast. The corners of her mouth had blackened against the chafing bit. The whole thing was fastened with a small lock behind her neck. Her eyes were red and wet in the firelight. After serving them she sat apart and fed herself by spooning broth carefully into her mouth and then tipping her head far back to let it run down her throat in the manner of a drinking bird.

Edward turned to the preacher and saw the man smiling at him as he ate. "Never seen one a them before, eh?" the reverend said, nodding toward the woman. "Called a brank. Scold's bridle. Come by it a few months ago in Galveston. From a German fella who'd got it from his daddy back in the old country. Fella's wife had just recent died with the cholera and he was sworn not to marry again and so he didn't have need of it no more. Said it to be a right common means in the old days for punishin a scold. Course now"—he paused to give the woman a hard look—"it'll do just as well for ary woman don't know to keep a proper tongue in her head." He spooned up the last of his stew and whistled to attract the woman's attention and beckoned her. She set down her supper bowl and hastened to replenish his. As she handed the refilled bowl to the preacher she looked at Edward with her pained wet eyes and he gestured that he wanted nothing more and she went back to the other side of the fire and resumed her awkward feeding.

"They got the serpent's tongue, boy," Richardson said, nodding toward his wife. "I mean ever one of them. Had it since the Garden. 'The serpent beguiled me and I did eat.' That's was Eve's side of the matter. Tryin to pass the blame, sayin the devil made her to do it and she couldnt resist him noway. 'The serpent beguiled me and I did eat.' And what's the first thing she done after? Why, turned right around and beguiled old Adam into eatin of the forbidden fruit too.

"He aint nary fool, the Devil. He always known which is the weaker spirit and which the weaker flesh. Knowed the way to get at Adam was through the woman. Knowed he could seduce her and she'd do the deed for him and pull down Adam to perdition right along with her and that's exactly what she done. Eve is the bitch mother of all of man's misfortunes, and ever woman since is got the same treacherous bitch blood as her. She damned ever one a us to a life of toil and sweat and fruitless effort. Made us to do disloyal to the Lord and turned His loving face from us and they been doin evil with they tongue ever since. When they aint scoldin or complainin, they tellin lies or gossip or speakin some other kind of evil meanness." He paused to spit off to the side and glare at the woman who did not look their way.

"'All wickedness is but little to the wickedness of a woman,'" the preacher declaimed. "Ecclesiasticus, twenty-five, nineteen. Mark me, boy, if ye pay heed to the words of a woman ye be lettin the serpent's tongue lick in you ear. The Good Lord put His faith in us and we broke that faith because of a woman and we been breakin the faith with Him and with our brothermen ever since. Ours not to question His ways, but if He'd seen fit to put a brank on that bitch Eve just as quick as he was done shapin her from Old Adam's rib we'd all be the better for it, you mark me. We'd right now be sippin the milk of Paradise at Old Adam's elbow and laughin for no damn reason a-tall except we didn't have a worry in the damn world."

He accepted the reverend's invitation to bed down in his camp for the night and rolled himself in his blanket beside the fire to keep warm against the encroaching cold. The reverend climbed into the covered wagon to sleep but the woman stayed outside and settled herself on the other side of the fire. Edward watched her through the yellow cast of wavering flames for a time and then turned over to put his back to her.

But he could not sleep. He could not rid himself of the vision of the brank in her mouth, the red pain in her eyes. He told himself it was none of his concern, that for all he knew the woman had it coming. Maybe she'd deserved to have her tongue cut out and the preacher had shown mercy by putting the brank on her instead. But still he saw her red eyes and ruined mouth. And he remembered now the damned Dutchman who'd bloodied his own daughter's mouth and run him off at gunpoint.

After an hour he got up and put on his boots and rolled his blanket. He saw the woman watching him, her eyes shining in the ruby glow of the low fire. The mare whickered softly as he saddled her. The half-moon was high overhead and bright white through the trees rustling in the cold wind and swirling their shadows on the ground. When he was ready to ride he went to the woman and she sat up quickly with the blanket drawn close about her and her eyes on him were red and frightened. He drew his bootknife and whispered, "Ye aint got to wear that goddamned thing." But as he made to cut it free of her face she whimpered and tried to ward away his hand.

"What the devil, woman!" he hissed. "I aint gone hurt ye. I'm tryin to help ye, dammit."

The woman shook her head like a dog shaking off water and her refusal enraged him the more. "Ye stupid damn woman!" She tried to scrabble away from him but he grabbed her by the hair and held her fast as he deftly slipped the knife under one of the metal straps behind her head and twisted the blade to get the keen edge on the strap and as he did so the top edge of the knifeblade dug into her scalp. She began shrilling through her teeth and struggling to get free of him and Edward could feel that the bit was digging into her mouth even harder now and the knife could not sever the metal. He cursed and she screeched louder and suddenly the Reverend Richardson's voice came from the wagon: "What in thunder are you *doing* to her?"

"*Damn* you!" Edward shouted, and shoved away the woman as the reverend clambered down from the wagon with a long rifle in his hand.

He ran to the mare and swung himself to the saddle and dug his heels into her and she bolted for the road just as the rifle cracked and the ball hissed past his shoulder. He heard the woman wailing as though lamenting the newly dead.

He cursed himself as he rode under the white moon.

Fool! It's all you can do to look out for yourself in this world. Damn the fools around ye. They got to watch out for theirselfs.

Fool!

An hour later he came to a willow grove hard by a creek and there reined up and put down for the rest of the night without a fire. He dreamt again of a barren waste laid red as blood in the setting sun. And again saw Daddyjack, this time squatting before a shadowed figure, doing something to it, grunting with effort and muttering curses. And now Daddyjack stood and backed away from the other figure and turned and looked at Edward with his one becrazed eye. And now Edward saw that the other figure was his mother, sitting on the ground with her hands in her lap and a breast exposed and its nipple a hard twist of scarred flesh. She had a brank strapped around her head. The bit cut deep in her mouth and blood ran down her chin. She looked at Edward with eyes like burning oil and showed a horrible red smile through the brank. And her laughter rang like a madhouse bell.

He woke gasping and sopped with sweat in the cold night air.

7

The pinewoods fell behind and the sky widened and the country opened up and assumed a gentle roll. He rode through bunch grass and along bottoms lined with hardwoods, passed through pecan groves and stands of oak. In time he came upon the first rocky outcroppings and cedar brakes at the edge of the hill country and saw farther to the west a low line of whiterock palisades shaped like wide steps leading to the high plains. There appeared now among the hardwoods scatterings of mesquite and occasional clumps of prickly pear. The west wind carried the scent of cedar and the sunsets seemed a deeper and brighter red, as if painted in fresher blood. The clouds were quicker to shape themselves and to change direction, to dissolve to pale wisps. A hard hailstorm drove him to cover in an oak grove and frighted the Janey mare.

He arrived at Bexar on a February morning bright with sunlight. He rode up over a grassy rise and there the town was. A clangor of bells carried faintly on the cool air and among the mission steeples stood a church dome shaped like a vision from an Arabian tale. The whitewashed buildings shone in the sun. Cottonwoods lined the banks of the river winding through town, their leaves shimmering in each huff of breeze. He spied the flag of the United States waving gently in the wind and beside it the Lone Star banner of the state of Texas. He hupped the mare down the rise and onto a loose sand road and headed in.

Despite the Stars and Stripes the place seemed a foreign estate. The public squares clamored with Spanish and the music of hurdy-gurdy and guitarron and castanets. The people were dark and toothy and dressed in white cotton. The air piquant with cooking spices and the droppings of stock. Lavishly saddled stallions carried mustached horsemen glowering under sombreros of enormous brim, bedecked in black jackets and tight pants seamed with silver conchos, their spurs huge and spike-roweled. The wide main plaza was abustle with rattling wagons and clunking ox-carts and bunches of clattering longhorns being driven to the butcheries by vaqueros hardly more than children. Burros laden with all manner of commodities. Coaches packed with passengers and heaps of topside luggage. Mangy curs everywhere. Beggars blind or maimed. Strolling vendors with trays strapped round their necks. On the wide steps of a municipal building women in black rebozos sat on blankets arrayed with foodstuffs and confectioneries, religious gewgaws, medicinal compounds of sundry sorts. Scribes at their tables with inkpots and sandbowls penned letters of declaration in behalf of illiterate lovesick clients. Garrison soldiers lounged on benches and ogled the passing girls behind the dueñas' backs. Men of business came and went from the courthouse. The high walls round the plaza were topped with shards of colored glass.

He watered the mare at a plaza well and then walked the horse down a narrow sidestreet that took him past stalls and shops where harness-makers and tinkers and seamstresses and cobblers of boots worked busily at their trades. He came upon a small plaza clustered with cafes and cantinas. He hitched the mare and went into an eatery and had a platter of roast kid in a chile sauce so potent he was obliged to mop steadily at his nose and eyes with his napkin as he ate. He was exhaling chile fumes when he came out but still had some coins in his pocket and so went next door into a cantina for a drink.

The barroom was dim and cool and had a high beamed ceiling and a polished clay floor. The floor gleamed in the slant of light from the entranceway. A half-dozen men stood grouped at the far end of the bar, all of them intent on something on the counter. Most of them looked Mexican and the talk was fast loud Spanish. But two were Americans speaking pidgin Spanish and using broad sign language. Both looked but a few years older than Edward. Their clothes were filthy with grease and dried blood. They wore slouch hats and each carried a brace of caplocks on his belt and a bowie on his hip and a knife in each boot-top

Suddenly the talk subsided and the men drew closer about the bar and for a moment no one moved. Then abruptly one of the Mexicans jerked back from the bar and the other men shouted in chorus and some laughed and the man who'd flinched cursed loudly and spat on the floor. Now Edward saw that on the bartop was a large jar of clear glass containing a coiled rattlesnake.

A grinning Mexican in a rancher's coat and leg chaps collected money off the counter. He dropped the specie into his poke and bobbed the bag in his palm to test its heft and looked pleased with himself. He glanced about at the others and said, "Pues, quien mas?"

Edward bellied up to the bar and rapped hard on the counter to catch the Mexican barkeeper's attention over the loud talk and laughter. The man came over and said, "Que tomas?"

He shrugged and said, "I don't talk but American. Give me a drink. Whiskey."

"Wickskey," the barkeep said with a nod. He poured a drink and picked out a dime from the coins Edward laid on the counter. Edward tossed off the drink and blew out a breath and felt his eyes fill. The stuff was vile but its hot rush down his gullet and warm burst in his belly were pure pleasure. He pushed the other dime across the counter and the barkeep refilled his glass and then went back down the bar to rejoin the others.

The two Americans were conferring with each other and then one loudly said, "Goddamnit, I'm gonna try er again! I know I can beat er!" He was short and broad, cleanshaved and drunk.

The other American was bearded and his sparse mustache was gapped under his nose by a bare pink harelip. His speech was thick and gluey. "Shit, Easton, you done lost five dollars to the sumbitch already. You aint gone have penny one left you keep on with that snake."

The Easton one waved him off and turned to the rancher. He nodded at the jar and jabbed himself in the chest with his finger and said, "Yo. Me. Again." The rancher grinned and rubbed his thumb over the first two fingers of his hand. The Easton fellow dug out a silver dollar and slapped it on the bartop and the rancher put his own dollar on top of it. Now the other Mexicans began jabbering excitedly and placing their own bets.

The American set himself directly in front of the glass jar like a man readying to jump into icy water. He took several deep breaths as the others gathered close about on either side of him. Edward leaned over the bar for a better look. He saw that the jar lid had holes in it and the glass was too thick for the rattler to break. The snake was drawn up into a tight coil, its thin black tongue flickering, its tail tip up and chattering in a blur. Now the Easton one laced his fingers together and cracked his knuckles and then dried his palms on his thighs. "Que esperas, hombre?" the rancher said and gestured impatiently.

The American put a finger to the jar and the snake struck at it and he jerked his finger away. Everybody laughed and shouted and bets were paid off. The rancher gathered his winnings off the bar and added them to his poke.

"I done *tole* you!" the harelip said to the muttering Easton fellow. "Didn't I *tell* you?"

Edward tossed off the rest of his drink and picked up his half-dime and walked over to the group and said to the rancher, "*I* can keep my finger on that glass." He held up the silver half-dime.

The rancher looked at him and at the half-dime and then grinned at the others and said, "Mira este con su monedita. Que gran apuesta, eh?" and everyone laughed.

He felt a rush of anger and turned to the two Americans. "What's so damn funny?"

"They aint too awful impressed with the size a your bet," the Easton fellow said.

Edward glared around at them all and pulled out the pepperbox and laid it on the bar. "I'll bet that."

The rancher picked up the pistol and examined it. "Mira pues," he said, looking amused. "Y cuanto vale esta cosa tan buena pa nada?"

Edward looked at the Americans. "How much he got to put up against the pistol?" the harelip said.

"Hell, I don't care." He looked at the rancher and held up a finger. "A dollar."

"Un dollar," the rancher said. He set the pistol on the bar and laid a silver dollar beside it.

Nobody bet on Edward's success. He set himself before the jar. The rattler coiled up tight. He knew it was impossible for the snake to hit him through the glass, impossible, and he put his finger to the jar.

The rattler struck and he yanked his hand away before he knew he'd done it. The Mexicans roared with laughter. The rancher grinned and slipped the pepperbox into a side pocket of his coat.

He was furious at himself and called for another try and this time lost his saddle. Then tried again and lost his horse. The Mexicans were tearful with laughter. The rancher slid a half-dollar across to him and made a drinking gesture with his thumb and little finger jutting from his fist. He was a good winner who would not leave a man without drinking money.

Edward sat at a table against the wall and drank in sullen anger while the Easton fellow lost yet another dollar against the snake and then another pair of Mexicans came in and wanted to try their hand at the game too. The Americans brought their drinks over and sat with him. The harelip introduced himself as Dick Foote and said the other was Easton Burchard. He told Edward not to fault himself too hard about drawing his hand away. "Aint a man here been able to keep from pullin back when that snake hits," the harelip said. "Couldn't do it myself. Don't believe it can be done."

"Just like a Mexican to think up a game nobody can win at," Easton Burchard said.

Dick the harelip said they were from just north of the Red River and were headed for Corpus Christi to join the Texas volunteers. "They sayin we gonna go to war with Mexico for damn sure and General Taylor's gonna be needin ever man he can get. We heard tell they's a bunch a rangers waitin on the Nueces right now and we aim to join it, by God.

They sayin Old Rough and Ready be movin south real soon."

"I'm pretty damn rough and ready my ownself, by Jesus," Burchard said.

"They say Mexico's just fulla gold for the takin," the harelip said in his glutinous voice. "Say they's rich people's houses and churches just full of sacks of gold and gold crosses and drinkin cups and the like. Damn near everything you caint eat's made of gold down there. And like they say, to the victor go the spoils."

"Aint no question we got the spoils comin too," Burchard said, glowering drunkenly. "We aint near forgot what them beaneaters did but ten years ago right out there at the Alamo. Nor what they done in Goliad. Half-breed bastards. Me and Dick weren't but stripling boys back then and couldnt do nothin but cuss about it when we heard, but we sure's hell can do something about it now."

"We aint forgettin neither what they done to them Texian boys a coupla three years ago just the other side of the Río Grande there at Mier," Dick the harelip said. Edward had heard about that business. A filibustering bunch of Texians had been captured at Mier by the Mexicans and each of the 176 prisoners was made to draw a bean from a clay jar holding all white beans but for seventeen black ones. The men who drew the black beans were blindfolded and stood against a wall and shot dead.

"Only some Mexican son of a bitch would think up a thing like drawin for them black beans," Burchard said. He drained off his drink and fixed his angry stare on the Mexicans gathered about the rattlesnake on the bar. "Damn half-breeds act like they still in Mexico, like this aint been Texas for ten damn years. If they aint gonna learn to talk American and start actin American they best get they asses down to Mexico where they belong. Greaser bastards. All the time talkin Mexican and laughin and actin polite and showin they teeth and they just as soon cut you throat as shake you hand. Winnin all you damn money from you with a goddamn sidewinder in a jar."

"I caint hardly wait to get down there and start killin the sonofabitches and gettin me some of that gold," Dick the harelip said.

Easton Burchard suddenly thumped the table with his fist and his face brightened. "Shitfire, *I* know how to beat that game!"

"No, goddamnit, not again," the harelip said as Burchard stood up. "We aint got but a coupla dollars left, bud."

"It just come to me how to do it," Burchard said. "You watch."

He went up to the bar and conveyed to the rancher that he wanted another try. The rancher smiled and shrugged and made the money gesture with his fingers. Burchard put his dollar on the bar and the rancher covered it. The other Mexicans were grinning wide and nudging each other.

"I don't even want to see it," the harelip said and kept his back to the bar. The crowd at the counter blocked Edward's view but he did not leave his chair either.

Suddenly the talk fell off and he knew Easton Burchard was set and ready. Then there was a chorus of shouts and Burchard let a loud whoop and the bartender yelled something and then everybody at the bar was yelling at once.

"La apuesta no vale!" the rancher said angrily to Easton Burchard. He pointed at the bartender and said, "Este te vio con los ojos cerrados, cabrón!"

"Oh shit," Dick the harelip said, turning around in his chair to look upon the commotion.

The bartender was nodding and jabbering at all the others and gesturing at Easton Burchard. "No vale!" said another Mexican. "No vale!"

"No valley, my ass," Easton Burchard said. "I don't care the sonofabitch saw me close my eyes. Didn't nobody say it was a rule against it. Only thing matters is I kept my hand on the glass and that means I won and that's my two dollars there."

He reached for the money but the rancher shoved him back and Easton Burchard said "God damn you!" and pulled both caplocks from his belt and discharged one squarely into the rancher's chest.

The rancher fell back against the bar and his legs gave way and he grabbed wildly at the counter to try to keep his feet and his arm knocked the jar off the bartop. It crashed on the floor and the rattler lunged from the broken glass and struck one of the men just below the knee. The man shrieked and kicked wildly at the snake and fell hard as the others all yipped and jumped away from the sidewinding snake and a man fixed eyes of horror on it as it slithered past his boots and he fired at it and shot himself in the toes in the same instant that Easton Burchard shot a Mexican not two feet from him and the man's brains flew from his head in a crimson streak. Edward dove to the floor as the harelip fired from one knee and a Mexican clutched at his face with both hands and fell. Several guns blasted at once and Easton Burchard yelped and dropped down beside the rancher who was struggling to pull the pepperbox from his jacket pocket. Burchard elbowed him in the face and took the weapon from him as the harelip fired his second pistol and put a ball through a Mexican's neck and Burchard cried out again and cocked and fired the pepperbox twice in fast order and a Mexican crashed against a table and crumpled to the floor. The last of the Mexicans dashed out the back door and the shooting was done.

Not a man in the room was standing and the air was an acrid haze.

The harelip got up and went to Easton Burchard and helped him to his feet. There was a thick patch of blood on Burchard's left side just below his ribs and another high on his thigh. "God *damn* it," he said, "didn't *nobody* miss me?" He tested the leg and it bore his weight and he said he could get along all right.

There was a clamor of excited voices in the street. The rancher lay on his back with a leg folded awkwardly under him and both hands over his chest wound. His breath came fast and shallow and wet and he seemed agape with wonder at some profound and private revelation as his life drained onto the clay floor. The foot-shot Mexican sat up and shoved his discharged pistol from him and showed the harelip his empty hands. The snakebit man clutched his shin and stared at the Americans without expression. His pistol was still on his belt and the harelip went to him and stripped him of it. The barkeep rose from behind the counter and the harelip pointed a finger at him and the man dropped from sight again.

Casting glances at the front door as he worked, the harelip swiftly went through the fallen men's pokes and took their money and their discharged pistols and powder flasks and shot pouches. Easton Burchard set the pepperbox on the bartop and gingerly examined his wounds. Edward went over and picked up the pistol and checked the remaining three loads. Burchard looked at him without smiling and said, "You lookin to buy that rotary pistola of mine?"

"Quit joshin the boy, we got to git," the harelip said, stepping between them and hurriedly sticking two of the pistols into Burchard's belt and hanging the shot pouches around his neck. The voices outside were louder now, their timbre more urgent. "Take a look and see is there any laws out there," the harelip said to Edward.

He eased up to the edge of the door and peeked around the jamb into the bright sunlight and saw a crowd of people lined across the street and looking and pointing his way. He turned around and saw the harelip helping Easton Burchard out the back door.

Amid the carnage on the floor the rancher let a last rattling breath. Five men lay dead. He spied the two dollars still lying on the bar and he went over and put them in his pocket. The crouching bartender glanced up at him and quickly dropped his eyes back to the floor. His bootsoles sucked through blood as he crossed the room. He went out the back door into the alleyway. Some Mexican boys stood by and looked curious. There was no sign of the two Americans. He walked to the end of the alley and emerged in a small plaza where people were haggling with street vendors and shopkeepers, shouting and laughing happily, a trio of fiddlers playing beside a splashing fountain. He circled back around to the street fronting the cantina and saw a crowd of people at the door. Soldiers with bayoneted rifles and several men brandishing pistols were pushing through the babbling throng. He waited till they'd gone inside and then strolled toward the cantina and begged pardon as he made his way through to the Janey horse. He mounted up and reined the mare carefully out of the crowd and hupped her down the street and through the plaza and rode on out of Bexar.

8

He bore south on the Camino Real for a few miles before abandoning the main road and once again taking up the less-traveled trails. Though he had not joined in the fray at Bexar he thought one of the survived Mexicans might have cause to identify him as in league with Dick Foote and Easton Burchard.

As he pushed deeper into brush country the land paled and flattened and thickened with chaparral. Grass gave over to prickly pear and scrub brush and rampant mesquite of bony thorned branches and niggardly shade. The air went dry and dusty, the noon sun white as a soda wafer. Sundown skies proffered visions of biblical firestorms. The air of the evenings was hazed red. He rode without hurry or destination through this alien wildland. He shot jackrabbit and rattler to roast for his suppers, put down early camps and regarded the setting sun at leisure. He felt swallowed by the immensity of the night skies, the riot of glimmering starlight from origins beyond ken. Firetailed comets streaked from pole to pole, plunging to infinity in the bare instant beheld.

He came one sunny afternoon to a village fronting a river running low and lined with scrub brush and scrawny dwarf oak. The place looked to be inhabited wholly by Mexicans. Dogs ran out with teeth bared and napes raised or slank away craven with tucked tails, depending on their blood. He walked the mare down the dusty street to the river followed by a small troop of yammering boys. After watering the horse he reined around and went to a small café whose front door showed a rough charcoal drawing of a bowl and spoon and he dismounted and went inside and sat at a table. The old proprietor came out of the back room bearing a clay cup of cool water which he set before him as he said, "A sus ordenes, caballero." Edward gulped down the water which tasted slightly of mud. He made gestures of eating and the old man said, "Sí, señor, inmediatamente," and went through a door in the rear of the room and returned with another cup of water and a small plate of warm tortillas and a wooden spoon wrapped in a white cotton napkin. He next brought out a steaming bowl of some sort of meat in a dark chile sauce and a smaller bowl with beans.

The old man sat at another table and watched him eat. "El hambre es la mejor salsa, no es verdad?" he said with an avuncular smile. Edward ate and smiled back and said, "Whatever you sayin, mister, you probly right." When he had done with the meal he gave the homunculus a dollar and received in turn three two-bit silverpieces.

Outside he found a pair of boys patting the Janey mare and talking to her. They continued stroking the horse as they scrutinized Edward from tattered hat to disintegrating boots.

"I don't reckon she speaks Mexican," he said.

"Jes," the larger of the boys said. "She comprende what we talk her."

Edward smiled and stroked the mare's muzzle. "That a fact? Well, it could be she met her a Mex stallion in a corral somewheres. Tell me, what river's that?"

"Ribber? Is el Río Nueces."

"No lie, the damn Nueces?" He looked about at the sandy brushland stretching to the horizon in every direction. "They's supposed to be a army readyin on the Nueces. At Corpus Christi. Where's Corpus Christi at?"

"Corpos Chrissie?" the boy said. He looked all around as if he might descry where it lay, then looked back at Edward and shrugged.

"How bout the rangers? You know where they're at, the Texas Rangers?"

"Los rinches!" the smaller boy said, and made an obscene gesture with his little arm.

"Well hell," Edward said. He looked off across the river and recalled the harelip's claim about gold for the taking. He doubted it, but why not have a look anyhow? He could not raise a single objection. Seek and ye may or may not find, but don't seek and you're even less likely to find a damn thing. He pointed downcountry. "Mexico. How far?"

The boys exchanged puzzled looks. The larger one looked at Edward and shrugged and pointed to the ground at his feet and said, "Mexico."

Edward laughed. "That so? Well, I hear tell they's a bunch of rough old boys fixin to change that." He pointed south again. "What lies yonderway?"

The two boys peered toward the hazy horizon with great concentration. Then the larger boy looked at Edward and said, "Bandidos. Much bad mens."

"Hell, there's them all over. What else is there? What towns?"

"Town? Is Laredo."

"How far's that?"

The boy swept his arm to the south in a gesture of much distance.

"I'm obliged for the information." He took up the reins and stepped up into the saddle and raised his hand to the boys in farewell.

At the end of the street he paused before a store along the front wall of which were hung a few plucked chicken carcasses and dark strings of jerky. On small wooden stands just below them were arrayed packets of parched corn and small sacks of dry beans and ground maize, woolen blankets and colorful sarapes, a variety of earthenware and goathide canteens. He bought beans and jerky and a small copper pot with a green-crusted bottom and an extra canteen, which the store's dueña promptly charged a small boy with filling at the river. He offered payment of six bits silver and the woman snatched the coins from his hand as though he might yet change his mind. Thus provisioned he tipped his hat to the dueña and hupped the Janey mare to the shallows and made a splashing ford.

He encountered few wayfarers on these trails so far removed from the main road and those few he came upon were not inclined toward amenities and vanished into the chaparral immediately on catching sight of him. Their wariness put him in mind of a biblical line his mother had ofttimes read to them in Georgia: "The wicked flee where no man pursueth." If that was true, he now thought, then *she* was likely fleeing every minute of the day and night. He looked about at the surrounding barrenness and smiled grimly and tugged down his hat and thought: *Like some other damned people we could name.*

Another week farther south he came upon a dead horse beside the trail.

It was bloated hugely under the white sun and its mouth and eyesockets boiled with maggots. The foreleg break was evident and on closer look he saw where the animal had received a large-caliber coup de grâce directly behind an eye. The following day he hove over a low sand rise and saw a Mexican but thirty yards down the trail sitting under a mesquite on his horseless saddle with a rifle across his knees. The man stood and grinned widely and raised a hand in greeting. "Amigo! Que tal!"

All in the instant of the man's salutation Edward noted his good clothes and boots and saw the two white-gripped pistols on his hips and another holstered under his arm and he knew the Mexican was either a bandit or a lawman and in either case he wanted a horse and here was the Janey mare.

He reined the mare hard left and dug his heels into her flanks and put her toward a thicket of mesquite fifteen yards distant. The Mexican threw the rifle up to his shoulder and fired and Edward heard the bullet crackle through the thick tangle of brittle branches. He held hard to the pommel and hung low on the mare's left side, using her for a shield, hoping the Mexican would not shoot the horse rather than chance losing her. And then he was in the thicket and thorns were tearing at his clothes and he slid from the saddle and let the mare go on. He ducked low and ran through loose sand along a dense line of brush, doubling back parallel to the way he'd come. He found a break in the thicket and went through it and paused at the edge of a clearing to check his bearings and yes, there was the trail up ahead and there, just a few yards farther on, the man's saddle lying under the mesquite.

He heard the Mexican call cajolingly, "Yegua! Ven aquí, mi hijita. Aquí, yeguita, aquí."

The mare came trotting into the clearing with the reins dangling and here came the Mexican behind, walking up swiftly but trying not to spook the horse, talking soothingly, saying, "Ay, que preciosa yeguita. Sí, de veras, que hermosa yeguita." And then he had hold of the reins and the horse tried to pull away and the Mexican was having trouble holding to both the rifle and the mare and so let the rifle drop and grabbed the reins with both hands and jerked the mare's head down and slapped her on the muzzle. She tried to pull away but he caught her by the ear and twisted hard and she quit struggling.

Edward came out of the thicket moving low and fast with the pepper-box straight out in front of him. The Mexican heard his boots scuffing through the sand and held the reins with one hand as he turned and grabbed for a pistol on his hip. Edward fired as he came and missed with the first shot and then with the second and the Mexican raised a revolver and fired and the round ripped through Edward's shirt under his arm and Edward's next shot hit him in the stomach from a distance of five yards and the Mexican discharged a wild shot as he sat down hard and the mare broke away. Edward clubbed the man in the face with the heavy pepperbox barrels and felt bone crunch and the Mexican fell back. Edward threw himself on the man's gun hand and wrested the revolver from him and scrabbled backwards and cocked the piece. The Mexican started to sit up and Edward shot him in the chin and the man fell back writhing with his lower jaw destroyed and Edward cocked again and shot him in the red gape of his mouth and the Mexican's writhing ceased.

He remained sitting on the ground for a time and let his breath and heartbeat slowly ease. The tips of the Mexican's long mustaches quivered in a frail breeze. His upper jaw showed a neat curve of bright white teeth and his lower was a bloody ruin of broken bone and molars. His tongue hung lank and purple against his neck. Already the ants and flies were converging onto the feast of his face, attending to instinctual duty as old as the earth itself.

The pistol in his hand was a Texas Colt, a .36 caliber five-shooter. So too, he next discovered, was the longarm, which wasn't a rifle at all but a smoothbore .62 caliber ring lever shotgun. The other two handguns were .44 caplocks. The Mexican had no badge about him but among his possibles Edward found a poke containing more than forty dollars in gold and silver.

He chased down the mare and calmed her and led her back to where the dead man lay and hitched her to a shrub. Shortly thereafter he was wearing the bandit's trousers and snakeskin belt and his pistol holsters and his leather boots, which were newly made and fit him only a little big. The man's bloodsoaked shirt was useless. The hugely brimmed sombrero was an excellent shield against the sun but felt alien on his head and so Edward kept to his own tattered hat. He put the Mexican's saddle on the mare. It was finely crafted with a great round pommel and in the wallets behind the cantle he found pouches of .36 and .44 caliber balls and two full flasks of powder.

He was glad of the lack of a shovel so that he need not debate whether to bury the corpse. Already the buzzards were spiraling overhead.

9

On a chilly night of rising wind he came into Laredo, but six years removed from its tenure as capital of the erstwhile and tumultuous Republic
of the Río Grande. The half-moon was brightly silver and lit the street
white. Blown sand stung his eyes as the mare clopped through the streets
faced by mostly darkened windows at this late hour. A guitar strummed
in a side street. In the weak cast of light from a small balcony on which
sat a shawled young woman he saw the suitor standing below in the
shadow of his sombrero and heard the soft croon of his serenade. This
tableau of courtly love as alien to him as the language of the love song.

The street led him to a ferry landing from which could be seen a row
of brightly lighted cantinas on the other side of the running river. There
carried on the air the music of piano and barrel organ and guitar. He
walked the mare onto the ferry and the clomping of her hooves brought
forth the ferryman who said something in Spanish. Edward extracted a
half-dollar and the ferryman took it eagerly and set to the pulley rope.

When they bumped against the other bank Edward hupped the mare
off the deck and up to the nearest cantina in the row and there dismounted and hitched the horse and patted her and whispered in her ear
and then went inside. The room was well lighted and a half-dozen men
stood at the bar, a handful of others sat at the few tables. They gave him
cursory attention and then turned back to their drink and talk. In a far
corner sat a man picking a guitar. Edward ordered whiskey but the barman shook his head. He pointed at the drink of the man beside him and
the barman said, "Tequila," and poured a cup for him. Edward drank it
down, liked it, gestured for another.

As he sipped at the second cup of tequila he became aware of someone
standing very close behind him and turned to face a husky hatless Mexican with an abnormally large head and webs of spittle clinging to the
corners of his gaped and awkwardly set mouth. The idiot's black eyes
bulged upon him and looked to be full of mute shrieking. He put his face
forth to within inches of Edward's. His breath was rancid.

"Get away from me," Edward said, and put his back to him.

The idiot mouthed a sound between growl and groan and prodded
Edward in the back with his fingers. Edward whirled and slapped away
his hand. "I said get the hell away, you damn softbrain."

He was aware of the sudden cessation of music and talk. The idiot's
eyes were the wilder now and Edward could not bear the terrible silent

shrieking he saw therein. The fool put his hand out supplicatingly once again and Edward knocked it aside and said, "Go bother somebody else, goddamn you. I aint givin you a damn thing but my fist you don't leave off me." He made a quick scan of the bar and tables, saw hard looks fixed upon him, said, "Some one of you best get this fool away from me quick."

The idiot brayed and reached with both hands as if he would embrace him. Edward punched him in the mouth and felt like he'd struck a tree. The fool stepped back and blinked and ran his tongue over his bloody lips and reached for him again and Edward pulled the Colt and hit him on the head with it and the idiot reeled on wobbly legs and fell to his hands and knees and began wailing like a frightened child.

A pistol muzzle pressed against his temple and its holder said, "Si te mueves te mato, chingado." Cocked pistols pointed at him from all sides. He let the Colt dangle against his leg and a man on his right cautiously took it from him. Then a fist crunched into his ear and he fell against someone who struck him in the forehead with a pistol barrel and he would have fallen had not someone else grabbed him and held him. He was again punched in the face and then hard in the stomach. As he spewed he was let to fall to all fours in his own vomit. Then he was hauled back up to his feet and held from behind with an arm twisted up high against his back.

His head rang and his vision was askew and mucus ran thickly from his nose. He felt hands disarming him. Now his sight cleared and he saw a man with a tarnished badge pinned to his coat standing before him. A pair of men were helping the idiot out the front door. Edward's ear felt the size of a potato, his cheekbone throbbed, blood ran into one eye. He tried to pull free and the man holding him from behind twisted his arm up higher and pain shot through his shoulder and someone began punching him in the ribs and belly. The man with the badge spoke sharply and the punching stopped.

The badged man scowled and said something to Edward in Spanish and then gave an order and Edward was conveyed out of the cantina and into the street and he saw that the Janey horse was gone. They took him up the street and around to the rear of what looked like a municipal building of some sort and up to a low whitewashed structure of stone fronted by a heavy wooden door and showing in the moonlight two small windows covered with iron bars. The guard at the door rattled a set of keys on the ring at his waist and worked one into the doorlock and pulled the door open just wide enough for them to shove Edward through. He sprawled face-first onto a stone floor thinly layered with straw and the door closed behind him.

The room was dark but for the glimmering of a few scattered candle stubs. The stench of the place seemed to rise off the straw in his face. He heard low voices all about. He pushed up on his elbows and made out the forms of men sitting against the walls, others lying about the floor. Now the smell was worse yet and he spied a slop bucket but a few feet from him. He crawled away from it and sat up.

And there in the sputtering light of a candle stub, sitting with his back against the wall, was the large blackbearded man who had robbed him at the Sabine ferry.

The blackbeard was watching him and grinning whitely in the dim light. "How do, friend" he said.

Edward jumped up and rushed at him and tried to kick him. But the blackbeard deftly dodged and rolled to his feet and absorbed the most of Edward's flurry of punches on his forearms as the other inmates scrabbled clear of them. The big man grabbed him and flung him against the wall and Edward bounced off and fell to his knees and the blackbeard yanked him to his feet and caught him up in a bear hug and squeezed until Edward could not draw breath. His vision flared redly and then came a dizzy swoon and then blackness.

When next he opened his eyes he was sitting propped against the wall and the blackbeard was squatting before him. Edward tried to lunge at him but the giant simply jabbed his forehead with the heel of a hand and knocked him back again. "Boy, you have got grit, damn if ye don't," he said. "But if ye don't quit trying my patience I'll truly put an end to this foolishness."

"You robbed me my whole damn outfit," Edward managed to say. His breath still came hard and his lips were bloated from the punch he'd taken in the cantina. He tried to spit off to the side and got most of the bloody gob on his sleeve.

"That I did," the blackbeard said. "But I didn't kill you, did I? I don't begrudge ye a try at me for robbing you, but now you have had your try and it fell shy and that it is all the attack I will tolerate from ye. Come at me again and I'll kill you graveyard dead."

Edward considered going at the man again but could not muster the fire for it. Every muscle and bone pulsed with pain.

"You stole my horse and sold her, damn ye. I had to thump a fella to get her back."

"Well hell yes I sold her. I needed the money. It's the usual reason for robbing somebody, don't ye know." He spat to the side and suddenly grinned. "The fella ye thumped, I hope he was a gambler with long mustaches."

"That be him."

"Good. I didn't much care for that sonofabitch. I'm real glad to know you got you horse back from him."

Edward adjusted his position against the wall and grimaced. "I believe you done bust my spine."

"Hell boy, if it was bust you wouldn't be able to move the least bit. You're just sore some."

A prisoner passing by stepped on Edward's outstretched leg and Edward kicked at him and cursed and the blackbeard snarled, "Cuidado, bruto! Ya te lo dije!" The man slank into the shadows.

"Where's my guns and knives at?" Edward said "My blankets? My goddamn slicker?"

"Done sold the guns. It aint much left of your possibles but for the blanket and slicker. They with my outfit over in the livery. But it's the alcalde's livery so we aint either one like to see our goods again."

"What's the alcalde?"

"The mayor, ye might say. The fella with the badge arrested ye. Set hisself up his own town this side of the river and calls it Laredo too. Some calls it West Laredo, some say New Laredo, take you pick. It's the same shithole whatever you call it."

"That son of a bitch." Edward told him of his trouble in the cantina.

The blackbeard said Edward wasn't the first to get locked up for abusing the idiot. "The softbrain is nephew to the alcalde's wife. What with all the sonofabitches in this town ready to kiss the alcalde's ass it's a damn wonder they didn't kill you like they have some others who provoked the fool."

"How come you to be in here?" Edward asked.

The blackbeard said he had been on his way to meet up with some partners in Monclova, Mexico, about 125 miles or so west by south from Laredo. He'd taken leave of the company in San Antonio and gone up to Arkansas to settle a matter involving his sister, who he said was the only living kin he had. He knew his partners would be taking their ease in Monclova as soon as they took care of some business they'd contracted to do in Coahuila state. He'd stopped in the south Laredo for a drink and a poke and a night's sleep in a bed, but the whore proved such a sullen bitch he'd refused to pay her and threw her out of the room. Next morning when he went to the livery he found the alcalde waiting for him and backed up by a dozen fellows with rifles. He was arrested for robbing the whore and clapped in the cárcel. That had been a month ago. He'd since found out that every whore in town had to give the alcalde half of her take and the alcalde had not appreciated being deprived of a dollar by some passing Yankee.

"How about a trial? Don't we get a trial?"

The blackbeard laughed. "You get you a trial when the alcalde gets around to taking you over to the courtroom where his brother's the judge. Damn greaser will fine you all you got, including your horse and outfit, and sentence you to six months at whatever labor the alcalde wants you for. You'll do it in leg irons and under watch of some hardcase guards. I aint had nary trial yet."

"Well damn," Edward said. "Looks like I'm here for a while."

"Could be ye are." The blackbeard said. Then he grinned "Or could be you got youself thowed in here at just the right time."

"What you mean?"

"Well now, just last week a bunch of us was took out in leg chains to dig graves for a family of a half-dozen who burned up when their house caught fire. Well now, as we was shuffling back from the graveyard with our shovels on our shoulders who do I see standing in the door of a cantina and grinning at me over his mug of beer but Charlie Geech. He's with the company I was headed to meet with in Monclova. He didn't say nor do a thing but give me a wink. I don't know what he was doing here but unless he's quit the company the rest of them's bound to be close by. I stopped to look at him and maybe say something but a guard come up behind me and poked me with his rifle and said I wouldnt be seeing the inside of no cantina for a good while and just keep moving, so I did. I looked back a minute later but old Geech was gone. I reckon they'll be here to see about me soon enough."

"You reckon? You must got some damn good friends."

"Look here boy, you ever done manhuntin? Bandits and Indians and the like?"

"I never."

"Well don't tell nobody you never. You strike me as you could learn the trade quick enough and this be ye chance. I figure the captain'll take you on when I tell him the kind a sand ye got."

"What captain?"

"Compny captain. Name's Hobbes."

"You think this captain's gonna get you out of here, no lie?"

The blackbeard laughed. "I know it for a fact he will. Take you out too if your ready to ride with us. The captain don't never leave a man of his company in a bad way if he knows about it. It's the only thing I can say about the man for sure."

"Well, it's the best thing about him I heard you say and I hope you be right about it."

Two days later as dawnlight was beginning to gray the jail windows they heard an outbreak of shooting and the rumble of horse hooves. Heard yeehawing and curses and screams. A minute later the lock rattled in the door and it swung open wide and admitted a rush of gray light and the door guard came running in with his hands to his throat trying vainly to stanch the pouring blood and he staggered and fell. And even as his life bled away into the filthy straw some of the inmates ran up and began kicking him. Others rushed toward the door but stopped short and moved aside as a man strode in with a revolver in one hand and in the other a bowie slicked with blood. Of unimposing height and build he yet moved with the mien of one who commanded whatever ground he stood upon. Black hair hung from his flatbrimmed black hat to just above the buckskin on his shoulders, his mustaches to his chin. His eyes looked cut from obsidian. He paused inside the doors and never glanced at the throatcut man. The shooting outside continued, the outcries and howls.

"Bill Jaggers!" the man called.

"You found him, cap'n!" the blackbeard replied. He started for the door with a wide grin and looked at Edward over his shoulder and said, "Let's go, boy!"

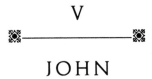

V

JOHN

1

On a warm forenoon of pale and cloudless sky they arrived at the Río Grande, known to the Mexicans as the Río Bravo del Norte. Taylor's scouts had reported that the town of Matamoros, positioned on the south bank of the river and about twenty-five miles inland from its mouth at the Gulf of Mexico, was fortified by a small Mexican garrison. The river along that stretch was a hundred yards wide and the Mexicans had confiscated every boat to be found and taken them all to their side and posted sentinels for miles along the riverbank east and west of town.

After sending a detachment to secure Point Isabel on the Gulf as the landing point for his seaborne supplies, Taylor chose to give the Mexicans a show of confidence. He marched his troops upstream along the north bank and hove into view of Matamoros with regimental bands blaring

173

and colors popping in the breeze. He halted the troops in a wide clearing and rode with his staff officers to the crest of a bluff affording an excellent view of the river in both directions and of Matamoros across the way. The river was the color of buckskin and its banks were lined with cattails except along the Matamoros riverfront and its opposite shore where the ferry had operated before the Mexicans dismantled it on learning of Taylor's approach. There were hardwood stands upriver and down along both banks and cotton fields shone in the distance on the Mexican side.

A crowd of townspeople had assembled on the Matamoros bank to gape at the Americans. In the midst of them was a troop of lancers sitting their handsome mounts and resplendent in green tunics with crimson sashes and tall black shakos with horsehair plumes. Alongside them an army band played rousing patriotic tunes hard and loud in competition with the strains of the Yankee musicians. Commanding the lancers was a major who now stood in the stirrups and brandished his saber at the invaders and addressed them loudly and at length in eloquent Spanish which Taylor's interpreter translated as a directive to the Yankees to go home or die.

As soon as the major had done with his address, the crowd started in with cursing and shaking their fists and the boys among them threw stones which all fell short in the water. The Americans in the ranks swore back at the Mexicans in explicitly profane terms. The cacophony of martial music and bilingual damnations shook the skies while Taylor conferred with his advisors about defensive positions.

John and Riley had by now been relieved of their gags but they had fourteen days more to carry ball and chain. When Master Sergeant Kaufmann went striding past them Riley called out, "Say now, sergeant, what if that fancy Mex cavalry comes charging across the river, eh? How are me and Johnny here to fight if we're chained down by these damn cannonballs?" Kaufmann gave him the barest glance and went on without a word. Riley looked at John and said, "I have prayed to the good Lord to let me have but five minutes alone with that son of a bitch, just five minutes to set things right with him and I can die a happy man."

"You best pray I dont beat you to him," John said.

The Mexican major now barked orders to his troop and the lancers reined their horses around and the unit trotted off in smart formation down the dusty street and back toward the garrison. The band marched along after, still playing as it went, its volume falling fainter as it moved away from the river. A moment later the only Mexicans still in evidence on the other shore were the sentinels and a few lingering civilians.

2

While diplomatic efforts to avoid war continued between Washington and Mexico City, Taylor was under orders to stay in place and take no hostile action except in response to Mexican attack. Rumors were rife, the most common of them that the Mexicans across the river were waiting only for the arrival of several more regiments before making their charge. Against that possibility Taylor ordered work to begin immediately on an earthen defensework to be called Fort Texas. It was positioned on the bluff and had would have five sides. Its outer walls would be nine feet high and fifteen feet thick. Toward its construction each regiment provided daily labor in the form of rotating fatigue details, and as compensation each man on the detail received a gill of whiskey at the end of the day's work. Required to work with the construction crews every day but denied the whiskey allowance were all men under punishment, including John Little and Jack Riley, who had to labor with ball and chain. They fetched and carried materials and tools, mixed buckets of mud mortar, applied pick and shovel, and all the while cursed the army that treated them less like soldiers than as beasts of burden.

Lucas Malone volunteered for the labor detail at every opportunity and so on most days found himself working in proximity to John and Riley. John introduced Lucas and Handsome Jack to each other one sultry afternoon when they were all shoveling construction debris into wheelbarrows along the fort's south wall. Thunderheads were rising like bloodstained purple towers over the Gulf and the sun gleamed off the whitewashed houses of Matamoros. Riley asked what part of Ireland his family was from. Lucas said County Galway and Riley grinned widely. "But that's me *birthplace*, man! Some Malones lived a few miles north of us. Could they have been kin?" Lucas said they might have been but he couldn't be sure. They'd had lots of Malone kin in the old country but his granddaddy had fled the sod after killing a man in a donnybrook. He'd kept on running after reaching New York and didn't' stop until he made Tennessee.

Riley asked Lucas why he volunteered for the labor gang. "Bad enough to have to do this as punishment," he said.

"Because I'd anytime ruther work like a man," said Lucas, "than march around on a drill field playin at being a soldier. March and drill, drill and march. That's all we do in this fuckin army camp."

"Dont be calling it an army camp," Riley said. "It's a bloody prison is what it is."

Remembering the penal camp in Louisiana, John thought Handsome Jack was wrong about that. "Hell Jack, it's only another seven days with these ornaments on our legs," he said.

"Only seven days left *this* time," Riley said. "Then comes the *next* time, and maybe we'll wear them sixty days, or ninety. Maybe next time it'll be the fucking yoke for a month or so. Maybe it'll be the bloody lash. These bastards can do any damn . . . *hello*, what's this?"

Their comrades were flocking to the riverside in high commotion, hollering and cheering and waving their hats. A dozen young women, all of them with long black hair and red laughing mouths, had come to the riverbank and there disrobed completely and entered the river to their brown thighs and now were busily soaping themselves and each other and blowing kisses the while to the cheering Americans across the way. Behind them a squad of Mexican soldiers stood at the water's edge with their rifles unslung and held the girls' clothes and pointed across to the Americans and laughed and said things to the women and quickly backstepped grinning when the girls splashed water at them. Some of the Americans removed their boots and walked partway into the river and called for the women to come over to their side. The women laughed and splashed water in their direction and jumped up and down so that their dark-nippled breasts jounced the more. They soaped each other's gleaming buttocks and threw their heads back and rounded their mouths in mock orgasmic delight as they worked a thick soapy lather into the hairy patches between their legs. The Americans were howling like penned dogs.

"Sweet Jesus," Riley said with a grin, "I been struck mad by the bleeding sun, I have."

Lucas laughed at the happy vision of all that lovely female nakedness in the bright sunlight. He clapped John on the shoulder and pointed to one girl after another. "Look there at *her*, Johnny—right over *there!* Oh, and *that* one, over there, with the bush like a beaver hat. You *see* her? God *damn!*"

Now officers had arrived on the scene with sabers in hand and were shoving their way to the forefront of the crowd of soldiers. The girls were beckoning to the Americans and cupping their pretty breasts to them and calling endearments to them in Spanish. And now some of the Americans had waded out to the river's depths and begun swimming for the other side and the officers ran into the water to their knees and commanded them to turn back immediately. Some of them did but several swam on and midway across the river one of them began to thrash wildly and quite abruptly sank from sight and his body would be found the next day caught against the bank on a tree root at a point more than twenty miles downstream near the mouth of the river.

Three made it across to the shallows opposite and one of them might yet have drowned even then except several off the girls came out and helped him to his feet. The other two Yankees were also helped to wade out onto the bank in their dripping pants. They all three looked back at their cheering comrades and waved and hugged naked girls to them and patted the girls' haunches and buttocks and squeezed their breasts. The girls playfully slapped away their hands and now hurried back into their clothes as the Americans kept at kissing and fondling them the while. The Mexican soldiers laughed and shook the Americans' hands and patted their backs in the manner of old friends. Again dressed in their loose cotton skirts and lowcut sleeveless blouses the girls put their arms around the necks of the American soldiers and the Americans stroked their hips and all of them walked away laughing together down the street and around a corner and out of sight.

A half-dozen officers now stood in the shallows on this side of the river with pistols in hand and commanded the men away from the bank and back to their units. The soldiers were still dazed and breathless from the spectacle of the Mexican girls and were slow to comply, but they did as they were ordered.

All evening the talk around the campfires was of the wonderful exhibition the girls had put on and of the grand time the three who swam across must be having. Bets were about whether they would return return, the odds favoring that they would, because the penalty for desertion was far more severe than for simply being absent without leave to have a good time with a girl.

They were struck that night by a violent storm that jarred them awake in fearful certainty that the camp was under artillery attack, so explosive were the thunderclaps. Lightning lit the night with a ghostly incandescence. The wind shook the trees and tore at the tents and carried some away. The river rushed and swelled and overran its banks. It ripped through the brush and made a mire of the lower reaches of the American camp. The storm raged through the night and finally broke just before dawn. The water receded swiftly and the sun rose red as blood over a landscape sodden and fetid with mud and littered with tents and roof straw and river reeds, with uprooted shrubs and drowned dogs and half-plucked chickens caught on driftwood at the river's edge.

That afternoon one of the three who'd crossed the river to be with the girls came back, rowed across by a pair of Mexican soldiers with a white flag attached to the muzzle of a rifle. They let him out of the boat in the shallows and quickly rowed back to their own side.

The soldier, Thomson by name, was brighteyed with excitement and told the men who gathered round him on the bank—John and Lucas and Handsome Jack among that avid audience—what a wonderful and generous people the Mexicans were, how religious, how beautiful and affectionate the women, how delicious the food and delightful the music. Thomson said the other two were not coming back. The only reason he himself had returned was that he did not want to break his mother's heart.

Now a guard detail showed up and the lieutenant in charge placed him under arrest and they took him away. None of them ever saw him again.

The next morning another seven soldiers swam the river, and then five more the day after that. Taylor increased the number of guards along the bank and gave specific orders that nobody was to go in the water except to bathe and then no deeper than his knees. The next day fourteen men swam across. Taylor posted a new directive: Any man seen swimming toward the other side would be warned to turn back and if he did not he would be shot. When one of Taylor's staff officers pointed out that desertion in peacetime was not a capital offense, Taylor responded gruffly: "Disobeying my orders can damn sure be."

The following day four men pretending to bathe in the shallows suddenly began swimming hard for the other shore and ignored the American guards' calls to turn about. In full view of the camp and the Mexicans watching from the other bank the guards opened fire and two of the swimmers spasmed and flailed and bright red billows spread around them in the brown water and they sank from sight. The other two made it across and were hastily hustled away by the Mexican guards.

3

A week after the exhibition at the river, the sergeant of the guard led John and Riley to the smitty's tent next to the main corral where each was relieved of his ball and chain. As they came out of the tent Riley clicked his heels and John laughed.

That evening dozens of copies of a Mexican handbill were somehow smuggled past the sentries and were soon circulating throughout the camp. They bore the signature of Pedro Ampudia, commanding general of the Mexican Army of the North:.

> *Know ye: that the government of the United States is committing repeated acts of barbarous aggression against the magnanimous Mexican Nation; that the government which exists under "the flag of the stars" is unworthy of the designation of Christian. Recollect now you men born in Great Britain; that the American government looks with coldness upon the powerful flag of St. George, and is provoking to a rupture the warlike people to whom it belongs; President Polk boldly manifests a desire to take possession of Oregon, as he has already done to Texas. Now, then, come with all confidence to the Mexican ranks, and I guarantee to you, upon my honor, good treatment, and that all your expenses shall be defrayed until your arrival in the beautiful capital of Mexico. These words of friendship and honor I offer in Christian brotherhood not only to the good men of Great Britain, but, as well, to all men of Catholic brotherhood presently enslaved in the army of the United States, whatever your nativity, and urge you all to separate yourselves from the Yankees.*

"What you make of it, John?" Lucas asked, reading the broadside over one of Riley's shoulders while John read it over the other.

"The man wants the Brits to quit this army and join his," John said.

"I know *that*," Lucas said. "Do ye reckon he means Americans too?"

"It dont say he'd turn a Yankee down," Riley said. "He's awful shy, though, aint he, about saying just how much he'll pay a man to go over?" They all three looked at one another but none said anymore about it.

All over the camp soldiers were ridiculing the handbill, pretending to wipe themselves with it and putting matches to it and pointing at each other and calling, "Catlick slave! Catlick slave!" But some among the Irish were not laughing, nor some of the Germans. They looked at each other and glanced repeatedly across the river. And each look they gave to the other side was longer than the one before.

That night John dreamt he was running hard through a wide marsh and every time he looked back he saw Daddyjack coming behind him at a walk, following a tracking hound on a leash and steadily gaining ground on John. And then it was no longer a hound on the end of the leash but Maggie, fully naked and moving on all fours as smoothly as a hunting dog, her face close to the ground and hard on his scent, leading Daddyjack on a zigzag course but always toward John, always closing the distance though John was running hard and gasping and felt his heart would burst in his chest. Daddyjack was closing the distance and now yelled, "Blood always finds blood! Always!" And now Maggie was upright and laughing, her pretty breasts jiggling as she trotted ahead of Daddyjack on the leash. . . .

And then he was awake, sitting up and gasping and pouring sweat, and Lucas Malone and Jack Riley were sitting up too and staring at him in the moonlit tent and he guessed he must have cried out. But neither said anything to him. After a moment he lay back down and heard them sigh hard and resettle themselves too. And each man of them lay awake late into the night with the rough company of his own thoughts.

4

One afternoon Colonel Truman Cross, the army's popular quartermaster, went out riding in the chaparral and did not return. There had been reports of Mexican guerrilla bands prowling on the north side of the river and now rumors flew through the camp that they had killed Cross. Some in the local populace told the American authorities that most of these guerrilla troops, whom they called rancheros, were nothing more than savage bandits who had for years terrorized the borderland, gangs of robbers, killers, renegades, rustlers and scalphunters. The two most notorious ranchero bands were led by Ramón Falcón and the infamous Antonio Canales, once president of the short-lived and violent República del Río Grande. Both men were long-time and bitterly despised enemies of Texans. They had been young officers under Santa Ana at the Alamo and had both been at Mier. Each with his own band had raided Texas throughout its ten years as a republic. The locals warned Taylor that in addition to robbing and killing Mexicans as they always had, the rancheros would now also plunder U. S. supply trains and freely murder Americans in the name of defending the fatherland. Testifying to this view of the rancheros as bloody marauders unworthy of military respect were the Texas rangers now serving with Taylor. Under command of Colonel Samuel Walker they were the first volunteers Old Zack had accepted into his army, and they had countless tales to tell of ranchero barbarities. Those familiar with the Lone Star way of warfare knew that many such tales could be told about the Texans as well. Indeed, Taylor had accepted the Texas volunteers in the belief that the best way to fight a band of savages was with his own band of savages. Still, some who heard the Texans' stories did not believe the larger portion of them. They attributed the rangers' gruesome narrative excesses to their well-known hatred of all things Mexican.

And then the ten-man patrol that had been sent out in search of Colonel Cross came back on five foundered beasts and none of their own good horses. Came back two men per horse and every manjack of them naked and tied belly-down over the animal. Two of the corpses were altogether headless and the rest dripping blood and gore from their scalped crowns and the raw wounds between their legs wherefrom the genitals had been severed. Some bore the detached privates in their mouths and some lacked hands and some had been docked of their ears or noses and some were eyeless. Many of the young Americans who looked upon them had never seen such things before except perhaps in nightmares or in imaginings roused by the vile tales of drunken old Indianfighters. And no man among them did now disbelieve the Texans' stories of ranchero cruelty.

Shortly afterward the body of Colonel Cross was found in the chaparral and it too had been mutilated.

The Yankees seethed with yearning for revenge.

5

The first handbill urging Americans to desert was soon followed by others, each more detailed and explicit in its arguments and inducements than the one before. The fliers pointed out that, unlike the U. S., Mexico was a devoutly Catholic country where slavery was outlawed. They asked why Yankee Catholics or any men who truly believed in liberty and justice for all should make war against one another. They argued that the Irish, especially, had stronger bonds with Mexicans in their common re-

ligious faith than they did with American Protestant soldiers. They
pledged that any Yankee who chose to fight in defense of Mexico and
the Holy Mother Church would be well rewarded for his honorable action. They promised an enlistment bonus to every American who joined
the Mexican side. They promised that every man would be given a rank
commensurate with his training and experience but in no case would he
hold a rank lower than that which he had in the American army and in
all cases he would be better paid. And they promised land. Every man
who came over to the Mexican side would receive a minimum of 200
square acres of arable land with at least another 100 acres added for every
year of service.

On a clear evening shortly after the most recent bunch of these leaflets
had as mysteriously as always found its way across the river and into the
Yankee camp, the three friends sat on the bluff and looked across at the
brightly lighted town where a fiesta was taking place. Taylor had now
posted sentries every few yards along the bank as much to keep his own
soldiers from absconding to the other side as to defend against infiltrators.
The guards were under order to shoot any man who set foot in the water.

The sounds of music and laughter carried to them from the fiesta. The
aromas of spicy Mexican foods mingled with the ripe smells of the surrounding countryside. Fireflies flared greenly yellow on the soft night air.

Lucas Malone was scooping handfuls of dirt and sifting it through his
fingers. His gaze was vague and far away.

"I was talking to this Mexie fellow today over by the corral who everybody thinks is a muleskinner but he's not," Riley said, speaking barely
above a whisper and looking off across the river. "He's from the other
side, dont you know. Name's Mauricio. He speaks good English and he's
been talking to lots of the fellas, he has. Other harps mostly, but to the
Germans too. Says there's forty or more of us already over there."

John looked at him but said nothing. Lucas looked at the dirt slipping
through his fingers.

"He says I'd be made an officer," Riley said, still not looking at them.
"Says Ampudia will know me for the soldier I am."

No one spoke. Then Riley said: "How else are you ever to get that
piece of land ye claim to want so dearly?"

Lucas looked at him sharply.

"I dont believe they can lose the war," Riley said in a whisper.
"There's too many of them. Hell, the country itself will beat this army.
Have you seen the maps? It's all mountains from one end to the other."

He turned to them now. "It's not everybody gets a chance for the thing he most wants. It's the chance for me to be the soldier I am, to have the rank I deserve. You, Lucas Malone, I know what ye want. This is your chance too, it is. And you, Johnny, what is it ye be wanting above all else? Is it your own plot of ground, like Lucas here? I've seen the look in your eye when he talks of it, but I've never heard ye say."

John looked from one to the other. What he wanted was unsayable. No way is there for a man to explain what he cannot put in words to himself, what he knows only in the pulsing of his blood. How might he tell that he wanted an end to the dreams of Daddyjack and Maggie? An end to waking in the night with his heart wild in his throat, choking on his own fear, feeling hunted by some dire nemesis drawing closer with every bloody sundown?

"Without a place to call his own," he said, "a man aint but a feather in the wind, now aint he?"

6

He favored waiting another few days until the moon waned out of sight— or at least until a cloudy night gave them better cover—but Riley and Lucas were set on crossing that very night. And so shortly after midnight they slipped out of the tent and worked their stealthy way through the cottonwood shadows upriver for a quarter-mile and then scanned the near bank from cover of the trees. They spotted a lone sentry singing softly to himself and strolling in the pale light of the cresent moon blazing brightly in a starry sky. No other guard close by. John attracted his attention by lightly rustling the brush and the guard warily approached with his longarm ready at the hip. As the sentry passed him by him Riley stepped out from behind a tree and drove the heel of his riflebutt into the back of his head with a wet crunch. He and Lucas then quickly stripped him of his rifle and pouch and the few dollars he had in his pocket and then joined John in the riverbrush. John asked if the sentry was killed and Riley whispered that he was not but he might have a bit of trouble walking a straight line ever again.

They stripped naked and bundled their clothes tightly and tied the bundles to their rifle barrels. They eased down the bank which was steeper here than it was down by the town and pushed through reeds that cut them like little razors and slipped into the moonlit water. The river tasted of mud and rot. They held their rifles and bundles above their heads and swam one-handed but the river was running faster and deeper than they had thought and they found themselves being carried swiftly downstream.

"Christ," Lucas gasp[ed as he pulled for the other bank, "we'll be in front of the camp in hardly a damn minute."

But they were all three strong swimmers and made an angled headway across the river. They were within twenty feet of the opposite bank when a voice cried, "*You there!* There in the water! Turn back *now* or we'll shoot!"

They stroked with furious desperation now, John in the lead as they reached the cattails and a rifle flashed and cracked on the far bank and the ball smacked the water a foot to his right. He wished the moon would die and go dark. His feet now touched a bottom of soft mud and his breath came hard as he grabbed at the cattails to pull himself to the sloping bank. He felt the reeds cutting his hands but did not feel pain. He flung his rifle and bundle up on the high ground as more rifleshots sounded and a ball buzzed past his ear and smacked the mudbank. He heard Lucas Malone grunt and curse softly behind him and he turned and looked but Lucas was not there. But here came Riley drifting fast alongside and John caught hold of the rifle barrel Handsome Jack extended to him and pulled him into the reeds. Riley slung his sopping things up on the bank and scrambled past him up through the cattails and crawled away into the dark.

As he followed Riley up the bank a half-dozen rifles discharged almost simultaneously and he felt a sharp blow to his lower leg and then a burning and he cursed and squirmed his way up through the reeds. He tumbled up on the bank and pushed his rifle and clothes ahead of him as he crawled into the brush and more shots sounded and rounds hissed through the scrub

He lay low in the thick scrub brush and looked to his left and saw the pale naked form of Lucas Malone crawling awkwardly into the darkness of a willow stand.

The shots were hitting scattered now and John knew the sentries had lost sight of them. The shooting continued for another minute before it finally ceased. He stayed put in case the shooters were simply waiting for him to give some sign of his position. His lower leg was throbbing and he felt of his shin and sucked a hissing breath when his fingers found the wound. He did not move from his hiding place for some time and then a passing cloud momentarily dimmed the moon and he crawled out of the brush and across an open stretch of ground and into the trees. And there found Riley dressed and waiting for him. Riley helped him to his feet and John quickly put on his muddy clothes. When he pulled on his left boot a white flare of pain behind his eyes made him momentarily dizzy. As they moved downstream through the shadows he felt the inside of his boot slickening with blood.

They came upon Lucas Malone sitting with his back against a tree. He'd been shot in the side and was bleeding freely but he could stand and walk. He'd lost his rifle and clothes and was naked in the world. John and Riley gave him their shirts and Lucas wore one in the regular manner and the other tied round his waist in the form of a skirt. "You fuckers laugh," he hissed, "I'll put my fist in your goddamn teeth." Riley and John grinned at him and Lucas Malone cursed them softly for sons of bitches.

They made their way through the trees and inland from the river and shortly came upon a sandy trace and followed it through the blue cast of the moonlight to the edge of town. John's boot was now heavy with blood.

A pair of sentries stepped out of the shadows with rifles pointed from the hip and challenged, "Quien vive?"

"Friends," Riley said. "Amigos."

And now an officer and two more soldiers and a man in civilian clothes came rushing from down the street and Riley again called out, "Amigos, we're amigos."

The Mexican in civilian dress said, "Está bien, Nacho. Son irlandeses." He pointed at Riley. "Yo conozco este grandote."

"Mauricio!" Riley said. "I didn't' bloody recognize ye."

Mauricio laughed and he and Riley hugged and patted each other in a rough abrazo.

The officer put up his pistol and grinned at them and said, "Bienvenidos, amigos. You are welcome."

7

The officer was Lieutenant Saturnino O'Leary by name, who took great delight in their faces when he told it to them. His father was an Irishman who'd come to Mexico by way of the United States some twenty-five years before and traveled all around the country before settling in Durango and marrying a Mexican woman of good breeding. Saturnino had grown up fluent in the tongues of both parents.

He had John and Lucas assisted into a muledrawn ammunition cart and then escorted them all to the main garrison on the other side of town. On the way to the main post they passed many smaller encampments and it was obvious that the Mexican ranks had been greatly reinforced since the American arrival on the north bank. With these troops had come hundreds of camp followers—wives and sweethearts, chiefly, but a goodly number of whores, as well—and their fires and makeshift settlements were everywhere. Riley and the lieutenant walked together and conversed in low voices but with much gesticulation. At the main garrison they went off while John and Lucas were helped into a large lamplit infirmary tent where they were received by several Mexican nurses. The women giggled and rolled their eyes at each other on seeing Lucas Malone's manner of dress. They laughed too at the men's acute embarrassment at being stripped of their wet clothes. The Americans were examined by a Mexican surgeon named Dr. Alonzo who spoke no English but was assisted by a muscular young man named Arturo who possessed a passable pidgin. One end of the tent served as Dr. Alonzo's work area and included a brazier full of live coals in which were propped a number of iron pokers. The rest of the spacious tent held some three dozen cots, only a half-dozen of which were currently filled, one by a man who looked to be dead.

The doctor treated Lucas first, permitting him several large swallows from a bottle of tequila to gird himself. Lucas pronounced it damn fine stuff. He was made to lie back and Arturo gave him a folded piece of leather to bite on and pressed down hard on his upper arms to hold him in place while the doctor probed the wound for the rifleball. A nurse held a lamp close by and moths fluttered and bumped against its sooty fire-bright glass and some flew too near the top of the lamp glass and fell withering upon Lucas and the doctor flicked them away as he worked. Lucas bared his teeth and cursed through the leather and the muscles stood in his neck like cords. Then Alonzo had the ball and held it up in the forceps for all to see before dropping it with a clank in a tin bowl. He now went to the brazier and withdrew a poker whose tip glowed orange and he told Lucas to bite hard once again. The muscles swelled along Arturo's arms as he once more pinned Lucas to the table. Lucas roared through his teeth as the iron sizzled into the wound and then it was over and the sweet waxy smell of seared flesh hung in the tent.

As he was being bandaged Lucas asked in a thick voice if he might have another drop of that fine Mexican spirit. Dr. Alonzo proffered the bottle and let him drink deeply that he might sleep soundly. Lucas was singing "Molly Malone" as a pair of soldiers carried him to a cot where a plump Mexican nurse covered him with a blanket and dried the pain-sweat off his face with a wet cloth and cooed to him as he drifted to sleep.

John's wound took longer to treat for the fact of the lead ball having glanced the shinbone and burst into fragments. The doctor pronounced that the bone was not fractured, though it was well bruised, and he was an hour picking pieces of lead from the torn flesh. He stared at John's fresh facial scar and pursed his lips but made no remark on it. As Alonzo tended to him John finished the tequila. Now Arturo held his leg fast as Dr. Alonzo pressed a glowing poker into the wound and again the tent filled with the smell of burning flesh and John shrilled into the leather he bit upon. And in that moment he remembered vividly a time somewhere in Alabama when he had cauterized his brother's shoulder with a redhot ramrod.

He let the leather fall from his mouth and gasped, "Edward."

"Qué?" the doctor asked. He looked at his assistant. "Qué dijo?"

"Egg word?" Arturo shrugged. "Quién sabe?"

8

They were confined to the infirmary tent for the next two weeks with little knowledge of what was happening in the world except what they could gather from reports delivered by Arturo in his malformed English. He told them that Riley had come by to see how they were just hours after the doctor had tended to them, but they'd both been sleeping and Alonzo would not have them wakened. In the days since, Riley had since been busy training with the garrison artillery batteries. Arturo referred to him as "teniente Riley." They found out too that General Ampudia had been replaced by General Mariano Arista who had recently arrived with additional troops and sent General Torrejón and his cavalry across the river at a point upstream where they'd fought and defeated a detachment of American dragoons. "Arista es el mejor general, the best most general," Arturo said fervently. A few days after Torrejón's victory a band of rancheros had ambushed a troop of Texas Rangers and killed ten of them. "Rinches chingados! Los rancheros they kill good the focking rinches, they kill them focking good!"

After their first few days in the hospital Alonzo permitted Lucas to get out of bed and walk around in the tent, but it was more than a week before he let John start getting about on a crutch. One day Arturo excitedly reported that Taylor had struck his tents and gone to Point Isabel on the Gulf with all his men and wagons save one regiment left behind to defend Fort Texas. The Americans were in bad need of supplies and Taylor knew it would take most of his force to protect the loaded wagons on the way back from the port. Now General Arista had taken the larger portion of his troops and headed downstream of Matamoros where he would cross the river in hopes of trapping Taylor between Fort Texas and Point Isabel.

"Arista he is kill Taylor," Arturo said gleefully.

Several mornings later they were wakened by the blasting of artillery fire. Though war had not been declared by either side, the Mexicans were bombarding Fort Texas. Except for the curfew cannon back in New Orleans these were the first artillery pieces John had heard in his life and his heart jumped at every thunderous discharge. He grabbed up his crutch and joined Lucas Malone at the tent's entrance flap where a guard was posted to ensure they kept to the hospital as Alonzo had ordered. The camp was in high excitement and hazy with gunsmoke. They saw a battery set up some forty yards away and spotted Handsome Jack Riley directing the gunners as a Mexican officer looked on.

"Whoooeee!" Lucas hooted. "Jack's got them boys shootin that gun like it's a goddamn revolver, they shootin so fast. I hope to hell Kaufmann's still over there and one of them rounds hits him square in the ass! Blast them, Jack! Blast that fucken Kaufmann to hell and gone!"

The bombardment went on until sundown. The last round lofted across the river was followed by a great cheering from the Mexican troops and their raucous threats to the Yankees on the other bank of more to come.

Shortly after dark that evening Jack Riley came to see them. He wore a Mexican artilleryman's uniform with its collar insignia depicting an exploding bomb and was grinning whitely through his powder-sooted face. He sat at the foot of John's bed and heaved a tired sigh and rubbed his face hard. Then cursed them both for lazy bastards and asked when they'd be ready to fight with the San Patricios.

"San Patricios?" John said. "What's that?"

"The Company of Saint Patrick," Riley said. "I formed her meself.

Taylor's had a lot more deserters than he's let on, you see. I found the Matamoros cantinas full of them. Plenty of them said they'd be willing to join the Mexies in exchange for some land of their own, dont ye know—and on condition that they can serve in the same outfit. So I had me an idea and soon enough found meself explaining it to General Arista face to face. And, lads, he liked the notion and gave it his blessing, he did! It's a company of soldiers all from the other side, almost all Micks, most of them run off from Taylor but a few come down here on their own. Some born in the States but most from the olde sod, by Jesus. We got some German in the bunch, naturally—there's not an army in the world dont have its Germans, now is there?" John had never seen Hand-some Jack so excited. "There's a few bloody Englishmen with us, and some Scots, and a fella from Canada, dont you know. But like I say, it's mostly harps like us. Forty-two in the outfit already and I expect we'll get plenty more as the lads get their fill of being nothing to the Yanks but Irish dogs to kick and decide no more, by Jesus, no more!

"Now the San Patricios aint official yet, you understand, but we soon enough will be. Arista told me so. A matter of paperwork is all. Mean-while we're the San Patricios just the bloody same. We wear the Mexie artillery uniform but we'll have our own banner, we will. Know what the Mexies are calling us? Colorados. The Reds. Because there's so many redhead Irish in the bunch. Aint it a hoot?"

He paused and looked at them narrowly. "I aint heard neither you fellers say what ye think of me insignia here." He touched the officer's brass pinned to his collar above the artillery insignia.

"What's it mean, Jack?" John asked with a wink at Lucas Malone.

"It means you'll damned well have to salute me is what it means," Riley said with a huge smile. "It's *Lieutenant* Riley to both you now, and a lieutenant always rates a salute from mere sergeants." He beamed at them.

John and Lucas exchanged looks.

"That's right, lads, I said sergeants," Riley said. "The CO's a Mexie, of course, but he's a good fella and a damn fine soldier and he's let me pick me own non-coms. Now I'm needing you boys at the ready, so ye'll have to quit your malingering, the both of ye. Doc Alonzo says he'll turn you loose tomorrow. He says ye'll be needing a cane still, Johnny, but me and Captain Moreno—he's the CO—we reckon it's better to have ye gimping about and learning how to shoot the big guns than leave you to laying on your lazy arse in here any longer."

He stood up and grinned from one to the other of them. "You've been too polite to ask, so I'll tell you: your pay will sixteen dollars a month, and dont that beat to hell the seven dollars ye were getting as buck privates for old Taylor? And that aint all. Ye'll be getting title to four hundred acres of land, each of ye. That's right, lads, I said four hundred. Pray the war lasts a year and ye'll get another 200 acres besides. This is it, buckos, the chance to fight for something worth fighting for—your own selves, your own land. Ye'll be men of property, ye will, when all the shooting's done."

He withdrew a pair of forms from his tunic pocket and spread them on the bed next to John. "All you got to do is just sign these."

John picked one up and saw that it was in Spanish.

"Arturo," Riley called, "bring the doc's pen and ink there on the table." The orderly retrieved the implements and Riley dipped the pen and handed it to John.

John hesitated. He looked up from the form and held Jack Riley's gaze. Handsome Jack's smile tightened. His blue eyes were hard and bright. "It's yay or nay, Johnny boy," he said softly. "A simple yay or nay."

John flattened the form on the bed and signed it and handed back the pen. Riley dipped it again and passed it to Lucas Malone and Lucas signed too.

Riley blotted the signatures with his sleeve and folded the papers into his pocket. He grinned at them and took a flask from his tunic and uncorked it and raised it in a toast. "To them of us who know the true brotherhood." He drank and passed the flask to Lucas Malone who turned it up and then passed it to John who raised it to each of the others in turn and drank.

Riley tucked the flask away and said, "See you at reveille, lads—I mean . . . *sergeants.*"

He was to the tent door when Lucas called out, "Say now . . . *lieutenant.* I got a question. What if we hadn't signed on?" Malone was smiling but his look was intent. "What would've become of us, do ye think?"

Riley looked at them both and grinned. "Why, what else, man? Ye would have stood against a wall in the morning and got shot for spies." He went out laughing.

9

They got the brunt of their artillery training during the daily bombardment of Fort Texas. They learned how to move an artillery piece from one position to another, how to unlimber the gun and charge it and set its elevation, how to swab out the piece with a sponge rod and how to cool the barrel with water every so often during firings. John was impressed by Handsome Jack's smooth proficiency with the big guns. Riley took them to the barricade overlooking the river and gave them a brass telescope and schooled them in the arts of the forward observer. The fort was holding well under the steady barrage and Lucas Malone said, "Christ, we really built that thing, didn't' we?"

Several times a day the crews broke off the shelling to take a rest or eat a meal. During these respites the fort's acting commander, Major Jacob Brown, would take a turn along the fort's front walls to inspect for damage. During a break on a windy afternoon when they sat at the emplacements eating a lunch of tacos and beans and watching Brown make his inspection, Riley suddenly said, "The cheek of the son of a bitch."

He set down his plate and ordered a pair of gun crews to charge two of the pieces with high explosive shell. The Mexican artillery was still using chiefly solid shot ammunition and Riley was daily petitioning Captain Moreno for explosive shell, arguing that their artillery would be no match for the Yankee guns without it. Moreno agreed but his requisitions to the high command in Mexico City were routinely denied without explanation or simply ignored. What little high explosive ammunition they had was precious but at the moment Riley didn't' care. He was set on killing Brown and shell was the sure way to do it. He positioned himself at one of the guns and posted a skilled gunner named Octavo at the other. He determined the elevation of the guns by eye and called it out to Octavo. As Brown strolled slowly before the wall and made his careful scrutiny Riley aimed his gun at a point directly behind him and had the Mexican gunner aim about fifteen yards ahead of the Yankee. Now he and the Mexican each lighted a cigar and puffed vigorously and then blew the ash off the tips and then held them down close to the touchhole. The soldados made bets and jokes and looked on intently. When Brown arrived at the spot Riley judged to be midway between the two target points he said, "Ya!" and he and Octavo touched the cigar tips to the vents and the guns boomed almost simultaneously.

Brown whirled at the sound of the guns and started to run back the way he had come and it was as though a deer in full stride had been led perfectly by the hunter's gunsights: He took perhaps three strides before the Mexican's shell exploded well behind him at the same instant that Riley's round landed at his feet and the blast threw him high and twirling in the air like a doll coming apart at its seams and flinging blood and losing limbs in every direction and he fell back to the earth in pieces.

The Mexican troops and the San Patricios cheered lustily as the smoky dust cleared from across the river and the figures of other Americans warily emerged from the fort to gather Brown's scattered remains. And now a large solitary figure came stalking forth to the very edge of the river and stood there brandishing a bowie knife and hollering imprecations only faintly heard at the Mexican emplacement yet clear enough to be understood as directed at Jack Riley and John Little. It was the Great Western cursing them for traitorous murdering bastards and vowing to shoot them dead and shed them of their manly parts besides. As she carried on in this way, Riley called John forward and gestured for a rifleman to give him his weapon and said, "Give her a recognition, Johnny, with that hawkeye of yours." John assumed a prone position and braced the rifle on a large rock before him and ripped up a few weed strands and tossed them in the air to gauge the wind. He adjusted his sights for Tennessee windage and Kentucky elevation and took a deep breath and released half of it and aimed carefully and squeezed the trigger. The Borginnis woman's high-crowned hat jumped off her head and described an upriver arc in the breeze and bounded along the riverbank and a dog ran it down and caught it and shook it from side to side like a hare.

Riley whooped. "That'll give her something to think about besides cutting off our peckers, by Jesus! Nice shooting, Johnny!"

The Great Western put her hand to her bare head and turned to see the dog worrying her hat some yards upstream. She looked back across the river and even at this distance they could see her white grin. She cupped her hands round her mouth and bellowed, "*I* won't' miss *you* . . . you *bastards*!"

A few days later Taylor would issue a general order renaming the place Fort Brown. But for months after, the Mexican Army of the North would be talking of the round the Irishman Riley put in the Yankee officer's pocket on the Rio Bravo.

10

They'd been shelling the fort for a week when late one morning they heard the thumping of distant artillery and spied dust on the horizon to the north and knew the two armies had engaged. They judged the fight to be about ten miles removed and centered near the Palo Alto pond. By late afternoon there was thick white smoke on the sky which they would come to learn was from grassfires ignited by burning powder wads of American artillery. Mexican wounded would burn to death as the fires spread through the chaparral. Riley cursed Arista's stupidity in having taken only round shot for his guns. "The Yanks are using explosive shell and he's shooting at them with iron balls. Jesus! Why not throw stones at them for all the good of round shot?" Captain Moreno took him aside and suggested he keep such insubordinate opinions to himself. Yet they soon enough heard of how the Yankees laughed at the solid shot and made a game of sidestepping it as it rolled past and was chased after by the dogs.

The battlesounds ceased at sunset but the grassfires continued to burn and the northern sky flickered redly through the night. Speculation was rampant in the garrison and wholly uninformed. The fighting resumed at dawn the next day at but half the distance, the crackling of small arms now audible between bursts of artillery. "Moreno believes they be round-abouts a dry riverbed called Resaca de la Palma," Riley told John and Lucas. "Says the chaparral's thick as Moses' beard out there."

Dust and smoke rose densely from that direction. And now they heard other sounds mingled with the booming of the field guns and the crack and pop of rifles. Heard the shrill of horses, heard war cries and screams of fury and fear and agony. And now they spied a scattering of lancers riding pell-mell for the river and every man of them clearly desperate for greater speed as they lashed at their mounts and dug rowels into the animals' bloody flanks and the lathered horses came hard with their eyes white with terror. Behind them came more riders and behind the horsemen came the greater mass of the broken and terrified Mexican infantry running headlong, some with their rifles still in hand, many devoid of all weapons, running as if from the devil himself. Never had John seen fear on such scale as this nor heard such collective wail of despair. The Mexicans ran wildeyed into the river and some spilled headlong in the shallows and were trampled by those behind and in some places men drowned in less than a foot of water. They splashed frantically for the south bank and some floundered and sank from sight in mid-river and none alongside or behind these drowning comrades thought to save them, caught up in their own frenzy to escape the Yankee demons on their heels. And those demons now hove into sight and came shrieking with bloodlust and ready bayonets and they skewered every fallen Mexican they came upon.

Thus did Arista's troops come back from their first full engagement with the Americans. Moreno and Riley had already resumed shelling the fort to hold at bay the troops within and keep them from joining in the slaughter.

John had cast aside his cane and was working with one of Riley's gun crews. And even as they fired round after round on Fort Texas across the way they caught each other's eyes, he and Riley and Lucas Malone, and all three knew the war had truly begun and the dice of their future days were tossed and tumbling.

Over the next nights Matamoros lay awake amid the moans of the dead and dying, the howls of encroaching wolves. The heat of day hummed with hordes of fat green flies. The walls of Fort Texas and the Matamoros rooftops were crowded with buzzards looking like solemn red-cowled priests attending a mass funeral.

Burial parties on both sides of the river worked round the clock to put the dead in the ground. But the going was slow and at night the lobos could be heard snapping and growling and tearing at the corpses.

Reporters traveling with Taylor's army claimed the wolves preferred to feed on American dead rather than on the degenerate enspiced flesh of the Mexicans.

Four days later the United States declared war on Mexico.

11

Arista's battered Army of the North abandoned Matamoros and all the sick and wounded and took with them a thousand camp followers and trudged southwest for nearly two hundred punishing miles to the town of Linares. The trek was through treeless brushcountry under a broiling sun that at last gave way to blessed rain which quickly became a two-day downpour that turned the countryside to mud. Wagons mired and animals bogged. They ran out of rations and slaughtered and ate pack animals and discarded the equipment they had borne.

At Linares they rested and regrouped and awaited further orders from Mexico City. They passed the rest of spring and the first half of summer in training and regaining strength. During this time yet more American deserters found their way to them and signed enlistment contracts and were placed with the new company of foreigners calling themselves the San Patricios but known to the Mexicans by several different names including "los colorados" and "los voluntarios irlandeses." When they were not training they were at local fiestas or the cockfights or the rodeos or in the cantinas, drinking and dicing and singing along with the guitar players. They larked with the girls in the bagnios. It was a mindless time of the sort familiar to all soldiers who have ever waited for the call to battle. But every now and then a look passed between the three friends, a look bespeaking a sad foreknowledge understood to them all though none could have explained it if he'd wanted to, which none of them did.

John now discovered that tequila in sufficient quantity did much to keep his dreams at bay. He learned how much and how fast to drink of an evening so that he could get back to camp under his own power and yet sleep dreamless as a stone. The hangovers were small price to pay for sleep undisturbed by visions of his past, but the nightly fights were another matter. He was now easily provoked and had again taken to carrying a knife in his boot. He cut out a local citizen's eye in an alley scrape, and in another tavern brawl cut two Mexican comrades so severely it was thought they would die, though neither did. The civilian was a known thief and despoiler of young girls and so nobody made a case for him, but in the latter incidents the army charged John with criminal assault.

At the trial Lieutenant John Riley argued on John's behalf before General Arista and his judicial staff, citing Sergeant Little as a valuable member of the San Patricio Battalion, a man who had risked his life crossing the Río Bravo to come fight for Mexico, and one who had simply been defending himself in the saloon fight in question. General Arista himself had presided over the court. He looked intently at John Little and remarked that he was most grateful to him for his allegiance to Mexico but hoped he would find no future cause to defend himself so well against anyone but the Yankee invaders. And then dismissed the charges.

Arista had greater problems than John Little. In July he was court-martialed for his blundering leadership at Matamoros and dismissed from the army. Again appointed commander of the Army of the North was

Pedro Ampudia, he who once cut off a rival general's head and fried it in oil the better to preserve it for display over the main gate of his hacienda.

Rumors were rife too that Antonio Lopez de Santa Ana would soon be back from exile in Cuba to take over the presidency as well as the army.

12

In midsummer the Mexican army moved to Monterrey, the capital of Nuevo León, a venerable old city on the north bank of the Río Santa Catarina. The city was encircled by jagged gothic-spired ranges awesome to the San Patricios, few of whom had seen mountains other than the Appalachians, tame inclines by comparison. They enjoyed the city's splendor and amenities for a few short weeks before word came in September of Taylor's advancing force. The Patricios were posted with the big guns in the Citadel, an impregnable fortress the Mexicans called the Bishop's Palace and which the Americans would come to name the Black Fort. Hundreds of residents fled the city in advance of Taylor's coming, taking with them all they could load on their animals and carry in their arms. Others remained and formed citizens' brigades and put up barricades in the streets. A party of Roman Catholic bishops performed a series of benediction rites on the front steps of the main cathedral.

On a gray Friday afternoon, the eighteenth of September, Taylor appeared at the edge of a woods on the outskirts of town in the company of a dozen officers. The San Patricios knew him even at the distance, knew his white horse and the attitude of its rider. At a wall of the Citadel Riley said he believed he could win the war right now. He adjusted the elevation of his gun and touched off the piece. The solid-shot cannonball keened through the air and struck not ten yards in front of Old Zack and bounced and cleared his head by less than three feet. Had Taylor been standing in the stirrups the ball would have taken off his head. Had the round been explosive it would have reduced the man to stewmeat. It was altogether a spectacular shot and the Mexicans cheered it wildly and pounded Riley on the back.

But Taylor wasn't standing in the stirrups and the round was not explosive and at the ball's passing he turned in the saddle to watch it bound into a pecan grove with a pack of camp dogs in yammering pursuit of it.

He leaned and spat and reined his horse about and said to his wide-eyed staff, "I expect you fellers'd feel more comfortable if we took ourselves back a bit, say to that fine little spring we saw the other side a them pecan trees?" And so they did.

All through the night Mexican bugles played the "Deguello," a chilling tune signifying no quarter, the piece inherited from the Spanish who first heard it as an ancient Moorish chant calling for the cutting of every last enemy throat.

And in the morning the battle began.

The fighting raged three days and nights. The U.S. artillery was of meager effect against the Bishop's Palace and the Mexican round shot was good for little save laughter in the American ranks. The early fighting was between cavalries, and then the infantries clashed at the town perimeters, and then the fighting was house-to-house in the streets. A thick haze of gunsmoke rose over the town. The bayonet ruled. Blood ran in the cobblestones, streamed from the rooftop gutters, spattered the white-washed walls. Came a thunderstorm and then another as the fighting raged on. The surrounding countryside went to mud. Rainwater ran pink in the streets. The carnage showed stark under shivering blue lightning. The San Patricios fired and fired their cannons into the Yankees until all shot was spent and then took up their muskets.. Curses carried in English and in Spanish. Men shrieked in terror and murderous intent, screamed for help, cried for God's mercy, begged for their mother's tender hand. Women joined the barricade defenses and proved fierce soldaderas. John saw one cleave a Yankee head with a two-hand swipe of her machete a moment before she was skewered by bayonets and blood gouted from her mouth and she cursed her killers and died. The Americans brought cannister to bear on the barricades and fired point-blank as with Brobding-nagian shotguns and Mexican defenders flew back with faces gone, limbs severed, viscera looping through the air, blood spraying and mixing with the falling rain. The air stank of gore and shit. The monstrous elephant was amok.

Three days of slaughter exhausted both sides. An armistice was struck and the shooting stopped. The dead lay everywhere. Mounds of mutilated men and women. A vast fly-swarmed bloating of horses and mules. Carrion birds blacked the sky. The howls and harries of wolves drove gravedigging parties to distraction. The stench of the dead was a continuing assault.

A joint commission of American and Mexican officers agreed to the surrender of Monterrey on the condition that the Mexican army be permitted to retire from the city with its weapons. The evacuation took three days. The Mexicans marched away with drums beating and banners waving high. The Yankees ranks muttered and watched them pass by and some recognized the deserters among them and let out cries of execration. Riley especially was the object of their curses and maledict warnings. He spat and stared straight ahead but Lucas Malone grinned at the Yankees' raging faces and recognized Master Sergeant Kaufmann among them and gestured obscenely at him and at them all. A platoon of Irishmen who'd kept the faith and hated the deserters for having blacked the reputations of all sons of Eire started for him but were driven back by their mounted officers. "We'll have at them in good time, boys," John heard a Yank officer say. "You'll see. They can only run so far and then we'll have them, by God."

13

They retreated two hundred fifty miles south to the silvermine city of San Luis Potosí, more than a mile high in the mountains, and there regrouped yet once again. Santa Ana had returned from Cuba as expected and was hailed by his countrymen as the Deliverer. He took charge of the army and reformed it as the Liberating Army of the North. He granted permission for the San Patricios to fly their own flag and Riley engaged the nuns of the local convent to fashion a banner of his design. Green silk it was, showing on one side a shamrock and a harp bordered by the Mexican coat of arms and its motto, "Libertad por la Republica Mexicana," and underneath the harp the motto, "Erin go Bragh." On the other side of the banner was a painting of Saint. Patrick with a key in his left hand and in his right a staff pinioning a serpent, and under the painting was the name "San Patricio." The men of the company cheered lustily at its first unfurling. John was surprised to feel himself stirred by this emblem of men like himself, by this bright green flag of the rootless and the damned.

They trained and readied and recruited for the next four months and in that time another fifty Americans deserted Taylor and made their way to San Luis to join the Saint Patricks. Riley was all business in the training of them. The loss at Monterrey had shaken his certainty that Mexico would win the war against the Americans—or gringos, as the Mexicans had taken to calling the invaders, deriving the name from "Green Grow the Rushes," a song the Yankees were often heard to sing. Handsome Jack tried not to show it but John and Lucas could see that his confidence in Mexican army leadership had shrunk considerably since Monterrey.

But if Riley's faith in their leaders was waning, his fidelity to the Saint Patricks grew ever greater—and he would abide no failure of the faith in his comrades. In November two men of the company deserted. They were captured a week later in civilian clothes as they tried to make their way to Tampico to get a ship out of the country. They were brought back to San Luis Potosí in manacles and put on trial for desertion. The adjudicating officers were a regimental infantry colonel named Gomez, Captain Moreno and Lieutenant Riley. All three voted for conviction. Colonel Gomez was against the death penalty but was overruled by Moreno and Riley. Riley requested and was granted command of the firing squad. He ordered all Saint Patricks to attend the executions.

"No one knows the seriousness of desertion better than those who have themselves deserted," he told the assembled company. "A man may have good cause to desert once, aye, but he who deserts twice proves himself a faithless vagabond deserving of no man's brotherhood. So it is with these two. At least from us they receive a bullet, but never forget that should you be taken by the enemy what *you'll* get is a noose."

The condemned were stood each in his turn before a side wall of the central plaza cathedral and permitted to say a few last words before being blindfolded. The first said he wanted someone to tell his mother he loved her. The second said he hoped the whole damned world went to heaven so he wouldn't have to see any of it again in hell. They were shot by a six-man San Patricio firing squad selected by lots and including Lucas Malone. That evening when they were drunk in the Oso Rojo, Lucas told John, "Damnedest thing. For minute there I thought I was takin aim at meself. Saw meself standin there blindfolded. Damnedest thing . . ."

John said nothing, though in truth the executions had made him wonder how much real difference there was between them and the army they'd deserted. And Riley's argument that desertion was permissible the first time but never thereafter struck him as self-serving horseshit. Every desertion was damnable or no desertion was. But he was an officer now, Handsome Jack, and John wondered if perhaps officers had more in common with other officers—officers of *any* army—than they did with the men in the ranks.

14

Came Christmas Eve, and while Jack Riley was at midnight mass and Lucas Malone with a Mexican girl he'd recently taken up with, John got into a fight with two men at the Oso Rojo. He gave one a kick to the balls that lifted him a foot off the floor before he fell in a vomiting heap, then broke the other's arm in shedding him of his knife and flung him from the cantina into the street. Not two minutes later this man returned with a pepperbox pistol in his good hand and shot John twice in the back as he stood at the bar. John slumped against the counter and turned around and the man now shot him once in the chest and then the pistol misfired on the next two tries and the assailant turned and ran away. John slipped to the floor and fell over on the hardpacked clay and felt the life running out of him. He heard Daddyjack's loud laughter and thought also he heard Maggie weeping. He lay with his cheek against the cold clay and felt eyes looking down upon him and he thought, *So this is how I'm done with.*

He was not however done with, though the doctors could not extract one of the pistolballs and so left it in him and it was two weeks before they were willing to say he might not die of his wounds. He was still very weak near the end of January when Santa Ana and the army departed north for another fight with the gringos. On the night before they left, Riley and Lucas paid him a visit in the hospital. Handsome Jack pressed a medallion of the Holy Mother into his palm. Lucas Malone said he would bring him Kaufmann's ears. After they left, John gave the medallion to one of the nurses.

He was up and walking in two weeks and another week after that was deemed well enough to serve as a wagon guard on an ammunition train to Querétaro a hundred miles south. But he was in truth still very weak and on arrival in Querétaro was taken with bone-wracking fever and a fierce case of bloody diarrhea. He was laid in the garrison hospital tent already crowded with men suffering from sickness of every sort. Day and night the dead were carried out and placed in the deadcart to be trundled to the graveyard and new patients were brought in to replace them.

The nurses were dedicated girls and women who brought in food and carted out slop jars, tried to feed those who could eat without throwing up, did their best to comfort the dying. He was for a time delirious more often than not but was sometimes aware of his hand being held. In his delirium he sometimes saw Maggie at his bedside dressed in black and weeping and sometimes he saw her naked and asking if he wanted to do it, saying that she would do whatever he wanted because he was her brother and she loved him and had no one else in the world who loved her. Sometimes she was so radiantly beautiful he wanted to weep. But sometimes her body was covered with ugly rankly suppurating sores and her face grotesquely distorted and his horror ran in his blood like ice.

Other times it was Daddyjack he saw sitting at the foot of his bed and grinning like a fleshless one-eyed skull and saying, "Look at ye now, laying in you own shit and caint hardly pull a proper breath thout it hurtin. Hell, boy, ye aint really worth a whole lot now, are ye?" And sometimes he was back in the smoky rainsoaked carnage of Monterrey, seeing the sundered flesh and the hearing the unworldly screams and smelling effluvia so horrid it might have come from the bowels of hell.

15

When at last he surfaced from the fever he found his hand in that of a young nurse who said her name was Elena. Her mestizo eyes darkly bright as indogo pools under moonlight. She had been educated by Jesuits and spoke English well. She called him Juanito and said they had been sure he would die but she had prayed every hour that he would not. He had been there nearly two weeks and was shrunken to hide and bone and he ached to his very marrow. She told him he had often screamed of people with strange names but he was all right now and needed only rest and nourishment and time to regain his strength. She told him of Santa Ana's victory over the gringos at Angostura—which the Yankees called Buena Vista—and of the high price paid for it. Many more on both sides had been killed at Angostura than at Monterrey. Much of the talk, Elena told him, was of the San Patricio Company that fought so valiantly, though almost half of them were reported killed. She knew little else about the battle but at his urging undertook to find out what she could. She learned that neither Juan Riley nor Lucas Malone was listed as killed, that in fact Juan Riley had been promoted to captain for his brilliant leadership and bravery in the fight. Moreno had been made a colonel. Santa Ana's army was now back at San Luis Potosí.

A week later he was sitting up and taking broth and his fever was much reduced. So great was the need for hospital beds that Elena was granted her request that he be discharged into her care. She took him home where she lived with her mother. Her father had been an educated man of Spanish bloodline, a Creole, and as an officer in Santa Anna's army in the war against Texas had been killed at San Jacinto. She had no brothers. The mother was a wizened thing who kept to her tiny room whose walls were hung with crucifixes and whose shelves held dozens of saintly icons and where she passed her days and nights in whispered prayers to them all.

She fed him and bathed him until he was strong enough to do for himself. She kept him apprised of the progress of the war. Taylor had returned to Monterrey and was apparently under orders to stay there.

In mid-March came reports of a Yankee landing just outside the Gulf port of Veracruz. The city was refusing American demands to surrender. Three weeks later she brought home the news that General Winfield Scott had bombarded Veracruz for three days and nights. The city had suffered terrible destruction before finally capitulating.. Everyone was saying that Scott would now begin marching inland to the mountains and then on to Mexico City and there the war would be decided. And there were rumors now, she told him, lowering her voice as though she might be overheard in her own house and perhaps thought a traitor, that Santa Ana had lied about Angostura, that it had truly been no victory.

By the first days of April he was strong enough to walk and he took most of his meals outside in the flowered patio behind the house. Swallows came to water in the small fountain and he fed them crumbs of bread. Elena was a wonderful cook and even when he was not hungry he could not resist eating at least some of whatever she prepared for him. She got clothes for him and he put aside his uniform except for his boots. They took walks down to the nearby creek and had picnics in the shade of the alamo trees along the banks where dragonflies drifted drowsily on the air.

One sunny afternoon at the creek she asked him why he had turned against the United States and chosen to fight for Mexico. He smiled and said, "Because I wanted to fight for you."

She blushed and lowered her eyes and said, "That is a pretty lie. You did not even know me then."

And he said, "I knew you. I just didn't' know your name or where you were. I just hadn't met you yet" He wondered where these words had come from. He felt they were true but wondered if maybe his mind had come unsound. Yet he smiled at her and at himself because he didn't' care if he was crazy. If this was what it was to be mad, he thought, then damn him to hell, it's mad he would be.

She looked at him closely, her bright black eyes roaming his face, her small smile sad in a way he couldn't comprehend. But when he leaned to her she raised her face to receive the kiss.

He felt he was home.

But still he was visited by dreams of Daddyjack who often came to him in the black heart of the night and showed a yellow grin and fixed his burning red eye on him and said, "Ye aint deservin and ye know it. She dont know ye for what ye are."

He'd wake sweatsoaked with Daddyjack's laughter in his ears and Elena would hold him close and coo to him and tell him not to feat, that the war was far away. And slowly his heart would ease from its runaway gallop.

She brought news one day that Santa Anna had sent a portion of the army east to cut off the American advance from Veracruz. The San Patricios were said to be part of that force.

He was surprised by his indifference. The war had come to seem somehow unreal, something far away and unconnected to him anymore.

He walked up the hills every day and ate with appetite and felt himself growing stronger. One moonlit evening they went hand in hand to the main plaza and listened to the guitarists and drank lemonade and ignored the disapproving looks of the women in their rebozos and the priests in their black gowns. And on the way back home they stopped under a wide shade tree through which the moonlight dripped like honey and they kissed. And when they got home they made love and all the while he held her naked flesh to him and breathed the redolence of her smooth brown skin and soft black hair he could hear the whispered prayers of the old woman in the adjoining room.

One day in early May she came home with a fever. "I will be all right in a few days," she said. "Many of the girls at the hospital get sick for a few days sometimes and then they are all right again. It is nothing serious, you will see."

But the fever worsened in the night. She tossed and moaned and the sweat poured off her and soaked the sheet. She was on fire all next day and night but she smiled weakly and told him in a hoarse whisper she would be fine in another day, he'd see. He stayed at her side and bathed her forehead with cool water and sang softly to her.

On the third day the fever was raging. She soiled herself and wept with the shame of it. He cleansed her and kissed her and begged her to get well. But the fever rose still higher and she became delirious and could not hear him telling her he would care for her as she had cared for him, telling her how beautiful her eyes were and her breasts and how he adored the sound of her voice. He dozed periodically, woke each time with a start and clutched her to him the better to feel her heart beat against him.

And then the fourth dawn broke through the alamo trees and eased in the windows and he started awake from a hazy stifling dream that rang with mean echoing laughter and she was in his arms with her eyes wide and dried blood on her chin and she was dead.

16

There was an evening wake and ancient women in black rebozos wailed and prayed loudly without pause until he thought he would go mad from the monotony of it. The mother did go mad, now shrieking like a cat and throwing herself on her daughter's bier, now pointing at him and screeching, "Tu! Tu eres la razón que ella está muerta! Tu, condenado gringo! Tu!"

In the morning she was buried and none among the mourners offered him a consoling word. Even in the graveyard some glared at him with open hatred.

He went directly from the funeral to a cantina and started drinking and did not stop until he passed out at a corner table. The barkeep knew him for a San Patricio and let him be. When he came to in the next forenoon he started right in drinking again. That night he ran out of money and so traded his tunic to the bartender for a bottle of tequilia. When that was gone he swapped his boots for two more bottles.

The next day he was arguing with the bartender about trading his trousers, which the bartender did not want, for another bottle when an army sergeant and two privates came in and told him he was under arrest. He broke a bottle over the sergeant's head and gouged the jagged end into his face as he fell. The privates fell to clubbing him with their rifle butts but he twisted the weapon away from one of them and shattered the boy's teeth with the butt plate and then whirled the rifle around and fired it point blank into the third soldier's heart. The boy with the smashed mouth fled through the rear door.

He was having his second drink on the house when a half-dozen soldiers came through the door and the sergeant-at-arms pointed a pistol at him and told him to put his hands up or he would kill him.

John laughed at him and spat on the floor between them and hooked his thumbs in his belt and leaned back against the bar.

The sergeant cocked the pistol as the bartender lunged over the bar and cracked John on the back of the head with a sap fashioned of twenty silver pesos in a leather pouch and he crumpled insensate to the floor.

17

Four days later the back of his head was still tender. He was in a cell and awaiting court-martial on a charge of murder when Colonel Francisco Moreno, Captain John Riley, and Sergeant Lucas Malone showed up and presented the garrison commander with a paper signed by President Santa Ana himself. They were immediately escorted to his cell. They all looked worn and none was smiling. While John's manacles were being removed Moreno him asked what happened.

John looked at him and shrugged. "Somebody got killed."

"They said something about a girl."

John looked away, then back at him. "There aint no girl."

Moreno turned to Handsome Jack but he looked away. Riley seemed irritable, impatient. Moreno studied John for a long moment and then sighed and his air became professional. He informed him that Santa Anna had reorganized the San Patricios into an infantry battalion of two companies of one hundred men each and named it the Foreign Legion. Moreno himself was battalion commander and Riley and Saturnino O'Leary commanded the companies. Santa Anna wanted the unit up to full strength right away and was granting pardons to every jailed foreigner willing to fight under the San Patricio banner. More handbills were being smuggled into Yankee camps urging desertion to the Mexican side and there were reports that dozens of foreigners in Mexico City had enlisted in the Legion in the past few weeks.

"Scott's pushing to Mexico City," Riley said. He was nearly twitching with agitation. "Santa Anna's pulling the whole army down there to make a stand of it. We got to get over there quick, man." It took John a moment to realize he was pleased to see Jack Riley so apprehensive about his own future.

"I guess the sooner we get down there and kick Scott's ass the sooner you get to be a general in this man's army, eh Jack?"

Riley's eyes narrowed. "Listen boy, I dont know what's happened to ye here and I dont care a damn, not right now. We aint got the time for it, goddamnit. You rather stay here and be hanged for a murderer, just say so."

Lucas Malone laughed tiredly and said, "Easy does er, boys. We all of us strung a bit tight just now. Come on, Johnny, let's get on over to Mexico City. It's nothin to do now but stick together and fight for our ownselfs."

John let a heavy sigh. "Our ownselfs, Lucas? Hell man, who *is* that?"

"Dont play the fool with me, boy," Lucas Malone said sternly. "Do it with Jack here all ye want but dont try it with me. Ye know damn good and well we of a kind—you and me and Jack here and all them other fellers in the compny who deserted the other side."

"What the hell you mean 'and Jack here'?" Riley said, but Lucas ignored him.

"Hell boy," Lucas said, speaking more softly now, "you think you the only one feels pure-dee no-count and lost in the heart? The only one the good folk look at like it's prison or the noose waitin for ye wherever ye go in this world?"

John looked at him.

"You know what the hell of is, Johnny?" Lucas whispered.

And he realized that he did know, yes.

"The true and burnin hell of it is, the good folk're right about us. We know they right. It be the drizzlin shits to know it. And it aint nothin to do anout it but admit it and live with it the best we can.

Riley hooted. Moreno gave them all a puzzled look.

"You're *so* full of bullshit, Lucas," Riley said. "Dont be including me in any such bunch of fools." He looked from one to the other of them and suddenly laughed. "If you two think you aint but common jacklegs, that's fine by me. Hell, it's what I think of ye both meself—*crazy* jacklegs, truth be known. But as for me, well, I'm a right fella and I dont mind who knows it."

John felt himself smiling. They were none of them anything for certain in the world but rogues, the lot of them, and their daddies all rogues before them.

He stood up and put on his hat. "Well *hell*, Lucas," he said with mock seriousness, "I feel ever so much better by them words of wisdom. I must of been simple not to understood it before."

"What ye mean, *must of* been?" Riley said. He nudged Lucas with an elbow and gestured at John, "Fella's talking like simpleness is some past affliction rather than his natural condition."

John grinned and said, "Piss upon you, Jack," and threw a lazy punch that Riley easily slipped with a head roll.

Major Moreno looked on the three of them laughing and punching each other on the arms and shoulders and shook his head. And then laughed along with them. And said, "Vámonos! A la capitál! Victoria o muerte!"

"Victoria o muerte!" cried Riley, making towards the door with a raised fist.

"I once knew a old gal named Victoria," Lucas said as they trooped away. "Tits like a milk cow and a ass like a mule. But *mean?* Whooo! That woman'd just as soon kill you as kiss you, and you never did know which she was gonna try."

"That aint the Victoria old Moreno's talking about," John said.

"Hell it aint," said Handsome Jack.

VI

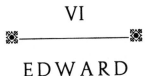

EDWARD

1

They left behind them in Laredo eleven dead and more than a dozen maimed or wounded on that cool March dawn when they broke the blackbeard Jaggers out of jail and accepted Edward into the company as well. Only one of the dead was their own. They were fifteen that departed at a gallop and in a great raise of dust bore due west, Edward on the Janey horse he'd recovered along with his guns and outfit from the livery where he saw a large painted Indian impale the stablebuck to the wall with a pitchfork through the neck. As he put heels to his mount he caught glimpses of men sprawled in the street in the awkward attitudes of death and splotched dark with blood. He saw a woman kneeling at a water trough with her back bloody and her face submerged in the gray-pink water. Saw a dog crawling on forelegs and dragging its bullet-smashed nether half. Saw a small boy staggering in the street with blood in his eyes and then abruptly trampled under the hooves of the horse express rumbling out of town and out to open country. In that galloping band the Janey mare looked like a blooded darling in contrast to the motley bunch of yet half-savage horses that only weeks earlier had been running wild on the desertland and now wore bridles of plaited human hair adorned with clicking bones and teeth.

The company went unpursued.

They made camp that evening in the hills. the Janey horse was white-eyed fearful at being tethered amid the mustangs. They jostled her and snapped at her with their teeth. One lunged and bit her flank and she spun and kicked the pinto so hard it trumpeted and shied away and thereafter the mustangs mostly let her be.

The company's fires tossed and swirled in the sandy nightwind and the men supped on the haunches of an antelope brought down with a Hawken gun at well nigh six hundred yards by a deadeye named Runyon who had been showing off. Jaggers introduced Edward to Geech and Finn and Huddlestone, who sat about the same fire.

They were going to Chihuahua under contract to the governor to hunt Apache. The deal had been closed in the neighboring state of Coahuila where the company had been recruiting itself and squandering its pay in Saltillo cantinas and cathouses after weeks of chasing down a fearsome bandit gang in the Sierras de San Marcos for the Coahuila government. They'd returned to the capital from the expedition with fifteen heads dangling on either side of a blood-stained pack mule including that of the infamous Pablo Contreras which of its own brought them one thousand pesos in silver. The alcalde himself identified the head as Contreras's and the governor ordered it displayed on a lance head over the main portal of the municipal building.

It happened that a party of officials of the Chihuahua government was at that time in Saltillo attending a federation council and these men were deeply impressed by the sight of the miscreant heads lined along the top of the front wall of the municipal building and being fed upon by crows. They invited Hobbes for an audience and informed him that if he could hunt Indians as well as he could catch bandits he should be interested in the state of Chihuahua's willingness to pay one hundred pesos for every Indian warrior scalp and fifty for the scalps of women and children. Hobbes claimed to have fought the heathen in the years he'd trapped in the Sangre de Cristo range and while with the Henry expedition on the upper Missouri and with the likes of Tom Fitzpatrick and Jedediah Smith along the lower Colorado River. He said that if the governor could see fit to pay the bounties strictly in gold—any mix of Mexican doubloons and American eagles being just fine—they had a deal. The governor's men were agreed, and and Hobbes set about readying his company.

While he took on supplies in Saltillo he sent a few men upcountry to Sabinas to buy and break fresh horses from the mustangers who regularly brought their wild herds there to market. Geech and another man he sent to Laredo for a supply of dependable blackpowder and new gangmolds for the company's Texas revolvers. When those two rejoined the company just south of Sabinas they brought with them as well the news that Jaggers was in the West Laredo jail.

"The captain don't like killing lawmen if he don't have to, not even Mexican ones," Huddlestone told Edward, then turned and grinned at Finn. "Which is more than I can say for some in this outfit." Huddlestone was burly and one-eyed and a pink cicatrix wormed from above his brow down under his eyepatch to midway down his cheek.

Finn spat into the fire and ignored him. He was a small but compact man lacking a left ear and the little finger of each hand. His hair flared from under his hat and his beard was a greasy thicket thriving with parasitic life. Edward would come to hear that Finn was a fugitive from the Kentucky hills who'd burned his wife to death for an act of infidelity. The man who put the horns on him he was said to have beheaded.

"They aint no money in killing a lawman," Huddlestone said, "and it can bring on trouble a businessman don't need. And that's what he is, the captain, a businessman, you see."

Finn snorted. "So's a undertaker a damn businessman. But I don't know no undertaker with five hundred dollars on his head."

Now Huddlestone ignored Finn in his turn. "But he warnt about to leave old Bill in that cárcel, the captain. A man rides with James Kirkson Hobbes is a man don't get left behind. But like I say, he'll try to keep from killing a lawman if he can. When we got to the outskirt of the west Laredo an hour or so before dawn, the captain went on in by hisself to talk to the alcalde and try to buy Bill out of the hoosegow. He come back before long and said the alcalde hadn't been too pleased about getting woke so early and wouldn't even come downstairs to talk to him. Had his manservant to tell the captain *maybe* he would have time to see him later that afternoon. Well hell, the captain didn't have time to waste waiting on some Mexican muckamuck who *might* see him. So we all rode

into town and up to the alcalde's house and the captain halloed the place
again and the alcalde come out looking all Señor Mucho Mighty. The
captain said he had to have Bill Jaggers out of the juzgado right now so
we could get on about our business. But it's no reasoning with some
people. The alcalde starts blabbering real loud at the captain in Mexican
and the captain stood for it for about a half-a-minute and then shot him
in the mouth and blowed his teeth out the back of his head. Not ten
minutes later you was heading for the outcountry with us. Could say it
was a lucky thing for you the alcalde didn't let the captain buy Bill out
of jail or you'd likely still be back there."

Edward looked over at the captain sitting apart from the company,
removed from the raillery and the fires, with a Mexican sarape over his
shoulders against the gusty chill, smoking his pipe and staring out at the
vast blackness to the west.

They were a band even more primitive of aspect than the horses they
rode and all had eyes that never did look on a living thing with a moment's mercy. They wore coarse cloth and animal skin, some of it not
fully cured, and their hats were of every description and appointed with
raptor feathers or snakeskin bands. They wore belts fashioned of human
skin and necklaces of gold teeth and of trigger fingers and ears withered
and black and looking like strung dried fruit. The one called Finn carried
on his belt a tobacco pouch tanned from a squaw teat, the hide the same
brown hue as its contents and black-nippled at its base. Some had themselves been docked of one or both ears and some lacked fingers or owned
but one eye. Among such mutilations Edward's severed ear was of little
note. In that company were tattoos of every sort and scars of every description, primitive sutures fashioned in dire circumstance. Some in the
company bore branded letters or numbers on faces and hands and inner
forearms. They were armed each man with bowies the size of machetes
and skinning knives and Colt five-shooters, and in that company were
longarms of every sort from Hawken guns to Kentucky and Jaeger rifles
to doublebarrels to hugebore muskets charged with shot or pieces of brass
or handfuls of silver dimes. And among them too were five Shawnee
trackers and scouts, their chief called Sly Buck, the large one who'd pitch-
forked the stableman.

This Indian conferred now with Hobbes and his lieutenants, a lean and
thinly blondbearded man named John Allen and a whitewhiskered and
rotund man of indeterminate age named Foreman who dressed in black
and was supposed to have once belonged to the Jesuit order and was

addressed by all as padre. When the confab broke up the Shawnees mounted and departed to westward.

By himself any man of the company would attract wary attention on the streets of any town. He would be regarded as a vagabond pariah, as a moral affront and a physical danger to ordered society, as the sort to be dealt with swift and sure by well-armed and strong-numbered legal authority. Many of them had been thus regarded and dealt with. Most every man among them had a price on his head. But conjoined in company they were more than an engine of outlawry. They were violent agency as old as human blood. They were a force as fundamental and terrible and beyond rational ken as death itself, as elemental as fire or temblor or howling wind.

2

Some in the company were curious about this new and youngest of their comrades who called himself Edward Boggs. At a night's encampment Huddlestone spat into the fire and leaned back against his saddle and his solitary eye gleamed in the firelight. He grinned at Edward and said, "Old Bill here says you've hunt the savages afore."

Edward shrugged and spat.

Geech laughed. He was skeletal and his face was redly raw with open sores. "That's right, lad. Don't say yay or nay and ye won't be lyin now, will ye? You're a right bright pup, ye are."

"Apache," Jaggers said, and winked at Edward across the fire. "That's the lad's specialty. Los tigres del desierto as the Mexes call them. Best hunting they is."

"If they be tigers, what do ye call the Comanch?" Geech said. "I reckon they be lions."

"No matter," Huddlestone said, lighting his pipe and billowing smoke. "We aint like to see comanch down here this time a year. Not till the harvest moon when the waterholes are full up."

"Ye best hope we don't see no damn Comanch," Tom Finn said. "It's some of us seen the sort a harvestin them mean bastards do." He'd been drinking from a bottle of mescal since before they put down for the night and the faint creosote smell of the spirit was detectable amid his other effluvia. Edward had come to know from others of the company that Finn and Huddlestone had once been friends but in recent weeks an animus had grown between them and none knew what their quarrel was.

"One heathen's hair'll bring the bounty quick as another's," Huddlestone said. "Makes no never mind to me. I hunt em all kinds."

"Price might be the same but you play rougher hell taking Comanche hair than Apache," Finn insisted. "It's some of us know what we're talkin about."

Huddlestone's eye narrowed. He leaned forward off his saddle and said, "I don't know what I'm talking about?"

Finn stared at him.

"The difference between them heathen sonsabitches aint worth arguing," Jaggers interjected quickly. "The one's as bad as the other. They got a saying down here: 'He'll make a good man if the Apaches don't stick him on a cactus.' "

"That aint hardly the worst them red niggers'll do," Geech said.

"Them of us who know what we're talkin about'll chase Apache all day long," Finn said, still looking at Huddlestone. "Just don't bring us no damn comanch."

Huddlestone laughed without humor. "How in hell you ever fool the captain into thinking you're a scalphunter?"

"I'm ever bit the scalphunter as any man here, especially you for damn sure."

They locked stares, their unblinking eyes glinting in the wavering light of the fire as they set their legs under them, the air charged with their ready violence.

But now Captain James Kirkson Hobbes stepped into the cast of firelight and every man held fast. He looked at each of them in turn, his face expressionless but his eyes as hotly bright as embers. He spat into the fire and took slow care in lighting a cigar and puffing it and checking its burn. Then he looked at them all again and turned and faded into the darkness. And Huddlestone and Finn sat back again, their stare now uncoupled, the moment expired.

3

They rode out of the brush country of northern Nuevo León and into the dustlands of eastern Coahuila under a sun as pale as a Spanish priest. They camped that evening beside a small rill running through a thin stand of willows under an amber cat's-eye moon. At the fire Padre Foreman asked Jaggers if he'd taken care of that matter in Arkansas.

"I did," Jaggers said. His sister had written to him in care of a hotel in Bexar some months before and told him her unarmed husband had been killed by a neighbor named Raitt in a dispute over the boundary between their properties. Her oldest son was but eight years old, not yet of an age to take his daddy's part, and so she was calling on her only brother to set the matter right. The company was then ready to leave for Coahuila to hunt bandits for the state, and as much as Jaggers hated to miss out on that enterprise, she was his only sister and he felt he could not refuse her. So he had gone to Arkansas and settled the matter by shooting Raitt dead.

Tom Finn asked if the man had sons.

"Aye," Jaggers said. "Two of em. One looked about eight, the elder near on to eleven. I come up on him in his field and was near as me to you when I shot him in the brainpan. His boys seen the whole thing and come running over and the way they looked at me I figure them to come hunting me soon as they get their growth. I guess I ort to killed them too."

"Ye damn well should of," Tom Finn said. "I known boys grown to old men hunting some fella who owed them blood. It's some like that who don't never quit lookin. But ye say these was so young, by the time they of age they maybe won't know where to start lookin for ye. It's a big world."

"Tis that," Jaggers said, "but it do have corners. And a man never knows when he's like to find hisself in one a them and no telling who else might show up there too."

"That's true enough," Finn conceded. "Never no tellin about them corners."

A man called Himmler walked by with an incurious glance their way. He was large and easy of movement and not much of a talker. He habitually wore his hat pulled low over his eyes. He settled himself alongside the rill and began to play softly on a harmonica. Sweet Betsy from Pike.

"Your mistake was in reading her letter in the first place," Huddlestone now opined. "Ye ought thow away any damn letter just as quick as ye get it. I never did know good news to come in any damn letter noways."

"How in the purple hell would you know?" Finn said. "You can't even read you own damn name."

Huddlestone's eyes cut to him but he held mute. He knew Tom Finn could at least recognize his own name in writing. He had lost a twenty-dollars wager to him when Finn proved it in a Saltillo cantina. He turned back to Jaggers and said, "Thow the goddamn things away soon as you get em. Don't even open em."

Jaggers gave him a narrow look. "Shit Lon."

Huddlestone spat and shook his head. "Oh I know, I know—she be blood. I don't understand why that counts so much with such as you. Bloodkin aint but a goddamn accident."

"Wait now," Padre Foreman quickly interjected, leaning forward with roused interest, eyes bright and quick. "Accident is no argument against obligation to kin. One can argue that beyond the creation of the world by the Lord Himself everything in life is an accident and man therefore has no obligations whatever except those he believes he owes directly to God. But is not the concept of accident itself a tenuous one? Much that seems mere accident in the world is later seen to be part of a larger design, and even if it is not seen so, the lack of witness is no disproof of the design's existence."

Huddlestone laughed. "Ye got some peculiar blather for a man of the cloth, padre, and that's no lie."

"I am not a man of the cloth," the padre said. "And the notion is not as peculiar as you think. Consider: What does obligation to God entail if not obligation to kin? Did not the Son sacrifice himself with the Father's blessing to make blood atonement for the sins of all His mortal kin? Did the Father demand more of Abraham than He Himself willingly surrendered?" The padre's eyes blazed. "But mark me now. The son was not literally of the Lord's flesh, was he? He was not conceived of blood passed by the brute coupling of the flesh, was he now? No. And yet who would deny that the Christus is kin to God the Father? The divine notion of kinship is far more encompassing than mere ties of the flesh, and the sheer scope of the Lord's sacrifice of his son—His *spiritual* kin—makes that clear."

"Aint a damn thing out you mouth *ever* clear," Geech said.

The padre smiled upon him, upon them all. "I am at this moment among closer kin than any I am connected to by line of birth. I am among men whose cast of spirit is most like my own, whose particular damnations, if you will, most closely resemble mine. No birth brother nor sister nor even my father himself, rest his soul, was as similar in spirit to me as are you all. Not one of ye has a soul darker nor fairer than mine. Not a one has more likely chance of heaven nor greater certainty of hell. Our very choice of trade, the common path we've elected to follow through this vale of tears, a path elected through the exercise of our independent will, has made us of blood more closely joined than that of any family comprised of mere lineage." He paused and grinned in return at the circle of grins and shaking heads about him.

"You saying I'm closer kin with this bunch a no-counts than with my sweet momma up in Michigan?" Runyon the deadeye said. "I'll be damned if that's so!"

The former Jesuit smiled more widely yet. "Aye, me good Teddy! Well and exactly said."

"Exactly said, shit," said Huddlestone. "A man'd have to be crazy as hell to listen to your bullshit, padre."

Others around the fire nodded at this, grinning.

The padre fairly beamed and spread his arms as if he would induce benediction and then sweep them all to his breast. "Indeed," he said. "Indeed. Quod erat demonstrandum."

4

Some days later they came upon the Shawnees waiting for them on a rise where a spring flowed down below. The company watered and made camp and the scouts conferred with Hobbes. "Aint likely we'll find sign of the heathen till we get the other side of them mountains," Jaggers told Edward. The range he spoke of stood darkly on the west horizon. These were the first true mountains Edward had seen since his early boyhood in upland Georgia and were different in every way: bare and sharp-edged and rawly purple against the red sky of late afternoon. As the company advanced on this rangeline they came to a low woodland about the Río Sabinas and rode through the cool shade of ancient ahuehuete trees and willows. The water here ran clear and sweet and in another two days they arrived at the pueblo of Sabinas where another six of the company were waiting with a caballada of mustangs freshly but barely broken to the saddle and with packmule supplies taken on in Saltillo and Monclova.

The new mounts were urgent with meanness, all snapping teeth and white rolling eyes. "These little sonsabitches as soon bite and kick you as not," Jaggers told Edward, "but they'll ride all day and night with but a sip of water and will eat any damn thing—rocks, dirt, you hat, anything. You won't see a meaner or tougher horse except under a Comanche."

A dozen of the company went into a restaurant where the local patrons gaped at this wild bunch of white men and Indians that seemed emanated from a realm of bad dreams. The company ate their fill and then repaired to a cantina that emptied of nearly all other customers within half-a-minute of their entry. Only a few machos stood their place at the bar and there were but two fights that night. A young but whitehaired Australian named Holcomb badly cut up a Mexican drover whom he took to have sneered at him, and a Mex-Indian halfbreed called Chato broke a bottle over a wrangler's head and gouged out his eye with the jagged end of it when the wrangler muttered something about "indio mugrioso." But no one was killed and no enforcers of law presented themselves and before sunrise the company rode out, trailing the caballada and packmules, every man sliteyed and testy with the dolor of hangover.

The country rose before them. They came to the southern reaches of the Sierra del Carmen and beyond them the Encantadas and over the next weeks crossed them on rising switchbacks and through narrow passes whose sides loomed dark and ever higher and to which clung drooping juniper and red-fruited prickly pear and stilted century plants with center stems long as Spanish lances. The clatter of their horses' hooves echoed off the stone walls. They shot and roasted wild pig for their suppers and filled canteens from icy creeks and in the moonlit evenings their breath issued like plumes of blue smoke. Their fires flattened and leapt and spun in erratic canyon winds. They heard cougars shriek in the barrancas. In this high country they had expected no sign of the savages and found none. In time the trail leveled and wound around the rocksides and cut through juniper and piñon growth and began its slow descent. They at last debouched onto the lesser bajada and spied a swirl of buzzards to the west and near noon the next day came upon a village in ruins still smoking.

The dead lay strewn and naked, caked in their own blackdried blood and swarming with ants and flies and partly consumed by canines and scavenger birds still picking clumsily over the corpses like drunken morticians. The remains of men and women lay eviscerated and throatcut and mutilated in the private parts. Not a corpse remained unscalped except for some of the infants who'd yet had no hair and who lay scattered and askew among the rocks on which their skulls had been crushed. The malodor was not yet at full ripeness but would achieve it by next day.

Only the blacksooted adobe walls still stood. Everything of wood was charred and smoking, everything of straw reduced to ash. The Shawnees quickly found out the survivors and rousted them from their hiding places in nearby arroyos. Fewer than a dozen and all appeared demented. A woman with eyes fixed on something far beyond the world around her held a dead babe to her teat.

The raiders had ridden off to the northwest with the stock and several young female captives. Hobbes looked about at the meager scattering of dead pigs and dogs and leaned out from his horse and spat and advised the elder in his fluent Spanish to strip and jerk all the unrotted meat they might find. The old man raised a hand as if he would point something out to Hobbes and then seemed not to know what he wanted to say and so dropped his hand and kept mute.

Hobbes spoke with Sly Buck and then the Shawnees galloped off on the trail of the raiders. The company mounted up and followed at a canter. They rode the rest of the afternoon and kept the moontains to their right. The sparse grass soon played out. They rode single file into the wider arroyos to avoid skylighting themselves to any watchers ahead. In this country of cactus spines and bloodstained rock and remnant bones the air was the driest Edward had ever breathed and it smelled of dusty death. Hobbes occasionally reconnoitered from the crest of a rockrise and studied the line of dark mesas standing squat on the far horizon under low reefs of clouds looking smeared with blood. They camped that night without fire. The moon came up from behind the Carmens and the wind blew cold and the sky was massive and congested with stars. Bright yellow comets flared across the sky and into oblivion. Edward rolled himself in his blanket and lay awake for a time, staring into the vastness of this desert nightsky and listening to the high yip of coyotes in the darkness and feeling in this alien wasteland a sense of rightful belonging he could not have put into words.

They rode another day and again made a fireless camp and in the forenoon of the following day they found a recently dead mule hardly more than hide and bones and with its flanks well butchered. Some hours later they spied the speck of a figure on the flatland ahead and after a time came upon one of the Shawnee outriders. Beside him a naked Mexican girl barely of age lay murdered on the hardpan. She bore no cut nor bullet wound but her inner thighs were coated with dried blood and her pudendum was crusted black and her eyesockets had been hollowed by the ants. Her arms were crossed over her breasts as though she would assert modesty even in death.

The Shawnee spoke in his tongue with Hobbes and pointed to the dark form of a mesa some fifteen miles distant where the sky was staining crimson about the lowering sun. Hobbes relayed the information to the company: the raiders were encamped at a place the Mexicans called Fuente de Dios, a waterhole set in the mesa ahead, and were apparently unaware of their trackers. He ordered the company to put down in a near gully and there rest up till nightfall lest their quarry descry their advancing dust. As he reined the Janey horse about, Edward saw the Shawnee bend to the dead girl with a knife in his hand. A moment later the Indian was remounted and catching up to Hobbes and her longhaired scalp dangled from his belt.

They moved out at dark with a pale half moon hung low in the sky behind them, proceeding at a trot, single file and well apart, their gear lashed tight against clatter. Still, had the savages had an ear to the ground they might have heard them coming. The moon gained its meridian and began its slow fall to the west. As they neared the mesa they slowed their pace to a walk. Their only sounds were of the horses' shoeless hooves whispering through the sand and the low creak of saddles and light chink of bitrings. Sly Buck and John Allen turned off with half the company in a wide arc to the left while Hobbes took the others around to the right. Both groups clung close to the shadows of the outcrops.

As they reached the yet larger outcrops near the base of the mesa the zodiacal light of false dawn was showing over the distant line of mountains in the east. Hobbes halted the party. They dismounted and the captain swiftly unfurled his blanket from behind the saddle and hooded the head of his horse with it and the rest of the band followed suit. Edward felt the Janey mare tremble and patted her neck and whispered in her ear and she settled. They walked the horses and mules further up into the rocks and into a ravine and now Hobbes scanned the men and Edward knew that as the youngest and least experienced among them he would be chosen to stay with the animals. But Hobbes instead pointed to a man called Patterson who had recently complained aloud about having to stand watch two nights in a row. Patterson scowled and gnashed his teeth but Hobbes simply stared at him and Patterson turned away and took each man's reins.

Hobbes led them swiftly and surefooted through the rock shadows and cactus growths and up the stone slopes and they at last crested on a tablerock. They followed Hobbes at a crouch through the sand and scrub brush and a figure suddenly stepped out of the shadows before them and Edward's skin jumped in the instant before he recognized Sly Buck. Hobbes and the chief parlayed in whispers and then moved up to the rockrim on their bellies and took a long look and then Hobbes motioned the others to come up. As they crawled toward the edge of the rock they passed within a foot of a dead Apache sprawled on his back in the scrub and Edward caught a scent like smoke and raw leather. His heart pounded against the earth.

In the first gray light of dawn they saw the raiders in a wide sandy clearing some fifty feet below. Edward's quick count numbered nearly two dozen. They were just roused and feeding off the low fires set hard against the rockwall so that the thin smoke carried through natural flues to disperse unseen from some other part of the mesa. Their horses and the stolen stock were bunched in a makeshift corral flanking a narrow pass. A pair of women huddled at the wall fire nearest the waterhole and a tall Apache kicked one of them in passing. Her yelp carried up to the men on the rock and the Apaches laughed.

Hobbes looked to the deeply shadowed rock wall across the way and then at Sly Buck who nodded and pointed to a brushy portion of the opposite rockrim. Edward figured that was where John Allen and the others were positioned. Now Sly Buck whispered to Hobbes and pointed to the tall Apache moving about the camp and talking to various of the braves. Hobbes nodded. He unholstered his two Colts and lay them close to hand and then brought the Hawken up to shooting position. Every man readied himself as well. The captain drew bead on the tall Indian as he moved across the clearing and then the Hawken's muzzle blasted orange flame and the report echoed deafeningly off the rock walls as the back of the Indian's head came apart and he spun as if drunk and even as he fell every gun along both rockrims opened fire.

Edward fixed on an Apache racing for the corral and led him perfectly with the smoothbore and the .62 ball knocked the man off his feet as if he'd been swatted with a mace. The mulekick recoil against his shoulder was more satisfying than Edward could have said. He recocked with the ring lever and aimed and hit his next target in the hip and as the wounded savage crawled on he aimed more carefully and shot away the forepart of his skull. He hurried the next two shots and missed both times and put aside the longarm and switched to his revolver and kept adding to the hellish crossfire raging into the hapless indigenes. On either side of him lay an angelfaced blond Jessup twin, three years older than he was and each at work first with a doublebarrel rifle and then going to their pistols too. A woman's lingering scream cut through the thunder of gunfire and then abruptly ceased. Apaches ran and spasmed and fell. A handful reached the corral and kicked down the rail and leapt to horse. They headed for the narrow pass but a fusillade from the rocks above where Sly Buck had posted his other Shawnees sent the Indian mounts down shrieking. Some of the riders rolled clear and jumped up and began running and then were shot down too.

And then it was done and not a single savage had made away. The company descended through the lingering blackpowder haze to the floor of the clearing and began taking hair. Edward watched Jaggers roll an Apache onto his stomach and squat beside him and run his knife edge hard all the way around the top of the skull and then put a foot firmly behind neck to serve as a fulcrum as he wrapped a hank of hair round his hand and with a sharp hard tug ripped the scalp from the skull with a sound like a booted foot being pulled from deep mud. He held it up lank and dripping for Edward to see. The same sound was all about them. Indians lay with the tops of their heads raw and bloody to the red light of the morning sun risen to the rimrock.

"Here's one needs trimming, boy." It was John Allen, standing beside him and pointing at an Apache lying hard by. Edward bent to the task and executed it with the ease of someone long practiced. The feel of the scalp tearing free of the bone sent a quiver through him unlike any sensation he'd ever known. He held the prize up high and felt the blood rivuleting down his arm and under his shirtsleeve and saw Padre Foreman smiling broadly at him and there rose now an exultant howling of the hellbound and his war cry carried with it.

5

They found the animals unattended in the ravine, Patterson gone. His trail led off toward a line of blue mountains to the north and he had taken two horses from the caballada. Hobbes dispatched Chato the Breed and one of the Shawnees after him and sent Sly Buck and the rest of the scouts as outriders to cut for sign in the west. Then the company got moving again, bringing the stolen Apache stock behind with their own horses. None of the captive Mexican women had survived the fight and so were scalped also and left to the scavengers with the other dead at Fuente de Dios. The only one in the company to suffer injury was Castro the Spaniard who hated mestizos as ardently as he hated Indians. Many of the indios at least owned courage, he often expounded, but the mestizos were craven mongrel dogs, shaped from the worst traits of both races and possessing nothing of the admirable from either. He'd slipped coming down off the tablerock and fractured his left arm. Doc Devlin had set it and bound it in a splint and the Spaniard had made a big show of how well he could yet handle and even spin his pistol with his good right hand lest Hobbes think him unable to carry his share of the load.

A Shawnee outrider returned at midday to report sign of the savages ten miles ahead. Hobbes appointed the Spaniard and the Shawnee to bring along the stock and the company set out riding hard and that evening caught up to Sly Buck and the other scouts. The Encantadas were a hard red rockline to their right. On the far horizon, visible between a pair of short low ranges, could be seen the ghostly forms of the Chisos standing on the other side of the Río Bravo del Norte where it formed a deep southern bend. The Apaches had made a jerkycamp at the foot of the nearest mountains. The Shawnees guessed them to be the rest of the raiders' clan. They told Hobbes it was composed mostly of women and children with but a few braves to watch over them.

"Easy pickins," said John Allen.

They attacked from the east at daybreak like demons unloosed from the hell-red sun itself, galloping through the heart of the camp and shooting down every man in sight and then reining about and riding through again and this time shooting anything still on its feet and setting afire the scattered hogans shaped of saplings and hides. And then they were off their mounts and shooting whatever still drew breath and one dying warrior rose to his knees and loosed an arrow into Runyon's lower belly that sat him down cursing and Himmler ran forward and with a twohanded swipe of his bowie lifted the archer's head from its mooring in a great spout of blood and sent it arcing to hit the ground and roll within reach of a stake-tied dog that fastened onto it and shook the thing viciously in its crazed excitement.

And then there was only the moaning and keening of the dying women and children and the company walked through the carnage and shot them dead every one. And when they had done with their business they had increased their harvest by thirty-eight scalps. Hobbes put the Shawnees to trimming the hair on most of the women's scalps the better to pass them off as belonging to warriors and reaping the higher bounty.

They supped on the meat the Indians had hung to dry on scrub brush and mesquite limbs, all but Runyon who had been helped into the shade of a rockface and now sat with his back to the rockwall and his hands holding tight on his belly around the protruding arrow shaft. Hobbes had come to have a look and then moved aside for Doc Devlin who made an examination and said he could do nothing.

"Soon's I yank her out you'll die."

"Well hell," Runyon grunted through his teeth, "I can't go around with no arrow sticking out my gut."

"No you can't," said Doc Devlin. And because there was nothing more to be said he and Hobbes repaired to the fire to join the others at supper and left Runyon to mull his circumstance.

At the fire Lionel and Linus Jessup were smiling and showing off their newly begun necklaces of Indian ears. They hailed from the northernmost reaches of Minnesota and had come to Mexico to see the elephant and had stayed to flay its hide.

Later that night Chato and the Shawnee arrived with Patterson in tow on his horse and with his hands bound behind him. They brought in the other two horses as well. But for a bloody arm wound received from Chato's longrifle Patterson was unhurt. He grinned down at the gathered men and called salutations to some but none hailed him in return nor even smiled at him.

Hobbes said for someone to yank the sorry son of a bitch off the horse for he would not look up to the likes of him now or ever. John Allen grabbed one of Patterson's feet from the stirrup and shoved his leg outward and up and thus unsaddled the traitor. Himmler pulled him to his feet by his shirt collar and stood him before the captain and Hobbes asked what he had to say for himself.

"If I aint to be but a horseholder I want nary more to do with this compny," Patterson said.

"I say what every manjack in this compny do and don't do," Hobbes said.

"I say I aint no damn horseholder."

Hobbes punched him in the mouth and Patterson went down and Himmler stood him up again. Patterson worked his tongue in his bloody mouth and spat a tooth at Hobbe's feet and said, "Put that on yer necklace, ye damn twistbrain." Hobbes hit him and blood flew from his mouth as he went down once more and this time no man made to pull him up.

"I won't abide a quitter," Hobbes said. He kicked Patterson in the short ribs and Patterson rolled against his horse's legs and the horse shied and nearly stomped him as though even it found him contemptible. One of the Jessups grabbed the reins and pulled the animal away.

"Man who quits on his compny's the lowest thing there is," Hobbes said, kicking at Patterson as the man tried to scrabble away from him, following after him, kicking at him again, trying for his balls. "Man quits his company is spittin on every man rode with him, but *he's* the one aint worth spit. He aint worth half that dog yonder." He gestured at the ropestaked dog glowering and snarling at every man to pass by. He kicked Patterson yet again and said, "Get him out my sight till I decide what to do with the sorry whoreson."

By sunup he'd decided. He had Patterson hoisted up onto his horse and tied to the saddle with his hands bound behind him still. He told him if he tried turning the horse to north or south or back to eastward the first outrider to spot him would shoot the horse from under him and leave him to die of thirst alongside his dead animal.

"Only way you can go is west," Hobbes told him. "Now go!" He lashed the horse's hindquarters and it bolted so fast Patterson nearly tumbled from the saddle. They watched him diminish into the vast flat desertland on the cantering horse until he was but a dark speck wavering in the rising heat and then he was visible no more.

"Why's he let him go, he hates quitters so much?" Edward asked Jaggers.

Jaggers looked at him. "He aint let him go but into the Apacheria. That's how much he hates a quitter."

Hobbes cut the rope holding the Indian dog to its stake and for a moment the animal stood crouched with its nape roached and teeth bared. It slowly circled away from Hobbes and the other men looking on and then sprinted over a low rise and was gone.

Now the company prepared to ride out and Runyon's eyes followed first one man and then another as they caught up their horses and made ready. The Spaniard had arrived with the caballada and the herd of captured stock and to it were added the newly taken Indian ponies. No man met Runyon's gaze. Then Hobbes went to him and asked if he had a charged pistol. Runyon removed one bloody hand from alongside the arrow in his belly and withdrew a loaded Colt from under his jacket and laid it beside him.

"It's naught I can offer ye, Teddy," Hobbes said, "except if you want it done I'll oblige ye." He already held a cocked pistol in his hand and he glanced now to the far horizons. "Others of em might be by before you're done."

Runyon stared up at him for a moment and then dropped his eyes to his wound and shook his head.

"You know how they'll do ye. Better a bullet than that."

"No," Runyon said. "Aint fittin."

"It's no shame in it, man," Hobbes said in barely above a whisper.

Runyon shook his head without looking up. He said no more.

Hobbes waited a moment longer and then uncocked and holstered his pistol. He went to his horse and mounted up and led the company out to westward. Edward looked back and saw Runyon sitting as before and looking after them, and then he turned forward and did not look back again.

6

They were now deep into the bloodlands, into regions labeled "unknown" on maps and marked by sharply rugged ranges interspersed with immense bolsóns and dry cracked playas that lay hazed and shimmering in the rising heat of the emptiness under the white sun. The fiercest of these wastes was the Bolsón de Mapimí whose northern reach they now traversed and whose gray wavering flatness lay unbroken to the horizon in every direction but for scattered low buttes and a jagged blue line of mountains showing far to the north.

The nights quivered with the crying of coyotes. He dreamt one night he saw Daddyjack sitting on a rock in an immense desert, watching the company go by and grinning as if he knew them all. And indeed Hobbes raised a hand in greeting of him, and Padre Foreman called out, "How do, Haywood!" and John Allen touched his hat brim and said, "Good to see you, Jack." Edward nodded as he passed and Daddyjack grinned and said, "Make youself to home, boy."

Three days out they spied a high noon dust cloud rising quickly from west by north and Hobbes ordered the company into a shallow gully and there every man unsheathed his rifle and set himself to stand against a heathen attack. After a time the source of the dust came thundering into view and went galloping past and was but a breathtaking herd of hundreds of mustangs wilder even than the company mounts had been at breaking. The scalpers had a devilish time holding their animals down against their trumpeting lunges to break free and join with their wild passing blood. They anyway lost four of the caballada to the mesteños.

Two days later they spied a small dark form in the vastness ahead and by and by drew near enough to make out it was a solitary and skeletal mesquite whose bare thorny branches were hung with something that on drawing nearer they saw was what had once been a man. It was Patterson hung upside down on the tree. His eyelids had been excised and his genitals cut away and put into his mouth and he had been scalped and completely flayed. Through the raw striations of his sunroasted flesh were visible his pale ribs and hipbones. His eyes looked to be cooked solid as boiled eggs. The ground beneath him was stained black with his fallen blood.

Edward had heard a hundred tales of things men did to one another in times of war. How the Creeks had done to the whites at Mims and how Jackson had done to the Creeks at Horseshoe Bend, how the Mexicans had done to the Texians at the Alamo, how Houston's army had done to Santa Anna's fallen soldiers at San Jacinto. He believed he himself had already seen all possible example of human cruelty and well knew its vast inventiveness. But he'd no acquaintance with such as he now beheld. He was at once informed with dread at the thing in the tree and with an admiration for the purity of its horror. And he felt now the certain realization that here in this maledict portion of the world was truly where such as he and his fellows in this company of the damned properly belonged—here where blood was both common instrument of commerce and venerated tool of art.

Finn dismounted and stepped up for closer examination and then took a quick step back and said, "God *damn*, it's alive!"

As if to prove him right the thing on the tree did emit a weak fluttering groan through the bulge of genitalia in its mouth. The horses sidled and tossed their heads and rolled their eyes white, sensing perhaps some tremor in the riders they carried. Hobbes pulled his pistol and drew bead and fired into the head of the wretched thing and only then did the muscles unflex and the body sag fully dead.

The company settled their mounts as Hobbes holstered his Colt and his horse whirled in a quick tight circle before he reined it steady. He pointed at the thing on the tree and shouted, "See him! See him who quit this company!" He looked and sounded like a crazed Old Testament prophet who'd known exactly what fate awaited this wretched apostate in the wilderness.

"See this one who broke faith with his fellows! *See* him!"

And he heeled his horse forward and the company hastened after him into the deeper wilds.

7

So much had Patterson's perfidy enraged James Kirkson Hobbes that he set the company upon the very next consort of Indians they encountered and said devil take it when Doc Devlin remarked that they were no relation to the Apache but a people who meant harm to no man. "Hair, boys!" he called as he pulled his Colt and raised his arm in signal for them to charge the luckless Indians. "Take it all!" And in less than ten minutes they did.

They rode on with nineteen more scalps freshly salted and hung on their mules and the smell of hard death holding close about them. Wolves trailed them in the open light of day and sometimes loped out on their flanks and some in the company shot at them but never hit even one. The nights were rent with their howling.

Now the company turned north and in time came to a range of nameless mountains and ascended the switchback trails through the scrubbrush and from the rimrock scouted the bolsóns below wavering in the rising heat. They saw but two nightfires over the next weeks and one proved to be that of a large bandit gang that gave them wide berth on the playa the next day. The Shawnees reported the other campfire as belonging to a unit of Mexican cavalry that rarely ventured into this portion of wildland and the company swung wide and rode through the night to put distance between them and the army by daybreak.

In Barrenitos they took an evening's respite and left behind them in the red dawn two maimed locals and one dead who'd confronted Himmler and Huddlestone in a matter of honor involving some women of the village. In San Pedro where they were greeted as venerable protectors from the demon aborigines Castro was obliged to kill a citizen who raised armed objection to the Spaniard's flirtations with his daughter. They crossed the Río Conchos in a brief hard rain that roused the smells of hot sand and creosote in its steamy aftermath. Then reached the Sierras de la Tasajera and ascended into forests of dwarf oaks and pine and manzanita. They scouted the ridges and scanned the flats below and then descended on the switchbacks and defiled onto the flatland and rode on. They saw no living thing for days on end save a few hardy lizards and some high-sailing zopilotes.

West of Gallego they could see four separate rainstorms raging blackly in the distances before and behind them but there was hint of neither shade nor moisture for miles around the ground they crossed. They blacked their eyes and the eyes of their horses yet the underside of the men's faces got burned from the sun's fierce reflection off the hardpan. In time they came to scrubland once again and to a minuscule muddy creek where they watered. Next day they arrived at a village whose name none in the company knew nor asked after. In the solitary cantina on the sole street of that forsaken place of a dozen adobe buildings they were informed of the rumor that the Apaches had only a few days before slaughtered a small train of pilgrims on the trail not fifteen miles westward at the foot of the Tunas range whose low blue peaks were visible from the doorway of the cantina where they drank.

Well before dawn they were headed for the Tunas. In time they came upon the remains of the train—charred wood and blackened axles and the scattered savaged corpses humming with flies and some few dead and bloated animals. Their spirits rose at this proof of Apache proximity and they set upon the raiders' trail and followed it to the mountains. But here the ground was all loose stone and the possible trails were various and even the Shawnees argued among themselves about which to follow and Hobbes in his urgency finally pointed up the mountainside and said, "That way." And that way they went.

But this trail did not cut through a pass as Hobbes had thought but rather climbed and narrowed and became yet more unsure as it steepened. A rock wall rose on their right and the earth fell away on their left as the night descended like a black shroud. Every man now knew the Indians had not driven their stock by this high trail and yet Hobbes pressed them onwards in the darkness thinking to get sufficient elevation to sight them come the dawn. They could see the pinpoint lanternlights that marked the village they had departed nearly a day earlier. Then Chato the Breed's horse lost its footing and Chato just did sprawl to safety before the pony toppled over the ledge and went twirling and screaming into the void and then vanished into silence. Sometime thereafter they arrived at a tablerock and there Hobbes put down their camp. They scanned the vast blackness but spied nothing but lightning jagging brightwhite and silent at the far end of the earth.

The following morning broke blood red over the eastern ranges and saw a sudden rising of thunderheads. The sky darkened in its entirety and then the rain came down in gusting torrents. They feared the narrow trail might wash out from under them but it held and that afternoon the sun reemerged and steam rose off their horses. They achieved a rimrock peak and scouted the horizon in every direction but saw no sign of the Apache. They were two days coming off the Tunas and it rained on them most of the way.

For weeks to follow they found no sign of quarry. They thought that word of their coming must have spread and the Indio was on keener watch and in better hiding. They rode deep into the night and set fires in one place and camped without fire a few miles removed to try to lure the heathen but no Indians did appear. They ranged in wide searching loops and the Shawnees cut for sign in vain. They traversed vast and shifting gypsum dunes as fine as lady's facepowder through which the ponies and mules labored for breath like bellows. The wind blew the sand like seaspray but only the whited bones of men and animals did they find there. They crossed shimmering flats empty of vegetation but for occasional saltbrush and stunted cactus. They rode up narrow arroyos to mesa tops and searched the terrain to every point of the compass and then descended again and rode out into the broiling cracked flats of the playas. They lay on their bellies to skylight the horizon for sign of men to kill. They dismounted and sat out a sandstorm for all of a night and most of the next day behind the shelter of their horses and were sitting in sand to their waists when it was past and their horses looked formed of silicate crystals. Some of the animals had gone blind and so were shot and butchered and their meat jerked.

They searched the night for flicker of campfire but saw none, saw only the distant flash of silent lightning casting its blue shimmer over the empty land. And then came a night they descriedthe bare glintings of fires to the north. They rode hard in that direction three nights running and on the third night they had closed to within two miles of their quarry. Hobbes put down a fireless camp and sent the Shawnees ahead. Just before first light they returned with the news that it was a party of forty Apaches returning home from a raid with many fresh scalps and driving a herd of some three dozen stolen horses and mules.

They struck at dawn in their usual strategy, one arm of the company led by John Allen closing from one flank and another led by Hobbes closing from the other side. They killed half the party in the first charge and pursued the others the day long before at last overhauling them at dusk at a low outcrop and there fighting them through the night and finally overcoming them at the first light of the following day. The company's only loss was one of the Shawnees and the keening of his four tribesmen was great as they sang the death song at his burial in the rocks. In addition to the forty-two scalps they took themselves they gained twenty-two more their prey had carried, and their horses and mules as well.

On their way back south they met with a band of thirty Indians of a tribe not recognized by any in the company. When the jefe of this band raised his bare hand in greeting of them John Allen said, "Looks a hostile move to me."

Hobbes drew his pistol and shot the jefe through the throat and the company fell on them and slaughtered them one and all.

8

On a hot bright August morning they trooped bloodcrusted and reeking through the gates of Chihuahua City, in that day the most prosperous trading metropolis of the Southwest. They'd hung some of the scalps on poles and bore these before them like regimental banners as they rode in to the city's clamorous reception, to cheers and flung flowers and the kisses of women and girls, to the blaring of brass bands and the shouted adoration of boys who ran alongside in the dust raised by their horses and the stock they now turned over to government wranglers for official accounting in the governor's corrals. They were guided to the governor's palace and led into the courtyard and followed by the cheering throng and there greeted with a speech most cordial and laudatory by the governor himself. They laid out their trophies on the courtyard stones and the governor's man made loud public count and when the last of the scalps was tallied the number totaled one hundred seventy-two and the acclamations of the crowd rose shudderingly to the sky. Hobbes asserted that all but thirty-one of the scalps were taken from warriors. If any thought this imbalance suspicious or wondered if every hair had in fact come strictly from Apache head none said so. Within the hour some of the scalps were dangling from the front wall of the palace and the other half from the portals of the main plaza and in both places coteries of young boys stood below and gaped in awe the whole of the afternoon.

The scalphunters repaired then to the city baths and there spent the greater part of the day scrubbing away the filth and blood and gore encrusted in the crevices of their flesh, in their ears and hair and fingernails. Spectators lined along and atop the walls nudged each other and whispered at the sight of these hairy northern barbarians in all their scarred and branded and tattooed nakedness. They pointed at Huddlestone's unpatched eyesocket and the earless side of Finn's head and the ropeburn scar around Chato's neck, at the branded number 12 over Himmler's eye and the assorted numbers on the inside of Geech's forearm and the patches of mange afflicting Castro's chest and back. So utterly ragged and befouled were these killers' clothes that only the fire would do for them. They purchased new raiment from the army of vendors arrived to besiege them. They submitted themselves to barbers of priestly demeanor and had their beards trimmed or shaved away and their wild locks shorn and even the hairs of their nose and ears were dealt with.

That evening they presented themselves each man including the Shawnees in a newly tailored suit and silk cravat in the main dining room of the palace, there to be honored and regaled by the governor who began the festivities by praising their fearlessness and martial skills yet once again. They learned now that their host country had been at war with the United States since early May, that even as they sat and drank in the palace of the governor of Chihuahua the U.S. Army was on the march to Monterrey which stood nearly four hundred miles to the southeast as the crow flies but was in fact much farther removed for being on the other side of the eastern Sierra Madre range.

"But the war is another business," the governor said in English, which was but one of the various languages he spoke admirably well, "and has nothing to do with our own." Neither he nor any man in that lavish room could know that in little more than six months Big Bill Doniphan's army of one thousand barbaric and ragged Missourians would blast into the city like the assembled wrath of God and kill and maim and wound more than one thousand Mexicans while suffering the loss of but one of their own.

The governor raised his glass high in salute to the company and they all saluted him in return. Padre Foreman was heard to whisper, "God *keep* those dear Yankee troopers . . . keep them far from our portion of this lucrative land!"

The governor now presented to Hobbes a handsome leather-and-canvas satchel bearing their recompense for the scalps and stock. Their captain's dignified aspect and the eloquent sound of his Spanish speech of acceptance impressed every man in the company even though few of them understood any part of what he said. At its conclusion even the Shawnees, who knew no Spanish at all and but few words of English, joined in the vehement applause that shivered the board's glassware.

There followed a sumptuous feast complemented by much proffering of toasts. So unrestrained was the company's subsequent libation that soon enough most of them were well drunk and calling loudly for women of ready affection. Hobbes suggested that the governor's attending officer show his men the way to the nearest well-stocked whorehouse before they surged into the streets and helped themselves to whichever women they found at hand. The governor laughed at what he was certain was the sort of rough joking one could expect from such men but then noted the absence of mirth in Hobbes's face and whispered in the ear of his adjutant. The officer clicked his heels and turned to the scalpers now pounding the table with tankards and knife heels and chanting, "*Gash!. . . . Gash!. . . . Gash!*" and raised his arms wide and proclaimed, "Attencíon, caballeros! Siguenme a la tierra prometida! Vamonos a ver las mujeres mas bonitas y mas cariñosas de la cuidad. Del mundo!" He gestured for them to follow him. "Siguenme. Siguenme por aca."

"What's that soljerboy sayin?" Geech asked Padre Foreman, who was already rising from his chair and mopping the grease from his lips with a napkin.

"Our brute but sincere prayers of supplication have been answered, me lads. It's this way to the ladies. Let's don't dally. Vita breve."

As Hobbes and John Allen rose to follow after the company the governor asked if the captain might spare a moment to speak with one Señor Aristotle Parras, who was not only the richest merchant in Chihuahua but a dear personal friend as well. He indicated an immaculately groomed little man sitting at his right hand who had spoken not a word thus far in the evening.

"Well, sir," Hobbes said, "I'm kinda itchy to attend the ladies myself at the moment, so maybe we can—"

"Please forgive my miserable manners, Captain," Señor Parras said in almost accentless English, "but I have a proposition for you that I believe you will find greatly worth your while. I am most eager to discuss it with you."

John Allen grinned at Hobbes and said, "I believe the gentleman's asking do we want to make some money, J.K."

"Please, sir, but a moment of your time," Parras said.

Hobbes shrugged and sat back down and said, "All right, mister, what's on your mind?"

9

He dreamt that night that he was drinking in a saloon hard by a transport wagon trace nearby the Del Norte River. The night was cold and wind-blown and the talk around him was of a whorehouse fire that just two weeks before killed ten of the twelve girls who worked there and burned to death as well five of their patrons. The place was called The Pink Passion and the locals were reminiscing about their favorites among the perished. He heard them tell of Jeanette with the talented cooter that could smoke a cigar. About Charlene who would give it free to any man who could last five minutes with her without coming and had not had to give a freebie but twice in three years. About Candy and Randy the red-head twins who liked to work together, whether with one man or two or three. About Eve, the moodiest and meanest of them, who some of them said was plain and simple crazy and could get a man killed quick. She liked to incite fights among the men and watch them go for each other's blood. But she was the best in the house and could damn near pull a man inside out if she was of a mood to. "Scared me, she did," one man said, "and I aint shamed to admit it. But ever time I was drunk enough, she's the one I wanted." Nods and knowing smiles all around. "She had the most scars of any gash I ever knew," said another, "but it was something about her. Ever time I had her it felt like I'd shagged the devil's wife and got away with it." They all agreed you didn't forget that one, that crazy Eve. "That nipple," someone added, "all twisted up thataway, like some-body sometime tried to bite it off. About the worst sew-up work I ever did see." He listened to them with his drink halfway to his lips and his heart thumping in his throat, his eyes cutting from one to another of them, thinking sure it was a devil's joke they had somehow figured to play on him. But they were all of them laughing and nodding at each other and paying him no mind at all. He knew then it was no joke, knew it had been her. Knew that here in this dusty patch of borderland she had burned to hell and gone. And then it was bright morning and he was striding along the trace and past the charred remains of the house and a little farther along there hove into view a cemetery. Then he was standing before the marker over the common grave where they'd laid the bones they'd found in the ashes.

THE GIRLS OF THE PINK PASSION
AND THEIR LAST RIDES

And in the mind of his dream he said: *I guess you suited well enough. Ye never cared much for talk noways.*

10

He came awake to a hand insistently shaking his shoulder. His head felt full of broken glass and his tongue savored of something dead a week. John Allen was grinning down at him through his sparse blond beard. "Let's go, lad. Captain's called a company meet in the yard below Let's up and about."

He saw the faint light of early morning in the window, then the naked brownskinned girl beside him. The girl was very pretty and she was smiling at John Allen's fondling hand at her breast.

"Hey, goddamnit!" He pushed John Allen's hand away and sat up and winced at the pain now augering his skull. John Allen kept his grin and winked at the girl, then said to Edward, "Come on, boy, let's go!" Then he was out the door and down the hall and rousting someone in a room adjacent.

They stumbled downstairs red-eyed and disheveled and exuding the rank effluvia of tequila and sexual fluids and whorehouse perfume. A half-dozen stableboys had saddled the company horses and behind each cantle tied wallets freshly packed with foodstuffs and new clean bedrolls and these boys now held the readied mounts in the brothel courtyard where Hobbes and John Allen were waiting for the men to assemble. Neither had slept at all but both looked eager for the day. Some of the men glared at them and muttered testily about spoiling a man's fun so damn early in the morning and before he could begin to enjoy his second wind.

"Say now, boys," Geech said, "lookit there them pistolas."

They saw now that each pony now carried a pair of holsters set before the pommel and each holster held a new model Colt. Hobbes had awakened the city's premier gun dealer in the middle of the night and presented him with the governor's immediate order for the guns. He now pulled a similar pistol from his own holster and held it up for all to see. "Gentlemen," he said, "I dislike to interrupt you at your fun, I do. But I want you all to look here at this new Colt."

It was a five-shooter like the Texas Colts on their hips but differed in that it had a ramming lever attached underneath the barrel. The company watched the captain closely as he put the pistol at half-cock to permit the cylinder to rotate freely and charged a chamber with powder from a flask and pushed in a ball and turned the cylinder to align the chamber under the lever and rammed the ball home. When he had thus charged all five chambers he capped them each in turn and the pistol was ready for use.

"See?" Hobbes said. "No call to take the thing apart to load the cylinder like with them Texas models. But a man wise enough to carry him a spare cylinder or two already loaded and he shoots up all five loads, then all he does is this." He pushed on a wedge key set alongside the barrel and slid the barrel and cylinder off their holding pin and swiftly exchanged cylinders and snapped the pistol together again and spun the piece on his finger as adroitly as any trick shooter. He reholstered it and spat to the side.

"Gentlemen," he said, "these pistols are the governor's present to us for the good job we done. A bonus, ye might say. Now a friend of his wants to make our hire. It's a sweet job and if we pull her off we'll be able to buy all the fun we want till we too damn old to remember how to have it. The thing is, we got to move on this right now."

He explained Parras's proposition in less than a minute and two minutes later they were all nineteen of them mounted and chucking their horses down the streets toward the gates of the city and outbound to the bloodcountry.

Three days before, a train of eighty mules bearing an immense store of merchandise from St. Louis had been attacked by a party of several dozen Apaches some thirty to forty miles northeast of the city and every member of the train killed but two. The survivors had walked the rest of the way to Chihuahua. One of them died within sight of the city and the other collapsed at the very gates. He lived only long enough to tell of the raid before dying with his head in his mother's lap. The entire train had belonged to Alexander Parras and his proposition to Hobbes was this: he could have half the mules and half the merchandise that he recovered from the Indians. Further, Parras offered to match the governor's bounty on every scalp Hobbes brought back. All Parras wanted was half of the recovery and to see those Indians' scalps on poles all around the walls of his hacienda as notice to every heathen redskin in northern Mexico of what would happen to those who robbed from him.

"We catch them red niggers we'll all be richern Midas," John Allen had told the company, and not a man among them begged to differ.

11

Hobbes sent the Shawnees ahead and they'd ridden swiftly out of sight. The company rode hard all that day and night and all the next day. In the late afternoon they arrived at the site of the attack and found one of the Shawnee outriders awaiting them. The shadows of nopal and yucca stretched long on the hardpan and the sky to the west looked awash in blood. The few mules killed in the attack still bore their goods but lay ravaged by vultures and writhing with maggots. The company collected the abandoned sacks of grain and crates of dried fruit and bore them on their pack animals to the next outcrop and there cached the goods among the rocks for retrieval on their return. Then set out on the raiders' trail leading eastward to the wasteland.

They pressed on through the night and rode through the next two days and nights and continued to come upon dead mules and disposed goods every ten miles or so and they every time cached the goods and cursed the savages for not taking better care of the animals. "Ever mule they run a lance through just cause it stumbles is one less mule we gone get to sell," grumbled Geech. "Fucken heathen sons a bitches."

They pressed on, feeding on jerky as they went and taking turns sleeping in the saddle. Late that night the land lit palely blue with lightning and then thunder blasted like cannonfire and the ensuing storm blew the rain sideways. The rain broke before morning and their horses splashed through the playa but before the sun was halfway to its meridian the land was again dry and becoming dust. They rode deeper yet into the great bolsón. On their eighth day out of Chihuahua City, as the eastern sky reddened like a fresh slow wound, a Shawnee outrider brought news that the raiders were but another day ahead at a mesa containing a spring and apparently thought themselves beyond all pursuit.

They caught sight of the mesa at sunset and hove up and waited for nightfall and then moved out quickly under a silver crescent moon with cusps upraised like horntips. They closed to within a mile of the nearest rocks and there dismounted. A pale cast of firelight was barely visible against the mesa walls. The company hooded the horses' heads with blankets and walked them to within a hundred yards of a connecting outcrop. Even at this distance they could now hear faintly the caterwaul and whoop coming from the other side of a high rockwall just ahead. Hobbes and Sly Buck went forward at a crouch and kept alert for sentries and saw none and reached the sloping rockwall and scaled it to the top as noiselessly as cats. They found themselves on a flat narrow rim with an excellent view to the Indian camp set fifty feet below in a wide mesa pocket. They were atop the pocket's eastern arm which curved around for perhaps three hundred feet and fell sheer on the side toward the camp. The opposite wall was part of the mesa's eastern face, a higher and even sheerer rockwall that extended straight and unbroken to the north for more than a mile.

Not a sentinel to be seen. A half-dozen fires blazed on the camp's sand floor. The deepest part of the pocket clearing had been roped off as a corral for the ponies and mules. Most of the mules still bore their cargo packs, though a number of packs had been broken open and lay scattered about the camp.

The savages were chanting and dancing and dressed in a carnival medley of fashions, wearing every combination of wedding dresses and top hats and overalls and hip boots and sunbonnets and vests and oil slickers and still more. Nearly every man of them had a bottle or flask in his grip and some were carrying small casks in both hands and drinking directly from the unbunged hole. Hobbes counted thirty-four of them and whispered so to Sly Buck who whispered back that there were thirty-eight. A mule lay dead with its haunches and flanks cut away and the packs it had carried lay burst apart in a wide litter of clothing. The mule meat was roasting on sticks over campfires that popped and lunged in a wayward wind and sent sparks rising up the rockface and vanishing into dark nothingness.

Now an Apache in top hat and stiff-looking overalls let a great shout and raced toward the largest of the fires and leapt over it laughing and staggered on landing and fell forward on his face and lay unmoving. The others around him laughed uproariously and grabbed up handfuls of sand and flung them at his sprawled form.

Hobbes grinned in the dark and nudged Sly Buck and they descended the slope and went back to the waiting company and told them the Apaches were drunk as coots and the time to strike was right-goddamn-now. He sent Sly Buck and his Shawnees and the Jessup brothers back to the top of the rockwall they had been on. John Allen, Huddlestone, Geech, Chato, Himmler and Holcomb he ordered to positions thirty yards east of the mouth of the mesa pocket. Then Hobbes and the rest of the company mounted up and rode north until they were out of visual range of the Apaches and then made a wide half-circle and angled back southward toward the Indian camp. When they closed to within a furlong of the mouth of the mesa pocket they hove up.

They were still under cover of darkness but could see clearly into the camp's firelit heart. Even at this distance the sight of the Apache celebration—their clownish dress and wild shrieking, their long shadows lurching and reeling along the rockface wall—struck Edward as a scene from hell's own madhouse. Hobbes dismounted and steadied his horse and braced the Hawken on the saddle and took careful aim. The rifle blasted with an orange tongue and at almost two hundred yards' distance an Apache in a planter's hat and with a woman's skirt belted around his neck like a cape left his feet in a backward arc as if performing a gymnastic feat. Even before he lit fully on the ground the rest of the Indians were racing in every direction and snatching up weapons and the Shawnees and the Jessups were shooting down on them from the rockwall above.

Every shot put down an Indian. Some of them ran for the horses and some came scampering out of the pocket with the intention of going up the slope to kill the snipers but as they came round the wall they presented themselves as stark silhouettes against the firelight behind them and John Allen's boys hardly had to aim to put down the first bunch of them with a rifle volley and then shoot the others with their pistols.

Now a dozen or so mounted Apaches came galloping out of the mouth of the pocket bearing north and away from the murderous gunfire coming from atop the rockwall and from their right flank. Hobbes and his team sat their horses in the darkness and watched the approach of the Indian riders' silhouettes and took aim on them with their rifles. When the savages closed to within thirty yards they fired a yellowstreaking fusillade that dropped the front seven horses and their riders with them and some of the ponies behind them tripped on these and went down screaming too. Now the scalphunters had pistols in hand and were urging their mounts forward and shooting every Indian to raise any part of himself from the ground. And then all of them—Sly Buck's shooters on the rock-wall and John Allen's party on the flank and Hobbes' mounted team—recharged their pieces and again shot every Apache who did not appear sufficiently dead. It was an attack of altogether perfect execution and they made short work of it.

As Edward chucked the Janey horse forward into the Indian camp the Shawnees skimmed down the rockwall as lightly as lizards and began scalping the dead. Their own technique for taking hair was to make a cut all the way around the top of the head and then sit with their feet braced on the man's shoulders and a tight two-hand hold on his hair and jerk the scalp off the skull with a wet sucking pop.

ohn Allen's shooters came jogging into the clearing, every man jaunty and loud with an ebullience peculiar to men of shared expertise in the blood arts. Some of the company set to taking acalps and some went to the mules in the corral and began rummaging through the packs to see just what it was they had come to own half of and would be selling at profit to the Chihuahua merchants. There was yet more clothing of every sort, men's suits and roughwear and suspenders and boots, dresses and parasols and women's shoes and ladies' undergarments of sundry sorts which roused cheers from this company of killers and many boastful proc-lamations of dire sexual intent on their return to Chihuahua. There were bolts of cloth in various colors and men's beaver hats and ladies' hats appointed with egret plumes as pale as cream. And yet more grain and dried fruit and sugar and angora wool and cotton, jars of preserves and candies, tins of meats and fish and sweets.

Now Geech gave a shout and from a mulepack pulled a bottle of French brandy and raised it high and the company fell to the cargo of spirits like wolves on a wounded beef. Edward joined the rush to the store of liquor and the melee thereat and fetched out a bottle of rye for himself. Had Hobbes been present at this discovery he likely would have stayed the company from the spirits until they first repacked the mules and made ready to start back to Chihuahua City at first light. Even then he likely would have held them to the sharing of a few bottles and nothing more until they were back in town where every man could addle his mind as he wished and exercise the license he desired and fend for himself with the consequence. But at the time the jubilant scalpers began unstoppering and turning up bottles of whiskey and jugs of wine their captain was with Doc Devlin on the other side of the rockwall seeing by torchlight to those in the company who had been wounded.

They were two. Himmler had taken an arrow through his calf and now lay on his belly with his teeth locked on a leather ball pouch as Doc Devlin first cut away the pointed end and then placed one foot behind Himmler's knee and the other on his ankle and carefully gripped the shaft with two hands just under the fletching of the remaining portion, setting himself to extract it with one hard pull. Himmler's face poured sweat and his jaw muscles looked like small fists and the veins bulged in his neck and across the number 12 on his forehead. As the arrow came free he let a strangled cry and arched backwards so far it seemed his spine might break and the pouch fell from his mouth on strings of saliva. His breath rushed from him and he fell forward with his face in the dirt and groaned like a man spent on a woman. Doc Devlin tossed aside the arrow portion in his hand and left Himmler to bind the wound himself.

The other casualty was a Shawnee who sat at the base of the rock slope gasping wetly with nearly a foot of the feathered end of an arrow angling down from just below his breastbone and two feet of the pointed end projecting upward from between his shoulder blades. Sly Buck stood close by without looking at him. Blood streamed from the Indian's mouth and nose and his eyes were set on some distant shore where his spirit would shortly alight. Doc Devlin stood over the man and studied his circumstance and then spoke to Hobbes who spoke in turn to Sly Buck in the Shawnee tongue. The chief made no response and the captain nodded and he and Doc Devlin walked away.

They found the company given over to riot. Castro and Geech and the Jessups were each armed with a bottle of whiskey and a knife and making bets on throws at a scalped Apache they'd sat up against the rockface some twenty feet away. One of the Jessups set himself and threw his knife in an end-over-end blur and sank it almost to the hilt in the corpse's stomach. This Jessup whooped in triumph and raised his bottle to his fellows and they all bubbled their bourbon. Padre Foreman sat pale and round beside a crackling fire, naked but for a woman's bonnet and a pair of great red drawers, smiling into the flames and imbibing from a decanter of Spanish wine. Jaggers and Huddlestone and Holcomb hefted magnums of champagne and were watching an Indian burn in the fire where they had pitched him and the smoke of this fire was greasily bittersweet.

Edward sat on a flat rock near the corral and sipped at his rye and beheld this carnival of the bloodcrazed.

John Allen appeared at Hobbes' side and made a dismissive gesture in response to the captain's glare. "I couldn't of stopped them if I tried, J.

K. You neither. I anyway figured they would of got into that liquor store somewhere between here and Chihuahua someways or other and no telling but it would come at a worst time. We best off letting them get it over and done tonight."

Hobbes stared hard at him a moment longer and then again looked about at his carousing company. "They at least take the hair already?"

"They did." John Allen pointed to the corral rope where the scalps hung dripping.

Hobbes let a long slow breath. "Well, hell. They done a smart of killing and the badger's done loose. Fuck it, John. We might's well have a drink ourself."

"Glad you feel that way, J.K.," John Allen said, and brought a full bottle of bourbon from behind his back and pressed it to Hobbes's hand.

12

They were most of them hungover and some still drunk when the captain roused the company at first light. Men had slept where they'd fallen and now raised themselves with the slow unsure action of rusted machinery, their heartbeats jabbing in their heads like cactus spines. Hobbes himself was redeyed and ensconced at the single campfire that still burned and which he'd mended to the right flame for making coffee. John Allen sat close to the fire too and nursed his own headpains with a cup of coffee laced with cornmash. The top of the mesa highwall was the color of raw beef in the first rays of the sun. The Shawnees were burying their kinsman under a shelf jutting from the lower rockwall and for the second time in his life Edward heard their quivering death song.

A few yards away sat Tom Finn, slackfaced and barechested and wild of hair, digging intently and deep down the front of his trousers. He withdrew his hand with the thumbnail and forefinger pinched together and studied his catch closely and then leant forward and pressed it into the sand and covered it over.

And now this way came Huddlestone and Holcomb and Castro, all three wretchedly besotted and trudging laboriously. As they passed by Finn, Huddlestone sneered down at him and then said something to his companions and all three men laughed lowly. Finn looked after them for a moment and then rose to his feet as smoothly as a snake uncoiling. He brandished an enormous bowie in both hands like a broadsword. Castro glanced back and saw him coming and fell aside and Holcomb too saw him and stopped walking as Finn stepped past them with the bowie over his head in the manner of one about to axe firewood. Perhaps Huddlestone heard the whisper of the blade as it descended. It clove his head with a wet *shunk!* to a point between his eye and his patched socket and for an instant they were joined, these comrades in arms, by the blade halfway through the center of Huddlestone's head and the haft tight in Finn's grip. Finn gave the bowie a grunting twist and the blade torqued apart the skulltop with a sound like sundering wood. He withdrew the blade as Huddlestone fell forward with all thoughts and plans and memories vanished from the spilling stew of his brains and blood. He lit on his face and gore jumped from his gaping head to shape a broad stain over the forward ground he never achieved.

Tom Finn turned and walked back to where his gear lay and his face read of no inward disturbance. He wiped the blade clean on his shirt and sheathed it and then put the shirt on and all the men looked to Hobbes to see what he might do. For a long moment the captain stared at Finn going about his business and then looked to Huddlestone on the ground and then he looked away from both and said: "Let's move."

Every man turned to the loading of the mules and assembly of his own outfit and within the hour the seventeen men remaining in the company set out to westward with their train of fifty-eight mules of recovered goods. Among the fallen and scalped aboriginal dead left to the gathering flock of buzzards were the cloven-skulled remains of Huddlestone whose bones the birds and coyotes would soon denude of all flesh and anyone to come upon them later would not know whose bones they had been. The bones would dry and crack and break apart in the sun and be blown over by the sand so that in time there would be no sign at all of what had once been Lonwell Pike Huddlestone of High River, Kentucky. And those few who had known him in manhood would be dead too and so not even memory of him would exist and it would be as though he had never set foot in the world.

None in the company knew the reason Finn had killed him. If Finn himself knew he did not say, not that day, which was the last left to them all but one.

13

Late that afternoon they were in the deep reach of a shimmering bolsón and sixty miles distant from the nearest ranges showing on the horizon as thin wavering lines of red stone when they spied a dust cloud swelling off the open horizon to southwestward. John Allen said that likely as not it was another wild bunch of mustangs headed for the grasslands. "Maybe so," Hobbes said. He glanced about uneasily at the utter lack of bulwark on the vast surround of hardbaked playa. He ordered a circle of pack-mules and every man drew his longarm and sat his horse inside the ring of mules and watched the dust draw nearer and billow higher and wider. It had to be a thousand head or more to raise such dust at that distance and none of them had seen a wild herd as large as that. They sat their horses and spat and watched as the first of the robust little mustangs took shape at the fore of the advancing dust and the faint thrumming of their hooves carried on the waveringly hot and dusty air.

"It's more horses than the boils on Job's ass," said John Allen. "Aint nobody can *drive* that many of them crazy jugheads. It's a wild bunch."

Now the alkaline dust rolled thickly over them and in the light of the low red sun the world assumed a crimson haze as if submerged in a blood-stained tide. The ground trembled beneath them as the pounding hooves came closer and now a mustang came racing past with tangled mane streaming and neck outstretched and eyes huge and white and froth flying from its flanks and behind it came the rest of the herd. The company's mules shied and lunged and Hobbes shouted for his men to hold the animals fast. Galloping mustangs swept past either side of the encircled company like a crashing river of horseflesh breaking round an island.

The men eased down the hammers of their guns and some resheathed their rifles and all of them grinned like lunatics in the red haze and every man among them felt kinship with this brute roving herd of the bloodland.

Then in that swirling dust they saw horses with trimmed manes and tails and with brands on their haunches and the men of the company exchanged fast looks and Edward heard John Allen yell out. He turned and saw him standing in the stirrups and staring hard into the dense red dust and there suddenly appeared a brightly fletched arrow through his neck. Allen's hand rose toward it and stopped midway and he fell forward onto his horse's neck and the animal shied and John Allen toppled dead from the saddle.

A great fluttering rain of arrows swooped upon them and mules and horses cried out and reared and broke from the train. An arrow sucked into Doc Devlin's chest. Another transfixed Castro's leg to his mount and horse and rider together went down screaming.

There came now a howling to seize the Christian heart. Out of the red dust and not eighty yards distant there appeared a horde of shrieking savages sounding like legions of Pandemonium, al in black faces and body paint of madhouse designs and brandishing bows and lances and clubs and clenching ready arrows in their teeth and even their horses were painted and seemed to be howling too with mouths open wide and huge teeth bared. A second flurry of arrows shuddered into the company before it had yet got off its first shot and another dozen mules and a scattering of horses and some of the animals in the passing herd too went down. One of the Jessups tumbled from his saddle and the Australian Holcomb grunted alongside Edward and clutched at the arrow in his arm. Hobbes was dismounted and shooting with a pistol in each hand and yelling orders never heard in that hellish din of war cries and curses and the screams of rent men and animals. The company sought cover behind fallen packmules and Edward slid off the Janey mare and ran past Padre Foreman lying prone and shooting even as a pair of feathered arrows angled from his back like fates come to roost. He threw himself behind a downed mule and fired all five rounds of his shotgun so quickly he thought he had fired but once and was enraged at the weapon and flung it aside and drew his revolver and shot a savage off his horse at twenty yards and fired again and an Indian pony went down at full gallop and flung its rider and the animal came tumbling head over heels at Edward who ducked behind the cargo pack as the paint pony went over him in a wild screaming flail of legs. He raised his head and an arrow flensed his cheekbone. And now the horde was fully on them and their demonically howling black faces everywhere and he shot one through the eye not five feet from him and then felt his chin strike the ground. His face was pressed to the sand and he wanted to rise but could not move and could not draw breath and then felt his hair clutched and his head was jerked up and directly before him was the wide-rent belly of a fallen mule and its huge welter of bloody viscera and he felt a sharp line of pain across the top of his forehead an instant before the very roof of the world ripped away and a great heaviness fell over him and then all was mute darkness.

14

And in darkness he awoke. He heard a heavy droning of flies. The crown of his head felt afire. His limbs would not obey his commands to move and he thought he was paralyzed, perhaps his spine severed, his neck broken. He knew his eyes were open but he could see nothing and so thought he was blind as well. Then his right arm flexed and he realized he was but pinioned under a heavy weight and he strained and struggled until at last he was able to wriggle out from between the dead horse and mule where he'd been snugged. He raised a raging swarm of greenflies as he came free. He felt something brush his back and he flinched and turned and saw an enormous black vulture tottering away, nodding its ugly redly naked head and holding its wings out in a perverse gesture of priestly blessing. He sat up and saw vultures everywhere in dusty twilight but could not tell if it was end of day or its beginning, could not for the moment determine east from west. He at last made out the brighter sky in the east and gained his directional bearings.

Wherever he looked was carnage. The carrion birds probed and tore and fed upon it with sounds like sloppy chuckling. He stood and swayed but held his balance. To the north he saw a long low cloud of dust that marked the savages' progress on the trail home to the high plains.

He wandered about like a drunk on ground sogged with blood and the void of animals and the rising stench might have originated in the bowels of hell. Mules and horses and men lay in grotesquely twisted attitudes. No man remained clothed or intact or unscalped. He recognized Padre Foreman's pale large-girthed corpus despite its missing face. The padre's private parts had been cut away and all other men the same. Here lay Tom Finn, yesterday's killer of Huddlestone, now tonsured to the bloody bone and with an arrow jutting from his eye and one arm hacked away. And here a Jessup sprawled and there another and vultures squabbled over the entrails of both. Yonder lay the unmistakable blackbearded remains of eviscerated Bill Jaggers who had reprieved him from prison and introduced him to the lucrative trade of Indiankilling. He found too what remained of John Allen and the Spaniard Castro. Holcomb the Australian. Doc Devlin. All of them with their forearms flayed and the bones of them removed to be fashioned into flutes for the warriors' favored children.

Himmler was gutted to the backbone and Geech so savagely mutilated Edward would not have known him but for the tattooed "Tess" over his heart. The only Shawnee he recognized as such was Sly Buck, who lay bellydown over a cargopack of rice with his hands cut away and his severed genitals stuffed in his mouth and a feathered lance in his rectum. Hobbes he found headless.

He searched for the Janey mare but saw none among the dead animals that looked like her and he reckoned the savages had her. His head was searing still and the sight of so many heads bared raw and bloody to the morning sun prompted him to put a hand to his own head and he howled at the white pain and his fingers came away sticky with coagulating blood and he knew then that among the scalps being carried in triumph back to the Comancheria was his own.

15

He scavenged intently through the slaughter and found three canteens that yet held water, one nearly half full. He found too a hat and was able to set it on his head so that no part of it pressed on his wound. He had the bowie he'd been wearing and the Colt he'd been clutching when he fell and he still had his charge pouch and he now loaded the pistol. The only packs the savages left behind contained commodities as useless to him as to them. He sliced out a portion of the flank of a horse and skinned it and cut it in strips and attached the strips to arrows to jerk in the sun.

The nearest range stood in thin red silhouette to the north-by-east and he made it for the Sierra Ponce mountains and knew that springs ran through the foothills there. He set out toward them, the meat-hung arrows stuck into his belt and positioned to catch the brunt of the sun. He walked the day long and his head flared with every heartbeat. He several times cried out against the pain and twice almost swooned and had to stop to rest. When the setting sun again bathed the bolsón in a blood-red haze the narrow line of mountains on the horizon appeared byt barely larger than when he had started for it. He had no idea how much distance he had covered. He'd gathered sticks he came upon as he walked and now had a small bundle of firewood under his arm when he put down for the night in that vast waste. He'd drunk up the two lesser canteens during the day and now vowed to take but five swallows of water from the remaining almost-half-full canteen but he took ten before he could stop. The wind blew cold and his little fire lunged and flattened and swirled and jumped like a thing desperate to escape its own essence. He roasted a few strips of horsemeat and ate them before they were fully cooked. Then he lay down and curled tight into himself and nearly howled with the pain of his scalp wound. He awoke with a start in the middle of the night and was not sure if the beast he saw in the dim cast of the moon was coyote or wolf or yet something else but in an instant it was vanished in the darkness with his horsemeat.

The next day he saw a storm raging blackly over the mountains ahead and the jagged blanched lightning and believed he could hear the faint rumble of its thunder but the rain did not come his way and he walked the day long under a relentless sun. He dreamt that night of firestorms rent with screams, of stone streets running with blood, and he wanted to wake but could not, not until the first gray line of light was showing along the east rim of the earth. He groaned to his feet and pushed on. By midday his water ran out. At sundown the mountains looked close enough to touch but he knew they were yet at least a dozen miles distant and if he did not gain them before the sun rose again he would never reach them. As he trudged on in the dark he thought he saw firelight flickering at the foot of the rockface but was not sure it was real. After a time he collapsed and got up and staggered on and then fell again and lost consciousness and did not come to until after first light. He pushed up to his hands and knees and made it to his feet and set out again toward the looming mountains. As the sun rose his tongue thickened and gagged him and he knew the next time he fell would be the last.

And now riders came toward him from the mountains. Three of them. Advancing slowly as if on the surface of a vast shimmering lake. He was afraid to stop walking for fear he would fall but when they drew within fifty yards he stopped and swayed and was surprised to feel the weight of the Colt in his hand and the hammer cocked under his thumb. When they closed to ten yards they reined up and studied him for a long moment. Then one of them, a Mexican with a flat-crowned black sombrero and a long droopy mustache put his horse forth another few yards and grinned at him with white perfect teeth. His eyes made inventory of him, pausing on the pistol in his hand.

"Hello, my friend," he said. His accent was pronounced but not as heavy as most Edward had heard from Mexican mouths. "You must are very tired, no?"

Edward shrugged. His lips were swollen and cracked and he did not want to speak if he didn't have to.

The Mexican unslung a canteen from his huge saddlehorn and heeled

his horse forward and handed it down to him. It was full and heavy and
Edward unstoppered it and raised the neck to his mouth and hesitated
and then gently put it to his lips. The pain jumped into his eyes and he
shut them hard and drank and gagged and nearly vomited the water. He
fought down the gagging and then took smaller, more careful sips. He
paused for breath and then sipped again.

"Basta," the Mexican said, and reached down for the canteen but Edward clutched it to his chest and stepped back quickly and nearly fell.
The Mexican quit his grin and his eyes thinned. He gestured impatiently
with his outstretched hand. "Damelo, muchacho." Edward took one
more drink and handed up the canteen and the Mexican stoppered it and
hung it on his saddlehorn.

"We see you desde ayer," the Mexican said. "Desde—how you say?—
yesserday. My friends, they say you don't reach la montaña, but me, I
say you do. We say, ah, una apuesta." He paused and turned to the other
two and said, "Una apuesta?"

Edward saw that one of the other two was a white man in a gray duster
with a pair of pistols at his belt. This one said, "A bet."

The Mexican turned backto Edward and said, "We say a bet. And you
have make me win." He showed the great white grin.

"I aint—" Edward began, his voice a croak, his cracked lips beading
with blood. He swayed and caught himself. "I aint there yet."

The Mexican laughed. "Pues, I think you are sufficiente close. I think
so, yes."

Edward thought this was funny and wanted to laugh but his legs gave
out and he fell forward and his hat came off and he heard a sharply
uttered "Jesus goddamn Christ!"

And a softly spoken "Ay Chihuahua!"

16

They laid him in the shade of a rock overhang and gave him more water
and a portion of food and treated his wounds except for his savaged scalp
for which nothing could be done.

"Your head's festering and you got a mean fever. I guess you'll either
die of it or you won't. But hell, I knew a fella was scalped to the bone
by Kiowas and lived to tell the tale for years till he choked to death on
one a his wife's biscuits."

Speaking was Jack Spooner, the sole white man in that gang of eighteen until now. "Even if you don't die you won't have need of any more
barbers or be turning the ladies' heads, that's sure." He studied Edward's
mutilated cheek for a moment, then his remaining portion of ear. "I gotta
say, boy, you missin more pieces off your head than just about any living
man I ever seen." He turned and spat and looked off to the open country
and then looked at Edward again. "We're ridin out tomorrow so we aint
gonna know if you live or die unless you ride with us. Manuel says you
can if you want."

"Who's Manuel?" Edward asked.

"The chief," Spooner said. He gestured toward the Mexican who had
given Edward water out on the playa. He was sitting in the shade of
another rock with several others, gesticulating, laughing with them at the
tale he told.

"I got no outfit," Edward said. His crown felt as if live coals were
pressing upon it.

"We'll outfit you. You can pay the chief for it later. If you die I don't
guess he'll hold you to accounts."

They rested that day and through the night there in the foothills of the
Sierra Ponce just south of the del Norte. The downcountry flatland was
bone-white under a pale half-moon and the Carmen range stood starkly
purple in the east. Comets described bright amber streaks across the black
void and vanished from existence in the same instant they appeared.

The gang was up before dawn and made ready to move out. Edward
was redeyed and dizzy with fever. The chieftain walked up to him trailing
his horse and grinned and asked if he was sure he wanted to go with
them. "Maybe you want be here hasta los Comanches come otra vez.
Maybe you want for to kill all them for because they kill you friends."

That got a laugh from the two or three other Mexicans who understood
English and they told the rest what the chief had said. All of them laughed
and slapped one another on the shoulder and pointed at Edward and
rubbed the crowns of their heads and laughed harder still. Spooner
smiled. Edward felt as if the world were slightly atilt under his feet and
he could not quite get his proper balance. All things looked to him sharp-
edged and hot to the touch in the red light of the rising sun. Every man
appeared swathed in a haze of a different hue. He felt becrazed.

He grinned through his pain to go along with the joke. He said he took
revenge only against insults and although the savages had killed his companions and taken his scalp they had at least known better than to risk

insulting him. He grinned like a lunatic as Spooner translated for the compañeros who howled with glee and pointed at him and tottered like drunks in their laughter and some made "fuck you" gestures toward the Comancheria to the north. They nodded at each other and agreed that Eduardo was muy chistoso y muy simpático, these dark-skinned hot-eyed men shaped of the violent mix of pagan Indian blood with that of the carriers of the Spanish Cross. Their teeth flashed white under thick black mustaches and every man of them was scarred of face and hands. They were loud in talk and laughter, in curses and melancholy song. They bore weaponry of every sort—firearms and knives and machetes, and some carried lances and some wore cavalry sabers and all of them expert with lassos to take a man off his horse and drag him to raw meat behind their galloping mounts. Some carried scalps strung on their saddlehorns but even in his fever Edward noted that much of the hair was shot with gray and had been taken by unpracticed hands.

Dominguez the chieftain was a Poblano, a man of the city of Puebla, which lay far to the south some sixty-five miles beyond the capital and whose beauty he said could not adequately be described in the words of any language but that of the heart. At the age of fifteen he had concluded that it was unjust for someone so handsome and strong and smart as himself to be so poor while so many fat, weak, stupid men were so rich. So he set about righting the scales of justice and quickly progressed from preying on drunks in the late-night streets to robbing isolate travelers on the mountain roads to holding up stagecoaches along the main highways. He'd been at the robber's trade six months when he got a price on his head for killing a diligence guard who refused to throw down the strongbox and grabbed instead for a shotgun. Other killings followed. When he was twenty-two he killed a famous bandit chief named Manolo Gomez in a knifefight in a cantina fronting Orizaba's main plaza and then dragged the body outside and dismembered it with a machete and scattered the bloody pieces to the plaza dogs. By the time the sun went down the town balladeers had composed a song about the fight and would sing of it for generations to come. Dominguez's reputation as a fearsome killer of men had thereafter grown swiftly.

He formed his own gang and over time it became the most notorious of the dozens of robber gangs ranging the high country between Mexico City and the Gulf, a region long infamous for banditry. The gangs became so rampant that no traveler or train of pack mules or cargo wagons was safe from robbery along either of the two major highways between the capital and Veracruz. The government assigned more and still more lancers to escort the wealthy merchants' trains and to patrol the main roads. Soon the richest trains were routinely protected by entire regiments and were virtually unassailable. Judicial formalities had furthermore been much relaxed and men only suspected of banditry as well as known bandidos were often executed on the spot of arrest. Highway robbery became such perilous enterprise that Dominguez and his band departed to the northern badlands where there was easy money to be made killing Indians—or so they had heard.

That had been a year ago. And the money did not prove so easy. Dominguez's trackers were unequal to the Apache and the gang never collected more than a dozen scalps at a time and most of the hair was of women and children and frail old men. Come autumn they were attacked by a huge war party in the Sierra del Hueso and of the gang's fifty-two men only eighteen escaped with their lives. The survivors repaired to El Paso to tell of their harrowing adventure and drink and whore away the last of their money. There they heard that the American army had defeated the Mexican forces at Monterrey the month before and the gringos now occupied the city. The Yankee supply trains from the Río Bravo into Nuevo León were said to be rich pickings for those with the balls to rob them.

Nuevo León was where the compañeros were headed when they spied the dust of the gringo mule train and then the greater dust of the savages closing upon it. The outriders came back at a gallop, wide-eyed and yelling of Comanches, and the gang sped to the refuge of the mountains and from there watched the dust of the Comanche attack on the gringo train. By evening the dust began to settle, and early the following morning the Indians resumed their northward trek for home. The compañeros held to their hiding place in the rocks and the next morning watched the Comanches pass by within a half-mile of their position, driving the stock before them, laughing and yipping, every brute of them coated with blackened blood and gore and their stink carrying into the mountain, many with scalps dangling from lances and some with blood-crusted heads strung from their ponies. Dominguez said they looked like devils heading home to hell. The compañeros waited the rest of that day and through the night to be sure they were well gone and at daybreak made ready to ride. But in the red light of sunrise they descried Edward's distant figure slouching toward them like the incarnation of their own folly in having come to this wasteland to chase their fortune.

"You are very much lucky," Dominguez said to Edward as they rode side by side. On Edward's other side rode Pedro Arria, a hawkfaced man who had been with Dominguez since his earliest bandit days and was the company's second in command. "All you friends they are died, but no you. Only you no die. Que buena suerte, hijito. Very much lucky, you."

"Yeah," Edward said. "I feel just awful damn lucky."

Dominguez laughed.

17

His next days were hazed with fevered pain, his sleep haunted by visions from hell which he then would recognize as out of his own recent past. At the village of Boquillas they took a night's respite. Pulque eased his suffering until morning and then heightened it with hangover, but his fever broke at last and some of the compañeros reluctantly paid off bets, arguing hopefully but without much conviction that the gringo might yet take a turn for the worse and die. The villagers thought him the most fearsome in the bunch because of his butchered head, the wound to his face where the cheekbone showed pale under the tight new growth of skin. Only the devil's spawn, they whispered to one another, could survive such savage wounds. There was little tribute the gang could exact from the frighted inhabitants save dried meats and clean clothes. And then they rode on. That evening two of them fell into dispute over ownership of a shirt and knives came into play. The fight fell off when one staggered away into the dark with his hands holding in place his exposed intestines. The other sat down by a campfire, grinning in victory and clutching at his slashed neck as the blood ran blackly down his arm and fell in gleaming bulbous drops and hissed on the firestones and its vapor smelled sickly sweet. A few minutes later he let a gurgling sigh and slumped over and was dead. One of the compañeros removed this man's boots and left his own worn ones there beside him and another took his pistol and knife but none made a move to bury him. A short while later they heard coyotes calling and drawing close in the night and then came the high howl of a wolf and the coyotes fell silent. In the morning they mounted up and hupped their horses to southeastward, A quarter-mile out on the hardpan they passed by the other one lying dead also, his abdomen hollowed of viscera. On a flanking ridge above them they spied a lone pale lobo looking down on their passing with its ears erect and its muzzle stained darkly red, but no man among them even thought to shoot at this wolf or any other ever.

They rode up into the blood-colored Carmens and wound through juniper forests and past century plants with stalks double the height of their horses. His scalp was scabbing now and the pain of it lessened every day. Fredo Ruiz, a rarity of a hulking mestizo and the largest of the compañeros, presented him with a wide black bandanna and showed him how to tie it over his head like a pirate headpiece to protect his crown from curious eyes whenever he removed his hat.

Over the next weeks they rode through the high country and its steep passes and deep gorges, rode along narrow mountainside trails that looked out to the ends of the earth. They could see below them the outspread wings of hawks circling slowly on the hunt. They camped on tablerocks and the flames of their fires played drunkenly in the wind. Now and then in the depths of the desert night they could see the tiny winking lights of other fires, though whether of pilgrims or savages or denizens of another world none would hazard to guess.

They came down in single file through a sequence of deep barrancas and rocky switchbacks overhung with piñon and catclaw and mountain cypress. The air was wet and blued with mist. Occasionally there came from the shadowed high rock the screech of a cougar that raised the hair on their napes and frighted the horses. Riding through this mean country of stone and sand and thorn, Edward felt himself drawing toward a reckoning he could not bypass whatever road he took.

They debouched at last onto the bajada. The horizons shimmered at midday and icy winds gusted through their night camps and their fires swirled and lunged and trailed furious lines of sparks into the darkling void. They rode long days through spiny growths of sotol and ocotillo and lechugilla and in a dusky twilight blinking with fireflies came to the village of Nacimiento on Christmas Eve of 1846. Here they learned that in the past months more than two thousand Yankee soldiers under command of a general named Wool had marched down from the presidio at the Río Bravo and crossed the river just forty miles ahead near the village of Sabinas. Their dust had been visible to the east for weeks. These gringo troops were now at Monclova seventy-five miles south and awaiting orders from Taylor in Monterrey. The compañeros listened to the news and feasted on cabrito and got drunk on mescal and several of them fought among themselves but none killed another and the combatants seemed the more refreshed afterwards despite their battered aspects. But tempers stayed short through the evening and the air remained charged with ready violence. Dominguez sat with Pedro, Spooner and Edward at a table against the back wall of the little cantina and his own face sagged with drink. He watched his men and sighed and said they had to find somebody to rob soon or most of them would start killing each other out of boredom.

18

Just south of Sabinas they waylaid a passenger coach in a chilly drizzling rain. At the sight of them the two mounted guards threw down their weapons and raised their hands as did the guard beside the driver. The box contained two hundred pesos in silver, all else was contracts and deeds and various other papers of no use at all to the bandits. Dominguez ordered the passengers out of the coach and had a compañero named Chucho search them for weapons and valuables. One of the five passengers was a woman of passing attraction enfolded in a hooded cloak, the wife of a prosperously dressed man at her side. After Chucho searched the man and extracted a small purse bearing eighty pesos in gold coin, he turned to search the woman. But the husband stepped between them and told Chucho he most certainly could not put his hands on her. Chucho pulled his pistol and looked up at Dominguez sitting his horse. Dominguez told the man it would be best for him if he permitted his wife to be searched, but the man said absolutely not. Dominguez shrugged and turned to Edward and said, "Mátalo," and made a shooting gesture with his thumb and index finger

He knew he should have expected it. Of course they would test him. Of course he would have to show he was of them. For a moment he thought of himself as one who had never killed in cold blood and then remembered some of the harmless Indians in whose slaughter he had joined. Still, those were Indians. This was an unarmed white man standing there and wanting only to protect his wife. He drew the Colt and pointed it at the man.

"Mira esa bonita pistola!" Dominguez said to Pedro Arria, admiring the five-shooter.

The man gently pushed his wife out of the line of fire, then glared up at Edward and said, "Crees que te tengo miedo, gringo? Nunca! *Nunca*, maldito!"

Edward cocked the weapon and sighted between the man's eyes and wondered how he might explain if he chose not to shoot. It occurred to him all in an instant that it made no real difference whether he shot this man or not, just as it made no difference why he did so if he did. In time both he and this man would be dead and all trace of their existence long vanished. It would be as if neither had ever existed at all. And yet they *did* exist, both of them, *now*, and although a man might do what he did in his time of existence simply because it was in his blood to do it, he might sometimes have the choice of rejecting his blood's urging. And so, at this moment, he could choose *not* to shoot.

What his choice of the moment would have been he would never know because just then the woman brought a small two-shot pistol from under her cloak and fired at him. Edward's hat brim twitched and his horse shied and he shot her through the top teeth. In the same instant Fredo shot the husband. And then all of them were shooting and wrestling with their spooked mounts and every passenger fell down bloodied and some screamed in the gunfire and the thickening mist of powdersmoke. The two mounted guards reined their horses around to escape and Edward shot one down and Dominguez dropped the other. The guard on the coach fired with a pistol and one of the compañeros toppled from his horse and Edward shot the guard and blood jumped from his neck and he fell from the coach as the driver stood up with his hands held high but Fredo shot him too.

Now some of the bandidos dismounted and used knives to finish those of the coach party who still drew breath. The fallen compañero had been shot in the stomach and his shirt was brightly thick with blood. Pedro Arria was bent over him, examining the wound, and now he looked up at Dominguez and shook his head.

"No! No, jefe!" the wounded man cried up to Dominguez. "Estoy bien! Ya lo verás, jefe!" He grunted painfully with the effort of trying to rise and then fell back with a grimacing moan.

Dominguez motioned Pedro Arria out of the way and raised the spare caplock already cocked in his hand. He leaned forward from the saddle and aimed carefully and shot the wounded man through the eye.

They rifled the pockets and purses of the dead and some could not resist fondling the woman as they pretended to search her yet again lest the previous searchers missed something. A few among them would not have been above ravishing her before she cooled had not so many of their fellows been present. A young compañero named Gustavo who had once studied in a seminary stood over the bodies and remarked aloud that it was interesting to see how the termination of these human lives now provided such abundant aliment for the ants and flies and the buzzards soon to appear. "De verdad nada se desperdice en este mundo," he said. "Todo que occure tiene algún resulto bueno." His fellows smiled at his banalities with avuncular indulgence though some were ever wary of him as one who had been maddened by the conflict between his abiding reverence for God's mysterious workings and his readiness to kill any of His creatures.

They took the guards' weapons and freed the coach team from its traces and strung the horses on a pair of lead ropes. As they recharged their arms Dominguez offered Edward fifty silver dollars for the Colt. Edward said he would not sell it—and then presented it to the jefe as a gift. Dominguez was effusive with gratitude and in turn gave Edward three fine caplock pistols and a .50 caliber Hawken with a sawed-off barrel charged with two dollars in silver dimes.

19

They followed the Río Sabinas to its junction with the Salado and held to the Salado's southeast course and arrived at the village of Anahuac on an afternoon bright with sun and piled high with deep white clouds. Flocks of grackles squawked in the trees and mangy dogs slank along the building walls and squealing children trotted beside the company's horses. The Laredo Road was another twenty-five miles downriver but the villagers informed them that the main American supply line to Monterrey was the Camargo Road, another fifty miles beyond the Laredo route. A large American army camp sited at Camargo, on the southern bank of the Río Bravo, was the major transfer point for Yankee supplies to General Taylor. The villagers had heard that the gringos were getting ready to move from Monterrey to Saltillo for a battle with Santa Anna and the road from Camargo was said to be heavy with wagon traffic bearing Yankee supplies.

Dominguez thanked them for the information and then told the compañeros to take from the village whatever they needed by way of commissary. Some of the compañeros forced the villagers to trade fresh sarapes or shirts or sombreros for their tattered own, and some went from hut to hut and stripped each one of its meager store of food. They took

all the jugs of mescal from the village's single cantina. Some paid a few
centavos for what they took and one or two who could write laughingly
scribbled notes of hand, but the more brutish among them spat into the
palms held out to them for payment. The village elders protested and
Dominguez politely apologized but told them his first duty as a chieftain
was to the welfare of his men. The few citizens so rash as to resist the
thievery were beaten to the ground. A dog composed of little more than
hide and bones barked and barked at them from the corner of a house
until Pedro Arria shot it dead and the quiet that ensued was greater than
that of the silenced dog and hung behind them as they rode away.

20

They found the Laredo Road but sparsely traveled. Only woodcutters and
parties of Mexican army scouts occasionally passed by. The gang moved
away from the river and rode south for the Camargo route. Two days
later at the Río Alamo they came upon a trio of Mexican cavalry scouts
replenishing their canteens at the bank. Two of the scouts stood and
turned just as the compañeros drew out their pistols on Domin-guez's
signal and opened fire. The two were knocked back into the water and
the third received his bullets while still kneeling and he too fell in the
shallow river. The hair of the dead soldiers wavered in the current and
blood rose off their wounds in red swirls and carried downstream. They
pulled the bodies from the water and went through their pockets and
Spooner claimed a pair of cavalry boots for himself and announced them
to be a perfect fit. They chased down the soldiers' horses and some of
the compañeros laid claim to the saddles and quickly strapped them onto
their mounts in place of their old broken ones. They added the army
animals to the company caballada.

Dominguez stood at the riverside and sang softly as he flicked powder
residue from the Colt and recharged the chambers. He saw Edward looking at him and smiled. Edward gestured at the dead Mexican soldiers
and said, "I figured you and them was on the same side."

The chieftain smiled uncertainly, his brow furrowed in confusion.
"Same side?" he said. He looked at the fallen soldiers and appeared to
consider Edward's question and then spat toward them and looked back
at him and said, "Me and *they? Noooo*. Not same side. Somos enemigos!"
He laughed and turned toward the compañeros and swept his arm to

include them all. "*My* side, Eduardito. *I* my side, *they* my side. You, tambien! *You* my side."

He grinned at Edward like a brother wolf.

21

They came the following afternoon to the Camargo Road and spent a few days reconnoitering. Some days later they attacked a poorly guarded American pack train and killed a half-dozen soldiers before the rest fled in the wake of the muleteers. The compañeros made away with a wagonload of Hall percussion rifles and two cases of Colt five-shooters and mules loaded with powder and ammunition. They armed themselves anew and sold the rest of the weaponry and the mules to a ranchero band operating out of the Magdalena Hills.

They remained in the region for the next three months. When U.S. trains were too well-guarded the company would set upon Mexican army or civilian transports, though these were never so lucrative in their yield as the Yankee trains. They recruited new members and at one point their band numbered nearly fifty but their ranks were always thinned in fights with the Americans. Then their number would again grow slowly.

During this time Edward learned to speak a passable Spanish although his natural reticence kept him from practicing the language sufficiently to allay his wretched accent. He habitually kept his own company. During respites between the company's forays he took to riding up into the higher country, to rimrocks facing west for miles to the wilder reaches of the sierras. He'd sit his horse and stare out to the horizon as the sky turned red as a jagged gash in the dying light of the sun. Had he been asked what thoughts he had while gazing on this ancient bloodland his only true answer would have been a howl.

On a chilly afternoon in January they went to Saltillo to attend the hanging of a compañero named Carlito Espinosa. He'd been shot off his horse and taken prisoner during their raid on a Mexican army pack train traversing the sierras between Victoria and Saltillo. The regional commander wanted him made an example to all other bandidos in the region and so announced his execution date and invited the populace at large to attend. The gang entered the town in scattered groups of three and four in order not to attract attention. They entertained no notion of rescuing Carlito, so grossly outnumbered were they by the garrison troops.

The streets were chockablock with soldiers ahorse and on foot and all of them grim of aspect. The gang sought only to bear witness to their compañero's execution. They joined the swelling crowd in the central plaza. A large alamo tree stood in the center of the square, the bark of its main branch scarred by the hanging ropes of generations. The air was festive. Music and song mingled with shouted talk and children's laughter and the hawking cries of street vendors. The redolence of roasting chiles and charcoaled meats carried through the plaza.

When Carlito was brought out in a flatbed wagon some of the spectators hissed and flung mudballs at him and some laughed and made loud jokes about his hanging. The compañeros made no show of knowing the condemned. Carlito stood in the wagon and a priest gave him final absolution and the hangman put the noose around his neck. The officer in charge asked if he had any last words. Carlito said, "Chinga tu madre!" The officer went redfaced and the compañeros had to stifle their laughter. The officer loudly proclaimed to the spectators that sooner or later all bandidos were killed or captured and this was what became of the captured. The children, especially, he said, should let it be a lesson to them.

His remarks drew applause and whistles of approval. The officer signaled to the teamster on the wagon seat. The teamster cracked his whip and the wagon rolled out from under Carlito and the crowd cheered lustily as he kicked the air. A second later he abruptly went slack in the way only the dead can do and he oscillated slowly under the tree limb, his pants freshly stained, his eyes upturned and solid white, his tongue bulging from his enpurpled face.

Watching Carlito suspended from the alamo branch Edward remembered a distant time when he had seen a Negro lynched in Mississippi, he and his brother John, and the thought of John reminded him of a recent dream in which he'd seen his brother wandering in a deep wood, the top of his skull flensed to the bone and his head cauled in blood. And in this dream he had again heard Daddyjack's voice crying, "Blood *always* finds blood. Ye best know it for the truth."

22

In February Taylor took his army to engage Santa Anna at Buena Vista. The skeleton force he left in Monterrey was hardly adequate to police the region and over the next few weeks the compañeros had their most lucrative raids yet along the Camargo Road north of Monterrey. They stole payrolls and clothes and food and new tack, stole horses and guns and ammunition which as always they sold to other bandits and to bands of Comancheros. Sometimes Edward and Spooner were recognized as Americans by surrendered Yankee guards who cursed them for traitors to the Stars and Stripes. Spooner was oblivious to their insults but Edward was incensed at being condemned by men who accepted army punishment as a natural condition of life. On one occasion he threatened to shoot a sergeant who would not leave off his slurs. The sergeant spat at him and said, "I bet you a goddamn dollar you won't shoot no real soldier when he's lookin ye square in the eye!" Edward lashed him across the mouth with the barrel of his pistol and the sergeant fell to all fours and spat bloody teeth. Edward asked if he had anything more to say and the man shook his head. He dug a silver dollar from his pocket and dropped it at the sergeant's knees.

Spooner laughed and said, "Damn, bubba, if you aint the sportsman."

They sometimes sneaked into Monterrey in groups of a half-dozen or so to sport in the city's finest whorehouses. For most of the compañeros it was a time of spree and prosperity never to be equaled in their lives.

Taylor returned to Monterrey in March, there to stay until the end of the war, and the gringo army patrols on the Camargo Road became more numerous than ever. On three consecutive raids the gang was driven off from a cargo train by the sudden arrival of Yankee dragoons and in every instance a dozen or more compañeros were killed or captured.

The compañeros had been reduced to eighteen when word came of General Winfield Scott's landing at Veracruz and his bombardment of the city into submission. When he heard the news Dominguez felt greatly cheered. Now the Yankee advance on Mexico City would be through his patria chica, the region of his birth and boyhood, through the lower eastern ranges of the Sierra Madres that he knew as well as he knew his own hands. The American supply trains would have to follow Scott up into the rugged high country where passage was difficult. It would be much easier to ambush them in the mountains and then elude pursuers than it had been in Nuevo León.

"In the mountains there," he told Edward, "they will never to catch us. I know *many* good hide places en esas montañas." The Mexican merchant trains would also be easier to rob now because every Mexican soldier would be needed to defend against Scott and far fewer of them would be assigned to guard the transports.

The whole gang was happy to be going south. That night they sat around the main fire in high spirits and drank mescal and each put five pesos in a hat and were agreed that he who told the best story would win the pool of money. Edward pitched into the hat but passed on a turn at a story. Most of the stories were morally didactic and the compañeros received them with nodding accord. The winning tale was told by the oldest member of the bunch, a graybeard named Lorenzo who was an uncle of Manuel Dominguez. He said the tale was told to him many years ago by his grandfather in Puebla who had heard it from his Spanish grandfather in Guanajuato who had heard it from an English mineowner. His tale was of three bandits who came upon an old man sitting by the side of the road one evening and decided to kill him for sport. The old man was but skin and bone and looked ready for the grave but he pleaded for his life. He said that if they would spare him he would reveal where he had hidden a strongbox full of gold. The bandits grinned and winked at each other and said all right, and the old man gave them directions to a hill a few miles away and told them the gold was buried under the highest tree atop the hill. The bandits thanked him and then killed him anyway. And then for lack of anything better to do they sought out the hill he had told of and dug under the highest tree and were astonished to discover a large strongbox full of gold, just as the old man had said. They laughed and hugged each other and danced all about, singing that they were rich. But the gold was too heavy to carry away all at once and so they decided to sleep there that night and in the morning figure out how to move the treasure to a safer place. The two older bandits then sent the youngest back into town for a bottle of tequlia with which to celebrate their good fortune and defend against the night chill. While the youngster was away these two talked things over and agreed that it made much greater sense to split the gold two ways rather than three, and so when the boy got back from town with the tequila they killed him. They then uncorked the bottle and toasted their rich futures and each took a deep drink and both suddenly felt a great pain in their bellies and fell down and died from the poison the boy had added to the tequila after deciding in town that he wanted all the gold for himself.

The compañeros laughed knowingly at this tale's ironic truth and applauded vigorously. Some pointed at others and said, "Esos tontos eran exatamente como tú!" And those pointed at affected astonishment and said, "Como yo? Carajo! Como tu!"

In the morning they were ahorse before sunrise and riding downcountry on an old burro trail well removed from the main road and the gringo army patrols roaming over it.

23

Southeast of Linares they came over a low sandrise and spied a pair of large covered wagons halted a half-mile ahead. A stiff wind tugged at their clothes and they wore their hats pulled low against the stinging sand. The overhead sun was huge and orange in the dusty haze. The two wagons were each pulled by a pair of mules but one of the animals of the lead wagon was holding up a foreleg and a party of six women and two men were gathered about the injured beast. One of the women caught sight of the riders and pointed at them and all the party turned to look their way and most then glanced around as if seeking somewhere to hide. But the land about was flat sandy scrub to the distant mountains and so they could but stand beside the wagon and watch the eighteen riders coming on.

One of the men was a muscular Negro in a sleeveless shirt, the other a tall clean-shaved white man in a yellow duster, and as the gang drew closer they saw that although the women were dressed in the Mexican style of loose colorful cotton skirts and bare-shouldered white tops they were all of them American and young and most of them pretty. The horsemen broke into grins and some whistled and raised a fist to each other and one said, "Ay, que bonita compañía de putas! Y puras gringas!"

"Esas gringas son tan puras como una pocilga," Pedro Arria said and they all laughed.

They reined up before the party and sat their horses and the white man shielded his eyes with his hand against the blowing sand and said in English, "Amigos! Hello, amigos, hello!" His face was tight with apprehension until he saw that two among this band of dusky mustached men appeared to be of his own race and he bellowed at them, "Howdy, boys! Damn good to see some fella Americans hereabouts!" He carried a pistol on his belt but the black man was unarmed. Some of the girls looked frightened but others boldly returned the grinning Compañeros' carnivorous leers. The injured mule had a broken leg, a compound fracture of a fore cannon, and the jagged ends of the break showed through the bloody hide. The animal stood in its traces with the bad leg held off the ground and seemed to be staring into its own unconveyable experience of the world.

"I was warned I ought not take this damn sandland route," the man said, addressing himself to Spooner and Edward in a strained voice striving for familiarity, "specially not with mules instead of oxen. But I just figgered they was exaggerating, the way folk tend to do. *Now* looka here this mule. Stepped in a hole yonder you got to practically step into youownself before you can see it. Bone just went *pop!* like busting a scantling under a boot heel." He looked at the mule with disgust, as if the animal had deliberately maimed itself simply to irritate him.

He introduced himself as Gene Segal of Tennessee by way of Mississippi and freely volunteered that he was in the whore business. The previous summer he'd recruited a dozen American girls in Louisiana and Texas to come with him and make their fortune servicing Old Rough and Ready's troops down on the Río Grande. But by the time they got there Taylor had moved the bulk of his force some eighty miles upstream from Fort Brown to Camargo on the tributary San Juan about three miles below its Río Grande junction. Segal and his whores made their slow way over a rough wagon trace and came at last to the American camp which proved a pesthole even in comparison to Fort Brown. The soldiers were elated to have these American cyprians come to ply their trade but life in Camargo had made their tempers raw as open sores and on the very night of the whores' arrival a pair of soldiers got in a fight over one of them and the bloodied loser limped away into the night only to reappear a few minutes later with pistol in hand and fire on his assailant but he was too drunk to shoot straight and instead hit the girl in the neck and killed her. The next day Segal solicited General Taylor for reimbursement for his loss of property and was laughed out of Old Zack's tent. A week later one of the other girls got her face and breasts razored badly by a drunken corporal who cursed her and repeatedly called her by the name of his faithless sweetheart back in Arkansas. This girl didn't die but the episode left her so badly disfigured and so unenthusiastic toward the trade that Segal was obliged to put her on a steamer back to Galveston.

Before they'd been at Camargo a month he lost two other girls to sickness. "You never did see such a place for sickness," Segal said, looking up at the half-circle of riders sitting their horses and staring down on him and the Negro without a trace of fellowship on their faces and all of them casting looks at the girls like dogs eyeing freshly butchered meats. The whoreman had been talking fast in his obvious belief that a steady flow of words might hold these men at bay. The Negro at his side didn't know where to look.

Segal said so many of Old Zack's troops had made use of the muddy and sluggish river for everything from a horsewash to a laundry to a latrine that the San Juan had quickly become a cesspool, and yet it served for the camp's drinking and cooking water. Hardly a man in camp was unafflicted by diarrheal distress the soldiers called the "blues." There was no escaping the stink of shit within five miles of the camp. The most common complaint from Segal's whores was of men fouling the bed as they humped. Dozens of soldiers were stricken daily by dysentery, yellow fever, measles, typhus, God knew what. The hospital tents were always full and the groaning carried through camp day and night. At every dawn and sundown the dead were taken from the tents and heaped on carts and trundled to the burying ground. Anybody with eyes, Segal said, could see that more troops would die of disease in this forsaken country than would ever be killed at Mexican swordpoint. Except for the two girls who took sick and died, however, the rest of his whores seemed immune to everything save the common venereal afflictions.

"When General Zack left for Monterrey, we followed along," Segal said, "and I tell you, once our boys took that town we did a better business than ever."

Dominguez watched the whoreman as if he were an enthralling freak of nature on par with a talking dog, but most of the compañeros now paid the gringo little mind, being far more interested in the smiling girls and stepping their horses nearer to them.

Segal and his party had then tailed Taylor's army to Saltillo and provided respite to the boys at Buena Vista, then returned to Monterrey in Taylor's wake. But by now other American whoremen had showed up with their stables and the Mexican clergy were complaining loudly that the Yankee cyprians were a disgrace to their noble city. Because he was trying to maintain cordial relations with the local population Old Zack ordered all the American whores and their mongers out of town. Some of the operations set up in tents just outside the city but Segal had heard that Taylor's next move would be to Victoria and he wanted his troupe to be among the first to get there. Rather than take the well-traveled Monterrey-San Luis Road down to Salado and then cutting through the pass to Victoria, Segal thought to take a shortcut via Linares and the open country to the south of it. They'd been trudging over that flatland for more than a week when the mule broke its leg not an hour ago. Segal scowled at the crippled animal whose breath was coming hard and whose eyes were white and rolling.

"Porqué no han matado esa mula?" Dominguez said.

"Why aint you shot that mule?" Spooner asked the whoreman.

"We was just talking about doing it, me and the Ethiopian here, when you fellas come along. We was thinking maybe—"

"Chingados!" Dominguez snarled. He pulled his Colt and shot the mule twice through the head and the whoreman flinched and the horses shied as the dead mule crashed to the ground in its traces and the girls squealed and huddled closer together.

Dominguez spat and reholstered the pistol. "Dijo que eran ocho," he said. "Donde están las otras?"

"You said it was eight of em," Spooner said to Segal, "but we don't count but six of the little darlins here."

"Two of em took sick just before we left Monterrey this last time," Segal said, speaking even faster than before. "Worked in that pesthouse of a Camargo camp for weeks and didn't neither of em even say a-choo and then they both of a sudden turn sick as dogs and been steady puking and shitting and just generally making a smelly awful mess so I put em in the other wagon by theirselfs and let the nigger drive it and hope none the other girls catch it from em. But I swear I'm bout ready to leave them two by the side of the road someplace cause it aint no damn hospital train nor deadcart I'm—"

"Is any a these sweeties sick?" Spooner asked. He smiled at the girls. They were grinning at the compañeros and letting the wind swirl their skirts up high on their thighs and folding their arms under their breasts to swell them in the low-necked Mexican blouses.

"*These* here girls? No sir, nary one," Segal said. He looked at his girls and then back at Spooner and abruptly smiled as if suddenly suspecting that not only might this proceeding yet be survived, it might even prove profitable. Edward looked on him in wonder. The man's turn of optimism struck him as lunatic.

"They're hardy stock as well as finelookin, these gals," Segal said, "not a tainted one in the bunch and each of them more fun than—"

Dominguez put his horse forward and the pony snapped at the whoreman's face like a mean-tempered dog and Segal's smile vanished as he fell back. The chief beckoned a tall redhead whom he'd been giving the eye and who had been smiling at him in return. The girl came forward and took his proffered hand and her thighs flashed whitely under her blown skirt as he swung her up behind him on the horse. A look passed between him and Pedro Arria and then Dominguez reined the animal about and hupped it into a canter toward a clump of mesquite some fifty yards away and there he halted and dismounted with the girl and drew her into the sparse chaparral.

"Yo no soy tan modesto como el jefe," a compañero named Julio said as he slid out of the saddle, his eyes fixed on a darkhaired vixen who smiled at him and stood her ground as he approached. "Aquí mismo me sirve bien." He grabbed the girl's arm and pulled her to him and her smile vanished as he ripped open her blouse to expose her breasts.

"Hey now, amigo!" the whoreman said. His protest was lost in the compañeros' cheers. The girl tried to pull away but the bandit twisted her arm and forced her to her knees and held to her with one hand as he unbuttoned his pants with the other. The compañeros laughed and dismounted and started for the other girls who were now all of them big-eyed with fear, their backs against the wagon.

The whoreman made no move for his pistol but only raised his hands and patted the air and shouted like a carnival barker: "Hold on now, boys, hold on! Let's do her in a orderly fashion! Just form up a line at the wagon here and all of ye have ye money ready and—"

Pedro Arria stepped up to him with a wide smile and put a hand on his shoulder in the manner of an old friend. A Green River knife appeared in his other hand and without losing his smile he thrust the blade to the hilt into Segal's heart and the man was dead even as he fell. The Negro turned and ran and two of the compañeros shot him in the back and the man collapsed with his feet still striving for purchase in the sand for a few seconds more before they stilled.

The compañeros fell to the girls and there followed carnal riot on that sandblown flatland. They took turns at holding some of the girls down for their fellows who went at them with their pants bunched at their boottops and their buttocks bared to the wind. Dominguez returned with the redhead whose hair was now wild and her mouth bruised and a pair of compañeros quickly set upon her. Most of the whores were acquainted with mean turns of the trade and bore their violation with little outcry. They would all of them survive the brutal visitations of that afternoon although two of the them would take ill and die before summer and one would perish a year later in a San Antonio hotel fire and one would be disfigured by smallpox and spend her remaining days attending in an East Texas pesthouse. The redhead would make her way to Saint Louis and within months enrapture a wealthy silverhaired shoe manufacturer who would die of heart failure while they made love on their wedding night and she would thereafter become a woman of fashion and a patroness of the arts and live a life of sophisticated ease into the next century.

The wind slowed and then ceased altogether as the compañeros continued to sport with the girls into the late afternoon. But now Edward's interest waned and he belted up his pants and went to rummage through the lead wagon. He there found a sealed jar of peaches in syrup and just as he opened the jar Spooner came over to join him. They shared the peaches and then went to see what might be found in the other wagon.

Spooner pushed aside the cover flap and the stench that befell them from the darkness within was a fierce and sickly composite of body wastes and mortifying flesh and it loosened their sinuses and watered their vision. They fell back from the wagon and hawked and spat and wiped their eyes and nose. "Sweet Mother Mary," Spooner said. They tied bandannas across their lower faces and again pulled back the flaps and peered over the wagon gate and saw the two girls the whoreman had spoken of.

They were lying naked on blankets befouled with their wastes. All Edward and Spooner could see of them in the dim light was that one was darkhaired and the other fair. They let down the wagon gate and pulled out the brunette by her heels and Edward felt the stiffness in her heelstrings and knew she was dead even before they saw her distended belly and that her eyes and mouth were full of ants. They gently lowered her to the ground so as not to jar the pent gases from her. Then they brought out the other and saw that she was yet alive.

She was wasted to skin and bone and crusted with filth. Her eyes were red slits against the light of the late afternoon. Her pale yellow hair was a rank tangle. Edward knelt beside her and saw her eyes move from him to Spooner and then cut back to him. She was breathing through her partly open mouth and showed a chipped front tooth. A white razor scar followed the line of her jaw from ear to chin. Her eyes showed a rim of blue and roamed over his face and her little breasts rose with a deep breath. A small choked sound issued from deep in her throat.

"I be damn" Spooner said, looking on her closely. "I believe I know this little thing. Sported with her in a Galveston house about a year ago or I'm a striped-ass ape. I gotta say she looked a sight bettern now. Drank like a fish but a load of fun. Hell, I went to that same house three nights in a row for the pleasure of her. I tell you I knew this gal real good but bedamn if I recall her name."

"Margaret," Edward murmured. And thought: *She lied, she lied!*

"No," Spooner said, staring hard at the wasted girl, "that aint it. Jeannie . . . Janey . . . Julie, more like, somethin like that."

Goddamn crazy bitch. I knew she lied and she did and oh sweet Jesus look what's come of it, just look. Because she lied, she lied, she lied. . . .

Her gaze held on Edward at her side and her eyes glimmered wetly. She made as if she would raise her hand to him but the pain of the effort was evident on her face and she groaned and let a long breath and closed her eyes. Edward clutched her hand and raised it to his lips and held it there.

"Hey pardner," Spooner said, puzzled and unsure if he should be amused. "What the hell's this?"

Edward did not say anything nor look at him.

Spooner watched him for a long moment, then said "Hey, Eddie," in a different voice. Edward kept his gaze on the girl, kept her hand to his lips. A while later Spooner went away.

After a time the girl opened her eyes again and looked at him and her hand pressed against his mouth with no more strength than that of a baby bird. She tried to speak but could form only a small rasp. Her breath labored. She worked her blackened tongue over her lips and tried again. "What they . . . *done* . . . to you." Her eyes brimmed and tears cut thin pale tracks down the sides of her face.

His throat felt as though hands were seized hard on it. Her face wavered and he brushed at his eyes to clear them. His hand tighted on hers but he immediately eased his hold for fear he'd break the bones of it.

"Ward," she rasped. "Ward." Her fingers applied the barest pressure to his lips and then her eyes again closed.

He watched the rise and fall of her breasts and would never in the rest of his life remember what he was thinking then or if he was thinking anything at all. The western sky was afire with the remains of the day. Two compañeros came and carried off the other girl. Dominguez appeared in the twilight and sat beside him without speaking. After a time got up and left.

Darkness rose over the country. He became vaguely aware of a campfire flaming near the lead wagon and of the movements of shadows and silhouettes. He smelled food and heard low voices and the soft singing of a compañero. Then again came shrieks of women, most now sounding more of pleasure than of pain.

He wondered if she would open her eyes again. He would not know it in the dark. He thought of fetching a torch to stick in the sand beside her so he could see her face but decided against it because he did not want to be away from her for even a second while she yet lived, nor did he want anyone else to look on her. Because he now could not see if she was breathing he placed his fingers to her parted lips and felt there her vague warm exhalations. He felt her breath become fainter until he felt it barely at all and then he did not feel it but kept his fingers on her lips for a time longer until he felt them cooling and knew she was dead.

At first light he took off his shirt and covered her nakedness and went to the lead wagon and there found a spade and used it to dig her grave at the foot of a sand rise some fifty yards away. Fredo and Spooner came to ask if they might help but he did not speak nor look at them and they withdrew. When the hole was deep enough to defy the scavengers the sky was burning red over the distant eastern range. He went to the wagon and picked her up and cradled her spare flesh against his chest and breathed deeply the entire mortal truth of her. Then he carried her to the grave and placed her in it and buried her. Then he went about gathering large rocks and when he had covered the grave with them he was done.

He had thought to ask among the whores what they knew of her, where she'd been and what she'd been doing and what she'd talked of, but then decided it was folly. He had seen what there was to know, seen it in the dying light of the day before, seen it and smelled it and felt it under his fingers and buried it this sunrise. What else was there to know that mattered?

The whores were standing around the smoky remains of the campfire, dressed now and hugging themselves against the morning chill and all of them watching the compañeros add the wagon mules to their string. Some of the girls asked how they were supposed to get out of there without mules to ride but no man paid them heed.

None of his fellows questioned him then or later about the girl. Dominguez gave him a shirt to wear and Chucho brought him his saddled horse. He mounted up and looked back once at the cairn he'd erected in that lonely waste and then hupped his mount forward and rode away with his compañeros.

That night and on many to follow he dreamt of her. Saw her laughing on the porch back home and putting her legs up on the railing and letting him and his brother see up her dress all the way to her cotton underdrawers. She was smiling wickedly and then reaching down and ruffling his brother's hair with her hand and his brother flushed and quickly ran the back of his hand along the underside of her leg and then snatched his hand away and blushed even more furiously.

And he dreamt too of Daddyjack, of course. Who pointed at Maggie and grinned at him and cackled, "I *tole* ye blood always finds blood! I *tole* ye!"

24

They rode the passes up into the Sierras de Tamaulipas and descended the eastern slope on the pine forest switchbacks and debouched onto the tierra caliente of the gulf coast plain. The air turned moistly heavy and smelled of salt and swampland. In the port city of Tampico they saw American soldiers and sailors everywhere who looked with suspicion on them and their half-wild ponies and rank aspects and clattering array of arms but none did confront them. Marimba music plunked and tinkled in every plaza. They entered a restaurant from which their mien and reek drove away a good portion of the patrons. A quartet of nervous policemen came in and sat at a doorside table and watched them noisily gorge on crab legs and shellfish and turtle steaks. When the gang had done with its supper it trooped out with their armament aclatter and hardly a glance at the police who kept their seats. They went to a bagnio overlooking the harbor and they bathed in large tin tubs and every tub was left with a thick and sudsy pink-gray surface of bloody filth. And then they each of them repaired to a room in the company of a girl.

Edward was attended by a young mestiza who did not seem bothered by his scarred face but she went pale when he exposed his mutilated crown so he put the bandanna back on. Her skin was smooth and honey-colored, her eyes black as a night of rain. She smelled of damp grass and earth.

She was astraddle him and working her hips smoothly when a man in the white cotton clothes of a peón crashed through the door and screeched "Puta!" and slashed at her with a machete. He hacked at her upraised arms and at her shoulders and blood flew to the walls and even through the girl's screams Edward heard the machete striking bone as he struggled to get out from under her and clear of the bed. The blade clove her neck and blood fountained to the ceiling and then Edward was on him and twisting his arm and the machete clattered to the floor. He beat the man to his knees and snatched up the machete and stanced himself to swat

off his head but was set upon from behind by several men who wrested
the weapon from his grasp and pinioned his arms behind him. A jabbering crowd was now at the door of the tiny room and Dominguez appeared and barked an order and Edward was instantly released.

Blood dripped from the ceiling and streaked the walls and slicked the
floor and soaked the bed where the girl lay nearly decapitated with her
dead eyes open wide. The killer was sobbing as he was taken away by
policemen. And now Edward learned that the girl was a newcomer to
the trade who had been working in the house but a few weeks and the
man who killed her was her brother. He had shown up three days ago
to take her back to their family's village in the hills but she'd refused to
go. When he tried to drag her out, the house guardian had evicted him
bodily. He'd since been drinking in the neighborhood cantinas and holding muttered conversations with himself and seemed at a loss about what
to do. Today he'd made up his mind.

25

They ascended the Sierra Madre and entered cold blue clouds that made
ghost figures of the trees. The trail narrowed as it rose. The steep rock
facings were dark and slick. They rode single file with their rifles across
their pommels and spoke hardly at all for days, their mounts' hooves
clacking on stone, bits chinking, saddles creaking. Birds whistled and flew
from the trees and deer bounded across the trail and small creatures rustled in the brush. The sundown sky looked like marbled, freshly butchered
meat. Timber wolves howled like woeful souls.

They met one forenoon with a pack train bound from Pachuca for the
coast. The lead rider reined up and grinned at them and took off his
sombrero and shielded his belt pistol with it. Dominguez did not wait to
see if he was going for his gun but simply pulled his Colt and shot him
in the face. The man tumbled from the saddle and rolled off the trail and
plunged into misty space and the other guards were still unslinging their
rifles as the gang gunned them down in a thunderous enfilade that echoed
down the canyon walls. They killed too all the muleteers but for three
who escaped into the forest. The compañeros made away with satchels
of freshly-minted silver specie and fifty mules loaded with coffee. The
animals and the cargo they sold to a broker in Tulancingo who asked no
questions.

They resumed the sierra trail and rode downcountry without haste. A week later a Mexican army patrol came wending up the mountainside behind them. They set up an ambush on either side of a narrow pass and caught the patrol in a crossfire and put down more than half the cavalrymen before the rest were able to retreat. They gathered up the fallen soldiers' mounts and weapons and then rode on toward Jalapa. A few miles north of that town they met with a guerrilla chieftain, a ranchero named Lucero Carbajal whom Dominguez had known since boyhood, and they sold the mules and all their extra horses and guns to him and then took supper in his camp.

Dominguez wanted to visit Jalapa, a lovely place of gardens and orange trees and weather unsurpassably fine. But Carbajal warned him away from there. A month earlier General Scott's army had crushed Santa Anna's troops in a ferocious battle at Cerro Gordo, some fifteen miles southwest of Jalapa, and sent the broken Mexican ranks running for their lives. The Napoleon of the West himself had fled the field on his pegleg and was said to have finally arrived at Orizaba and begun to reorganize his army for the defense of Mexico City. Scott's army was now ensconced in both Jalapa and Puebla and all the talk in the cantinas was of the gringos' preparation to begin their move on the capital. The only real resistance the gringos faced between Puebla and Mexico City, Carbajal said, was that of the ranchero bands led by such as himself, Padre Colombo Bermejillo, Annastasio Torrejón and José Miñon. They had each been harassing the Yankees with hit-and-run raids on their supply trains and with sniper attacks on their columns. They regularly trailed the gringo patrols and killed the stragglers and mutilated their remains in order to frighten their comrades who found them. But despite the rancheros' continuing guerrilla raids, the American victory at Cerro Gordo had cleared their route to Mexico City and the war was sure to reach the capital soon.

The Yankees weren't the only problem, Carbajal said. The alcaldes of Jalapa and Pueblo had told the gringo commanders that most of the local ranchero gangs were nothing but bandidos looking to enrich themselves under the banner of patriotism. The bastards had given the gringos a list of names. They were all on that list, Carbajal said angrily—himself, Dominguez, Bermejillo, Torrejón, everybody. He knew the local people hated them for bandits and wanted to see them all dead or at least behind bars but he'd never thought they hated bandits so much they'd turn to the goddamned Yankees for help. Dominguez smiled over the rim of his tequila cup and said it surely was amazing that some people could hate a bandit just because he robbed and killed a few of their friends and neighbors every now and then. Carbajal grinned back at him and shrugged. He said the locals knew Dominguez and his gang were back in the region because two surviving muleteers of the Pachuca pack train had brought back the tale of the robbery and of the killings of the guards and the other drovers. It was widely supposed that Dominguez was headed back to his native city and both the local police and the Yankee army were on the lookout for him. It would be unwise to show his face in Jalapa, Carbajal told him, and even riskier to appear in Puebla.

Dominguez shrugged and thanked him for the information and advice and then they passed out bottles to their compañeros and there ensued an evening of drinking and singing and two chieftains told stories of the old days when they were boys just starting out as bandits. And before daybreak Dominguez and his gang were mounted and on their way.

26

They came through a high pass and into view of Puebla on a bright late afternoon and sat their horses on a high ridge overlooking the city and listened to the tolling of church bells. Dominguez sighed and said, "Ay, que linda ciudad!" Beyond the city's perimeter rose the presidio of Loreto with the American flag fluttering over its gates and some few of the compañeros cursed through their teeth but most were as indifferent to one flag as another and shrugged at their fellows' ire. Dominguez put his mount forward onto the downward trail and the company followed after.

It was Mexico's second largest city and the tidiest Edward would see in his life. The streets were perfectly-paved with cobblestone and shaded by trees. In every plaza there stood churches and convents ornately trimmed with colorful glazed tiles. In the central plaza loomed the imposing Cathedral of the Immaculate Concepcion built by the Spaniards two hundred years before. It was Sunday midday and the last masses of the morning had just finished. The streets and squares were thronged with people in their finery and priests and nuns in flowing black robes and habits. Fredo Ruiz, who detested the Catholic Church as a personal enemy, looked about at the multitude of clerics and spat. "La Roma de Mexico," he growled.

The plazas sparkled with fountains and were lively with musical bands and fireaters and jugglers and clowns from the local circus. There were

street vendors of fresh fruit and tamales and charcoaled meats and gim-
crackery. Patrons crowded the arcade shops and cafes. And everywhere
they saw Yankee soldiers, most of them strolling wide-eyed with wonder
at the city's ancient beauty and agape at the lovely girls who smiled at
them over their lace fans as they were hurried along by scowling dueñas.
The Yankees paid the gang no mind, but in the shadows of the arcades
were some who watched intently as the compañeros passed by and they
recognized the bandit Dominguez and some of the other riders as well
and made visual inventory of their weapons. And then them followed at
a distance.

They boarded their mounts in a livery off the main plaza and there
washed themselves thoroughly and then bought new clothes at a haber-
dasher's and had themselves barbered and pomaded and shaved and powdered. Their longarms they stored with their horses but those who were
following and watching took notice that every man of them wore a pair
of Colts under his coat. They sat for dinner at a banquet table in a fine
restaurant where Dominguez several times had to hiss at some of the less
urbane of his fellows about their faulty manners. They attracted much
sidelong and murmuring attention from the surrounding tables and many
of the compañeros were pleased by it, but not Edward, who felt most of
the attention was of the sort one saw at a zoo and most of it was directed
at him for the bandanna on his head. He was tempted to remove it and
really give the gawkers something to whisper about but he checked the
impulse.

They next repaired to the corrida and bought seats in the shade and
drank beer and cheered those matadors who braved the bulls' horns most
daringly and artfully and cheered too the bulls who fought and died well.
They ridiculed and cursed those few matadors whose ineptness or fear
made for an awkward show and was taken as insulting to a noble bull.
Several among the compañeros joined other disgusted aficionados in tossing cupfuls of piss down upon these disgraces to the matador's art. It was
Edward's first witness of the corrida's pageantry and blood rituals, and
the good fights stirred him in a way he had not felt since his young
boyhood in Georgia when he saw Daddyjack stab Tom Rainey dead.
Each time he shouted "Ole!" in unison with the crowd as the bull lunged
at the matador's swirling cape and its horns brushed the front of his
spangled jacket he felt a tight excitement all the way down to his balls.

Exiting the plaza de toros into the encroaching twilight of early evening
the compañeros were all mildly drunk and eager for women. Dominguez

said La Mariposa was the best house in the city, but Pedro Arria, who was also a Poblano, believed Las Flores Picantes was a better place. Half the boys wanted to go to the one and half to the other. Dominguez said he would meet them all the following afternoon in the main plaza and then headed off by himself.

"Where's *he* off to?" Edward asked Spooner.

"See his wife, most likely," Spooner said. He laughed at the look on Edward's face. "Hell, boy, ole Manuel's been married since before I met him. Bout four years, I believe. Name's Laura. I aint seen her myself, but some of the boys have, and they say she's a right beauty. Know what his great sorrow is? Him and his wife? They aint got no kids. Tells me they try like hell ever time he comes home but they just aint had no luck that way."

Spooner went off with Pedro and his group to do their sporting in Las Flores and Edward and Chucho and the rest made their way toward La Mariposa. As they passed the lamplit main plaza they paused to admire the pretty girls promenading in the company of their dueñas at the evening paseo. A brass band played merrily as the women strolled about the perimeter of the plaza in one direction while the men circled in the other, smiling and giving each other appraising looks as they passed. The moon showed bright white through the trees. "Andale," Chucho said after a minute. "Éstas hermosas me tienen de rabia por una mujer. Vámonos!" They left the plaza and went another two blocks and turned down a long and darkened alleyway and arrived at La Mariposa.

27

Edward's girl was a sexy but sullen wench who coupled like the act was an imposition. When he had done with her he did not want to linger and got dressed while she lay naked on her side, smoking a thin cigar and watching him with hooded eyes. But neither did he want the compañeros to make fun of him for having been so quick about it and so he rolled a cigarette and sat on the bed and smoked it. The room was small and lighted by a single candle and their smoke swirled blue and clung to the ceiling in webs. Neither of them spoke. When the cigarette was down to a nub he crushed it under his boot and went out and shut the door behind him. Chucho just then came out of another room down the hall and they grinned at one another and headed down the stairs and at the middle landing found themselves staring down at more than a dozen cocked rifles pointed at them from the brightly lighted parlor floor. Some of the riflemen wore police uniforms, some did not.

"No se muevan, carajos," said a man with a raised pistol in his hand. He was the chief of police and his authority was proclaimed by his uniform, the most elaborate in the room, topped by a stiff-crowned cap with a silver badge pinned to its front. Two of his minions came warily up the stairway and relieved Edward and Chucho of their Colts and prodded them the rest of the way downstairs. They were made to sit on the floor with their hands under them and their backs against the wall. The chief told them that if they so much as shifted their weight they would be shot for attempting to escape. He examined their Colts and smiled and handed his flintlock to an aide and cocked a revolver in each hand and turned his attention back to the stairway landing.

A few minutes later Cisco appeared on the landing and his face fell at the sight of the ready rifles. He put up his hands and was disarmed and ordered onto his hands beside Edward and Chucho. In this way were all the compañeros in La Mariposa put under arrest. All but Gustavo the seminarian who as always was the last to finish his business with the girls because after sating himself on them he always spent a while trying to persuade them to give up the whore's life. When he finally came down to the landing and saw the riflemen and the chief said, "No te mueves, cara—" he went for his Colts and the rifles all fired at once and knocked him back against the wall amid splatters of blood and he pitched headlong down the stairs and rolled to a crumpled heap and the chief stood over him in a gunpowder haze and emptied both Colts into him as Gustavo's blood soaked the carpet in a widening red stain. Not until both pistols were done blasting did Edward hear the high steady screaming of the women of the house.

They were eight of them manacled and taken out to the street and led off toward the jail. People had come hurrying from the plazas to see what was happening and the chief told them to keep their distance. The gawkers followed along on either side of the line of chained men in the wavering light of the street lamps, talking excitedly about these captured bandidos and heaping imprecations on them. One of the plaza brass bands joined the procession and added to the festive air with a lively tune. Now some of the boys snatched up stones and pelted the prisoners who cursed and tried to shield themselves with their arms and the police laughed at them along with everyone else.

The jail was a comunal cell, a long stone room set in the rear of the main municipal building of the central plaza. It had a wide door of steel bars and the floor was covered with straw the color of mud. A single heavily barred window was set a dozen feet above the floor and rose almost to the ceiling. The compañeros were unmanacled one by one in the anteroom and shoved inside. The cell was dimly lighted by small candles set on the floor and by lamplight falling through the door from the anteroom. It stank powerfully of sweat and human waste. Slop buckets stood in the corners. Most of the two dozen inmates already there had been comrades of some the compañeros in earlier bandit gangs and there were greetings and nods of recognition and bittersweet abrazos.

Barely an hour later the eight compañeros who'd gone to Las Flores Picantes were brought in. Julio had a broken wrist and Fredo's cheek had been fractured by a rifle butt and the half of his face was swollen grossly and purple as a plum. Spooner had lost his hat. He sat down beside Edward and sighed. "Aint we the dumb sonsabitches, lettin em slick up on us easy as that?"

"They aint got Manuel," Edward said. "Could be he'll get us out of here some kind a way." He surprised himself by saying it and more so by believing it. He was recalling how Captain James Kirkson Hobbes had dealt with the arrest of one of his company.

"Don't believe he will," Spooner said, and spat into the straw.

"And why not?" Edward said, irritated by Spooner's air of defeat.

"Because right there he is."

A knot of policemen led by the chief had brought Dominguez into the anteroom. He was held by a policeman on either side of him and his hands were manacled behind him and his mouth was bloated and bloody and he was naked save for a jacket draped over his shoulders. The hair about his right ear was matted with blood. A knot of compañeros converged on the cell door and were warned back by the jailers. The police chief grabbed a fistful of Dominguez's hair and directed the bandit chief's attention to the men in the cell. "Ya lo vez, cabrón? Hay están tus chingado compañeros, lo mismo como te dije! En dos días los colgaremos todos. Todos! Te lo prometo!" He rammed his knee up between Dominguez's legs and the bandit groaned and sagged in the grip of the men who held him. Now Ortiz stepped back and said, "Tíralo adentro!" and the men holding Dominguez dragged him to the cell door and flung him inside and a jailer clanged the door shut and turned the lock.

28

Later that night they sat around a guttering little chunk of candle and Dominguez told Spooner and Edward how he'd been mounted on his wife and was right on the brink of coming when his head suddenly burst with stars and the next thing he knew he was on his face on the floor with his hands manacled behind him and a boot sole pressing hard on his neck. He'd always been careful in going to his house, always taken roundabout routes through side streets and back alleys and crowded marketplaces, always taken precautions against being followed. But this time he obviously hadn't been careful enough. The police had with them a pair of Tarascan Indians who sneaked into his house and up the stairs and into the bedroom and went right up to him as he was fucking his wife and he'd never heard a thing until his head exploded.

When he regained consciousness a pair of policeman were holding him fast, one on either arm. He was surprised they hadn't simply shot him in the back and been done with it. Then he saw that the police chief was Huberto Ortiz and he understood why they had not. Ortriz greeted him with a wide smile and a punch to the mouth that smashed his lips and loosened his front teeth.

"Ortiz, he hate me since we are little boys," Dominguez said. "We fight and I win him. We race and I win him. We dance and make love with the señoritas and I win him. All the times I get the more pretty ones. He hate me because he never can win me. When we are hombres I make together my gente, my compañeros, but he don't want to call me el jefe and so he make together his own gente, but they never can steal so much like my gente can steal. He never so good like me at nothing, Ortiz, from the time we are muchachos. So he hate me, you see. Is simple. Is why he want for all the peoples to see me hang. Is more shameful for me than he shoot me, and is more better for him if the peoples see me to hang. He can say to everbody, 'You see all this bad mens? You see this bad hombre Manuel Dominguez? I am going to hang him for you and you can see him to die with your eyes.' He will be more famous, you see."

"And now the bastard's the chief of police?" Spooner said. He chuckled. "Aint that always the way?"

Dominguez's smile was twisted on his bloated lips. "The peoples, they want a policemens who can make them to feel safe, you know? Somebody strong for to protect them to the bad mens like Manuel Dominguez." He laughed without humor. "They *want* for to see me be hang, this damn peoples." He looked up at the high dark window as if he might scale the wall to it and look out on all his fellow citizens who wanted him dead. He spat.

He made no account of his wife and neither Edward nor Spooner was so impolite as to ask after her. It was sufficient to know she had been naked in the bed when the police came in. It required little imagination to know what happened thereafter, and they knew that had it been otherwise Dominguez would have said so. But he had not.

The morning brought verdicts rendered by a judge they had none of them ever seen or ever would. All of them had been found guilty of "undeniable" acts of murder and robbery and rape and all of them had been sentenced to death. They were to be hanged in the municipal square at four o'clock that very afternoon. Hanged four at a time from branches of the Hanging Tree, one bunch after the other until only Dominguez was left and then he would be hanged by himself.

Ortiz delivered the news. He grinned through the bars at Dominguez and said he was now going to pay Dominguez's wife a visit but would return in time to watch his execution. Dominguez stared at him without expression and Ortiz laughed. "Quieres que la daré un besito por tí?" he said, puckering his lips. He was laughing as he left.

29

The condemned spoke little as their final hours passed. Each man of them sat with his back to the wall and kept to his private thoughts. Edward leaned back with his eyes closed and was surprised by the rush of memories of the days in Florida. He recalled the ripe swampland smells and the feel of the long summer's wet heat. He saw vividly the creek where he'd witnessed one of his dogs killed by an alligator, where he and his brother caught catfish and turtles and where farther upstream he'd once spotted his brother hidden in the reeds and spying on their sister as she bathed. He had himself remained hidden and watched her too. He felt himself hardening as he recalled his naked sister—and now remembered the softbrain girl who had been his first—and the girl's momma who only minutes later had been his second. And recalled too the countless sunsets when he sat on the stump next to the stable and looked to westward and envisioned some vast territory burning red under a noonday sun fierce and pitiless as the Devil himself.

And remembered feeling absolutely certain, in a way he would never understand, that only out there did he truly belong. Only out there.

30

Two hours before they were to be hanged they could hear through the high window the sounds of the gathering crowd in the municipal plaza. A band was playing merrily. Laughter and shouts of children. Cries of vendors hawking snacks. The head jailer appeared at the barred door and called for Dominguez to come forward. Dominguez stared at him from where he sat against the wall and said if the jailer wanted to see him up close he was welcome to come in and sit beside him. The compañeros laughed maliciously.

"Ven aquí, cabrón!" the jailer commanded. 'Ya te lo digo."

"No," Dominguez said. "*Tú* ven *aquí*, hermanito."

Now a pair of American army officers stepped into view and peered into the cell's noisome gloom. The compañeros turned to each other with puzzled glances and their murmur snaked through the room. The jailer motioned the Yankees back and said he would take care of this but the officers ignored him. The jailer put his hand on an officer's arm as if he would guide him away from the door and the Yankee turned and shoved him hard against the wall and the bonk of the jailer's head resounded loudly. Several of the inmates laughed and the jailer slank from sight.

"Captain Dominguez," the other officer said into the dimness. "General Winfield Scott wishes to speak with you in his headquarters, sir. Right away."

Dominguez turned to Spooner. "El General Escott quiere hablar conmigo?" Spooner arched his brows and nodded.

Dominguez looked back at the Yankees. "For why he want to talk with me?"

"I'm not at liberty to say, Captain," the officer said. "If you'll just come with us, sir."

"Pues," Dominguez said, getting to his feet. "A ver que pasa. Si me van a colgar, que me cuelgan de una vez."

The other officer went out of view momentarily and then reappeared with the jailer's keys. He worked the lock and swung the door open. Some of the other inmates made for the opening but the officer drew his pistol and said, "Get back, damn you," and they did.

Dominguez stepped out and the officer relocked the door and then the three of them walked off with their bootheels clacking on the stones. The prisoners heard an outer door creak open and then slam shut and then nothing.

The compañeros exchanged looks and shrugs. "What you reckon it's about?" Edward asked Spooner.

"Could be they aim to hang him for all them U. S. of A. trains we robbed. Only I never heard of no general wanting to talk to somebody he was about to hang, and specially not no Mexican. And specially not asking so nice as all that." He scratched his chin thoughtfully. "General *Scott*, by Jesus! Old Fuss and Feathers hisself. No sir, I don't believe they'll hang him. I'd say the general *wants* somethin. And if that's the case, then maybe, just goddamn maybe . . ." He left the thought unspoken.

But now Edward too was thinking, "Maybe, maybe . . ." as the high window above them admitted the rising clamor of the crowd so eager to see them die.

31

At ten minutes to four the gloomy cell was resounding with the carnivorous rumblings of the crowd outside when Dominguez reappeared at the jail door. Edward's heart jumped at the sight of the chief's wide grin. The jailer eased up next to Dominguez and turned his key in the lock and then quickly stepped back. Dominguez looked at him and laughed. He entered the cell and the compañeros gathered around him with a clamor of questions and the other inmates closed in behind them. The jailer did not reshut the door. There were fresh dark bloodstains on Dominguez's shirtsleeves and Chucho asked him if he'd been wounded. The jefe laughed and shook his head and said for them to shut up and listen, he had some things to tell them. His high spirit was infectious. Edward felt his own blood racing.

Dominguez described Winfield Scott as having the face of a Roman emperor whose picture he had once seen in a book. His uniform was the most splendid he had ever seen on a Yankee. In addition to Scott, there had been several others at the meeting. General William Jenkins Worth was there, silverhaired and mutton-chopped and nearly as dazzlingly outfitted as Scott. He had commanded the U.S. forces in Puebla for the two weeks preceding Scott's arrival and had an air of vanity about him. Also present was Scott's adjutant, a trim and quick-talking colonel named Ethan Allen Hitchcock. And a rugged-looking colonel named Thomas Childs, Scott's appointee to serve as Military and Civil Governor of Puebla. And a strange man named Alphonse Wengierski, tall, lean and goateed, who served as translator in the proceedings. Wengierski said he was from Poland, and though his Spanish was excellent it was the most strangely accented Dominguez had ever heard.

Hitchcock did most of the talking, occasionally glancing at Scott to assure himself of the general's concurrence with a point. Worth sat with his arms folded over his chest and showed little expression through most of the meeting. Childs watched everyone closely, especially Scott, who kept his eyes on Dominguez.

They gave no time to amenities. Through Wengierski's interpretation Hitchcock told Dominguez that General Scott was in need of someone who had been raised in this part of Mexico and knew the region very well. Someone who could serve as a scout during the coming advance on Mexico City. Someone who could gather accurate intelligence information for him. Someone who knew every foot of the main highways and where guerrilla gangs might position themselves to attack military supply trains, who knew the high country and where the guerrilla camps might be. Above all, General Scott needed someone who could be depended upon to organize—and quickly—a counterguerrilla force to seek out and destroy these gangs and thereby spare the general the necessity of appointing any of his regular troops to that special duty. The general's forces had been greatly reduced of late with the expiration of many of the volunteer units' terms of enlistment and every soldier of the regular ranks was needed for the push toward the capital.

Hitchcock paused to give Dominguez a moment to absorb this information. Dominguez looked to Scott and the general smiled slightly. In that moment, Dominguez told his compañeros, he knew they might yet escape the noose.

Then Hitchcock said: "The question, of course, is whether such a man as we are discussing might have reservations about fighting against his fellow countrymen."

Dominguez affected to mull Hitchcock's point for a moment, then said that he knew of such a man as they were discussing, a man with no reservations whatsoever about fighting against his fellow countrymen. This man had in fact been fighting his countrymen for most of his life and even now could name several fellow countrymen whose hearts he would dearly love to cut out. The real question, Dominguez said, was whether such a man as they were discussing would be relieved of any legal difficulties he might now be facing from his fellow countrymen.

Hitchcock smiled and said, "Such legal difficulties as being scheduled to meet with the hangman within the next two hours, for instance?"

Dominguez said yes, that was a perfect example of the sort of legal difficulty he had in mind.

Hitchcock assured him that *all* legal problems such a man might be facing from his own government would be resolved immediately. Furthermore, he said, such a man would likely be interested to know that the American army would not now or ever charge him with any U.S. military train robberies he might have committed, or with any other crimes alleged to have transpired during those robberies—notwithstanding any official reports of his own government that might name him as the culprit in any of those crimes.

Dominguez said that such a promise by the American government would certainly give comfort to such a man as they were talking about. Would such assurances, he asked, apply as well to all members of the man's company?

Hitchcock looked to Scott and Scott nodded at Dominguez.

This man, Hitchcock told Dominguez, would be granted the rank of colonel and be paid fifty dollars a month. He would be authorized to raise a special cavalry unit to be called the Spy Company. It would consist of thirty men, including two captains and two sergeants of his own appointment. The captains would be paid forty dollars per month, the sergeants thirty. The other members of the company would each receive twenty dollars a month—more than a U.S. sergeant was paid. The entire company would be enlisted in the Army of the United States for the duration of the war and would be provided with the best of arms and horses and its own distinctive uniform bearing U.S. Army insignia. Colonel Childs and he himself, Hitchcock said, would be the intermediaries between the company and General Scott, under whose direct orders they would operate.

Dominguez said that such a man as they were discussing might find it perilous to remain among his fellow countrymen at the end of the war. Could provision be made to remove him to some safer location when the war was over—to the United States, for example?

Hitchcock looked to Scott. The general nodded. Dominguez smiled.

"Now tell us, Captain," Hitchcock said, "who is this man you have in mind who might meet General Scott's requirements?"

Dominguez faced General Scott, stood at attention, saluted smartly, and said, "Coronel Manuel Dominguez de la compañia de espías—a sus ordenes, mi general!"

Even General Scott had joined in the laughter.

And now, facing his grinning compañeros in the dim jail cell, Dominguez said that whosoever among his compañeros would ride with him as members of General Scott's Spy Company should come with him now to the U.S. garrison where they would sign enlistment papers and be given temporary lodging and fitted for uniforms. Tomorrow they would draw weapons and horses and begin planning their campaign against the region's ranchero gangs.

Every compañero rose to his feet to go with him. And from the clamoring throng of other inmates who also wanted to join, Dominguez swiftly selected the thirteen most capable to fill out his authorized roster of thirty. They filed out of the cell and into the anteroom and out the door into the municipal building courtyard where a dozen U.S. soldiers were waiting to escort them to the garrison. Fredo kept calling for the jailers but none would show himself.

They swaggered through the plaza, laughing and making obscene hand signs to the gaping and frightened crowd that had collected there to be entertained by the spectacle of their hanging. The policemen kept their distance but many of the compañeros pointed at them in passing and said they would come back to see them again. Dominguez spoke to the sergeant in charge of the escort detail and the sergeant shrugged and said, "Hell, Colonel, you're giving the orders. We'll go any way you say."

Dominguez turned them off the main avenida that led directly to the garrison and took them instead down a series of back streets where people saw them coming and ran out of sight. At the corner of a narrow residential street shaded by oaks and brilliant with flowers he halted the procession. No one was on the street but for a handful of small children who stood gaping up at the huge front door of a house midway down the short block. Dominguez pointed at the house and told the compañeros it was his and that after leaving the meeting with Scott he had come directly home to get his wife and move her to another residence where she would be safe from the police and from anyone else who would do him harm by harming her. Edward now recalled Ortiz's parting words to Dominguez in the jail and he saw that others of the company remembered as well, and they all shifted about uncomfortably and none would meet their jefe's eyes for the shame his wife must have been made to suffer at the hands of that son of a whore.

But Dominguez was grinning wide and telling them that he had been lucky because he found Ortiz at his house and lingering over his wife when he arrived.

The compañeros exchanged looks of confusion. Dominguez laughed. "Miren!" he said, striding quickly toward the house where the children were gathered. The compañeros followed after and he pointed to the large crosstimber above the imposing front door that opened into a courtyard. "Miren!"

And there in the center of the crosstimber was the badged cap of the chief of police held fast to the wood by their jefe's Green River knife that pinioned as well a shriveled cock and dangling bloody balls.

32

A week later they rode out of Puebla on their first mission, every man of them mounted on a fine American stallion larger than most Mexican horses and seated on a well-tooled saddle and armed with a pair of new Colt five-shooters and a Hall percussion rifle and some with a shotgun besides. A half-dozen of them carried a lance they had learned to use when they served in the Mexican army and some were armed with sabers and some with bowies as big as machetes. They wore high black boots and gray trousers and short-tailed gray coatees with red collars and cuffs and flat-crowned black felt hats banded with a blood-red scarf. The effect of the uniforms was heady. Edward felt cloaked in power.

With Hitchcock's approval Dominguez had organized the company into two units which he named the Eagles and the Serpents, a patriotic allusion he found amusing in its irony but which outraged the local populace. Mexican newspaper editorials condemned the company as a reprehensible collection of society's dregs, as a crew of despicable and utterly damned murderers and convicts who lacked even the single saving grace of allegiance to their native land. The more the good citizens ranted the more pleased did Dominguez seem. "This people are want to hang me," he said to Spooner and Edward, "and now they are want me to fight the gringos for them. This people are very stupid, no?"

Edward was assigned to the Eagle squad, which was captained by

Spooner and had Fredo as its sergeant. The Serpents' captain was Pedro Arria and their sergeant a new man named Rogelio Gomez whom Dominguez had known in the old days and who had served as a sergeant in the Mexican army before deserting. As they rode out of town on their fine prancing stallions they were looked upon by the citizens on the streets as a damnable spectacle but a fearsome one even more and thus no one cursed them audibly as their horses clopped past on the cobblestones.

Two weeks later they found Padre Colombo Bermejillo's ranchero band encamped in the hills a few miles east of the junction of the National Highway and the Orizaba Road. So confident of never being discovered by Yankee scouts had the guerrillas become that they did not even post night guards. Dominguez positioned Spooner's men on one flank of the camp and himself with Pedro Arria's men on the other and they waited for first light. When it came they opened fire and killed a dozen as they slept on the ground and shot the other fifteen when they jumped to their feet and ran about in confusion. They then descended into the slaughter and killed off the wounded. Padre Bermejillo was easily identified by the priestly robes he had persisted in wearing despite his excommunication from the Church. Dominguez sent the padre's tonsured head and the twenty-six noses of the other rancheros back to Hitchcock in a bloody sack.

The trophies appalled many of the Yankee officers in attendance in Hitchcock's headquarters when they were delivered to him, and the next time Hitchcock and Wengierski met with Dominguez the colonel told him not to send any more such evidence of his successes. Dominguez said he simply wanted him and General Scott to know the Spy Company was doing its duty. Hitchcock said he understood, but there were some officers in their ranks who were set on making trouble for General Scott with the politicians back home and these men would not hesitate to provide American newspapers with a lot of muck about Scott's sanctioning of "barbarities" in Mexico. General Scott believed that Dominguez and his boys should do whatever they had to do in order to achieve their missions, but Dominguez must henceforth be very careful in his reports to exclude all the unpalatable particulars. And now it was Dominguez's turn to assure Hitchcock that he understood perfectly.

Dominguez thereafter omitted from his reports even the details of the interrogation techniques they were sometimes obliged to apply as they sought information from villagers in guerrilla territory. When a response seemed to him evasive or untruthful Dominguez would permit the Yaqui half-breed Bernado—whom they called El Verdadero because of his talent for eliciting truth—to exercise his own persuasive methods of questioning, methods he'd learned as a scout for the Mexican army in its endless war with the Apaches. No man could hold to a lie once Bernardo began to burn his feet or cut out his teeth or slap at his bare testicles with a little rawhide quirt or press the burning end of a stick to his asshole or to the head of his dick.

In early July they caught up to Annastasio Torrejón's gang in the highlands near Las Vigas where they were lying in ambush for a U.S. pack train coming from Veracruz. The company had been informed of the rancheros' plan and came around from the west and behind them and caught them by surprise in a drizzling rain. The ensuing fight lasted an hour and four of the company were wounded although only two seriously enough to be of no further service. They killed all twenty-two of the Torrejón bunch. Dominguez sent to Hitchcock a courier report of their success and a string of the guerrillas' horses

Ten days later they tracked down the Miñon gang to its hideout in a canyon just north of Orizaba. The rancheros made a run for it and the fight carried for three days and covered nearly fifty miles before the last of the Miñonistas went down. As a warning to other bandits and rancheros in the vicinity the company hung naked Miñonista corpses by their heels from a tree every few miles along the road between Orizaba and Córdoba. Mexican officials of both church and state complained in outrage to the American authorities and Hitchcock sent a detail to cut down the bodies and bury them. But there was no reprimand of the Spy Company.

The company next rode into the sierras north of Jalapa and searched out the ranchero band of Lucero Carbajal. The fight was fierce but quick and when it was done Dominguez found his old friend still alive among the fallen though he'd been mortally wounded in the belly. Dominguez sat and cradled Lucero's head in his lap and mopped his brow and rolled cigarettes for him. Edward and Spooner sat close by and waved away any others who approached. Dominguez and Carbajal spoke of the old days and sang songs they had learned together as children and every time Lucero screamed with a new rush of pain Dominguez gripped his hands tightly and whispered to him to be strong, be strong. They watched the western sky turn bloody red behind the mountains and Carbajal said the sight was the most beautiful in all God's world and Dominguez agreed. A moment later Carbajal was dead and Dominguez and Rogelio Gomez who had also known Lucero since boyhood dug his grave in the dark and buried him. The rest of the rancheros they left to the scavengers.

33

They arrived back in Puebla in the first week of August to find Scott ready to begin his move on Mexico City at last. He decided that one squad of the Spy Company would go with him, one would stay behind in Puebla under the authority of Colonel Childs. Dominguez selected Spooner's band to go with Scott and he put himself in command of it. They set out on a red-streaked daybreak—foot soldiers, cavalry, artillery limbers, caissons, supply wagons, a military train that stretched for rumbling miles and wound about the mountain trails like an enormous martial snake.

The Spy Company rode well ahead of the main force and through the day Dominguez alternated between Spooner and Edward as his report riders to Scott, thinking the general would be grateful not to need an interpreter. And grateful Scott was, but he and his fellow officers had as well been surprised to learn of a pair of Americans riding with the Spy Company. Spooner had carried the first report and on his return he warned Edward of what to expect, but still, the first time he rode to the main body, Edward had suddenly felt every eye in the column fixed sharply on him as he rode past on his way to Scott's wagon. And then in the general's quarters he'd been subjected to the severe scrutiny of the half-dozen other officers in attendance. He'd removed his hat and reported that the road ahead looked to be all clear for at least the next ten miles and Scott thanked him and was about to dismiss him when General Worth asked his name and where he hailed from.

"Edward Boggs, sir, from Tennessee. Nashville."

A bullnecked, whitebearded general named Twiggs asked if he'd ever worn the uniform of his true country. Edward said he'd never been in service before signing on with the Spy Company. Twiggs looked around at his fellows with a narrow smile and said it might be interesting to check the deserter rolls for the name of Edward Boggs. He started to say something else but Scott broke in and asked Edward why he wore the bandanna over his head.

"An accident, sir," he said. "It's to cover it over."

"Let's have a look," said a general with muttonchops joining his thick mustache though his chin was shaved close. Edward looked at Scott and the general returned his stare blankly. So he took off the bandanna.

"Damn, son," the muttonchops said.

"I fell down drunk one night, sir, I'm ashamed to say, and my hair caught aflame from the cookfire. My own fool fault." He quickly retied the bandanna over his crown.

Several officers exchanged smiling glances and one said, "I once saw such a—" but Scott silenced him with a raised finger.

"I too have seen similar scars on some few other heads," Scott said. "Curiously, all the heads belonged to men who had been fallen upon by savages yet were lucky enough to escape with their lives, if not the entirety of their hair." The officers laughed and Edward felt his face flush hotly.

"No, Davy," Scott said confidently to the general named Twiggs, "I do not believe this young man is likely to prove a deserter. No one with such, ah, *campfire* scars on his head could be so cowardly as to desert his ranks." He smiled at Edward and made a gesture of dismissal and Edward hastily saluted and exited the wagon.

A group of enlisted men stood nearby and watched him closely as he went to his horse and mounted up. He heard one say something about "a damn deserter in that Mex scout outfit."

But another quickly said, "How's he be a deserter if he's reporting to General Scott and got the U S. insignia on his coat?"

"He's riding with Mexicans, aint he."

"*Those* Mexes are on our side, you damn fool!"

"Shitfire, *you're* the damn fool if ye believe *any* Mex be on our side!"

34

Three days west of Puebla they came up through a wide pass flanking the great volcano called Popocatepetl and crested a ridge and of a sudden found themselves looking out upon the entire Valley of Mexico three thousand feet below and spread out before them like a vast map of bright green felt. It lay engirt by a sharp and darkly rugged range, a mountainous circle 120 miles in circumference. And there, directly ahead and blazing like some vision conjured of medieval magic was the fabled city of the Aztecs. The towers of Mexico City stood so vivid in the sharp cool air they seemed to Edward close enough to hit with a rifleshot but were in fact some twenty-five miles distant. The three great lakes about the city blazed like silver mirrors. It was a vista to awe even Dominguez and the few others who had seen it before, and those who looked upon it for the first time could not put into words what they beheld, this portion of earth fashioned by ancient gods unknown.

When Scott arrived and gazed at the panorama he too was bedazzled. Dominguez beamed as if the vista were his personal gift to him. "Look!" Scott said, spreading his arms toward the valley in the manner of a munificent war lord bestowing wondrous spoils upon his minions. "Look there, my brothers! The very seat of the Montezumas!. And soon, *soon*, by all that's right and holy, that splendid city shall be ours!"

VII

THE BROTHERS

1

In Mexico City Santa Anna made ready. He put the federal district and surrounding states under martial law. He emptied the prisons into military training camps. He ordered every able-bodied Mexican male between the ages of fifteen and sixty to enlist in the army. Press gangs prowled the streets round the clock. Civilian construction crews were conscripted to build new defenseworks and reinforce existing ones. They flooded the surrounding marshland flanking the narrow causeways to prevent Yankee artillery from wheeling over it. Private livestock and conveyances were confiscated by the army in the name of national emergency. American civilians were ordered to join the Mexican military or get out of town.

The San Patricios were quartered in the citadel, on the western side of the city. From there they could look across the flat marsh to the spectacular castle of Chapultepec less than two miles distant on a hill at the far end of the Belen Causeway. Awaiting their orders they passed the days training recruits and seeing to their weapons and gear. They gambled and wrote letters and got up fistfights to break the boredom. In the evenings and on Sunday afternoons they made rounds of the city and found spectacle on every side. The bullfight plaza was larger, its pageantry more expansive, its aficionados louder than they had witnessed in Puebla. They stood agape before the National Palace and then wandered across the the vast main square of the Zócalo thronged with vendors, viejas, beggars, musicians and street entertainers of every stripe. They stepped timorously into the incensed shadows of the gargantuan National Cathedral whose vaulted and groined ceilings were dizzying to look upon and whose altars blazed with polished gold. They remarked upon the realistic renditions of the violence visited on Christ and the various saints depicted on the walls and windows. Moreno had seen much human flesh impaled by arrows during his tour of duty in the Yaqui lands of Sonora and he attested to the accuracy of the wounds inflicted on the statue of Saint. Sebastian. It was not the first time John had been struck by such fidelity to violent detail in Mexican religious art. The nailed hands and feet of the sculpted Christ on the Cross, the gash in His side, looked as though they would bloody the fingers put to them. The world, he reflected, was naught but killing and rites of blood, even among the pious. The stronger killed and ate the weaker, and the weakest of all fed on the leavings. It was Nature's ruling principle, the most ancient of its immutable laws.

They toured the National Museum and saw bones of man and beast thousands of years older than the first writ word of history, saw gleaming Aztec daggers of obsidian that had religiously excised, steaming and still abeat, human hearts beyond number. They strolled through the sundappled park at Chapultepec and were poled on dugouts across the flowerstrewn beauty of Lake Xochimilco.

And when they had done with enjoying the wonders of the city proper they repaired to brothels as finely appointed as aristocratic salons and staffed with the most desirable whores in Mexico. But not even the pleasures of the girls in La Casa de la Contessa, girls as lovely as daydreams and whiteskinned as any of the Saint Patricks themselves, could long distract them from the knowledge that the Americans were marching their way.

2

Hearsay of every sort came to them, the most disturbing being that they would not be used in the defense of the city at all. One rumor had it that Santa Anna did not trust them to fight against their fellow Americans. Another, that if the defense of the capital did not succeed, he intended to turn them over to the Americans in exchange for certain concessions. When some of the Patricios said they sure enough wouldn't put it past any damn general, Yank *or* Mex, to doublecross his men that way and wondered aloud if maybe it would be wise to slip away while the slipping was good, Riley said he would beat the shit out of the next man who said such a thing and would personally shoot any among them who attempted desertion.

The San Patricio ranks had in fact increased in recent weeks and both companies were now but a few men shy of their full strength of one hundred men each. In U.S. camps from Veracruz to the advance units now within fifteen miles of the city, Santa Anna's English handbills called on Yankee soldiers to reject the unjust American cause and come to Mexico's noble defense of true liberty and the Mother Church. The fliers had drawn a new influx of deserters eager to reap the promised rewards of "rich fields and large tracts of land, which being cultivated by your industry, shall crown you with happiness and convenience."

Handsome Jack himself wrote a handbill for circulation:

> *"My Countrymen, Irishmen! I urge you to abandon a slavish hireling's life with a nation who treats you with contumely and disgrace. For whom are you contending? For a people who, in the face of the whole world, and who in their greed for more and yet more territory, and more and yet more peaceloving peoples to rule over as despots, trample upon the holy altars of our religion and set firebrands to all sanctuaries devoted to the Blessed Virgin! My Countrymen, I have experienced the hospitality of the citizens of this true Republic, and I say to you that from the moment I extended to them the hand of friendship I was received with kindness. Though I was poor, I was relieved; though undeserving, I was respected; and I pledge you my oath, that the same feelings extended toward me await you also."*

Lucas Malone read a fresh copy of it over John's shoulder and said, "Bedamn but Jack can scribble a sermon, caint he? Makes me wish I was back on the other side just so's I could desert all over again."

In his fervor for recruits Handsome Jack made daily visits to the erstwhile monastery of Santiago Tlatelolco and proselytized among the captured American soldiers imprisoned there. Most cursed him for a turncoat son of a bitch and said they would see his head on a pike, but others succumbed to his suasions and the promised Mexican rewards and found themselves in a Saint Patrick uniform within the hour of accepting his offer.

3

On a sunny Thursday morning came the order for them to proceed at once to the village of Churubusco about five miles south of the citadel and reinforce the defense of the Río Churubusco Bridge.

"About damn time!" Lucas Malone said. The bunch of them were grinning fiercely The order dispelled their apprehension that Santa Anna was reserving them as bargaining pawns.

"Sure now Señor Napoleon finally come to realize we got lots more to lose than any Mexie does if we get took prisoner," remarked a Patricio named Tom Cassady. "Hell man, it's *us* got the most good reason of anybody to see the Yanks beat back."

"Churubusco," said a redbeard named O'Connor as they readied to move out. "Is that be the name of some famous Spanish general or somebody?"

"No," Colonel Moreno said. "It is Aztec, that word. It means, ah, where the war god—how do you say—the place where the birds come to their nest? In the evening?"

"A roost?"

"Si! Churubusco. It means the roost of the war god."

"The war god be a *bird?*"

"Like a ferocious bird—like an eagle. And also like a snake. The war god is like Mexico. He is like all the wild things of the blood."

4

They crossed the Río Churubusco that afternoon under a glaring sun veiled in thin ragged clouds. The sight of the Saint Patrick banner snapping in the breeze drew cheers from the two infantry regiments defending the stone bridge. "Viva los Colorados! Viva los San Patricios!" The infantrymen had constructed a bridgehead marked by a high U-shaped parapet behind which were posted two battalions of riflemen and three artillery pieces. The parapet afforded an excellent field of fire and was fronted by a watery ditch some twenty feet wide. The bridgehead overlooked a causeway flanked on both sides by deep ditches and soggy marshland. The causeway ran south for nearly two miles to the pueblo of San Antonio. It was one of only two approaches the Americans could take to the bridge. The other was the Coyoacán Road. On either causeway they would be open targets.

The Patricios raised their fists in salute to the cheering Mexicans. They veered from the bridgehead and trooped onto the Coyoacán Road and followed it southwestward for two hundred yards to the imposing Convent of San Mateo. The convent consisted of several monastery buildings and a church with a high thick steeple. A half-mile southward lay a lava bed called the Pedregal, some fifteen square miles of blackly adamantine volcanic rock sharp enough to cut through bootsoles and savage even the shod hooves of horses. Together with the surrounding marshland and dense cornfields, the Pedregal blocked all approach to Churubusco except by the Coyoacán and San Antonio roads.

They filed through the huge front gates to the stirring music of an army band and the resounding vivas of the two battalions already there under the command of General Manuel Rincón. The convent was enclosed by twelve-foot-high stone walls containing rifle loopholes and a wide scaffolding on which were positioned a quartet of eight-pounder guns. In the center of the cobbled courtyard was a large fountain bordered by a brick walkway lined with cypress trees and flowering shrubs. Along the base of the eastern wall bloomed a vivid red rose garden. Rincón bade the Saint Patricks welcome and made a brief but eloquent speech about their nobility and heroism. More vivas and march music followed and then the general took Moreno aside and conferred with him briefly, pointing here and there around the convent as he spoke, leaning close to him to be heard above the din of the band. The two men exchanged salutes and Moreno returned to his men and apprised them of their specific duties.

The convent walls would be manned by Rincón's infantry but the four big guns would be crewed by San Patricios. Two of the guns were trained on the San Antonio Road and two on the southern stretch of the Coyoacán Road by which the Yankees would have to come in order to attack the convent. The road was flanked on one side by marsh and on the other by a muddy field of ripe corn and was visible all the way to a small rise almost a half-mile to the south where stood the tiny village of Coyoacán and a squad of lookouts posted there. Beyond the rise, the road ran west to San Angel, a mile farther on.

The flat roofs of the monastery buildings were edged by low protective walls and made excellent ramparts. Saturnino O'Leary's company was assigned to them. The core of the convent's defense was the church itself. Its huge steeple was girt by a wide stonewalled walkway that commanded a clear view of the surrounding countryside. The position was ideal for riflemen as well as for the six-pounder gun and the pair of four-pounders Rincón had already placed there. Its defense was given to Handsome Jack Riley's company and a platoon of Mexican riflemen.

The order from Santa Anna, Moreno told his battalion, was that the convent must be held at any cost. "If the Yankees should break through our southern positions and advance this far, only the tête du pont and this convent will stand between the barbarians and the capital. We cannot fall, compadres. We cannot."

"You aint lying," Lucas Malone murmured.

5

Not an hour after they'd settled into their assigned positions the booming of artillery came to them from the far south side of the Pedregal, some three or four miles away. The convent defenders gathered at the south walls and gazed out to the Pedregal as the big guns resounded in the distance beyond. General Rincón and Colonel Moreno joined Riley's Saint Patricks in the steeple but even from that vantage point all they could see of the faraway battle were vague billows of dust and smoke. The lookouts at Coyoacán were gathered on the crest of the rise and all of them peering to southward.

"General Valencia ya emprendio la lucha," Rincón said. Moreno told Riley and John that General Valencia had been charged with blocking any Yankee attempt to go around the south end of the Pedregal and then advance on the convent by way of the San Angel Road.

The distant artillery battle continued through the afternoon and seemed to be advancing slowly toward San Angel. Now the sun set in a crimson riot behind a swelling rise of thunderheads dark as slate. Sheet lightning

flashed ghostly pale in the mountains. The camp women prepared a supper of spicy kid stew, beans and tortillas, and the San Patricios fell to it.
They had just done eating when the sounds of artillery abruptly ceased.
The army band had earlier let off its blaring and now a soft strumming
of guitars began to carry through the convent. Many of the Mexican
soldiers were accompanied by their women and huddled close with them
in the shadows.

And now the night rose fully. The sky was densely dark with rushing
clouds and the wind picked up and smelled heavily of a coming storm.
Thunder rolled over the valley in long rippling cracks and every clap came
louder than the one before. The wind gusted and shook the trees and
shrubs. The convent was suddenly illuminated in pale blue light followed
on the instant by a shuddering blast of thunder that made John flinch
and Lucas whoop and then the sky broke open and the rain came slashing
down.

6

Past midnight the wind at last fell off and the rain eased to a drizzle but
did not quit altogether until just before sunrise. The morning was wet
and cool, ripe with the fecund smells of the marshland. The sky reddened
over over the eastern mountains. As the sun broke over the peaks the
sounds of battle renewed in the southwest distance.

John and Lucas stood at the stone rail of the steeple walkway and
sipped coffee as they scanned the far rise of the Coyoacán Road where
the Mexican lookouts were posted. The lookouts were tiny figures once
again bunched on the road and looking south. Now several of them began
to gesticulate excitedly. The sounds of artillery and small arms grew more
distinct. Riley came up beside John and trained his field scope on the
Coyoacán rise. The lookouts mounted up hurriedly and reined their
horses about and spurred them toward the convent. A moment later Moreno came running up the steeple steps and out to the walkway and
peered out on the dozen horsemen galloping up to the gates and clattering
into the courtyard yelling, "Hay vienen! Hay vienen!"

They were indeed coming but they were not Yankees, not yet. The
men riding hard over the rise and followed by soldiers afoot and running
headlong were Valencia's troops retreating from San Angel. As they
passed by on the road they did not even look toward the comrades calling

to them from the walls and the open gates of the convent but pressed on all the way to the bridgehead and there took their refuge.

The crackling of American rifles grew louder. Still more soldiers came up the road at a gallop and on the run. And now there were cries of "Mira! Mira!" from the east wall of the convent and the Patricios on the walkway dashed to that side and saw that the San Antonio Road too was now athrong with Mexican troops in full flight for the bridge.

John and Lucas looked at each other and John thought he saw in the old man's eyes a tiredness he had never seen before. His own mouth had gone dry. He could not have said how much of his excitement was fear, how much anticipation.

Mexican soldiers continued retreating north along both roads for nearly an hour more, the last of them shooting behind them as they came. As these rear-guard infantry made it to the bridgehead, the first Yankee soldiers hove into view, a company of dragoons, and there they halted. The gringos were reconnoitering the road ahead when all three guns at the bridgehead opened fire on them.

The Yankees reined hastily about on the narrow causeway and all started galloping back the way they came and some were forced off either side of the road and into the watery muck and two of the cannonballs were solid rounds and landed with high splashes in the marshwater off the road but the other round was explosive and blasted against the causeway embankment and cut down two horses and their riders. A great cheer went up from the tête du pont and the walls of the watching convent. One of the fallen Yankees jumped to his feet and limped to a comrade who pulled him up to ride double but the other downed trooper was pinned under his dying and weakly kicking horse in the shallow water off the road. The men at the convent could see him beckoning frantically for his comrades to help him, could hear dimly his shrill cries as the last of the dragoons spurred away before the big guns could fire on them again.

"Lookit em leave him," Lucas Malone said. "Sorry sons a bitches."

"Finish him, Johnny," Riley said.

John looked at him. "Hell, Jack, he *is* finished."

Riley scowled. "He gets loose of that horse and gets back in the fight and he might be the very one to shoot *you* an hour from now. Worse than that, he might be the one to shoot *me*! Now do it!"

"I got a dollar says Johnny'll do for him with one shot in the head,"

Lucas Malone quickly called out. "No matter the fella's wiggling like a snake and it's two hundred yards if it's a damn foot."

"You're covered, Malone!" somebody said. "The lad's a deadeye, sure enough, but he aint *that* good!" Immediately there was a clamor of bets. As money changed hands Lucas gave John a broad wink.

John braced his rifle on the walkway wall and cocked the piece and took careful aim. The trooper was sitting up in the water with pistol in hand and had almost managed to free his leg from under the horse. John squeezed off the shot and in that instant thought he could see the ball flying out of the muzzle in a flare of smoke and cutting through the still noon air and traversing the distance to its target in less time than a heartbeat and in John's inner eye the Yankee's head loomed from hardly more than a speck to its full size as the ball crunched into it just above the left ear and bore through bone and brain and burst out the other side of the skull and took the right ear with it in a red spray. The man's head abruptly tilted to the right and he fell over dead with his face in the water.

The Mexicans raised another great cheer and Lucas Malone laughed and collected bets and clapped John on the shoulder.

John felt no joy in the shot. The man had been no more threat to him than a bottle on a fence. Lucas caught a look at his face and leaned close and said, "Jack was right, what he said. And the son of a bitch was anyway one a *theirs*, goddamnit, and it aint never nothin but right to shoot one a theirs no matter he's standin or sittin or sleepin or takin a shit or gettin laid or sayin his goddamn prayers. You hear me, boy? You done right. And *you* done it cause you the best of us at it."

John shrugged. And thought that whoever it was that said a man was no more than what he did best was right for damn sure.

A half-hour later American troops hove in view once again, this time on both the Coyoacán and the San Antonio causeways—and this time in numbers. The bridgehead guns opened fire and took down another horse. And now the wall guns at the convent fired—and mingled with the round shot was a high explosive shell whose blast put down a pair of dragoons and several foot soldiers and the Mexican cheers overwhelmed the screams of the animals and the fallen men.

And then, along both causeways, the Americans attacked.

7

The Spy Company did not engage in the initial assault. General Twiggs, directing the attack on the convent via the Coyoacán Road, held them in reserve in a willow copse a half-mile south of San Angel. They sat on the ground smoking and talking, their saddled horses close by, their rifles at hand. The day had dawned cool after a night of pouring rain but had warmed quickly as the sun rose, and now in the late forenoon the air was hot and thick. They could hear the battle raging, the steady blasting of Mexican artillery and the continuous clatter of small arms, the war cries and the screams of men, the shrieking of downed horses.

They'd heard rumor that Twiggs did not trust the Spy Company to fight its best against their own countrymen, and now old Lázaro said it looked like it was true. "I hope to hell it be true," Spooner said in English and grinned at Edward.

But Dominguez was insulted. "This Tweegs, he don't think I fight hard against Mexicanos?" he said. "Bermejillo, he is not Mexicano? Torrejón? Miñon? My good amigo, Lucero, I kill *him*. *He* is not Mexicano?"

"Hey Manuel," Spooner said, "just listen to what's going on out yonder. You *hear* that shit? You want to get into *that*? I sure's hell don't. Twiggs can leave us out of it till hell freezes over, be fine by me."

But two hours into the battle Twiggs sent orders for them to mount up immediately and join the attack. They stepped up onto their saddles and rode hard up the Coyoacán Road toward the hellish din and crested a small rise just as an artillery shell struck the causeway not forty feet in front of them and the first six riders in the column, including Dominguez, went down with their shrieking horses.

Edward's mount was struck by shrapnel and it trumpeted and veered wildly off the causeway and into the adjoining cornfield and its legs buckled and Edward was unseated. He scrambled to his feet, his hands thick with mud but still grasping his rifle. The horse was gone. He knocked the rifle barrel against his bootsole to clear the muzzle of mud. The cornstalks were almost as tall as he was and the field was hazed with gunsmoke. The earth shook with cannon rounds. The convent looked ghostly in the distance ahead. He scrabbled up the causeway embankment and peered over it and saw the battered San Antonio Road a furlong or so to the east. Saw the small vague shapes of bodies sprawled over the road and bobbing in the shallow marshwater. General Worth's infantry was slogging through the marsh toward the bridgehead as artillery shells continued to blast in their midst. He looked to the convent and saw a cannon flare orange on the wall and he rolled down the embankment as the roundshot whined overhead and struck the ground with a shudder a bare fifteen yards behind him.

Now a shell exploded on the other side of the causeway and flung up body parts in a shower of blood and black water. Dominguez came tumbling down the embankment and sprawled beside Edward and sat up wildeyed and muddy. He was bareheaded and blood ran out of his hair and over his face and mustache. He wiped his chin with his fingers and stared at the blood on them and looked at Edward in outrage. "Esos chingados casi me mataron!" He glared all about as if those who would kill him might be fast closing in on him, then snatched up his hat and put it on and looked at Edward fiercely. "Pues, vamos a ver quien mata quien! Andale, Eduardito, sigame!"

He followed Dominguez into the cornstalks and toward the convent looming a hundred yards away. Just ahead of them a regiment of Twigg's infantry was pushing forward through the cornfield too. The causeway was littered with dead and dying men and horses and continued to receive heavy artillery fire. Edward was sure that if he stopped moving he would be killed on the instant. He sensed that the only tactic of the moment was the same as in any fight—keep going toward whoever was trying to kill you and get to him and kill him first. Other compañeros converged about them as they advanced. The greater portion of the company was yet alive. Spooner materialized from the smoke like some malevolent spectre bent on annihilation. His sleeve gleamed bright with blood. "Kill em!" he demanded of Edward as if the idea had only just come to him. "Kill em all!" They went forward at a crouch through the corn, moving past corpses, past wounded men begging for help, for water, cursing, praying aloud for an end to their agony. The compañeros pressed on. The ground quivered under them with every blast of artillery. Rifle balls hummed over their heads. The screaming of the world was incessant.

As Twiggs' forces closed in on the convent the cannons on the walls and steeple began firing canister and grape and dozens of Yankees fell shrieking at each blast. The compañeros dropped to the ground and grasped tightly to the muddy earth. Edward heard himself cursing at he knew not what. Grapeshot ripped through the stalks. He smelled blood through the muck in his nose. Then came a blast of different timbre—an explosion not against earth but against stone, and there followed a chorus of cheers from the Americans in the corn ahead. He got to his feet and peered over the stalks as another blast resounded from the convent and he saw a great spray of broken stone rising high on the far side of the church and come raining down again.

"It's Worth's boys!" Spooner shouted. "They musta took the bridge! They using the Mexes' own guns on that damn church is what they doing!"

A round struck the steeple above its walkway and gouged out a great chunk of it and set the church bells tolling madly. The infantrymen in the corn let another lusty cheer. A shell blasted on a monastery roof and flung up a scattering of riflemen like rag dolls. Now a section of the wall before them blew apart—an explosion of such force it could only have been a powder store struck by a shell or set off by a spark. At the sight of the sudden breach directly ahead, the lead wave of infantry rose up in the cornfield with a huge and quavering war cry and led by their captains with sabers raised high surged toward the convent.

"Adelante!" Dominguez yelled. *"Adelante!"* He was on his feet and brandishing a bayoneted Hall and running for the broken wall and the compañeros rose and charged behind him.

Edward's field of vision now narrowed to that small segment of the world immediately before him. He was but dimly aware of the riflefire storming down on them, of the men before him and alongside him whose hands flew up as they fell and over whom he leaped or on whom he stepped as he kept running for the wall and the gaping rift in it where the first Americans were now plunging through to the interior. He glanced up at the top of the wall as it loomed closer and saw there the dark white-eyed faces of Mexican riflemen and saw a gun crew clustered about a cannon but now they too were shooting with rifles and he knew they had run out of artillery rounds. As he arrived at the breach he looked up again and saw that the gun crew was of white men.

And then he was in the courtyard and shooting a little Mexican soldier who came rushing at him with poised bayonet and looked about fourteen years old and the boy fell at his feet with blood gushing from his mouth and his eyes rolled up. Mexicans were everywhere shooting and stabbing at the first rush of Yankees and at their sides their women with bared teeth flailed with knives and now the courtyard was aflood with American troops pouring through the broken walls and scaling over the others and dropping down into the rose bushes with high tremulous howls.

He was knocked down from behind and rolled quickly against the base of the fountain and saw high on the steeple walkway a pair of Mexican riflemen with white flags tied to their rifle barrels. But the men were grabbed from behind and the white flags ripped away and one of them who would surrender was shot in the head by a big hatless redhaired man and the other was lifted bodily by a graybearded man and pitched into space and he came wheeling down screaming but barely audible over the din and struck the rim of the stone fountain and his head burst open and he flopped to the cobblestones as if his bones were turned to sand.

Cisco fell beside Edward with a face masked in blood, slashing up with his saber at a pair of Mexican soldiers trying to bayonet him. Edward jumped to his feet and thrust his bayonet through one soldier's throat and as the other turned to him Cisco skewered him through the thigh and the Mexicanscreamed and fell with blood jetting from the wound.

The courtyard was a pandemonium of outcries, screams, curses, the crack and pop and ricochet whines of gunfire, the ringing clash of bayonets and sabers. The air was thick with dust and smoke and the smells of shit and blood. Edward wielded his rifle with both hands like a club and felt every strike break bone. He stumbled on a body and went down again and saw the hazy sky for a moment before it was blocked from view by a crush of bodies slashing over him with rifles and bayonets and someone in a Spy Company uniform rent the belly of a Mexican soldier with a bowie and the Mexican's guts poured down beside Edward like a tangle of bloody blue snakes. The bowie-wielder was Fredo Ruiz who yanked him to his feet and pulled him away toward the stone steps of the church where a dozen compañeros were already rushing inside. The cobbles were slippery with blood, the whitewashed walls spattered and smeared with it.

Edward had a Colt in his hand and took the steps two at a time. But now Fredo fell and Edward nearly tripped over him and he bent to help him to his feet and saw that he had a large red hole just behind his ear and was dead. He holstered his pistol and took Fredo's two Colts and raced up the steps and into the dimness of the church where the compañeros were shooting and clubbing and stabbing at a horde of Mexicans slashing with bayonets. Edward fired the Colts till both were empty and he put down five Mexicans. He threw aside Fredo's empty pistols and drew his own but the compañeros now had the rest of the Mexicans backed against a wall and in quick order shot or bayoneted them every one.

"Por acá!" Dominguez was at an inner door, pistol in hand, gesturing for them to go up the stairway just beyond. "Arriba! Arriba en el campanario hay una bola de artilleristas. *Mátanlos*, muchachos, mátanlos to-dos!" He let Chucho and a dozen others lead the scramble up the winding stairway to the door leading out to the steeple walkway and fell in beside Edward and showed him a crazyman's grin. Clambering up the stairs behind them came a surge of Yankee riflemen with a bellowing captain in the lead.

"Está abierta!" Chucho shouted, surprised to find the door unbolted. He kicked it open wide to admit a blaze of daylight—and a deafening blast of canister tore him and five others to pieces and sprayed their bloody bits over the men below them on the stairs.

8

The canister was their last artillery round. Jack had charged the gun and turned it toward the door and ordered the bolt shot back and said, "We'll give them a warm welcome, by Jesus!." They had not a rifle bullet left among them, only a few loaded caplock pistols, only their ready knives and bayonets now as the Yankees came howling through the smoke and the destroyed doorway. But the first of them weren't Yankees at all—they were Mexicans in flat black hats and strange uniforms that bore the U.S. insignia and one of the Mexican defenders blurted, "Oye, pero qué—?" and the Black Hats fired from the hip and dropped a dozen dumbfounded San Patricios where they stood before they all came to-gether in a clash of bayonets and rifle butts and slashing sabers and knives and curses and shrieks. Men fell in sprays of blood from gashed throats and ripped bellies and punctured femorals. Those San Patricios armed with pistols shot whom they could with their single round and then flailed wildly with the empty guns. John was thrusting with his bayonet and clubbing with the rifle butt and falling back along the blood-slicked walk-way as the Black Hats and now regular Yankee soldiers too pressed in on him and the dwindling Patricios around him. He impaled a grayhaired Black Hat through the stomach and but the bayonet would not come free so he let go the rifle and drew his charged pistol with one hand and his knife with the other and now saw Lucas Malone wrestling with a Black Hat over a bayoneted rifle and he slashed the Black Hat's neck to the bone. Lucas grinned at him and then a numbing blow on the side of his face sat John down hard. A Yankee loomed over him and made to slash at him with a saber but John was the quicker and stabbed him between the legs and the soldier screamed and dropped his sword and fell away. And there was Edward in his black hat not six feet distant and staring at him open-mouthed and in that moment a San Patricio ran a bayonet into Edward's side. John shot the Patricio in the head a bare second before he himself was knocked back and his head struck stone and then the wavering image of a grinning Yankee soldier clarified into that of Master Sergeant Kaufmann who stood astraddle him and raised a bayoneted rifle to run him through—but a forearm appeared around Kaufmann's face and a knife moved across his throat and blood leapt from the open wound and Kaufmann died as he fell. Edward stood with knife in hand and blood slogging down his side and he was gaping at his brother—and then abruptly doubled over and grabbed his kneees and then spasmed and fell forward and John scrambled atop him and embraced him tightly and tensed himself for a bullet or blade in the back but now someone was hollering, "Cease action! *Cease action*, goddamnit, it's done!"

9

He awoke on a stretcher laid on the courtyard stones. The sun glared just above the west wall and the air smelled of smoke and carnage and was snarling with flies. There was moaning and weeping all around, cursing loud and low in both English and Spanish, pleas for water, for medical attention, for a bullet to end the pain. To one side of him lay a man with no face who yet breathed. On his other side lay a blond and dead-eyed American soldier whose viscera were visible through a large raw hole in his flank.

His knee throbbed and his side was on fire and every heartbeat pounded his skull with pain. The sky looked atilt. Now he heard a voice shrieking curses in Spanish, vilifying someone as turds, as filthy snakes, the vomit of pigs, the bottoms of shit pits, as even worse traitors to Mexico than La Malinche, the whore of Cortés.

He struggled up onto his elbows to see over the dead man beside him and caught sight of a column of Mexican prisoners being led across the courtyard with a general at its fore and it was he who was cursing so stridently. He had an arm bound up against his chest and a bloodstained bandage over one eye and the objects of his vilification were the onlooking members of the Spy Company. Dominguez stood by with his coatee open and his thumbs hooked in his belt and he stared back at the passing general without expression or remark. Spooner stood beside him and stared back too, grinning largely, one arm in a sling and a bandage around his thigh. The other compañeros were all looking off in various directions and none of them meeting the eyes of the general who so vehemently denunciated them. The general swept them with an accusing finger as he limped past and swore that Mexico would extract its vengeance on them for the miserable turncoat whoresons that they were. The women accompanying the prisoners spat at the men of the Spy Company, and the compañeros backed out of range until the women had gone by.

Then came the captured Americans in Mexican uniforms and now the great crowd of U.S. soldiers began excoriating them and spitting at them and pelting them with rocks and mud and dogshit and calling for their blood, calling for them to be shot on the spot, to be hanged from the cypress trees. Their most sulfurous fulminations were directed at a tall redhead whom Edward recognized as the man who had shot the Mexican in the steeple for trying to wave a white flag. "We'll all of us piss on yer grave, Riley, ye miserable bastard!" one hollered at him. The one called Riley looked at the man and clapped a hand on his bicep and raised his other fist. The Americans howled with rage and began surging forward and they would surely have torn Riley and his fellows to pieces had not Generals Twiggs and Worth, sitting their horses in the forefront of the crowd, ordered them to stand fast.

"You're the lowest scum on the earth!" A wildfaced Irishman shouted at the passing prisoners. "The filthiest bastards to ever shame the face of God is what you are!"

"You'll see these sons of bitches hang, boys!" Twiggs bellowed. "Every last traitorous dog of them!"

Edward strained to hold his head up, scanning the column of American prisoners and finally spying John as he trudged past in his bloodstained tunic, hatless and indifferent to the maledictions raining on him and his fellows. Hardly flinching as a rock glanced off his shoulder. Staring dead ahead as if fixed upon an impatient fate.

Edward fell back and the sky above whirled and he spun into darkness.

10

When next he woke he was in the U.S. Army hospital at Tacubaya, within two miles of the heart of the capital. He had been unconsciousness for nearly three days. He'd lost much blood through the bayonet wound in his side and his kidney had been damaged and the doctors had thought he might die. Then his fever began to ease and the worst was past. But his knee had been shattered by a pistol ball and they debated whether to amputate and finally decided the leg could stay. But the knee would never again bend more than slightly and so he would limp for the rest of his life. "At least," a doctor told him, "you'll be limping on your own leg and not on a wooden stump." He'd suffered a concussion as well, and the ringing in his ears would likely prove permanent. When one doctor asked what had happened to his scalp, Edward looked at him without expression and the doctor asked no more about it.

Over the following week he mostly slept, waking occasionally to gulp water as if trying to douse a fire in his belly, to slurp soup spooned to him by the nurses. But even the effort of trying to think clearly was exhausting, and so he slept. Slept and dreamt of Daddyjack with his single eye and in his bloody-crotched trousers wandering through the charred and smoky remains of a large razed house and muttering angrily to himself as he kicked at the smoldering cinders. He spotted Edward where he lay wounded and in a sweat on a blanket under a drooping willow. "Ye done good," he said. "The both ye. Bloodkin's all ye got in the world and ye got to protect ye brother and him to protect you. It's how it be with brothers and no matter their blood's been tainted." He scratched his whiskered face and looked at Edward slyly. "Aye—tainted I say! Poisoned! Poisoned sure as if she put rattler venom in ye veins while ye were yet curled in her belly, you and ye brother and ye sister too. She poisoned my tree, that demon whore! Poisoned it and made it to bear a bad bitter fruit." He went back to sifting through the ashes of the house and Edward wanted to speak to him but it was as if he'd been robbed of all language shaped of words.

11

When he finally sat up in bed and began eating with appetite and again taking notice of the world around him eleven days had passed since the battle of Churubusco. He was informed that Colonel Dominguez and others of the Spy Company had come by to see after him several times but he'd each time been asleep when they came and the doctor would not have them wake him. Two days ago the company had left as an escort to a military train bound for Veracruz.

From the nurses and fellow patients Edward learned that General Scott had halted his army just at the outskirts of Mexico City and struck an armistice with Santa Anna in order to discuss peace terms. On their pledge not to take up arms again for the rest of the war, Scott had released most of the three thousand Mexican prisoners captured in the push to the capital's perimeter, and there'd been a good deal of muttering in the American ranks about that. "Lots of fellas think he ought to of shot them all," said a man in the bed beside his, an artillery corporal named Walter Berry who'd lost a foot. "A dead man's a lot less like to fight you again than a fella who promises he won't."

"Leastways Old Scotty didn't turn loose a one of them deserter sonsabitches call themselfs Saint Paddies," said a man named Alan Overmeyer who lay in the bed on Edward's other flank. Overmeyer had lost his right arm and right leg and so he looked like he'd been halved by length.

"Hell no, he didn't!" Walter Berry said. "Scotty'd let *them* go, his own army would of hung *him*, you bet!"

"That goddamn Santa Anner saying if he'd a had him a hundret more like them Saint Paddies he'd of won the fight. Shit! All the more reason to hang all the sons of bitches, I say. Saint Paddies, my sorry ass—Saint Judases more like it."

They told Edward that more than half of the Saint Patrick Battalion had been killed at Churubusco. Nearly two dozen were unaccounted for and a few of them were presumed to have escaped. Some ninety had been captured and seventy-two of them charged with desertion from the United States Army. Scott wasted no time bringing them to trial. Forty-three had been tried at Tacubaya the Monday before last and three days later the other twenty-nine were tried at San Angel. Every man of them but two were found guilty and sentenced to hang.

"Ye should of heard the cheer in that San Angel court when the judges passed sentence on Riley," a nurse named Marlin Grady said. "I was right there and I mean to tell ye I thought the roof would blow off the place, so loud it was. Oh, that's one right hated bastard, Riley. It's him formed that bunch of rebel Paddies and him that had the blasphemous balls to call them by good Saint Patrick's name. He's done naught but blacken us Irishmen each one, he has, the filthy son of a bitch."

"They hung them all?" Edward asked, feeling his own throat constricting tightly. He saw John's face before him now as clearly as he had up on the steeple walkway in the instant they'd caught sight of each other, his astonished bloodsmeared face.

"Not yet they aint, but it's good as done, by Jesus," said Walter Berry. "It's only for Old Fuss and Feathers to approve the sentences all official-like and then it's the noose for them Judas bastards."

The trials had been covered by *The American Star*, a Yankee newspaper that had begun publication in Jalapa and followed after the U.S. Army since, and Marlin Grady brought Edward some back issues so he could read the accounts for himself. He thereby learned that one of the Saint Patricks, a fellow named Ellis, was ruled never to have been properly enlisted and so was acquitted on that technicality—and two hours later was attacked in the street by a bunch of U.S. soldiers and beaten nearly to death before a crowd of Mexicans rescued him and spirited him away. Another Saint Patrick, Lewis Prefier, had not been in a Mexican uniform when captured, had in fact been completely naked, and he besides proved to be crazy, so loony he didn't even know his own name and could not be made to understand the simplest questions put to him any more than could a dog, and so the court granted him a discharge paper and he was shortly thereafter driven from the gates of the garrison under a hail of flung stones.

Only six of the accused pled guilty. Most of the others all professed their innocence of deliberate desertion and claimed to have been coerced by one means or another into joining the Mexican side. A few held their tongues throughout. But the prosecution brought forth two Saint Patrick prisoners as witnesses, an Englishman and an Irishman who had been residents of Mexico since before the war and had never been in the American army. They were willing to testify against their fellow Patricks in exchange for early release from prison. They pointed at each of the accused in turn and said that they had seen him willingly put on the uniform of the Mexican army and bear arms against the Americans.

Included in the reports was an alphabetical list of the seventy men condemned to hang. And there—between "Klager, John" and "Logen-hamer, Henry"—Edward read the name of his only true brother in this world. And wanted to howl.

The newspaper also carried several sardonic accounts of the Mexican outcry against the death sentences passed on their beloved San Patricios. Civil and military officials of every rank protested publicly. The Arch-bishop of Mexico himself made a plea to Winfield Scott on their behalf, as did the British foreign minister. The Irish leader of the deserters, John Riley, whom the Americans held as the most detestable of the loathsome lot, attracted the most ardent defenders. A petition for clemency toward him was submitted to Scott and signed by nearly two dozen "Citizens of the United States and Foreigners of different Nations in the City of Mexico." It read, in part:

> *We humbly pray that his Excellency the General in Chief of the American forces may be graciously pleased to extend a pardon to Captain John O'Reilly of the Legion of St. Patrick and generally speaking to all deserters from the American service.*
>
> *We speak to your Excellency particularly of O'Reilly as we understand his life to be in most danger; his conduct might be pardoned by your Excellency in consideration of the protection he extended in this city to persecuted and banished American citizens by nullifying an order he held to apprehend them and not acting on it. We believe him to have a generous heart admitting all his errors.*

In response to the clamor for leniency toward the Saint Patricks, General David Twiggs told *The American Star* that it was Generals Santa Anna and Ampudia and Arista who had solicited and "seduced from duty" the men who deserted the American ranks, and so it was they who were responsible for the price the "poor wretches" would now pay for their crimes.

12

Over the next week Edward fast regained strength. The wound in his side knit tightly and he got out of bed and for longer periods every day and walked up and down the ward, the first two days with the aid of a crutch before he switched to a cane. Yet he felt like a man in a dream. The world about him was starkly clear but seemed to move slowly, as if underwater. He felt an unyielding dread. Each time he closed his eyes he saw his brother's face. He had no thoughts at all.

Now came Scott's rulings on the verdicts of the courts. For various reasons he granted outright pardons to five of the condemned. In fifteen other cases he found that the men had deserted before the war's official declaration and therefore could not, according to the Articles of War, be legally executed. These fifteen would instead receive fifty lashes on the bare back and be hot-iron branded on the cheek with a *D* for "deserter." They would thereafter remain imprisoned until the U.S. Army removed itself from Mexico, at which time they would have their heads shaved to the scalp and the buttons ripped from their uniforms and be drummed out of service to the tune of "The Rogue's March":

> *Poor old soldier, poor old soldier,*
> *tarred and feathered and sent to hell,*
> *because he would not soldier well.*

The sentences of the fifty others he let stand. They would hang.

On learning that John Riley was one of the fifteen to be spared the rope the hospital went into uproar. Chamber pots were pitched through windows and plates of food sent crashing against the walls. Scott was cursed for a stupid bastard. Walter Berry shouted, "Riley's the *main* whoreson of them! He's the one most goddamn well *ought* to hang!" Overmeyer wept with fury. The outrage was rampant through the ranks. The *Star* quoted Scott's aide-de-camp as saying the general had walked the floor each night as he struggled with his decision. He had known the troops would be inflamed by the commutation of Riley's sentence. His staff officers had argued that it would be preferable to spare all the other turncoats than to reprieve Riley. Scott rebutted them with the point that the law was the law, that the Articles of War prohibited Riley's execution, and if he did not cleave to the law he would as much violate his own duty as John Riley had violated his. He would sooner be killed in the assault on Mexico City, he reportedly said, than to violate his duty to the law.

Edward wanted only to know who besides Riley had been spared from execution, but he could not of course reveal he had bloodkin amid the traitors. He hobbled through the ward trying to cadge a newspaper but none of the few who had one would part with it while they read and cursed and re-read the hard news about Riley. Marlin Grady finally went out and bought more newspapers and Edward took one and sat on his bed and spread it before him and scanned the names of the fully pardoned five and recognized none. He cursed lowly and then ran his eye down the list of fifteen whose sentences had been commuted and did not see John's name. He saw Riley's but not John's and his breath caught and his throat tightened and he felt like screaming, like shooting somebody.

Then he slowly went down the list again, this time with his finger, and this time touched on "Little, John" and he looked and looked at the name and was afraid to take his eyes from it for fear it would not be there the next time he looked.

13

On the tenth of September he rose before daybreak and joined some of the other wounded aboard a hospital wagon transport for the three-mile trip to the central plaza in San Angel to attend the punishments of the San Patricios who had there been convicted. Dominguez had not yet returned from Veracruz. The armistice had come to an end three days before and the outskirts of the capital shook steadily with artillery blasts and crackled with small arms. The air again smelled of rotting flesh, smoke, gunpowder and dust.

La Plaza de San Jacinto was packed with spectators a dozen deep in a wide semicircle in front of the church. Every American soldier in San Angel not then engaged in the fighting had turned out to witness the punishments and most of the local citizenry was in attendance as well. The eastern sky was a scarlet riot as the sun broke over the mountains. People watched from rooftops and wagon beds, from their horses and from up in the trees. The town dogs raced about in a yapping frenzy. An army band played "Hail, Columbia" while across the square a Mexican string band strummed out a sequence of extemporaneous ballads in praise of the San Patricios. A gallows had been erected in front of the church, a simple scaffold of four thick beams—an overhead stringer some forty feet long supported by a fourteen-foot beam at either end and another in the center. Sixteen nooses dangled from the stringer and positioned directly below them were eight muledrawn flatbed wagons, each facing in the direction opposite to that of the one beside it and each with a Mexican driver at the reins. At one end of the gallows, resplendent in full-dress uniforms, General Scott and his officers sat their horses. Near to them stood seven black-robed priests. At the other end of the scaffold a squad of soldiers in their undershirts tended a large blacksmith's brazier shimmering with heat and holding several branding irons and throwing off sparks with each puff of the bellows. A wooden stool was close at hand and a pile of spades. A few yards beyond stood a large oak tree with a coil of rope lying at its base.

Now the drums began to roll and the murmur of the troops rose to an excited babble and then erupted in execrations as a small group of Saint Patricks in their blue Mexican uniforms with their hands manacled in front of them was led into the plaza from around the side of the municipal building. They were seven and John was the second man in the column, directly behind Riley, who was the only one among them being vilified by name. Edward's heart turned over at the sudden thought that these were the men about to be hanged, that he had misunderstood the newspaper reports, that Scott had changed his mind and decided he'd yet hang them all. But the prisoners were not put aboard the hanging wagons. They were made only to line up facing the gallows.

Then came another column into the plaza and these men had their hands bound behind them and were the men about to die. They were led to the wagons and helped up onto them, two men to a wagon. Their boots were removed and pitched aside and they were made to stand toward the rear of the flatbeds. "How come it's only sixteen of em?" Edward heard someone ask. "It was twenty spose to hang here." Someone said he'd heard the other four would be hanged tomorrow at Mixcoac, about a mile and a half away.

"How come's that?" the first man asked.

"Hell, old son," the second said, "who knows why the army does anything the way it do?"

Most of the seven prisoners standing witness to the executions were staring down at their own feet, but not John or Riley. Their gaze was fixed on one of the condemned, a graybeard who looked down at them and grinned. "So long, Johnny boys!" he called down through the steady drumbeat. "See you in hell!" A white hood was draped over his head and the same done to the others and then the nooses were set round their necks and snugged up tightly. The drums abruptly fell silent and now the only sounds in the square were the susurrant prayers of the priests and the squawking of crows in the high branches and the sudden barking of a solitary dog. The hoods of the condemned were pulsing against their faces with their quickened breath.

A captain stepped up to the end of the scaffold nearest General Scott and raised a pistol in the air. The muledrivers made ready with their whips. The drums again rolled, louder and faster than before. The captain was watching Scott intently. Scott's gaze was set on the sixteen hooded men. He looked to Edward like an old man tired with killing. He appeared to sigh. Then his mouth tightened and he nodded and the captain fired the pistol and the drums cut short and the drovers cracked their whips and four wagons clattered to the east and four to the west and sixteen men dropped off the flatbeds. The crowd gasped and there followed immediately a medley of male laughter and cursing and of women's wails and sobs. Some of the hanged died on the instant and some kicked wildly for a moment before going limp in the unmistakable attitude of death, but one of them, the graybeard who had called down to John and Riley, was kicking in a way that made it clear his neck was not broken, that his noose had been poorly set and he was slowly choking to death. Soldiers were pointing at him and laughing.

"Pull on him!" John cried out. "Pull on him, goddamnit!" The sergeant of the guard strode quickly down the line to John and punched him full in the mouth, staggering him, shouting, "No talking, prisoner!" Riley looked as if he might kick at him but the sergeant pulled a club from his belt and squared off and Riley held back.

Two of the priests dashed forth and each grabbed one of the graybeard's legs and tugged down on him and more soldiers joined in the laughter as the graybeard's pants went dark with piss. John was gaping at the strangling man in anguish with blood running from his mouth. The graybeard yet struggled weakly and there issued from under his hood a horrid croak as the redfaced priests hung their weight on his legs. The man's neck was now stretched grotesquely and Edward thought his head might tear off. But now a pair of Mexican muledrivers ran over to the priests and took the graybeard's legs from them and they lifted the man up about two feet and jerked him down hard and snapped his neck and killed him.

The dead were then cut down and the priests bore away seven of them in handcarts, seven who were devout Catholics and had taken Holy Communion and the last rites prior to being ushered to the gallows. They would be buried in a monastery graveyard a mile north of San Angel. The other nine were dragged by the heels around to the side of the church and laid in a line. Already the flies had found them and swarmed over the hooded faces and stained trousers.

The drums began anew and the punishments continued. The seven prisoners spared hanging were now made to form a line before the oak tree and Riley was the first of them ordered to step up to it and strip to the waist. He was stood with his chest against the tree trunk and his arms were bound tightly around it. The muscles stood like cords along his arms and back. General Twiggs was in charge of carrying out the punishments and had appointed a pair of burly Mexican muleteers to take turns delivering the floggings. He considered the turncoats unworthy of being whipped by Americans. Now one of the skinners stepped out with a rawhide lash in hand and set himself a few feet behind Riley. "Tell them to lay on with all the severity they can muster!" Twiggs called out to his interpreter. "Tell them if they do not, I will have *them* whipped to blood pudding" The interpreter relayed the order and the muleteers nodded grimly.

The first lash popped like a pistolshot and laid a red stripe across Riley's back and the onlooking troopers cheered. His muscles bunched and spasmed. Again the whip flashed and Riley's head threw back and his teeth showed white in his grimace. The muleteer worked with the steady rhythm of a man hewing timber, laying the strokes on hard and with barely a pause between them. The whip cracked and cracked and the stripes cut one over the other and blood stippled the branches and leaves overhead and streaked down Riley's back to darken his trousers and still he did not cry out, not until the nineteenth stroke, and his first yowl and each he let thereafter on every lash that followed roused louder cheers yet from the American troops. At thirty lashes he was groaning between the cracks of the whip and the soldiers were laughing at him and chiding him for a weakling. The muleskinner was pouring sweat. He grunted with every stroke. By the fortieth lash Riley was sagging against his bonds and the bloodstripes were no longer distinct one from the other but had shaped now a single massive wound and his pants were bloodsoaked to the thighs. Edward thought he might die before the last stroke was laid on. And then it was done. At the count of fifty Riley hung limp on the trunk but was yet conscious. His bonds were loosed and he crumpled to the ground and some of the soldiers cheered this too and derided him for a little sister. The sergeant of the guard prodded him with his boot toe and said something to him too softly for Edward to hear. And Riley, grunting, got to his feet without assistance and turned toward the ranks of troops watching him. He spat at his feet and grinned a crooked wavering grin. Those who had not let off taunting him howled in rage and cursed him and threatened to kill him at the first opportunity. The sergeant of the guard took him aside and sat him down near the brazier. The men tending the fire made mean gibes and the smitty raised a redly glowing branding iron and shook it at him and said he was going to burn him right through to his teeth. Riley muttered for him to fuck his mother. The smitty's face went livid and he started toward him but the sergeant told him to get back to the fire and mind his duty. "We aint quits," the smitty said to Riley.

Now John was shed of his shirt and brought forth to the flogging tree and quickly made fast to it and the other muleteer took up the lash while the first recruited himself with a dipper of water and a cigarette. This time Edward flinched with every crack of the whip. Like Riley, John was limp but still sensible after the fiftieth stroke. "Bedamn if it don't look like wolves done et on that boy's back," said a man near Edward with an arm that ended at the elbow.

"Hell, it aint so bad," someone else said. "I seen men flogged open to the backbone and all they ribs showed through. I don't see much bone showing on these boys. They aint hardly getting whipped, you ask me."

John was made to sit beside Riley and neither man looked at the other as the floggings continued. The blood ran off their backs and soaked their pants and stained the cobblestones beneath them. Whipcracks and outcries and cheers echoed off the plaza walls. Then all seven had received their fifty lashes and the trunk and underbranches of the tree were bespattered with blood. Only two of the Patricks had been unconscious when loosed from the tree and one of them recovered his senses within a few minutes. It was thought the other would die and bets were made among the soldiers but the prostrate Patrick at last bestirred himself after a second dousing with a bucket of water and sat up and his back wore a coat of bloody mud. Those who lost the wager cursed him now more hotly than they had damned him for a traitor.

By the time the last man was set free of the whipping tree the army spectators were chanting, "The iron! The iron! The iron!" in anticipation of the brandings.

Now the prisoners' hands were manacled behind them and they were again formed into a column with Riley at its head. He was made to sit on the stool hard by the brazier and a burly soldier on either side pinned him fast by an arm and a third man, a huge barrel of a corporal, stood behind him and put an armlock on his head and twisted it tight against his chest so that the right cheek was turned outward. The grinning smitty drew a red iron from the fire and said, "Hold the bastard fast now."

He put the brand to Riley's cheek and there was a low sizzle and Riley screamed and the troops cheered and in the next moment Edward caught the sickly-sweet odor of the seared flesh. But now the sergeant of the guard was gesturing angrily at the smitty and calling him a stupid shit and the smitty only shrugged and smiled a wide foolish grin and said,

"Hell, it was a accident is all, I can easy enough make it right." The other members of the branding detail were grinning too and now Edward saw the reason for their good humor: the *D* brand on Riley's cheek had been applied backward.

General Twiggs hupped his horse over to the branding party and asked what the hell was going on and the sergeant told him. Twiggs looked down at Riley and chuckled and said, "Well now fella, I guess we *all* make mistakes, don't we?"

Word of Riley's botched branding spread among the soldiers and there was laughter and cheering and cries of, "Well done, smitty!" Twiggs smiled at the blacksmith and said, "Do him proper on the other cheek, soldier, and let's have no more accidents. General Scott wants to be done with this in quick order."

The big corporal twisted Riley's head to the other side and exposed his left cheek and the smitty pressed a fresh red iron to it and Riley screamed again.

And then it was John screaming on the stool. They all of them screamed in their turn and soon each bore a dark *D* on his misshapen right cheek.

The prisoners were then handed spades and ordered to dig nine deep graves alongside the church. They swayed and stumbled like drunks at their painful labor to the amusement of the watching soldiers but yet they achieved the task. And when they had done with the digging they lowered into the ground the nine dead men still with the hoods on their faces and covered them up.

They were ordered to put their shirts on and some among them grimaced at the touch of the cloth against their flayed backs, but not John, whom Edward was watching. As they were marched from the plaza one of the prisoners collapsed and the soldiers cheered and chanted "Die! Die! Die!" Riley pulled the man up and draped him over his shoulder and bore him onward. Others of them looked ready to fall but managed to keep their feet. The bloody seven staggered by within ten yards of Edward. As they were passing, John looked over as if drawn by the intensity of Edward's gaze andtheir eyes met and Edward wondered if his brother could read in his face the anguish he felt, the fury, the rage to howl and wreak destruction. In John's maimed face he saw naught but indifference so vast it was frightening. The look of one who cared not at all if the sun should never rise again.

14

On the following day he went to Mixcoac and saw hanged the other four Saint Patricks convicted at San Angel. He'd not intended to witness any more of the executions after the Tacubaya hangings but that night Daddyjack had come to him in a shadowy dream, eye aglitter and bloody hair wild, whispering, "It aint done, it aint done." He'd asked what he was talking about but Daddyjack only shook his head and hissed again, "It aint done, I tell ye!" He seemed nigh to lunacy.

The dream upset Edward, filled him with foreboding that John might yet be hanged, and so he went to Mixcoac to see for himself that he was not. He kept his own company all the rest of that day and all of the next, his thoughts consumed by his brother.

That evening the Spy Company returned from its Veracruz mission and Dominguez and Spooner showed up at the hospital and secured Edward's release. The three repaired to a cantina and there drank beer and tequila and ate chicken mole. Dominguez and Spooner grinningly accused Edward of malingering.

"A damn limp aint no excuse for staying off a *horse*, goddamnit," Spooner said. "There *we* been, riding all over the damn mountains and all through lowland brush and risking our lives to rid Mexico of bandidos, and here *you* been, laying about and acting like it's a chore to walk and eating three meals a day and getting fat."

Dominguez laughed. "If we get rid of all the bandidos in Mexico there would not be one hundred people left in this country."

"Well for damn sure I'll be with them other ninety-nine," Spooner said, "but I caint say about you boys."

Dominguez and Spooner wanted to witness the execution of the thirty Saint Patricks convicted by the court at Tacubaya. Edward agreed to go with them. He did not tell them of his brother, but his apprehension that John was still in peril of the noose would not dismiss until he had seen the last of the executions carried out.

15

They arrived as the sun broke over the mountains in a shattering vermilion blaze. The gallows was of the same design as at San Angel but twice as long in order to accommodate the thirty condemned at once. It stood on a hill just outside of Mixcoac with a clear view to Mexico City and the castle of Chapultepec on a higher hill just west of the capital. The branding brazier was set close by and a smitty already at work on the bellows. The artillery assault on the castle had begun before daybreak and the booming strikes and smoke of the shells were easily visible from the Mixcoac hilltop. So too were the ranks of dragoon and infantry troops down in the valley awaiting the order to attack.

In charge of the executions was Colonel William Selby Harney whose decision to hang all thirty at a stroke was in keeping with his reputation, which as his obituary in 1890 would record was that of a "right hard hater always; somewhat ferocious, too, in the award of punishments." He was said to have beaten a recalcitrant female slave to death in Saint. Louis some dozen years before. During the Indian Wars in Florida he was given to decapitating prisoners and posting their heads on stakes along the riverbanks as warning to the savages. There were tales throughout the army of his prodigious appetite for Indian girls whom he afterwards prevented from bringing charges against him by hanging them for spies. He would now hang the last thirty turncoats in his own fashion.

The three compañeros sat their nervous stamping horses alongside a troop of dragoons posted hard by the gallows and watched a column of ten mule-driven carts come clattering up the hill with three men seated in each cart but for the last, which held only two. The men were bound both hand and foot and when Edward saw that John was not among them his relief was so utter he suddenly felt exhausted. Harney demanded to know of the lieutenant in charge of the prisoner detail why only twenty-nine men had been brought out. The lieutenant explained that one of the condemned, a man named Francis O'Connor, had lost both legs in the Churubusco fight and the doctors had said he was not expected to live more than another day or two.

"Day or two, hell!" Harney thundered. "The bastard will not outlive the morning! Get that sorry son of a bitch out here right now! If any goddamned doctor interferes, tell him I'll hang *him* too!" The lieutenant rode off at a gallop

The carts were aligned under the gallows and the prisoners made to stand and the nooses put around their necks. They would wear no hoods. Harney wanted them to witness what was happening at Chapultepec. "You sons of bitches see that Mex flag on the tower?" he said, pointing toward the castle where the infantry assault had begun and riflefire crackled and smoked and the army band marching behind the troops had struck up "Yankee Doodle" with all its might. "When that piece of shit comes down and the Stars and Stripes go up, *that's* when you'll hang, the whole bastard lot of you. Now you just think about that in the time left to you."

Dominguez glanced at Spooner and Edward. "Pero que modo de matar es este?" he said in a low voice. "A man does not kill like this. Is no a children's game."

"If we got to wait till your flag flies over that tower," a goateed Saint Patrick called out, "we'll by God live to eat the goose that fattens on the grass over *yer* fucking grave, ye damned blowhard bastard!"

The other Patricks laughed and the three compañeros exchanged grins. Harney hupped his horse over to the cart holding the Patrick who spoke and slashed at him with his saber, gashing open the man's face.

"Damn ye!" the Patricio shouted. "Damn ye for the cowardly rascal ye are!" Blood poured off his rent face and his teeth were visible through the open flap in his cheek.

"He's ruined yer looks for sure, Larry!" a Patrick in a neighboring cart yelled out. "Ye'll not turn the head of a pretty girl the rest of your born days, I'll wager!" The bleeding man called Larry laughed along with his comrades.

Harney was red-faced with fury but everyone knew he could not make them cease their mockery nor their mirth, not short of shooting them, which would but deprive him of the pleasure of seeing them hang.

"Laugh, you whoreson bastards!" he said. "We'll see how you laugh when Old Glory rides up that pole and you're dancing on the air. We'll see who'll be laughing then!"

They carried on in jocular fashion, these condemned men, as the American infantry advanced steadily up the Chapultepec hill through the fierce defending fire and made the castle walls.

The legless Saint Patrick, O'Connor, now arrived in a hospital wagon and was transferred to a hanging cart where a board was laid across the slat sides to set him upon with his hands bound behind him. A noose was snugged round his neck and the rope made taut to keep him from toppling. The bandages around the man's leg stumps were red-brown with blood and stained yellow with pus and gave feast to a growling riot of flies. His eyes were black hollows and he looked nearly dead where he sat.

Now the infantry had breached the walls of the castle and a pale haze of smoke and dust rose from within where the fighting was hand to hand

and the bayonet would decide the day. For nearly another half-hour the battle raged at Chapultepec. When some of the Patricks mockingly complained that they were awful damned tired of standing, others of them joked that they'd be a far sight more discomforted if they tried to sit down. And then the last of the gunfire fell off and a minute later a faint but prolonged cheering from the castle came to the men on the hill. Harney came alert and stood in the stirrups as if he might thus be able to see over the distant walls.

And now the Mexican flag began to descend and Harney reined his mount around and trotted his horse along the front of the gallows and grinned up at the array of condemned men fallen silent who only a moment before had been joking about their tired legs.

"Ready your whips!" Harney ordered the muleteers at the wagon reins.

"Look there now!" he shouted at the condemned and pointed toward the castle tower where the Mexican flag was now gone from sight. "Look there at the last sight your traitorous eyes will ever see. Look there at the flag you betrayed, damn your souls!"

Over the tower of Chapultepec castle now rose the Stars and Stripes, shining in the sun. And every noosed man stared at it and beyond to his own eternity.

"Laugh *now!*" Harney bellowed. And cackled like a lunatic. And slashed the air overhead with his saber to send the wagons clattering forward and in the next moment the renegades were kicking wildly at the emptiness under their feet like crazed marionettes—all but one who lacked the legs to kick with—and then the thirty were dangling dead in the haze of that ancient Mexican hill.

There followed the floggings and brandings of the eight whose death sentences had been commuted and who would be made to bury their hanged comrades. And as those punishments were taking place Edward told Dominguez he wanted his help and Dominguez asked for what and Edward told him, "To help my brother escape from prison."

16

In the *North American*, yet another American newspaper publishing in Mexico City at this time, appeared the following editorial:

We can paint no man, however cursed by conscience and despised by all, so perfectly unmanned, so infamously degraded, as the deserter. There is no punishment too severe for the traitor; no infamy too blackening for his name. There is no word in the language that implies so much shame as that of deserter. With Americans it expresses more than all the epithets of the language; for if all crimes were bundled together and stewed down into one, they could not convey the strength of the blackest of all—DESERTER!

And on the eve following the executions at Mixcoac, an editorial in the *Diario del Gobeirno,*. a Mexico City newspaper, proclaimed thus:

Mexicans: Among the Europeans whom the American army has hired to kill us, there are many unfortunate men who are convinced of the injustice of this war, who profess the same Roman Catholic religion that we do, and who, following the noble impulse of their hearts, passed over to our army to defend our just cause. From them the president formed the Foreign Legion, known under the name of the San Patricios. At Angostura and Churubusco they fought with utmost bravery and after the enemy took this last place, they were made prisoners. Well then, would you believe it, my countrymen? This day, in cold blood, the barbarian American army, from an impulse of superstition, and after the manner of savages and as practiced in primitive times, have hanged these men as a holocaust.

Mexicans: in the name of our dignity as men and of God Himself, we should all unite in one unanimous and continuous effort to revenge those great outrages. . . .

Such was the opposition of American and Mexican sentiments on the subject of the San Patricios. Americans everywhere castigated them as damnable traitors while Mexicans of all stations venerated them as heroes. Scott refused the Mexican entreaties to free the Saint Patricks from prison. But he did permit the city council to send a team of inspectors to see for themselves that the Saint Patricks were being humanely treated. They were locked up in the Acordada penitentiary, an imposing whitewashed colonial building that covered almost a whole city block on the wide and lovely Calle Patoni. Armed guards manned the walls of the large central courtyard where the prisoners passed their days playing cards, exercising, writing letters, napping in the shade of the ahuehuete trees around the fountain. In the early evening they were locked into a common cell that took up half of the second floor. Tall barred windows afforded them a clear view of the busy sidewalk and street below and of the lovely Alameda with its smooth stone walkways and dense green trees and flower gardens bursting with colors. The inspectors saw that each man had been given a shirt and pair of trousers, shoes, and a sleeping mat and blanket, and they verified that the men were adequately fed. The council requested that the prisoners be permitted to receive social visitors and gifts, and against the protests of his advisers Scott consented. Newspapers began to report on the daily parade of people, mostly priests and women, let into the prison to visit with the San Patricios and bestow upon them rich foods and pastries and clean clothes and books. Every man of them had been presented with a bunk with a soft mattress and received a daily change of freshly laundered linens. One of their benefactors had furnished the cell with a long table and benches where the men might sit to write letters and consult with their attorneys. All this generosity to the traitors made the editor of the *North American* wax choleric:

> *The guard over these prisoners is importuned daily by persons apparently occupying a respectable position in society, who drive to the place in their carriages, and carry in to these miserable apologies for humanity, these fat rascals, all sorts of luxuries, while their own countrymen, prisoners also, the sick and wounded officers and privates, are utterly neglected. The greater portion of these ostentatiously benevolent people are women.*

One such woman was the Señora Olga Maritza Martinez de del Castro, a wealthy widow of middle age and regal aspect whose father was a retired ambassador and whose husband, a colonel of lancers with Ampudia's army, had died a hero's death at Monterrey. Señora del Castro would evermore dress in mourning and vehemently despise all things American but for the men of the San Patricio Battalion, whom she regarded as saints for their devoted defense of her beloved country. She had contributed lavishly to the Mexican war effort, and as one of the capital's leading social luminaries she was often quoted in the Mexican press regarding her views on American barbarities and San Patricio heroism. She made regular visits to the Patricios and was afforded every deference by the prisonkeepers on directive of General Scott who'd been informed of her social standing. She had shaken the hand of each Saint

Patrick in the Acordada and ensured that they were fed on ample cuts of meat every day. It was she who arranged for them to have mattressed bunks to sleep upon. And because she was a woman of liberal sensibilities who well and frankly understood the needs of men, she sent an emissary to General Scott with a special petition. Scott had already quietly granted to the half-dozen married Saint Patricks the same right of weekly conjugal visitation that Mexican law conferred on its own convicts, and now Señora del Castro asked that he extend to the unmarried Patricios an equal right of intimate relations with their sweetheart or, lacking one, with a woman of the trade. She herself would arrange for the women and bear all costs associated with their visits. On learning that such amatory privileges were routinely sanctioned by Mexican penal authorities, Scott shrugged and acquiesced to the señora's request. The Mexican newspapers applauded her efforts on behalf of more civilized treatment for the San Patricios but the American papers excoriated Scott for extending his excessive benevolence to the traitors to such lengths as this immoral Mexican practice.

Came a morning when a trio of men—two Americans and a Mexican and all three in well-tailored business suits—presented themselves at her door and informed the mayordomo that they desired an audience with la Señora del Castro. They claimed to be friends of the San Patricios and in possession of information about them which la Señora might find of great interest. The mayordomo asked them to wait and while he was within they wondered if he might be sending for the authorities to arrest them for trespassers or worse. Then he was back and politely ushered them into the parlor where la señora awaited them. Her appraising look at the two Americans was openly suspicious, yet she bade all three sit and had a servant pour tea. The Mexican spoke for the visitors, applying his most formal Spanish although it was well known la señora owned a flawless English. He introduced himself as Capitán Jorge Amado and his two friends as Lieutenant James Walker and Corporal William Meese, all three of the San Patricio Battalion, lucky survivors who had eluded capture at Churubusco and were now under Santa Anna's direct order to reorganize the unit as quickly as possible for return to action against the Yankees.

La señora was thrilled by this revelation and there followed much expression of mutual admiration, on her part for their valorous struggle in the defense of Mexico, on theirs for her generosity toward their imprisoned comrades and fierce public support of their organization. The two

Americans apologized for their wretched Spanish but la señora dismissed the notion with a wave of her hand and said in English, "In the language of bravery you are both supremely fluent."

The visitors shortly came to the point. Their new unit was almost fully manned and was eager to resume operations against the Yankee supply lines between the capital and Veracruz but it lacked an explosives expert, and the best explosives man they knew of was now among the prisoners in Acordada. Although there was absolutely no chance to free all their imprisoned fellows, it might yet be possible to help *one* to escape. And that was why they had come to her. If she were willing, she could be of great service to her country.

But of course she was willing! Just tell her what to do!

Barely an hour later the mayordomo brought before them a half-dozen men closely fitting the description given by the youngest of the three Patricios, he with the gouged face who limped on a cane and wore a black bandanna over his crown. The six men were lined up in front of this young man who carefully studied each of them in turn before pointing out his selection. La señora smiled and nodded. Like everyone else on her staff, the chosen man, Luis by name, was completely devoted to her and would do whatever she asked.

17

Edward had several times gone to the Alameda park and stared across the street at the Acordada and pondered his brother's plight but he had not yet been to see him. He felt at fault for John's present circumstance. He was certain his brother had not voluntarily enlisted in the army and so must have been pressganged in New Orleans. If they had been at each other's side that wouldn't have happened—or at least they would have been forced into the army together. But he had abandoned his brother in Dixie City and John had been dragooned. And then had deserted. And then for some damn reason joined the Mexicans and had narrowly missed being hanged for it. But he had been whipped and branded and locked up in prison, and Edward had felt he could not face him without some ready offer of atonement.

On the morning after he'd gone with Dominguez and Spooner to the house of La Señora del Castro he went to the Acordada in his Spy Company uniform and presented himself to the officer of the guard as Sergeant

Edward Boggs of General Scott's Life Guards and said he wished to see John Little, a former comrade in the Fifth Infantry who might know what became of some old friends they once had in common. He was granted admission and labored up the stairway on his stiff knee to the second floor and was allowed to pass through the barred door at the landing and then permitted to go to the wall of iron bars that sealed off the prisoners' common cell. The heavy wooden floor was swept clean and was bright with soft yellow sunlight falling through the tall windows. Visiting hours began early and already a dozen people were at the bars—wives and sweethearts, reporters, Mexican lawyers. The room hummed with low conversations. The prisoners would not be let out to the courtyard for another hour yet and from various braziers within the neatly ordered cell came the aromas of coffee and grilled chorizo and fried eggs. He scanned the cell as he approached the bars but didn't see John. Men were playing cards or reading newspapers or talking in small clusters or simply standing mute at the sunlit windows and staring out at the world beyond.

He took a place at the bars that gave him the widest berth on either side. A few feet to his left a Mexican woman whispered low to a San Patricio who listened glumly. To his right a lawyer in an expensive suit and bearing sheaves of legal documents was murmuring with a prisoner whose raw cheeks were flayed from cheekbone to jaw. Edward recognized him as John Riley. He had picked the flesh off his face to rid himself of the brands.

"Used to be he was called *Handsome* Jack."

The first words Edward had heard from his brother except in dreams since a rainy night in New Orleans a lifetime ago. John stood at the bars and looked at him, studied his uniform, smiled. The *D* brand on his face was crusted darkly red and his other cheek bore a deep cresent scar. His eyes were shadowed hollows. He regarded the cane in Edward's hand, the disfigured cheekbone, the bandanna showing under his black hat. "Had you some near times, looks like."

"Bout near as yours, I guess."

They gazed upon one another.

"Listen," Edward said. "Maggie's dead." He'd meant to tell him later, under better circumstances, but he'd suddenly felt the need to say something of import and it was the thing that came to mind.

John's face seemed to go hollow. He stepped back from the bars. "Dead?" He ran a hand through his hair and looked about as if searching for the word's meaning. Then he looked back at Edward. "Dead how? Where?"

"Some bad sickness," Edward said. "I buried her. Five, six months ago. Up near Linares."

John clutched the bars and then released them. He turned in a circle, looked up at the ceiling, heaved a huge breath and rubbed his eyes hard with both hands like someone trying hard to wake fully from a bad dream. Edward thought he would reserve the fact of their sister's whoredom for another time. "She ought not of come to Mexico," he said. The words sounded lame in his own ears.

John looked off to the sunbright window for a long moment and then turned back to Edward. "Aint nobody ought come to Mexico. Place aint all that kind even to the Mexicans."

They stood in awkward silence for a time and then Edward took off his hat and put his face close to the bars and whispered, "You're coming out."

John looked at him without expression.

"Tomorrow night," Edward said. He glanced to either side of him to ensure that no one was paying them mind. "The Castro woman'll be here. Do like she says. I'll be waiting with a ready mount for you. Come sunup we'll be sixty miles gone."

John looked at him and said nothing. His aspect was indifferent, the cast of his eyes somehow alien. Edward had the sudden sensation of facing a stranger.

"You understand me?" he asked.

John stared at him. "Understand?" He echoed the word as though it were of some foreign language. He looked off to the window again and there was another period of strained silence. Then he said: "You know something? I had that noose coming. Not for deserting. For what we done to Daddyjack." He looked at Riley on his left and continued in a lower voice. "What *I* done, I mean, since it's me the reason he's dead. If I hadn't tried to kill him he wouldn't of tried to kill me and you wouldn't of had cause to shoot him. So it aint really your doing he's dead, you see, it's mine. It aint been much to do here but think about things and I been thinking plenty and that's the way it works out, no matter how much I think on it. Our *daddy*, Ward. He was a son of a bitch sure enough but he was our *daddy*."

John's eyes seemed at once strange and familiar. And then Edward realized they reminded him of the eyes of their mother.

"I been wondering something," John whispered. "If it's proper to hang a man for deserting a bunch a strangers, what ought be done with one kills his own daddy? A hanging rope don't hardly seem sufficient. I anyhow had it coming for other reasons, reasons I can't even—"

"Quit it!" Edward said so sharply that Riley and his lawyer looked over at them, then turned back to each other. His grip was tight on the iron bars and he pressed his face against them and hissed lowly, "It's *done*, goddamnit. It's *done*. It aint no bringing it back and making it something other than what it was and it aint no making up for it. A hanging rope don't make up for a damn thing, it only makes a live man into a dead one."

"I dream about him, Ward."

"So do I! But I aint letting it eat on me." He abruptly drew back, abashed by his own intensity. He eased his hold on the bars and blew out a breath and glanced about. Then leaned in close again. "Look, Johnny. It's like the Mexicans say—what you can't make no different ye got to just stand it. It aint but the simple truth."

John regarded him closely. "You telling me true? You really dream him or you just saying?"

"Hell yes, I dream him! Ever goddamn night. And he don't never quit trying to make me feel like I aint fit to live. But he's dead goddamnit and to hell with him."

They stood there with the iron bars between them, searching each other's eyes for something neither of them could have given name.

"Listen Johnny," Edward whispered. "I wanted to . . . I mean . . . I shouldnt of lit out like I did. . . ."

"Lit out?" John said. "Where from?"

"Where *from?* From *Dixie*, goddamnit. If I'da stayed they might not of got you."

"Who? You mean the constables?" John now recalled how Maggie had disabled the boniface of the Mermaid Hotel as she fled through the door and the memory made him smile. And then he remembered what he'd done the night before the constables came crashing through the door and he ceased smiling. "Hell, you couldn't of done nothing. You didn't know where we were."

Edward squinted at him. "Who's *we?*" he said. "*What* constables?"

But a throng of visitors had just then arrived on the floor and his questions were lost in the clamor as they pressed up hard by him on either side and more prisoners were crowding John's flanks and what small bit of privacy they'd had was lost.

He stepped back from the bars and put on his hat. "Listen. I got things to tend. I'll see you, Johnny. Soon."

John nodded.

And in that moment they each one saw himself in the eyes of the other as in the closing fist of some destiny long determined.

18

At a few minutes after ten o'clock of the following evening la Señora del Castro's carriage arrived unexpectedly at Acordada where she debarked into the misted amber light of the streetlamps in the company of three men wearing broadbrimmed hats and black cloaks and carrying brief-cases. Two of the men wore black beards. At the door beside the main gate she informed the officer of the guard, a young lieutenant in charge of the prison detail, that the men were Veracruz attorneys from a firm of long standing with her family and she had engaged them to assist several San Patricios who had petitioned for their release from prison. Because the gentlemen would be departing the capital in the morning it was im-perative that they consult with their clients this evening. The matter was important but could be concluded rather quickly.

The lieutenant was hesitant to permit them entry, for the hour was late and long past the close of the daily visiting period. One of the attorneys sighed audibly and consulted his pocketwatch. La Señora del Castro won-dered aloud if perhaps they ought to intrude on General Scott's repose to see of he might persuade the prisonkeepers to be more cooperative. Thus reminded of the latitude General Scott permitted Señora del Castro regarding visitation to the San Patricios, the lieutenant suddenly envi-sioned himself reassigned to some remote desert outpost.

"Well now, ma'm," he said, "I don't guess there's any real need of disturbing the general at his ease."

The señora and her trio were admitted and then escorted up the stairs. At the landing the three men were searched to ensure that they carried no weapons on their person or in their briefcases. When the sergeant of the guard stood before the señora as if considering whether to search her as well, she fixed him with a defiant stare. He looked at the lieutenant who pursed his lips and looked away. The sergeant shrugged and stepped aside and the señora and her attorneys were let into the dim recess of the cell. A guard was posted just outside the bars to keep an eye on the proceedings within.

Most of the prisoners had bedded down for the night and were snoring soundly. The room's weak light came from the two small candles by which a pair of men were playing dominoes at the table and from the streetlamps glowing through the windows and throwing striped shadows on the wall. The place smelled of charcoal and flatulence and the muskiness of men in close habitation.

The two men at the table stood up at her approach. One of them was a Patricio named George Killian, the other John Little. She smiled at John and whispered to George Killian to sit with them and do nothing but look serious and nod when spoken to and sign his name to every paper placed in front of him. Killian grinned and nodded excitedly, happy to be included in the game. She fixed him with a look and he assumed a serious mien. She directed John to sit across from her, with his back to the door and next to one of the bearded associates, a man of similar size and build to his own and of the same sunbrowned hue of face and hands. The associates all removed their hats but only the two on her side of the table took off their cloaks. As these two extracted sheaves of papers from their briefcases and began addressing John and Killian on such matters as rights of petition and precedent law, the bearded man beside John removed the false beard from his face and surreptitiously passed it to him. John leaned forward on his elbows in the manner of a man listening closely to the advice of the attorneys across the table and applied the beard to his own face. It reached high on his cheekbone and covered the brand but the adhesive had been diluted by the other man's nervous sweat and the beard felt loose on his skin. He looked at the señora across the table and she smiled and nodded once.

Their doings attracted the attention of several others of the Patricios yet awake and they started toward the table but la señora gestured for them to keep their distance and they shrugged at each other and did as she asked. Still speaking loudly enough to be heard by the guard at the cell door, the associates were showing John and Killian where to append their signature on a half-dozen different forms.

Now John Riley emerged from the shadows with his ruined face. He sat beside the señora and smiled tightly at John across the table. "Why *him?*" Riley said in a low voice. "Why not me?"

"Because," la señora said, "he's the explosives expert."

Riley looked from her to John and back again, smiling uncertainly, as if he thought they might be playing a joke on him. "Who says so? I know more about explosives than this pup ever will."

"Captain Amado told me so."

"Captain *who?*"

"Keep your voice down!" she hissed, glancing toward the door. "He is an officer of the San Patricios, as you very well know. He escaped capture at Churubusco, he and Lieutenant Walker and Corporal Meese."

"The *hell* you say. I never heard of any of them."

La señora's look was scornful. "Really, captain, I am very disappointed that you should affect such pretense simply to indulge your own pique."

Riley looked narrowly at John. "What the fucking hell is this? You aint no powderman and it aint no Saint Patricks springing you. Why aint I in on it?"

John looked at him but said nothing. He felt oddly detached from the proceedings. His heart beat steady as a clock. His only sense was one of curiosity. He wondered if they were going to get away with it.

Now the associates were returning the paperwork to their briefcases, checking their watches by the candlelight, reminding la señora that they had an early coach to board in the morning.

Riley said, "I'm of a mind to whistle on ye if I aint let in."

La señora's face went fierce. "If you interfere in any way, captain, I promise that life in this prison will become very uncomfortable for all of you. I promise you that not another woman will set foot in this cage for the remainder of the time you and your men are here—and I promise you I will tell your men why the women do not come."

Riley smiled but his eyes were raging.

She looked toward the guard at the door and saw that he was engaged in watching a cockroach skitter across the floor. She nodded at the man who had given John the beard and he stood and shrugged out of his cloak to reveal the Mexican uniform he wore and he slipped the cloak over John's shoulders and quickly moved off into the shadows. La señora gestured for Killian to leave the table as well. The two associates put on their hats and cloaks and John folded his cloak about him and tugged down the brim of his hat. La Señora del Castro came around the table and drew close to John and so deftly did she withdrew a five-shooter from her purse and hand it to him and so adroitly did he slip it under his cloak that not even Riley saw that something had passed between them.

"What's to become of your man here?" Riley asked the señora, nodding toward the rear of the shadowy cell.

"Luis will answer to the name of John Little until all of you are discharged," she whispered.

Riley sneered hugely. "Pardon me bluntness, lady, but that's plain cuckoo. You can't pass that Mexie for a Mick. He'll be found out just as soon as they get a look at him in the daylight."

"If he should be found out he will confess nothing," la señora said.

"They'll give him some goodly pain to persuade him otherwise."

"No matter. He will not talk. Unless some one of you here tells them who he is, the gringos will never know how the switch was made. They might suspect me of it, but they will never know for certain. Tell the others that if they wish continuation of their comforts and pleasures they had best keep the secret."

Riley snorted and spat on the floor.

The visitor party went to the cell door and the guard worked the lock and let them out and gave but a cursory glance to the three attorneys, looking closely only at the woman who bedazzled him with her wide warm smile and told him he reminded her of a painting she'd once seen of Sir Gawain of the Round Table.

Then they were down the stairs and past the rest of the guards and out in the misty amber air and on the broad sidewalk of the Calle Patoni dappled with tree shadows under the light of the steetlamps. They were within feet of her waiting carriage when someone just inside the prison door shouted, "Stop them! *Stop* them!"

Guards ran out with rifles in hand and the two associates lunged for the carriage and their weapons within and the carriage driver sprang down from his seat and grabbed the señora and shielded her with his body as he pulled her away from the coach and John whirled around with the Colt in hand and fired three quick shots and two guards fell and another threw himself to the sidewalk and the rest turned and scampered back through the door as he fired twice more and the trailing soldier cried out and fell headlong through the door.

He turned and raced westward down the street as a staccato of gunfire burst behind him. He glanced over his shoulder as he ran and he saw the associates exchanging fire from a distance of six feet with two of the guards lying on the walkway. The associates fell and the other guards ran back out to shoot them several times more and none among them was looking his way as he rounded the corner of the Avenida Dolores and vanished into the shadows.

19

Five blocks east of the prison Edward sat on a bench on the Calle Patoni where it intersected with the Avenida de Perdidos. His horse was hitched to a post and beside it a fully outfitted black stallion he'd readied for John. He wore his Spy Company uniform and had a second uniform in John's saddlebags. Though the night was hazed with mist he could see the front of the prison from where he sat. He'd been waiting since shortly after nightfall and both street and pedestrian traffic had been light all evening. Finally, just as the street watchman passed him by, calling that it was ten o'clock and all bore well, the Castro woman's carriage arrived at the prison. She and three associates alighted and crossed the wide sidewalk to the door beside the main gate. An officer appeared and there followed a prolonged discussion and Edward was certain they had been denied admission. Then the door opened wide and the señora's party went inside and the door closed behind them.

He waited and passed the time thinking of how he and his brother would within the hour be riding hard to the north on the Querétaro road. Since his visit to John he'd thought of little else but their return to the other side of the Río del Norte. He'd thought about his brother's long yearning for a portion of timberland to call their own, about his desire to be a man of property, to be settled. And he was determined that John would have what he wanted. It was nor more than he deserved. They'd settle in Texas, way up east, a good long ways from this murdering Mexico. Up hard by the Sabine someplace, where the pines grew thick as grass and high as the damn clouds. They'd buy themselves a goodly parcel of woodland and work it for timber and maybe operate their own sawmill as well, and why not? Like John said, it was work they'd been trained to since they were big enough to swing an ax. John was right— he'd always been right. As soon as they got clear of Mexico City and into the north country he'd tell him how much he'd come to favor the idea. Edward grinned in the amber streetlight as he fancied the exchange between them, as he imagined the moment when John would lament that they lacked the money to buy a timber tract of sufficient size. That's when he'd show him the pokes of gold and silver he'd collected as his portion of the spoils with Dominguez's company. *Just watch Johnny's face* then, *by Jesus.*

"Las diez y media y todo sereno!" The watchman's cry started him from his reverie. They'd been in there now for half-an-hour, which seemed to him a lot longer than necessary. He was suddenly seized with a sense that something had gone wrong and now they were all of them held prisoner within.

Then the prison door swung open and here they all came out and he knew John was one of the three cloaked men. He stepped up onto his saddle and took up the black's reins. The carriage was to come down the Calle Patoni and turn onto the Avenida de Perdidos and out of sight of the prison and there discharge John. His horse sensed his excitement and stamped and snorted and he patted its neck and told it to stand fast, Johnny would be here in just a minute, by God.

But now soldiers came running out of the prison and shooting broke out and several soldiers fell down and the others retreated into the prison and then the shooter was running down the Calle Patoni in the other direction as yellow tongues of fire blasted between the soldiers on the ground and the other two cloaked men and now all of them were down and more soldiers ran out and shot the two cloaked men many more times as the third one disappeared around the corner.

Edward put spurs to his mount and led the black behind him as he galloped up to the prison and several of the guards swung their weapons on him as he reined up, yelling, "Scott's Guard! I'm a Scott's Guard!"

"Hold fire!" a lieutenant shouted. "It's one of ours, hold fire!" He turned to a soldier beside him and said, "Check that coach!"

Edward slid out of the saddle and went to the two cloaked men lying in spreading black blood on the sidewalk. One was on his back and was bearded and Edward bent and looked closely and saw that it was not his brother. The other was on his side and he pulled him over to see his face. The man was cleanshaved and showed a hole over one eye and another through his upper lip and neither was he John.

"Aint nobody in here, sir!" the soldier at the carriage called.

"Hufnagel! Reedy!" the lieutenant ordered. "Check that alley across the street! Johnson! Get down to the corner there and see can you spot him. Move!"

Edward looked after the soldier running to the corner. He turned to mount up and there stood la señora with her arm in the grip of a soldier and beside her the carriage driver had his hands up high. She was looking on Edward's Spy Company uniform as upon some alien horror. She glared at him with a mix of confusion and disbelief and visibly surging fury. The soldier holding her was looking off across the street to where his fellows searched for the third man and Edward put a finger to his lips for the barest instant.

For the moment the cozen worked. The woman followed him with her eyes but held silent as he swung up into the saddle.

"What were you doing, sergeant?" the lieutenant called to him, grinning. "Looking to see did we kill em sufficient?"

Edward smiled back. "They pretty well dead enough, sir," he said.

"Dont see nothin of him, sir!" the soldier named Johnson yelled from the corner. "Nought but a bunch a Meskins on the sidewalks. He musta run down around the next corner."

"*Shit!*" the lieutenant said through his teeth. ""If he's got friends in town we'll never find the sonofabitch."

"Mugrioso *condenado!*" la señora suddenly cried out. "Eres de la compañia de traidores! La compañia de Dominguez!" She was struggling in the guard's grasp as though she would lunge at Edward and batter him with her bare hands. "Maldito mentiroso!" She spat at him.

"Lordy," a soldier said, "these Meskins sure aint got no love for you Spy Compny boys, do they? Even if you aint no damn Mexican."

"*Por qué?*" the woman shouted. "Why did you liars come to me? What was the purpose? *Tell* me!"

'What the hell she talking about?" the lieutenant said.

"Damn if I know, sir," Edward said. "Woman's loony, you ask me. Like the fella there said, this uniform makes lots of the locals crazy to see it." He took up the black's reins. "I got to get, sir. Got a report to deliver to General Scott and this here horse to Colonel Hitchcock. I was on my way to do it when I seen you-all shooting."

"*Why*" la señora cried. Her face was bright with tears. "What did you *want?* You and damned Dominguez, the filthy traitor! It was him with you that day, wasn't it? *Wasn't* it?"

The lieutenant looked quizzical. "Dominguez is your C.O., aint he?"

"Damn good man," Edward said. "All these Meskins hate him cause he's fighting for us. They'll tell any lie about him."

He chucked up his horse and rode off down the Calle Patoni and glanced back to see the woman speaking to the lieutenant and then he turned the corner of the corner where John had gone.

20

He ran down the Avenida Dolores with the pistol held under his cloak and wove through the pedestrian traffic on the sidewalk and came to a plaza where a band was playing to a festive crowd and the trees were hung with colorful paper lanterns. He turned onto a side street and strode past brightly lighted shops and cafes and spied now a dark alleyway and he entered it and paused to catch his breath. He listened hard for sounds of pursuit but heard none, only the clopping of horses and the rumble of wheels on the cobbled street and the laughter and song of evening revelers. The beard felt askew on his sweated face and he readjusted it as best he could by feel. He wondered where Edward was, if he knew what had happened, if he'd been close by and seen it.

On the busy street a few feet away the indifferent world passed by. The alley was dark and long, extending about sixty yards to the street bordering its far end. The sole illumination was an oily cast of yellow lamplight spilling from an open door midway down the alley where a line of horses was hitched to a long post and even at this distance he could hear a raucous din from within. Thinking it the wiser course to avoid the bright lights of the streets he made toward the door. Its clamor grew as he approached.

The alley reeked of piss and rot and the cobbles were slippery under his bootsoles. He tucked the pistol into his waistband and closed his cloak over it and stepped to the doorway and peered around the jamb. It was a tavern inside hazed blue-yellow in the smoky lamplight. A raucous crowd of men cheering and cursing and shouting bets was gathered around a small rectangular cockpit enclosed by wooden walls about three feet high. Through gaps between spectators he could see the cocks leaping and coming together again and again in a flurry of feathers and flash of spurs and beaks and flicks of blood. There was a row of tables along the wall to the left and a bar ran the length of the right side of the room and he could see the swinging-door front entrance at the other end of the long cantina. The air of the room touched his face like hot breath and carried on it the smells of smoke and sweat and spirits. He thought to have his first drink in weeks while he pondered his next move.

He eased through the door and skirted the crowd around the cockpit and went to the bar and ordered tequila from a cantinero with wavy hair so heavily pomaded it shone like black satin.

The cantinero poured tequila in a small clay cup and set it before him. "Dos reales." he said.

Only now did he remember he was penniless. He patted his empty pockets and grinned abashedly at the bartender. "Bedamn if I aint a bit shy here."

The cantinero sighed and shook his head and reached to retrieve the cup but John snatched it up and drained it in a gulp and banged the empty vessel on the bar and grinned at him. The tequila burned its way to his belly in a wonderful rush.

The bartender scowled and muttered, "Hijo de la chigada," and pulled away the cup and made an abrupt backhand gesture for John to remove himself.

"How bout another?" John said. "Otro mas. Te lo pago mañana."

"Quitate de aquí, carajo!" the bartender said, "Andale."

"Uno mas y me voy" John said. "Por amistad, amigo."

"Ya no te digo mas," the cantinero said, his face darkening. "Ya, vete!"

"Shit, boy, don't beg the greasy sonofabitch." He had not been aware of the American soldier standing a few feet to his right and leaning over a mug of beer on the bar, a sergeant with a white scar angling across one eye. "Aint no greaser gonna give us one on the house," he said, "and it don't matter a damn you can speak Mexican." He snapped his fingers at the cantinero and jerked his thumb at John and said, "Give him one."

The cantinero rapped his knuckles on the bar and turned his palm up for payment. With his fingertip the sergeant slid two coins away from the pile of specie before him and pushed it across to the cantinero who picked them up and gestured at the cup John had emptied and held his palm out again.

"Son of a bitch," the sergeant muttered and slid another two reales toward him. The cantinero replaced the cup in front of John and filled it. John raised the drink to the sergeant and said, "Obliged," and but sipped at it to make it last.

Now the cheering at the cockpit rose to a crescendo and a moment later came a piercing cock crow and the cheering abated amid curses and happy whoops and the crowd began to break up. One grinning gallero cradled his gamecock to his chest while the other disgustedly flung his dead bird against the wall and another man kicked it out the back door into the dark alley. Now John became aware that some of the excited talk was in English and he saw a handful of Yankee soldiers advancing on the bar to join the sergeant, some of them bragging about their winnings on the fight and some cursing the cowardly nature of the losing cock. All of them wore sidearms.

As they pressed in close against the bar one of them jostled John's arm and some of his cup's contents slung out and splashed on the countertop and splattered the soldier's sleeve. The trooper turned a hard face to him and then saw that John was an American and his thick black handlebar widened over his grin. "Sorry, friend. I'll buy you another."

The cantinero poured John's cup full once again and John smiled and raised it to the Handlebar in thanks and saw that the soldier was not grinning now but staring fixedly at his face. "Shitfire," the handlebar said. "You boys lookee this here."

The other troopers were joking and laughing and now turned to look at John and their smiles vanished too.

And John knew what they saw. He could feel now the false beard gone awry. He put his hand to his face and his fingers brushed the crusty proud flesh of the exposed brand on his cheek.

Well, hell. He pulled off the beard and held it up with two fingers like something dead and tossed it and all eyes followed its arc over the bar and out of sight and then swung back to him.

The cantinero's eyes were on his brand too and now he quickly removed himself from behind the bar and went out a side door. Other of the Mexicans now saw what was happening and hastened for the exits as the soldiers formed a loose half-circle in front of the branded boy.

"What we got here," the sergeant growled, "is a fucken *deserter.*"

John tossed off the rest of his drink and let the cup fall to the floor and the soldiers flinched back a step as it shattered at his feet. He grinned at the lot of them. *About damn time,* he thought. *About damn time.* He heard Daddyjack's laughter from somewhere in the outer dark and he pictured for an instant Maggie's smiling face.

"What you got here, you sonofabitches," he said, feeling his smile tight and fierce on his face, "is John Little come to give what ye got comin."

He threw open his cloak and they saw his Mexican uniform and the cocked Colt already in his rising hand and John grinned hugely at the sagging look on the sergeant's face as he pointed the pistol squarely in his eye and pulled the trigger.

The hammer fell on the empty chamber with a dull tick.

For one long moment the soldiers all stood gaping. Then John lashed the sergeant across the mouth with the pistol and teeth flew in a spray of blood.

And then they were on him.

21

He trotted his mount up the Avenida Dolores, looking in the doorways of cantinas and shops and cafés as he passed. A string band was entertaining at the plaza at the end of the street and he turned left onto a side street and paced the horse slowly as he scanned the sidewalks and open doors, peered into every dark alleyway. He passed a church with a wall bearing the freshly painted exhortation, "¡Mueran los yanquis!" Some passersby glanced curiously at him and the saddled horse he led alongside but most paid him no mind.

A gunshot cracked somewhere in the near distance—and then another, and then two more. Some of the people hurriedly removed themselves from the street but most merely looked about and then went back to whatever they'd been doing. Gunfire in the capital had been more frequent than usual since the Yankees took occupation of the city and snipers were everywhere. Small skirmishes sometimes broke out in the crowded streets. But the capitalinos were long familiar with sudden public violence and most of them went on about their lives in much the same way as always.

He hupped his mount back to the plaza and crossed it to the next street and now spied a flock of Mexicans, some mounted but most on foot, rushing out from an alley two blocks away, a few glancing behind them as they turned onto the street and scattered. He spurred his horse forward and drew the black along and clattered into the alley and almost ran down some stragglers before he reined up. He spied the lighted doorway farther down the alley and faintly heard voices, laughter, shouts from within— then saw a handful of American soldiers come running out the door whooping and laughing.

They sped away down the alley in the other direction and then around the corner and were gone. He unholstered a Colt and put his horse forward and slowly advanced on the lighted door. When he hove to within a few yards of it he reined up and dismounted and hitched the two horses to a post. He drew the other Colt and with a pistol in each hand stepped up to the doorway.

John hung by the neck from a rope slung over a ceiling beam. Blood dripped from his boot toes, from his chin. He had wounds to his crotch and leg and one of his eyes was gone and a bullet hole showed red-black under his remaining and wide-open eye.

There was no one else in the room. Edward sat at a table and stared up at his brother and thought of nothing and felt as if his chest were utterly hollowed.

After a time he got up and cut him down. Then he went out to the black stallion and took the Spy Company coatee from its wallets and went back inside the tavern and stripped John of his Mexican jacket and put the coatee on him. He went to the bar and poured himself a drink and drank it and then went back to John and carried him outside and heaved him belly-down over the black's saddle and tied securely him in place. He put a Spy Company black hat on him and snugged the tie tightly under his chin. Then he went back in the cantina and retrieved two full bottles of tequila and stuffed them in his wallets and mounted up. He hupped the horses out to the street.

People on the sidewalks stared as he went by, stared and whispered to one another and pointed after him.

He rode through the city and encountered no army patrols either horsed or on foot until he came to the pickets at the north end of the Tlalnepantla causeway. He told the officer in charge that the dead man was a comrade who'd been killed not an hour ago by a goddamned Mexican sniper and he was taking him back to their unit's reconnaissance camp near Pachuca so Colonel Dominguez could decide where to bury him. The officer expressed his condolences and cursed the Mexican snipers for the cowardly bastards they were and waved Edward past.

22

He rode at a canter all that night and all the next day over the tableland between towering violet ranges to east and west. He slept in the saddle, pausing only to water the animals. He thought on little but the physical world about him. The skies drew his intent reflection, the shifting clouds. He studied distant rainstorms trailing across the horizon like mysterious purple veils.

The following day he angled northwestward into the brown foothills and then through a steepwalled canyon where the light was dimly blue and the horses' hooves echoed like hammered anvils. He put down in a clearing ringed by junipers and catclaw, nearly numbed with exhaustion. A cold wind whistled in the rocks and his fire lunged and twisted frantically as if in mute agony with its own burning. A baleful yellow eye of moon fixed narrowly on this hard dark world below. He wondered about the origins of comets streaking across the black void and wondered too where their fires did extinguish. He woke before dawn to find a sidewinder coiled beside him. The snake's eyes might have been fixed on his or might have been staring at some inner vision forever the secret of snakes. He closed his eyes and slept again and when he next awoke the snake was gone.

He was in the saddle before daybreak and followed trails made by no man before him, winding routes formed by runoff and rockslide and the passings of wild animals, cutting through the thorny growth so narrowly in places that his clothes were soon rent to rags and he and the animals streaked bloody with deep scratches. The going grew tenuous as they ascended. The horses shrilled and laid their ears back as they struggled for purchase and moved forward in lunges and yaws and loosed great clattering slides of rock behind them. The next sunrise found him on a climbing siderock trail jutting from a sheer rock wall and barely wide enough to accommodate the horses before dropping away into misty nothingness.

He came that afternoon around a long curve in the mountainside and arrived at a broad clearing overlooking a vast and darkly dappled bolsón that lay a half-mile below like a roughly tattered rug all the way to the blue-misted northern rim of the world. The clearing was shaded by a growth of pines and water trickled from a fissure in the rockwall and issued into a small pool. He let the horses drink and then bent to sate his own thirst and gave a momentary start at his reflection on the water's surface. He found that the ground to one side of the pool and at the base of the rockwall was soft enough to be dug up with knife and hands. He sat on his heels and considered. Then looked to the black horse where the body of his brother yet carried. Then looked for a time out to the vista below. Then set to work with the bowie and his hands and dug quickly and easily until he had fashioned a shallow grave. And there he laid the mortal remains of his brother, John Jackson Little.

He set his hat over John's face and then covered him over with dirt and tamped down the soft earth and then sought out heavy rocks he could barely heft in both arms and he grunted with the effort of carrying them to the grave and positioning them on top of it. And when he had covered the entire grave with stone to keep the scavengers from his brother he retrieved a bottle from his saddle wallet and took several deep swallows of tequila. He sat down crosslegged at the rockrim and looked out in the closing twilight at the vast and hazed horizon to the north where their home country lay in the mists.

Long low reefs of clouds burned redly to the west. And now, without turning to the grave behind him, he addressed his brother. Told him he was sorry. For everything. Sorry for their mother and their daddy and their little sister. Sorry for being a no-good brother. Sorry for deserting him in New Orleans and now in Mexico. Sorry for not even getting him to that part of Mexico where Maggie now lay.

"It's the wrong country, bubba, but leastways you both in the same one." He took another deep drink. "Hell, boy, I would of had to sleep sometime. The wolves would of had at you while I did. The damn coyotes. You know it's true."

He looked off toward the faraway end of the world. "Sorry," he said, "is all in the hell I am."

In the gathering darkness he looked out upon the empty waste and could feel the world spinning under him as it had been spinning since before time was measured and as it would spin long after time ceased to exist for lack of anyone to mark its passing.

"Hell, bud, I hate to say it right out, but you'da started rotting pretty bad before too much longer. I expect you'da pretty soon been dropping off in pieces ever coupla miles. Being in pieces all over this damn Mexicio—*that'd* be a hell of lot worse than buried up here all in one piece. You know that's true too."

And then as he took another drink he was abruptly moved to laughter and the tequila came up through his nose in a fiery gush and he choked and his eyes flooded.

Gasping, he turned to the grave and said, "God damn, bud—you'da been ate by crows and buzzards and vultures, and Lord knows that's plenty bad and shameful enough, but it aint the worst of it, no sir. The *worst* of it is they'da soon enough shit you out again!"

He threw his head back and laughed with all his teeth. Thumped his fist on his thigh and swayed and snorted and snuffled with laughter. The horses turned to see what affliction had befallen him and the alarm he perceived in their shadowed faces made him laugh the harder. His jaws ached with his laughter, his belly cramped. His eyes burned.

And then suddenly he let a piercing keen and was crying. Weeping without restraint. Wracked with great fierce sobs that shook him to his bones.

He drew his knees up to his chest and hugged them tight against himself and rocked back and forth like a child and wailed his grief with all the heart left to him.

And his wails echoed off the rockwalls down in the empty canyons and carried out to the wasteland and faded into the darkling void.